"I hope they're friendly," Lynnley said.

"Of *course* they're friendly!" Paul replied. "They're just coming out to greet us!"

The shipboard alert clamored in their minds. *Now hear this, now hear this,* intoned the voice of the Marine detachment's resident AI. *Battle stations, battle stations. All hands man your battle stations.*

A precaution only, she thought. Here, almost nine light-years from what was known and understood, it paid to be doubly cautious.

"Damn," she said. "I sure hope you're right, Paul."

She began to disconnect from the noumenal feed. Battle stations for the Marines was in the Squad Bay aft, suited and armed, ready to repel an attack on the ship or to deploy planetside in their TAL-S *Dragonflies* to meet an enemy. There was no planetside here, and the golden ship—or whatever it was—had made no hostile moves as yet, had it?

Just a precaution . . . just a precaution.

Then something made her hesitate, to look again at the approaching golden vessel.

And then she felt her soul and her mind being dragged from her body.

She began screaming . . .

Eos Books by
Ian Douglas

STAR STRIKE: BOOK ONE OF THE INHERITANCE TRILOGY

STAR MARINES: BOOK THREE OF THE LEGACY TRILOGY
BATTLESPACE: BOOK TWO OF THE LEGACY TRILOGY
STAR CORPS: BOOK ONE OF THE LEGACY TRILOGY

EUROPA STRIKE: BOOK THREE OF THE HERITAGE TRILOGY
LUNA MARINE: BOOK TWO OF THE HERITAGE TRILOGY
SEMPER MARS: BOOK ONE OF THE HERITAGE TRILOGY

BOOK TWO OF
THE LEGACY TRILOGY

BATTLESPACE

IAN DOUGLAS

An Imprint of HarperCollinsPublishers

EOS
An Imprint of HarperCollins*Publishers*
10 East 53rd Street
New York, New York 10022-5299

Copyright © 2006 by William H. Keith, Jr.
ISBN-13: 978-0-380-81825-9
ISBN-10: 0-380-81825-6
www.eosbooks.com

First Eos paperback printing: February 2006

Printed in the U.S.A.

10 9 8 7 6 5 4

To CJ,
who's helped me with my own battlespace.

BATTLESPACE

Prologue

Star Explorer Wings of Isis
Sirius System
1550 hours, Shipboard time

Lance Corporal Lynnley Collins, UFR/US Marines, drifted free within inexpressible beauty.

From her vantage point, she seemed to float in the depths of space, but a space turned glorious by the blue-silver-white beacons of two nearby stars: gleaming Sirius A and its tiny white-dwarf brother, Sirius B.

The Sirius system was thick with dust and debris that caught the starlight and twisted it into hazy knots of pale color. The noumenal display revealed the hard radiation searing the encircling sky as a faint purple background glow.

Noumenal space—such a bland and uninformative description of the sheer miraculous. If a phenomenon is something that happens in the world around us, within that collection of events and happenstance and knock-on-wood solid matter humans are pleased to call reality, then a *noumenon* is that which happens within a person's mind.

Thought, wonder, visualization, imagination . . . such are the bone and sinew of the noumenal. With the appropriate nanochelates forming hypolinks and neural access stacks at certain points within the sulci of the brain, with implanted microcircuitry and perhaps twenty grams of other hardware grown nanobit by nanobit into key nerve bundles to provide sensory input, a human could link in to the data feed from a computer or an AI and become an organic SUI, a sensory user's interface, experiencing downloads not on a computer monitor or wallscreen, but as unfolding visual and aural imagery within the mind itself.

Lance Corporal Collins, then, was not *really* adrift in open space, bathed in the fiercely radiant glare of Sirius A. Remote cameras and other sensors on the hull of the explorer ship *Wings of Isis* provided the cascade of data flooding through her brain by way of the ship's communications systems. The sky around her was dramatically, impossibly beautiful, bands of dust and gas aglow in actinic Sirian light. Sirius A was distant enough that she didn't even show a disk, yet still was so brilliant that even within the artfully massaged illusion of the noumenal sensorium it was difficult to look at the star directly.

Closer by some hundreds of millions of kilometers, Sirius B radiated its own hot light, illuminating the stellar debris within which it was imbedded in blues, silvers, violets, and harshly glaring white. A white dwarf, a shrunken star the size of Earth and so dense that a teaspoonful possessed the mass of a good-sized mountain, Sirius B was too small even at this relatively close range to show as more than a blinding spark embedded in its glowing cloud of dust.

Lynnley was not watching the stellar panorama, however. Opposite the two arc-brilliant suns—and harshly illuminated by them—drifted the Wheel.

Ten kilometers away from *Wings of Isis*, and at least twenty kilometers across, the thing was clearly an artifact, something deliberately created by intelligence, a hubless wheel of roughly the same proportions as a wedding band. Under magnification, the outer surface was black, cracked, and broken, which might indicate that the Wheel had been constructed from asteroidal debris. The inner surface was smooth, almost polished, marked by geometric shapes and lines, and here and there lights glowed like neatly ordered stars, indicating power usage and the possibility of life. Gravitometric readings, however, teased and confused. If they could be believed, the Wheel was incredibly dense, the mass of a large planet collapsed into an enigmatic, clearly artificial hoop.

In fact, there were no planets in the Sirian system. Sirius A was far too hot and bright a star to allow for a comfortably Earthlike planet, and it was young, too young for life to have evolved, even had there been such a world; once Sirius B had been nearly as bright as its big brother before it had vomited part of its mass and collapsed into its present shrunken state. The background radiation, barely held at bay by the *Isis*'s magnetic screens, would have fried any unprotected lifeform in seconds. Whoever had built that structure had come here from somewhere else.

Why? What was the ring for?

And who had built it, here in the harsh and deadly glare of the Sirian suns?

Unseen, but sensed in the imaginal space at her side, Sergeant Paul Watson watched and wondered with her. Paul was a shipboard lover, but, more, he was a friend, a bulwark against the loneliness. John Garroway, the man she loved, was another Marine, one now even more distant from the *Wings of Isis* than was Earth. As much as she liked Paul, she wished John was here now instead.

"My God!" Paul said suddenly, his voice sharp in her mind.

"What?"

"Look! There in the center. You'll need to magnify. . . ."

She set her attention on the center of that massive Wheel, giving the mental command to narrow in on the field of view. Yes, she saw it now . . . something drifting out from the center of the artifact. If the known diameter of the Wheel was any indication, the object must be a couple of kilometers long at least, as slender as a needle and gleaming in the hard starlight like pure gold.

"What . . . is it?" she said.

"A ship!" Paul replied in her thoughts. "Obviously, a ship!"

"Why obviously?" Lynnley said. "We don't know who these people are. Or what they are. We can't take anything for granted!"

"Bullshit," Paul replied with a mental snort. "It's a *ship*. That Wheel must be some sort of enormous habitat or space station. I think we're about to meet Berossus's friends!"

Berossus's friends. The phrase at once chilled and excited.

The *Wings of Isis* had voyaged to Sirius—8.6 light-years from home, on a long-shot gamble. Berossus had been a Babylonian historian living about three centuries B.C.E. Only fragments of his writings remained, but from those fragments had come the story of Oannes, an amphibious being who'd appeared at the headwaters of either the Arabian Gulf or the Red Sea—there was some confusion as to which—and taught the primitive humans dwelling there the arts of medicine, agriculture, writing, and of reading the stars. Oannes, Berossus insisted, was not a god, but one of a number of beings he called *semidemons* or "animals with reason," intelligent beings like men, but not human. The Greek word he used for them was *Annedoti*, "the Repulsive Ones," and they were said to have the bodies and tails of fish with the heads and limbs of men.

The tale, like so many other fragments of lost or nearly lost history, from Quetzalcoatl to Troy to the Iberian Bronze Age copper miners of Lake Superior to the nuclear holocaust described in the *Rig-Veda* to lost Atlantis, had long been relegated to myth. The twenty-first- and twenty-second-century exoarcheological discoveries on the moon, Mars, and Europa, however, had demonstrated once and for all that many such myths were history in disguise.

The rise of human civilization was *not* what it long had seemed.

The Annedoti of Berossus were associated with the star Sirius, having claimed to come from there. The Nommo of the myths of the Dogon tribe in Mali also purportedly hailed from the Sirius system, which the primitive Dogon had described in intriguing, impossible detail. The Dogon traditions were so anachronistically detailed in fact that even in the twentieth century some writers had speculated that the Nommo might represent memories of an encounter between early humans and visiting extraterrestrials.

The only problem was the fact that Sirius couldn't possibly have planets.

The *Wings of Isis* had departed Earth orbit late in the year 2138 and traveled for ten years, objective, most of that time at near-c. For the 245 men and women onboard, 30 of them the UFR/US Marines of the Shipboard Security Detachment, relativistic effects reduced ten years to four, and they were unaware even of that passage of time since they were in cybernetic hibernation in order to conserve food, air, and other consumables. Awakened out of cybehibe as they approached the Sirius system, most of the men and women not actively on duty at the moment were gathered now in noumenal space, linked in through the ship's comm network, watching . . . and wondering.

"I hope they're friendly," Lynnley said after a moment. "The *Wings of Isis* wouldn't make a decent lifeboat for that thing!"

"Of *course* they're friendly!" Paul replied. "All the legends about gods from Sirius emphasized that they were friendly, taught humans how to plant crops, that kind of thing. They're just coming out to greet us!"

The shipboard alert clamored in their minds. *Now hear*

this, now hear this, intoned the voice of the Marine detachment's resident AI. *Battle stations, battle stations. All hands man your battle stations.*

A precaution only, she thought. Here, almost nine light-years from what was known and understood, it paid to be doubly cautious.

"I hope to the Goddess you're right, Paul," she said. "But whoever they are, they must be damned old, and someone once said that the old are often insanely jealous of the young. And . . . there are the Hunters of the Dawn, remember?"

She felt his noumenal touch. "Nah. It's Oannes's descendents, and they're coming out to see how their offspring have done. Everything'll be fine. You'll see."

"Damn," she said. "I sure hope you're right."

She began to disconnect from the noumenal feed. Battle stations for the Marines was in the squad bay aft, suited and armed, ready to repel an attack on the ship or to deploy planetside in their TAL-S Dragonflies to meet an enemy. There was no planetside here, and the golden ship, or whatever it was, had made no hostile moves as yet, had it?

Just a precaution . . . just a precaution. . . .

Then something made her hesitate, to look again at the approaching golden vessel.

And then she felt her soul and mind being dragged from her body. . . .

She began screaming. . . .

$$\boxed{1}$$

The NNN Interactive World Report
WorldNet NewsFeed
0705 hours, PST

Visual: A heavy Trans-Atmospheric Transport slowly descends through a night sky on shrieking plasma thrusters, its blocky, massive outline wreathed in swirling clouds of steam and illuminated by search-lights from the ground.

". . . and in other news today, UFR/US Marines of the **First Marine Interstellar Expeditionary Unit** returned to Earth early this morning, touching down at the **Marine Spaceport Facility at Twentynine Palms, California**, at just past midnight, Pacific Time. The First MIEU departed Earth twenty-one years ago in order to safeguard human interests on the planet **Ishtar**, in the star system designated **Lalande 21185**." [Thought-click on highlighted links for further information.]

Visual: Enormous cargo containers, each twenty meters long and massing a hundred tons, are lowered on hydraulic arms from the grounded TAT's belly and onto ground-effect cargo carriers. Marines in full battle armor stand guard around the perimeter.

"The unit's marines, numbering over a thousand men and women, were brought down while still in cybernetic hibernation from the **EU** stellar transport *Jules Verne*, the vessel which brought them back from Ishtar on a **voyage lasting ten years**. They were taken at once to a hibernation receiving facility at Twenty-nine Palms for revival."

[Thought-click on highlighted links for further information.]

Visual: A succession of scenes of Marines in battle armor on the planet Ishtar—beneath a sullen, green-tinted sky and the swollen orb of the gas giant, Marduk, about which Ishtar orbits. In the distance, a stepped pyramid rises above purple and black vegetation. Other buildings, crude things of mud brick, are visible in the foreground.

Scenes of battle, the Marines firing their weapons at unseen enemies.

More scenes of battle, Marines holding off an oncoming wave of humanoid creatures waving spears and banners. Marine Wasp fighters twist through the green sky.

"Fighting on Ishtar was, reportedly, savage, and the First MIEU suffered heavy casualties. According to reports, the alien **Ahannu** inhabiting Ishtar were holding a number of humans as slaves, the descendents of humans taken from Earth when the Ahannu, or **An**, possessed a starfaring empire **ten thousand years ago**.

[Thought-click on highlighted links for further information.]

Visual: Images of Ahannu—primitive, carrying spears and wearing crude armor. They are humanoid, with elongated, crested heads, finely scaled green or brown skin, and enormous, golden eyes bearing horizontally slit pupils.

*A scene shows several richly dressed Ahannu appar-
ently in conversation with a number of Marines, one
identified by a floating ID label as Colonel Ramsey.
The Marines tower over the diminutive aliens, who appear submissive and afraid. A caption reads "Formal-
ization of peace accord between the UFR and Ahannu
leaders, June 30, 2148."*

"The Ahannu, primitives who no longer possess the
advanced, starfaring technology of their ancestors,
surrendered to the Marines after two days of hard
fighting. The commanding officer of the First MIEU,
Colonel T. J. Ramsey, reportedly established a **treaty**
with the Ahannu guaranteeing the freedom of Ishtar's
human population."

[Thought-click on highlighted links for further information.]

*Visual: The scene shifts to Earth and an angry crowd
numbering in the thousands, filling a street, shaking fists
and hand-lettered signs, chanting slogans. A woman in
an elegant green cloak speaks passionately into the Net-
Cam. "The Ahannu are gods! As the An, they came to our
world thousands of years ago and brought with them the
seeds of civilization—agriculture, medicine, writing!
The Ahannu are the An's descendents. We should be worshipping them, not killing them!" A caption reads:
"Live: Demonstration in Portland, Maine, by members
of the Anist Church of the Returning Gods."*

"Reaction to the return of the Marines has been
mixed. Many groups protest UFR involvement in the
Lalande system, which has now fallen under joint
EU–Brazilian–UFR control. Numerous religious
groups here on Earth protest what many are calling
heavy-handed **interference in Ahannu affairs**. And
there are nations which disagree with UFR policies on
Ishtar as well."

[Thought-click on highlighted links for further information.]

Visual: Another mob, this one obviously Islamic, with a mosque visible in the background. An imam speaks to the NetCam in Arabic, which is translated by the broadcast's AI. "These so-called ancient gods are demons and upset the order of God, may his name be blessed forever! It is a sin to have any traffic with them whatsoever!" A caption reads: "Imam Selim ibn Ali Zayid, speaking in Cairo, the Kingdom of Allah, earlier today."

Visual: Another mob, many waving American flags. A prominent sign in the foreground reads HUMANITY UNITE! *A wild-eyed man shouts into the NetCam, "The An enslaved people! They set up a colony on our planet and took away people to be slaves on other planets! They should be nuked. What the hell are we doing signing treaties with these monsters, for God's sake? They're demons! Kill them! Kill them all!" A caption reads: "Fr. Ronaldo Carrera, Church of Humankind, La Paz, Baja, earlier today."*

"Meanwhile, tensions continue to mount between the UFR and the EU–Mexican–Brazilian Accord over the question of Aztlan independence. President DeChancey announced that . . ."

*Cybernetic Hibernation Receiving
Facility
Star Marine Force Center
Twentynine Palms, California
0920 hours, PST*

Lance Corporal John Garroway, UFR/US Marine Corps, struggled upward toward light and consciousness. Tattered shreds of dreams clung to his awareness, already slipping away into emptiness. There were dreams of falling, of flame and battle and death in the night, and of an endless, empty gulf between the stars. . . .

He drew a breath and felt that terrifying no-air feeling you got when the wind was knocked out of you. He tried to inhale, harder, and a flash of white-hot pain stabbed at both sides of his chest.

He was drowning.

Garroway tried to breathe through the blockage and felt his body convulse in paroxysms of coughing and retching. A viscous jelly clogged his nose, mouth, and windpipe. A giant's hand pressed down on his chest; another closed about his throat. Damn it, he couldn't *breathe*. . . .

Then, with a final, explosive cough, the jelly was expelled from his lungs and he managed his first ragged, burning lungful of air. He managed a second breath, and a third. The pain and the strangling sensation faded.

There was something wrong with his vision, he thought. He could see . . . a pale, faint green glow that nonetheless hurt the eyes, but there was nothing to see, save a flat, smooth, plastic-looking surface a few centimeters above his face. For a moment claustrophobia threatened, and his breathing became harsh, rapid, and painful once more.

Something stung his arm at the angle of his elbow. A robotic injector arm pulled back, vanishing into a side compartment. "Lie still and breathe deeply," a voice that was neither male nor female told him in his thoughts. "Do not try to leave your cell. A transition medical team will be with you momentarily."

Memories began surfacing, as other sensations besides pain and strangulation returned to his body. He'd been through this before. He was in a cybehibe tube and he was awakening once more after years of cybernetically induced hibernation. The voice in his head was coming from his own cerebral implant, which meant they were monitoring his revival.

He was awake. *He was okay.* . . .

The gel that had moments before filled the narrow tube, providing, among other things, protection from several years' worth of bed sores as well as a conduit for oxygen and cell-repair nano, was draining away now into the plastic padding beneath his back. Garroway concentrated on breathing, gulping down sweet air . . . and ignoring the stench that had collected inside the coffin-sized compartment for the past ten years or so. His empty and shrunken stomach threatened to rebel. He tried to focus on remembering.

He could remember . . . yeah . . . he could remember.

He remembered the shuttle flight up from the surface of Ishtar, and boarding a European Union transport—the *Jules Verne*. He remembered being told to remove all clothing and personal articles and log them with the clerk, of lying down on a metal slab barely softened by a thin plastic mattress, of a woman speaking to him in French as the first injection hit his bloodstream and turned the world fuzzy.

Ishtar. He'd been at Ishtar. And now . . . Now? They must be at Earth.

Earth!

The thought brought a sudden snap of energy and he thumped his head painfully against the plastic surface of the hybe tube as he tried to sit up.

Earth! . . .

Or . . . possibly one of the LaGrange stations. The pull of gravity felt about right for Earth, but that could be due to the rotation of a large habitat. He might even still be on the EU ship.

Gods and goddesses, no. He didn't want to have to deal with *them* again. Let this be Earth!

The end of his hybe cell just above his head hissed open, and his pallet slid out into light. Two Marines in utility fatigues peered down at him. "What's your name, buddy?" one asked him.

"Garroway," he replied automatically. "John. Lance Corporal, serial number 19283-336-6959."

"That's a roger," the other said, reading from a compboard. "He's tracking."

"How ya feeling?"

"A bit muzzy," he admitted. He tried to concentrate on his own body. The sensations were . . . odd. Unfamiliar. "*Hungry*, I think."

"Not surprising after ten years with nothing but keepergel in your gut. You'll be able to get some chow soon."

"Ten years? What . . . what year is it?"

"Welcome to 2159, Marine."

He held up both hands, turning them, looking at them a bit wonderingly. They were still wet with dissolving gel. "2159?"

"Don't freak it, gramps," the other Marine told him. "You're all there. The nano even stopped your hair and nails from growing."

"Yeah. It just feels . . . odd. Where are we?"

"The Marine Corps Cybernetic Hibernation Receiving Facility," the Marine with the board said. "Twentynine Palms."

"Then I'm home."

The other Marine laughed. "Don't make any quick judgments, timer. You'll null your prog."

"Huh?"

"Just lie there for a minute, guy. Don't sweat the net. If you gotta puke, puke on the deck. The auts'll take care of it. When you feel ready, sit up . . . but slow, understand? Don't push your body too hard just yet. You need time to vam all the hibenano out of your system. When you feel like moving, make your way to the shower, get clean, and rec yourself some utilities."

Garroway was already sitting up, swinging his legs off the pallet. "I've done this before," he said.

"Suit yourself," the Marine said. They were already moving away, beginning to cycle open the next cybehibe capsule in line, a few meters away. As the hatch cycled open and the pallet extruded itself from the bulkhead, Garroway could see the slowly moving form of Corporal Womicki half-smothered in green nanogel.

"What's your name, buddy?" one of the revival techs asked.

"Wo-Womicki, Timothy. Lance Corporal, serial number 15521-119—"

"He's tracking."

"Welcome to 2159, Marine."

The routine continued.

Elsewhere around the circular, fluorescent-lit compartment, other Marine revival techs were working with men and women emerging from cybehibe, dozens in this one room alone. Some, nude and pasty-looking, were already standing or making their way toward a door marked SHOWERS, but most remained on their pallets.

"Hey, Gare!" Womicki's voice was weak, but he was sitting up. "We made it, huh?"

"I guess we did."

"Whatcha think the pool number is?"

His stomach gave an unpleasant twist. "Dunno. Guess we'll find out."

The deathwatch pool was a kind of lottery, with the Marines betting on how many would die in cybehibe passage.

How many of their buddies had made it?

And then his head started swimming and he vomited explosively onto the deck, emptying his stomach of yet more of the all-pervading foamy nanogel.

A long moment later, his stomach steadied, and he began working on bringing some focus to his muddled thinking.

Twentynine Palms. This was the place where he'd been loaded into cybe-hibe preparatory to being shuttled up to the

IST *Derna* like a crate of supplies. That felt like a year ago or so . . . not twenty years.

Well, his various briefings had warned him that he'd have some adjusting to do. Between the effects of relativity and the cybehibe sleep, he'd been just a bit out of touch with the rest of the universe.

He thought-clicked his cerebral implant. "Link. Query. Local news update."

He expected a cascade of thought-clickable headers to scroll past his mind's eye, but instead a red flash warned him that his Net access had been interdicted. "All shoreside communications have been restricted," the mental voice told him. "You will be informed when it is permissible to make calls off-base or receive information downloads."

A small flat automaton of some sort was busily cleaning up the mess he'd made on the deck.

So far, he thought, *this is a hell of a welcome home. . . .*

Headquarters
Star Marine Force Center
Twentynine Palms, California
1750 hours, PST

"Why," Colonel Thomas Jackson Ramsey said as he took a seat at the conference table, "all the extra security? My people have calls they want to make, and they're justifiably curious about the Earth they've just come home to. But we appear to be under quarantine."

"Quarantine is a good word for it, Colonel," General Richard Foss told him. "Operating policy now calls for a gradual insertion of returning personnel into ordinary life. Things have changed a lot in twenty years, you know."

"How much?"

"The political situation is . . . delicate."

"It usually is. Damn it, what's going on?"

"The European Union has recognized the independent nation of Aztlan, along with Mexico, Brazil, and Quebec. All U.S. military bases are on full alert. The borders are closed. War may be eminent."

"Jesus." Ramsey frowned. "An EU ship brought us home."

"The crisis flared up for the first time a year ago, about the time you were beginning deceleration, a half light-year out. Geneva recognized Aztlan independence, at least in principle, and was offering to broker talks. There was . . . concern, in some circles, that you people might be held hostage if war did break out."

Ramsey nodded. The Aztlan question had been smoldering for some years, even before the *Derna* had left for Ishtar, and it really was only a matter of time before there was a final showdown. The *Aztlanistas* wanted a homeland—to be carved out of the southwestern states of the Federal Republic of North America, land they claimed had been unjustly taken from Mexico in the wars of 1848 and 2042. Since that homeland would consist of some of the United Federal Republic's choicest and most populous real estate—southern California, Arizona, New Mexico, Texas, Baja, Sonora, Sinaloa, and Chihuahua—Washington flatly refused to negotiate.

Unfortunately, there were a number of players in the world arena, including China and the EU, who would like to see the UFR taken down a notch or three, and breaking away 8 of the Federal Republic's 62 states would certainly accomplish that.

"Things were smoothed out," General Foss continued. "Our AIs talked to their AIs, a summit conference was held at Pacifica, and things quieted down a bit.

"But two weeks ago, while you were still inbound out beyond the orbit of Saturn, *Aztlanistas* managed to smuggle a small AM bomb into the Federal Building in Sacramento. Twelve hundred dead—and the heart of the city leveled. At this point in time, Colonel, as you can imagine, there is considerable ill feeling toward people of Hispanic descent. Three days ago, anti-Latino rioting in New Chicago and in New York resulted in several hundred dead and over a thousand injured."

"That still doesn't explain why my people are being held incommunicado, sir."

Foss didn't reply for a long moment. His eyes seemed a bit unfocused and Ramsey waited. Possibly he was talking with someone else over his implant or downloading some key information.

"Colonel," Foss said at last, "there are people in the current administration who were suggesting MIEU-1 shouldn't be allowed back to Earth."

"What?"

Foss held up a hand. "You were working with the EU on Ishtar," Foss said. "And you pulled that cute stunt that pulled the rug out from under PanTerra. There are some who question your loyalty, Colonel, and the loyalty of the Marines under your command."

Ramsey came to his feet. "*Who*?" he demanded.

"Take it easy, Colonel."

"I will *not* take it easy. Sir. *Who* is accusing my men of disloyalty?"

"Sit down, Colonel!" As Ramsey grudgingly took his seat, Foss folded his hands on the table and continued. "You know how rumors spread, Colonel. And how poisonous they can be. They take on a life of their own, sometimes, and do some horrific damage."

"That does not answer the question, General." Ramsey was furious. "If I screwed up with the Ishtaran state, then court-martial me. But I was responsible, not my men!"

"No one is talking about courts-martial, Colonel. Not yet, at any rate. You did overstep your authority, true, but there were . . . extenuating circumstances."

"Like the fact that my orders were coming from eight-point-three light-years away? And that something had to be done immediately?"

"Well, yes. More to the point, however, your mission required you to support the PanTerran representatives and their interests."

"Which, it turned out, involved 'liberating' human slaves from the Ahannu, so they could be shipped to Earth as contract laborers. Slavery, in other words."

"Not slavery, Colonel . . ."

"Oh? What are you calling it these days?"

"Liberational relocation."

"Bullshit. Sir. The *Sag-ura* have been shaped by ten thousand years of Ahannu selective breeding and conditioning." *Sag-ura* was the name for the descendents of humans removed from Earth thousands of years before and taken to other worlds of the Ahannu empire. "PanTerra was planning on shipping them in cybehibe tubes back to Earth to be trained and sold as 'domestics.' With no understanding of Earth–human culture, what chance would they have had for *real* freedom?"

"You made certain political decisions, Colonel." He gave a grim, hard smile. "Do you realize that they're calling it 'Ramsey's Peace' now?"

"Yes, sir. We helped facilitate the creation of an independent Sag-uran state, which should be able to look out for the interests of humans living on Ishtar."

"And it was not within the purview of the Marines to dabble in local politics."

"No, sir. Except that the Ahannu had surrendered. Earth was eight-and-a-half light-years away, and the EU–Brazilian military expedition was due to show up in another five months. Do you think they would have tried to guarantee the safety of the *Sag-ura*?"

"Probably not. Especially since they have PanTerran connections as well." Foss cleared his throat. "The point, Colonel, is that you *did* overstep yourself by making the decisions you did. But that's not why I called you in here."

Ramsey worked to control his anger. "Yes, sir."

"There is widespread suspicion that MIEU-1 was working with the EU on Ishtar."

"Reasonable enough. We *were*. Under orders."

"Indeed. And by brokering that agreement with the natives and creating that Sag-uran state, whatever it's called . . ."

"*Dumu-gir Kalam*, sir."

"Whatever. You *did* steal a march on the EU. They couldn't very well abrogate treaties you'd written and signed, not without an incident and some very bad press back home."

"So the Accord is holding up?"

"Has for the ten years since you left, Colonel, yes. As for the future? Who knows? The EU have established a diplomatic mission on Ishtar, now."

"So they're playing by the rules, at least."

"For now. But my concern is what's happening on *this* planet. On Earth. Specifically, we have people—both in the government and ordinary Joes and Janes on the streets—who think you were somehow collaborating with the EU on Ishtar. And they know that the EU brought you back to Earth on one of their transports."

"Well, it was that or have us stay there with them."

"It was decided to have MIEU-1 return to Earth, Colonel. Protecting UFR interests on Ishtar is the Army's job now." An Army occupational force consisting of elements of the First Extrasolar Special Operations Group had accompanied the EU and Brazilian joint expedition. "However, that has caused some serious problems for us here."

"My men are loyal, General," Ramsey said through clenched teeth. "You can't lock them away without a fair hearing."

Foss sighed. "Colonel, it's not just the loyalty question. You should know that. The Ahannu are the focus of the biggest religious brouhaha since Adam and Eve got their eviction notice in Eden. Some people think they are gods—or the descendents of gods—and that our proper place is at their feet, worshipping them."

"Crackpots."

"Some think they're demons and think it's wrong to have any political dealings with them at all. Some think they're the underdogs, poor, misunderstood little primitives, and the big, bad Marines are out to commit high-tech genocide. Some think they're your stereotypical bug-eyed monsters lusting after human females, slave masters who must be punished. The Papessa is saying the Ahannu ought to be stopped from keeping slaves. The Anti-Pope is saying we have to treat the Ahannu as friends and equals and to respect their traditions. The list goes on and on.

"The point is, Colonel, you and your people have come back to Earth at a rather sensitive time. You can't help but be caught up in the politics—and the religious controversy. You've just stepped off the boat, Colonel, and smack into quicksand."

"If you're looking for a scapegoat, General, you're free to take a shot at me. I'll fight it, but you can try. But it is a monstrous injustice to blame the men under my command for—"

"No one is blaming them, Colonel. Or you. But I needed to make sure you understood the . . . ah . . . delicate nature of your position here."

"You've got my attention, sir. That's for damned sure."

"We have a new situation, one that calls for MIEU-1's special, um, talents."

"Another deployment, General?"

He nodded. "Another deployment."

"To where?"

"To Sirius. Eight-point-six light-years out. The brightest star in Earth's night sky."

That pricked Ramsey's interest. "The *Wings of Isis*, sir? She found something?"

"Link in, Colonel, and I'll fill you in with what we know."

Ramsey closed his eyes and felt the familiar inner shiver as data began to flow, downloading through his cereblink.

Visual: A wedding band adrift in space. Two stars, arc-brilliant and dazzling to look at, hung in the distance, suspended against wispy clouds of hazy light.

"These images were laser-transmitted to us as they were being made," Foss said. "They arrived two years ago. The star on the left is Sirius A. The other is Sirius B, the white dwarf. And the Wheel. . . ."

Visual: The NetCam zooms in and the structure is revealed to be enormous. Data scrolls down one side of the visual, indicating dimensions and mass. The structure is titanic, twenty kilometers across, but massing as much as a small start. The density of the thing—better than 6×10^{18} grams per cubic centimeter—is astonishing.

"An alien artifact?"

Foss nodded.

"What is it? A space station? A space habitat of some kind?"

"No. At least . . . we don't think so."

"That density reading," Ramsey said, examining the data. "That can't be right."

"According to gravitometric scans made by the *Wings of Isis*, it is," Foss replied.

"Neutronium? Collapsed matter?"

"The density's not *that* high. Most of that thing is actually hollow. But we think we know what's going on. Think of that hoop as a kind of particle accelerator, like the hundred-kilometer supercollider at Mare Humorum on the moon."

"Okay. . . ."

"Now imagine, instead of subatomic particles, what you have whirling around inside that giant racetrack are tiny black holes. And they're moving at close to the speed of light."

"*Black holes*? My God, why?"

"Best guess is that what we're looking at here is an inside-out Tipler Machine."

"A what?"

"Here's the data."

Frank Tipler had been a prominent physicist at the turn of the twenty-first century. Among other things, he'd suggested the mechanism for a means of bypassing space, of jumping from here to there without the tedious process of moving through the space in between. His scheme had called for building a very long cylinder, one hundred kilometers long, ten kilometers wide, and made of neutronium—the ultra-dense collapsed matter of a neutron star. Rotate the thing two thousand times a second, so the surface is moving at half the speed of light. Theoretically, according to Tipler, the rotating mass would drag space and time with it, opening paths through both above the surface. By following a carefully plotted course around the rotating cylinder, a starship pilot could cross light-years in an instant . . . and would be able to fly back and forth through time as well.

The whole thing was just a thought experiment, of course. No one seriously expected anyone to ever be able to squash neutron stars together in order to make their own time machine.

But someone, evidently, had figured out another way to do the same thing.

"So that thing's a time machine?" Ramsey asked after he'd had a moment to digest the download.

"Space *and* time," Foss replied. "Space-time equivalence, remember? We think this must be one of several identical

gateways, constructed around different stars. You fly into one
and come out another. We don't know if they use the time
travel component at all, though the smart money says they
don't. They would screw causality to hell and gone if they
did. Now. Watch. . . ."

> *Visual: The stargate appears from a different angle,
> suspended against the background haze of the Sirian
> system. Something appears in the middle, a little off-
> center. One moment there is nothing there; the next,
> there is* something, *a golden object rendered tiny by the
> scale of the vast Wheel. The scene magnifies, zooming
> in for a closer look. The object appears to be a ship of
> some sort, needle slender, but somewhat swollen aft,
> golden-hued. Data readouts show the object to be over
> two kilometers long.*

Ramsey felt his scalp prickle as he watched the ship grow
rapidly larger. The vessel appeared to accelerate suddenly,
leaping toward him. . . .

The image cut off in a burst of white noise and electronic
snow.

He blinked. "Okay," he said slowly. "We have first contact
with a high-tech civilization. Who are they?"

"That," Foss replied, "we don't know."

"What happened to the *Wings of Isis*?" The words were
hard, grim.

"We don't know that, either. Whatever happened, of
course, happened ten years ago, while you were still on
Ishtar. We have to assume that the *Wings of Isis* was destroyed, since two more years passed after these images were
recorded and transmitted, and we've heard nothing from
them. That might have been an accident or . . ."

"Or enemy action. The Hunters of the Dawn?" Ramsey's
heart was beating a little faster now and he felt cold.

"Again, Colonel. We don't know. But we hope you and your people will be able to tell us."

"Huh. You don't believe in *easy* assignments, do you, sir?"

"This is the Marine Corps, son," Foss told him. "The only *easy* mission was the last one."

2

Marine Receiving Barracks
Star Marine Force Center
Twentynine Palms, California
1825 hours, PST

"So what's the dope, Gare?" Lance Corporal Roger Eagleton asked. "You hear anything?"

"Nope," Garroway said around a mouthful of steak-and-cheese. "You think they tell me anything?"

"You're the one with the famous Marine ancestor," Kat Vinton told him.

"I guess. So why would that mean they'd tell me what's going on?"

"I don't know. With your name, we figured they were grooming you for a recruiting tour, y'know?"

"Yeah," Corporal Bill Bryan added. "Just to keep you happy, so's you can be convincing with your sales pitch. You know. 'Join the UFR/US Marines! Travel to exotic climes! Explore strange new cultures! Meet fascinating people! Kill them.'"

"Ooh-rah."

They were seated at a long mess table, showered, dressed in newly issued utilities, and packing in their first meal in ten years. The chow was first-class and there was lots of it, but now that their stomachs had gotten rid of the last of that damned packing gel and had some time to settle, they were *hungry*. Even three-lies-in-one field rations would have seemed like food of the gods under the circumstances.

"How about you, Sarge?" Kat asked the big man at the end of the table. Staff Sergeant Richard "Well" Dunne was acting platoon sergeant now and the platoon's liaison with all higher authority. "They tell you what's going on?"

"Negative," Dunne said. "The word is to sit tight and all will be revealed."

"Hurry up and wait," Garroway said. "The litany of the modern Marine Corps."

"Fuck that shit," Sergeant Wes Houston said. "It's been that way since Sargon the Great was a PFC."

Garroway continued to eat, but he was somewhat unsettled. Kat's crack about his famous ancestor had caught him by surprise. His great-grandfather had been Sands of Mars Garroway, a tough old-Corps Marine who'd led his men on a grueling march through the Vallis Marineris during the U.N. War of 2042 to capture an enemy-held base. The man was one of the legends of the Corps, another live-forever name like Dan Daily, Smedley Butler, and Chesty Puller. When he'd gone through his Naming Ceremony, he'd deliberately chosen his mother's maiden name—Garroway—hoping, perhaps, that some of the luster of that name would rub off on him.

Now that he was a Marine himself, though, he frequently found himself wishing it wouldn't rub off quite so much. Officers and NCOs tended to expect more from him than of others, and everyone else assumed the name meant he had things easy.

The fact was that there was no favoritism in the Corps—not below the rank of colonel, at any rate, not that he'd been able to detect.

"There's one piece of good news," Dunne said. "The TIG

promos are probably gonna go through. That's something, at least."

Appreciative claps, whistles, and cheers sounded from around the mess table. It *was* good news.

In the service, being promoted from one rank to the next required passing advancement tests, but more it required TIG—time-in-grade. Garroway had boarded the *Derna* right out of boot camp as a wet-behind-the-ears private first-class, pay grade E-2. The voyage out to Lalande 21185 had taken ten years, objective time, though relativistic effects contracted that to four years, ship's time.

His promotion to E-3, lance corporal, had been pretty much automatic. Technically, he'd needed six months as an E-2 and four years subjective counted, even if he'd slept through most of it in cybehibe. He'd received his chevron above crossed rifles while serving on Ishtar.

He'd been on Ishtar for less than a year, however, before being packed onboard the *Jules Verne* and popped back into cybehibe for the return voyage. The promotion to the next rank, corporal, required a year in-grade plus a test. He would be an NCO, a noncommissioned officer, at E-4, with more responsibility and higher expectations regarding his performance.

So here he was . . . ten years objective and four years subjective later. Technically, he had the time in grade. What he did *not* have was the experience.

Still, it was embarrassing to be a Marine with—according to his Earthside records—twenty-one years in, and he was only an E-3. If he'd not gone to the stars, if he'd stayed in and stayed out of trouble, he would be a goddamned sergeant major by now, at the exalted pay grade of E-9.

Scuttlebutt had it that the brass was considering a blanket set of promotions for the men and women of Operation Spirit of Humankind, with everyone bumped up a pay grade and given a hefty out-system combat bonus to boot. There was talk of a special download training session to implant the necessary skills and knowledge that went with the rank.

Of course, if they kept *that* up, they'd have a whole platoon of gunnery sergeants. He wondered how they would handle the tendency for units to go top-heavy like that.

"There's also some other news," Sergeant Dunne went on, "though I can't vouch for it. Word is they may be about to offer us another deployment."

That brought shocked silence to the table. "Another deployment?" Kat asked. "Where?"

Dunne shrugged. "I was talking to the senior revival tech a while ago. All he knew was that we were being kept here for a while, possibly with the idea of letting us volunteer to go out-system again."

Out-system again? Garroway thought about it, and he didn't care for it. He'd just gotten back, and there were things he wanted to do, damn it. Like see how things had changed in twenty years. And, oh yeah . . . see if he could find his father and kill the bastard.

Anyway, the usual routine in both the Navy and the Marines was to rotate personnel between ship and shore assignments or between overseas or off-world duty stations and duty back in the World.

"This is just gonna be for volunteers, right, Sergeant?" he asked.

"I'd imagine so," Dunne said. "Unless the Corps's changed one hell of a lot in the past twenty years."

"On the other hand," Houston said thoughtfully, "we *are* all Famsit one or two. I'd imagine that's a resource kind of scarce in the Corps, y'know?"

"Yeah," Corporal Regi Lobowski said. "Maybe there's no one else to send."

"The question is," Kat said, "send where? Any idea, Sarge?"

"Nope. Not that there are that many possibilities."

Garroway had already uplinked to the platoon net, with a search query. How many out-system missions were going on right now?

And the choices were fairly limited. Marine detachments had been assigned to several extrasolar archeological missions, but most of those had been recalled due to budgetary constraints. The Chiron mission, at Alpha Centauri A, had been reopened two years ago after a ten-year suspension, and the *Diego Vasquez*, with exoarcheologists, planetologists, and Marines, was now en route to begin again the exploration of that desert world's dead cities, but Kali/Ross 154 and Thor/61 Cygni A both remained abandoned. There were Marines stationed at Rhiannon/Epsilon Eridani and at Poseidon/Tau Ceti, both worlds with ruins apparently going back to the long-vanished Builders.

And there was a detachment onboard the *Spirit of Discovery*, a deep explorer now en route for 70 Ophiuchi, and another on the *Wings of Isis* expedition to Sirius. That brought a wistful pang to Garroway. Lynnley was assigned to that shipboard detachment. He wondered where she was now . . . en route home? She ought to be by now. He hoped so.

What else? Outposts on Janus, on Hecate, and on Epona. There were no Marines stationed on those desolate worlds, but if there was trouble, Marines might be sent—assuming the need justified the colossal expense of an interstellar military expedition.

"Betcha it's Rhiannon," Corporal Anna Garcia said. "I heard the Builder ruins there are even bigger and more extensive than on Chiron, and the EU would just love to snatch that little gem right out from under our noses."

"Nah," Lobowski said. "Gotta be Chiron. Makes sense, right? I mean, we have a base there, we're diggin' up all kinds of cool shit, and then we pull out when the money dries up. But now we're sending out another expedition to the place. Either there's some highly classified shit goin' down out there, stuff the big boys don't want to talk about, or the EU is about to make a grab for the place. And the Feds want the Marines to handle it."

Womicki laughed. "Shee-it. Y'wanna know what I think?"

"Not really."

"I think they're sending us back to Ishtar. Wouldn't that be just like the Corps? Send us out there to fight the Frogs, haul us back, and then as soon as we're back, they ship us out to the same place again. SOP—standard operating procedure."

"You're full of it, Wo. Your eyes are brown."

Garroway wasn't sure what to think. Alpha Centauri . . . Epsilon Eridani . . . Tau Ceti . . . Sirius. Which was it?

Sergeant Houston's comment about Famsits was a good one. Where possible, the Corps only sent Famsit one and two personnel to the stars . . . men and women who had no close family on Earth. That was for the simple fact that travel between the stars took years objective; between relativity and cybehibe, a starfaring Marine might age a few months while a wife or parents back home aged a decade or two. Military service had always placed a strain on families, but time-lagging brought a whole new level of complexity to the problem.

How do you find Marines who have no family attachments at home?

"I'd sign on for another cruise," Womicki said.

"Fuck, not me," Houston said. "I've put in six years subjective—and twenty-six objective. Done my time, and now this gyrine's gonna be an *ex*-gyrine."

"There's no such thing as an ex-Marine, asshole," Dunne said good-naturedly. "Once in the Corps, *always* in the Corps!"

"Yeah," Kat put in. "They own you, body and soul, for all eternity. Didn't you read the fine print on your enlistment contract?"

"Anyway, Sarge," Lobowski said. "Maybe they won't give

you a choice. Maybe they just say 'Jump,' and you say 'Aye aye, and how high, *sir*!'"

"Aw, they ain't gonna ship us out without us sayin' they can," Corporal Matt Cavaco said. "It's against the law."

"The law," Dunne said slowly, "is what the brass *says* the law is. They want us to go fifteen light-years and tromp on some bug-faced locals, then that's what we'll do."

"*Semper fi*," Kat said.

"Do or die," Garroway added.

He wondered if they would at least be allowed leave before being shipped out-system again.

He had an old debt to settle with his father, and if another twenty years passed on Earth before he returned again, it might well be too late.

Virtual Conferencing Room 12
Star Marine Force Center
Twentynine Palms, California
1904 hours, PST

"Colonel Ramsey? Thank you for nouming in for this meeting. I know it's late there . . . and you must be tired after your long journey."

The others in the noumenal space laughed. "My pleasure, General," Ramsey said. "Not as late for me as for some of you."

In point of physical reality, Ramsey was lying on a padded recliner in a small room behind Foss's office. To his mind's eye, however, he stood—if that was the word, since there was no trace of a floor—in Sirius space, surrounded by the illusion of glowing gas and dust. Sirius A and B were hard, brilliant pinpoints beneath his feet. Ahead and above hung the enigmatic Wheel.

"Gentlemen," the welcomer said, "ladies, this meeting

will initiate Operation Battlespace. This information is classified, of course. Code Seven-Orange."

General Foss stood beside him. They were being addressed by Major General Franklin Kinsey, a man with the unwieldy title of CO-USMCSPACCOM, the commanding officer of the UFR/US Marine Space Command, based in Quantico, Virginia. Also in attendance were Brigadier General Harriet Tomasek, the coordinator of SMF space transport assets; Brigadier General Cornell Dominick, SPACCOM's liaison with the Joint Chiefs; and Colonel Gynger Kowalewski, SPACCOM's senior technical advisor. Two civilians were present as well, a Dr. James Ryerson, from the Federal Exoarcheological Intelligence Department, or XID; and Franklin T. Shugart from the President's Federal Advisory Council. Other men and women, some in uniform, others in icon-civvies, hovered in the near distance, staff members, aides, and advisors.

Their images—computer-generated—hung in a semicircle in space, watching the immense Wheel. To one side, the explorer ship *Wings of Isis* appeared to be drifting toward the artifact, a long and slender assembly of hab and cargo modules topped by the broad, full mushroom cap of the water tank that served as both reaction mass and shielding against deadly impacts of particulate radiation encountered at near-*c* velocities. The star transport's deceleration drive had been deployed, rising up through the center of the shielding cap to keep the hab modules safe in the cap's shadow.

"Is this a computer simulation of the ship's approach?" Dominick wanted to know. "Or the real thing?"

"Actually, it's built up from data transmitted from a half-dozen robot probes deployed as the *Isis* entered the Sirius system," Kowalewski said. "It's a sim, yes, but it's based on direct data, not extrapolation."

"It's the real thing, Corny," Tomasek said with a laugh. "In so far as we can know what *is* real."

"Here comes the hostile," Kinsey pointed out. The golden needle of the alien spacecraft appeared. Under heavy magnification, it seemed to materialize out of empty space, but a ripple of movement visible against the background stars visible through the opening suggested that space itself was being warped out of shape within the center of the ring.

"We are pretty sure that the ring is serving as a kind of artificial wormhole," Kowalewski said, "connecting two distant points in space. The mass readings suggest that black holes are being accelerated through the lumen of the ring and that this is radically distorting both space and time."

The needle changed course slightly, as though aligning on the *Wings of Isis*. They watched it accelerate in silence, growing large . . . growing *huge*. At the last instant, the alien vessel seemed to shimmer slightly, and then it was gone, *everything* was gone, stars, Wheel, alien vessel, and the *Wings of Isis*. The watchers hung in blackness absolute.

There was a long silence, and then the scene reappeared—*Isis* drifting toward the Stargate, with Sirius A and B gleaming in the distance.

"So where do these guys come from?" Dominick wanted to know.

"There's no way to tell," Kowalewski replied.

"Can we use this, this gateway?" Foss asked.

"Again, we don't know . . . though the physics of the thing suggest that the answer is yes. A ship would just fly right through, like threading a needle. But there's also the possibility, if this thing works like a Tipler Machine, as some have suggested, that we would have to fly a very precise, specific course through the gate. The problem, though, is that we have no way of knowing what that course is—or where it will take us."

"So how do we learn how to use the damned thing?" Kinsey asked. "Trial and error?"

"Essentially, yes," Kowalewski replied. "It may be possible to send remote probes into the gateway on different trajectories and record the results. The bad news, though, is that coming back is not as simple as retracing your steps. It may be a completely different course into the gateway on the other side that brings you home."

The group watched in grim silence for several moments more. The scene repeated itself and again they watched *Wings of Isis* attacked by the huge alien.

Or was it an attack? "We don't really see the *Isis* being destroyed," Foss pointed out. It looks like the alien is still some five hundred meters away when the transmission ends. Maybe the alien took the *Isis* onboard."

"It's possible," Tomasek said. "*Isis* wouldn't even make a decent lifeboat for that behemoth."

"The fact that we've had no transmissions from the *Isis* since suggests that she *was* destroyed," Ryerson said. "At the very least, our people are being held prisoner. Not exactly a friendly act."

"Which brings us back to the billion-dollar question," Kinsey said. "Who are these guys? Are they the Hunters of the Dawn?"

The question hung in the virtual conference space for a long and cold moment. During the course of the last two centuries, exoarcheologists had uncovered the debris left behind by several sets of alien visitors to Earth's solar system in ages past. The Builders had raised awe-inspiring structures on Mars and on Earth's moon. They'd terraformed Mars, briefly bringing shallow seas and a decent atmosphere back to that arid world, and they'd evidently set their mark on the genome of the primate that later would be called *Homo erectus*. All of that had transpired some half million years ago.

The Ahannu—also known as the An in the myths they sparked in ancient Sumer—came along much later. A starfaring culture, but one not nearly so advanced as the godlike

Builders, the Ahannu had colonized Earth and enslaved several human populations between twelve and ten thousand years before. They'd introduced mathematics, agriculture, medicine, writing, metallurgy, and other important skills to their slaves, who came to worship them as gods.

The gods had been helpless, however, before the onslaught of yet another alien race which they referred to as the Hunters of the Dawn.

Almost nothing was known about the Hunters. An expedition to Europa in 2067 had uncovered an immense robotic warship, the Singer, trapped deep beneath the Jovian moon's ice-locked ocean, the only Hunter relic so far discovered. In almost a century of intense study, very little had been learned about them.

What was known was that the Hunters of the Dawn had eradicated the Builders from Earth, Mars, and the moon half a million years ago, as well as Builder colonies on half a dozen worlds of several neighboring star systems. Presumably, they'd also, five hundred millennia later, destroyed the An empire as well, though that idea was still hotly debated. *Someone* had dropped several large asteroids onto Earth eight or ten thousand years ago, however, wiping out the An colonies and leaving a few human survivors to pick up the fragments of civilization and press forward. They'd also wiped out An colonies on numerous other worlds; the surviving Ahannu outpost on Ishtar evidently had been overlooked because the world was an unlikely place for them—the moon of a gas giant far beyond its star's habitable zone, kept warm by the flexing of tidal forces.

Were the Hunters of the Ahannu the same as the beings who wiped out the Builders? It seemed unlikely that a civilization could remain intact for half a million years, and yet clues linking the two genocides had been uncovered on both the moon and in the Europan world-ocean. If they *were* the same race, might that race still exist today, somewhere among the stars?

The Singer had released a powerful signal of some kind when it reached the surface of its icy prison. Even at the crawl of light, the signal had crossed over ninety light-years already and would still be traveling starward today. The possibility existed that the beings who'd destroyed both the Ahannu and Builder cultures yet survived, and that it now knew of the existence of humankind, or would, very soon.

That single chance, no matter how remote, continued to cause sleepless nights for those charged with Earth's defense. The main reason xenoarcheology continued to be well-funded and—for the most part, at least—strongly supported by several Earth governments was the hope that a dig somewhere would uncover more clues to the Hunters, to where they came from and what they were. The evidence suggested they were out to eradicate *all* possible competitors in the galactic arena.

If that were true, and if the Hunters of the Dawn still existed, Earth was in terrible danger.

"Obviously," Dominick said after a long silence, "that is something we need to learn. If the Sirian Wheel is a Hunter artifact, or a base, or a way back to their home worlds, we need to know that as well. And that is why we are authorizing Operation Battlespace."

The term *battlespace* was a relatively new Marine concept with some very old roots. As far back as the twentieth century, combat was seen in terms of control of the battlefield, which included the terrain, approaches, and the airspace above the combat zone. Control all of those factors tactically through fire, force, and movement, and a commander dominated the battlefield.

Modern combat made the concept a bit trickier than it had been back in the days of the Old Corps. Space was a completely three-dimensional medium and controlling the approaches to the battlefield when you had to take into account the possibilities of a strike from space was a lot tougher than worrying about air strikes from a carrier at sea or from the other side of the mountains. The MIEU-1's attack against the Ahannu on Ishtar had been carried out by troop transports approaching from the opposite side of the planet, then skimming in from over the horizon.

Ramsey looked up at the huge ring floating in the middle of a vast emptiness above him and wondered how they would approach *that* target.

It wasn't going to be easy.

"Colonel Ramsey," Dominick went on, "it is the consideration of the Joint Chiefs that your group would be best for this mission. They have experience taking a fortified enemy-alien position, the Legation Compound on Ishtar, and they have experience deploying in a hostile alien environment. They were superb on Ishtar. More, they have already been screened for Famsit one and two considerations."

"Sir," Ramsey said, "with respect . . . is this a voluntary deployment? Or are you just shipping us out?"

"Well, consideration will be given to each Marine's personal wish, of course," one of Kinsey's aides said. She was a colonel, and her electronic ID label read CHENG. Ramsey mentally requested further information, and a window opened in his awareness, silently scrolling words identifying Cheng as an expert in sociopsychological engineering.

"Forgive me, Colonel Cheng," Ramsey said, "but in the Corps that doesn't mean squat. I want to know if you plan on shipping these boys and girls out again without even hearing what they have to say about the matter. These people have fought hard for their country and for the Corps. They deserve to be treated right."

"I think what Colonel Cheng is saying," Franklin Shugart told him, "is that we will listen to what your people have to say. Those who wish to remain on Earth should be able to, after . . . appropriate retraining."

" 'Appropriate retraining,' " Ramsey repeated. He didn't like the sound of that. "What's that supposed to mean?"

"Earth has changed in twenty years, Colonel," Shugart told him. "You don't yet know how *much* it's changed. The culture. The language. The political spectrum. The religious splintering."

"Twenty years isn't so much."

"No? You haven't been here. We have. I sub you not glyph us on our n-state stats until you've DLed the gamma-channa."

Ramsey mentally checked his noumenal link and saw that Shugart had disengaged a consecutive translation function for his last few words.

"Okay, so your speech patterns have shifted a bit. We can learn. People who've been alive for more than twenty years *have* learned."

"Yes, but gradually," Shugart pointed out, restoring the translation function.

"Right," Kinsey added. "We didn't get hit with it all packed into one incoming warhead. I was . . . what? Thirty-eight when Operation Spirit of Humankind set out for the Lalande system. There've been astonishing changes in the years since, but I adapted to them incrementally, step by step, like everyone else. Like everyone *except* the Marines of MIEU-1."

"The truth of it, Colonel," Cheng said, "is that there are certain, well, *legal* problems with simply loosing your men and women on the country, unprepared. It's not fair to them. It's not fair to the civilian population."

An old, old joke about cybernetic hibernation for Marines spoke of keeping them frozen in glass tubes with sign plates reading: IN CASE OF WAR, BREAK GLASS. Marines were warriors—arguably the best damned warriors on the planet—and their skills could be embarrassing, even disruptive, in peacetime.

But it was still wrong to treat them that way.

"So you're keeping them prisoner?" Ramsey asked. He could feel the anger rising within, a burgeoning red tide. "Lock them up and then ship them out? What kind of shit are you trying to shovel at us?"

"Colonel Ramsey," Shugart scolded. "Some decorum, if you please. No one is going to be locked up, as you put it. But we will have to introduce certain safeguards. It's for their own good, as well as for the protection of the civilian populace."

"And as for shipping them out right away," Tomasek observed, "why don't we wait and see what they would prefer?" Her noumenal icon shrugged. "With no family attachments, with Earth changed so much, they might actually prefer another going back to space."

"Gentlemen . . . ladies," Ramsey said, "you're asking them to give up another twenty years objective for the dubious pleasure of facing the Hunters of the Dawn. It's too much!"

"Too much for the Marines?" Shugart said with an unpleasant smile. "I didn't know there was such a thing."

"They'll go as volunteers," Ramsey told him, "or not at all." He owed *that* much to his people, at least.

"I have to agree, Mr. Shugart," Kinsey said. "These are Marines, *people*, we're dealing with. Not chess pieces."

"I don't believe you or the colonel fully understand," Shugart said. "This will be a direct presidential order. The Federal Directorate has precedence over national interests."

And that, Ramsey had to admit, was one aspect of modern politics he did *not* understand, and it was becoming more confusing by the decade. The sudden growth of the old United States of America during the collapse of Canada and the wars with the U.N. and Mexico in the last century had resulted in huge, new territories added to the continental United States. To manage those territories, and to prepare them for admission as new states, the United Federal Republic of America had emerged as an organizational step above the United States.

And so, technically, the Corps was now the UFR Marines. Still, tradition dies hard in the Corps. So far as most Marines were concerned, they were still the *United States* Marines, a title *no* leatherneck would surrender without a fight. While the President of the United States was also President of the Federal Republic, technically the two were not the same, and, legally, it was the United Federal Republic that called the shots now . . . in the name of organizational efficiency.

Not that bureaucrats ever seemed that concerned about efficiency.

Ramsey didn't like the change, which had been well under way before the MIEU's departure for Ishtar, and which was now very well entrenched with the new Federal capitol being constructed in New Chicago. He felt, he imagined, much as an advocate of states' rights might have felt as the Federal government superseded mere state governments around the time of the American Civil War.

The upshot of it was that the political situation—always something of concern for the Corps—was becoming damned hard to understand.

"We can offer inducements for volunteers," Kinsey suggested. "Surely that is preferable to simply ordering them to turn around and keep marching off into the future."

"Perhaps," Shugart said. "The Federal Advisory Council will leave those decisions to the Marine brass and to the American Congress. But Mr. Ramsey and his people *are* going to Sirius. One way or another."

Ramsey wondered if the phrase *United States of America* even had meaning any longer. Just who was the Corps supposed to be fighting for now?

3

5 NOVEMBER 2159

Starstruck
Condecology Tower Raphael
Level 486
East Los Angeles, California
2028 hours, PST

The magflier public transport deposited them on the landing shelf of the tower, almost five hundred stories above the brilliantly lit sprawl of Greater Los Angeles. Garroway, Anna Garcia, Roger Eagleton, Regi Lobowski, Tim Womicki, and Kat Vinton stepped onto the platform, resplendent in newly issued Class A dress uniforms. A stiff wind off the ocean chilled and Garroway pulled his formal cloak a little closer about him. Eagleton paid off the transport with a wave of his newly issued asset card.

"You sure we belong here, Gare?" Kat asked him.

"I gave the flier's AI the address," Garroway told her. "This must be it."

"It" was a graceful series of curving walls and partial domes built into the side of one of Greater LA's newer skytowers. The landing platform was broad and edged with walled gardens and gene-tailored landscaping. Several other skytowers gleamed in the night in the near-distance, self-contained arcologies, some 5 kilometers high and each holding a small city in its own right. The one named Raphael, an implant download told Garroway with a whispering in his mind, had been completed ten years ago and packed 950 stories into a column 3.8 kilometers tall. It housed 15,000 people in spacious luxury, as well as hundreds of shops, stores, restaurants, theme malls, indoor parks and plazas, recnexi, and tobbos . . . whatever *those* were. People could live out their entire lives in Raphael or one of the other condecologies and never set foot outside.

To Garroway, that seemed a sterile kind of life, hardly worthy of the name. Still, different people, different customs. . . .

"Hey, even if it's the wrong address, it's worth it just getting offbase for a bit," Anna Garcia said. "I didn't think they were going to let us go."

"I sure don't know what the hassle is, that's for damned sure," Womicki said. "With all the form screens we had to thumb, you'd've thought we were trying to smuggle in ancient high-tech artifacts or something."

"Whoa," Eagleton said, nudging Garroway in the ribs. "Look at this!"

A woman walked out to meet them in a swirl of luminescence. She was strikingly nude; nanoimplants within her skin glowed in constantly shifting colors visible through the translucence of her skin, pulsing between deep ultramarine blue and emerald green. Her delicate tuft of neatly coiffed pubic hair had been treated as well; it glowed brightly, cycling from bright yellow to orange to red to gold to yellow again, creating interesting contrasts of hue against the deeper, inner glow of her thighs and belly. Her face and hair, however, were masked behind a silver, visorless helm. A spray of optical threads created a dazzling cascade of moving green and amber light rising over her head and spilling down each side to the ground.

"You didn't tell us we had to *dress* for dinner, Gare," Anna whispered at his side.

"Johnny!" the woman cried. "So glad you downjacked!"

"Uh . . . Tegan?"

"Who else?"

He gave an awkward grin. "Sorry. I didn't recognize you . . . uh . . . dressed like that. I appreciate your asking us out here tonight."

"Hey, no skaff." The cold didn't appear to bother her. "The mere the meller, reet? These your hangers?"

He blinked. Her speech was quite rapid and laced with unfamiliar words. "I guess so. Uh . . . these are my friends, the ones I told you about. This is Corporal Kat Vinton, Corporal—"

"Vix the IDs," Tegan said, waving a glowing hand. "Leave it for the noumens."

"I beg your pardon?"

"You don't expect me to downrem *names*, do you?" She laughed. "Grampie, you *are* synched out! C'mon!"

"Does 'grampie' mean what I think it does?" Anna asked.

" 'Grandparent'?" Eagleton replied *sotto voce.* " 'Grandpa'? That's my guess."

"Are you understanding any of this, Gare?" Kat asked him in a whisper as they followed the woman toward the building entrance.

"Oh, a word here and there," Garroway admitted.

" 'Johnny'?" Eagleton said and snickered.

"That was my civvie name," he said. "John Garroway Esteban. But I dropped the Esteban on my naming day, and I lost the John in boot camp."

He wondered just how much in common he had with Tegan now. He'd given her a netcall as soon as they'd been informed that the com interdict had been lifted, and she'd sounded happy to hear from him. She'd invited him and anyone he cared to bring along to a *numnum* . . . whatever the hell that was. They'd approached Staff Sergeant Dunne and, after a few frustrating hours of red tape and a *lot* of question-

ing, received passes. Garroway had the impression that there
were some high-level complications in the request, but he
didn't care about the details. Just so long as they could get out
of Twentynine Palms for a few precious hours.

"So who is this Tegan?" Anna wanted to know.

He shrugged. "A friend. I met her down in Hermisillo a
few years ago. A few years before I joined the Marines, I
mean. She was on winter vacation at a resort down there."

"Just a friend?" Womicki asked.

"Well, no. More than that." That had been before he'd
started seeing Lynnley.

"I got news for you. She's too old for you now, son,"
Lobowski said. " 'Out of synch,' huh?"

"Oh, she looks pretty well-preserved," Eagleton said, eye-
ing her glowing back as she led the way through a high,
curved archway and into the party proper.

"Yeah," Womicki said. "Almost as well-preserved as us."

Garroway shook his head. The objective-subjective time
difference was taking some getting used to. Cybehibe did not
entirely stop aging, but it did drastically slow all bodily processes by a factor of something like five to one. That, coupled
with the effects of time dilation, meant that Garroway and his
fellow Marines had aged less than a year biologically, while
Tegan had aged twenty.

Of course, anagathic treatments were becoming more
common and less expensive on Earth. At the base, Garroway
had already met people who were over a hundred years old,
but who looked no older than fifty. Someday, perhaps, thanks
to nanomedical prophylaxis, age might not matter at all.

But in the meantime, it could be disconcerting. Tegan had
been a year younger than he when he'd left Earth.

Inside the doorway, the floor dropped away in a large,
roughly circular room sunken in the middle, with alcoves and
balconies at various levels on all sides. A warm, indirect
ruby-hued lighting made walls and ceilings hard to discern, a

dreamscape of subtle, sensuously curving forms. Everything appeared to be made of moving red light, and it was tough to see what was solid wall or floor and what was not.

And the place was packed.

The six Marines stopped and stared, their mouths comically open. There must have been hundreds of people present, standing, sitting, or lying a-sprawl on the thickly scattered divans that appeared to have grown out of the floor. Many, men and women both, were nude or nearly so, though most wore bangles and elaborate high-tech helmets that completely masked their faces, and their skin glowed with myriad inner hues. Those not stripped down were wildly dressed up. Garroway wondered if there was a competition under way for the most elaborate and eye-popping costume.

"Is this your home?" Kat asked the woman.

"What? Are you seerse? This is a sensethete, of course! It's called the Starstruck, and it's part of the conde. Part of the service, y'know?"

"Take your cloaks?" a gleaming, streamlined machine floating above the floor asked. Garroway and the others removed their cloaks, draping them across the robot's waiting and multiple arms. "And your clothing, ladies and sirs?"

"I beg your pardon?" Womicki asked.

"When in Rome, Mick," Garroway said, gesturing at the crowd.

"I think I'll keep my uniform on, thank you," Kat said.

Garroway agreed. "We're fine," he told the hovering robot. It hummed in what seemed a disapproving manner, but then floated off into the encircling red mist. Casual and social nudity had long been accepted throughout most of the southern and western states, and there was little privacy for males or females in a Marine squad bay or on board ship. Privacy wasn't an issue.

However, this was different. The other guests weren't completely bare, but were adorned in myriad ways, with nanoinduced internal lighting, with devices that appeared to be grown into the skin itself and with various items of jewelry. There was, Garroway thought wryly, a large difference between *nude* and *naked*. The six Marines would have looked somewhat akin to plucked chickens in this gaudy company, and at least their blue with red and white trim Class A's gave them some ornamentation.

"You'll need these, grampies," Tegan said, returning to them. She held out a pair of delicately shaped and filigreed helmets. A helmed, winged angel with fluorescent violet tattoos and a handsome man wearing a low-cut seventeenth-century ball gown handed them four more.

"What are these for?" Lobowski wanted to know, turning one uncertainly in his hands.

"You don't viz techelms?" the angel asked. He laughed.

"G'wan!" the guy in the ball gown told them. "Put 'em on and down 'em! You'll jack!"

Hesitantly, Garroway slipped the helmet he'd been given onto his head. The visor was opaque, blocking all vision. He felt a warm tingle at the back of his skull and at the temples.

And then . . .

Color and light exploded around him, and he heard a murmuring ripple of multiple conversations in his head. He could see now, despite the opaque visor. Somehow, the helmet was taking in his surroundings and transmitting them directly to his implant. He could see more clearly, more crisply than before, and was aware of a tumbling avalanche of detail.

It was, in fact, a little like being linked into a tactical net in combat, except that this was accompanied by an odd, very deep, and very sensuous inner movement of feeling and emotion. It took him a moment to identify it: *pleasure*.

"*How's that feel?*" Tegan asked him, her voice sliding into his mind like liquid silk. "*Nice?*"

"It's . . . interesting."

And it was going to take some getting used to. It wasn't

that he minded the sensation of pleasure itself. It was the fact that these pleasurable sensations were coming and going, emerging, building, exploding all without any thought, movement, or input from him.

In fact, the sensation was like what he'd always imagined a nano-induced high might be like, one that involved all of his senses. As he looked about, he realized that the bodies of the people around him were subtly—and sometimes not so subtly—enhanced. The men seemed more handsome, more muscular, more athletic, while the women were slimmer, more beautiful of face, more generous and perky of bosom. The man in the ball gown was now a lovely woman, and the gown itself an explosion of blue and silver starlight. Many of the guests were no longer even human; a radiantly green and golden lion with eagle's wings stared at them from a nearby dais. Other shapes were more outlandish—zoomorphic, angelic, demonic, or mixtures of the three. Were they real? Or illusion? Or some subtle combination of the two? Some shapes morphed and shifted from one thing to another as he watched.

And he could hear things, conversations he'd not been able to hear before, and it was impossible to tell whether he was hearing actual sound or picking up on a mingling interchange of surface thoughts.

"*Oh sure, and the flam did the jug out of a whiter, reet? . . .*"

"*And so she was neg way, and then I was yeah, way, and then she was neg way, and then . . .*"

"*So'dja hear the zit on Chollin and Vashti? . . .*"

"*Well, Ran and Silva and me, we all vammed down to Cancun for a bit of a vaccshi, and . . .*"

"*So I was getting bored, totally weed, and there was this new religion, Galaninism, and I thought, reet, why not, it can't be as moomy as the Church of the Mindful Stars . . .*"

"*So why'd Teeg invite them? Fascists. . . .*"

That last had cut through the other conversations with a peculiar bitterness. He tried to focus on it, and picked up a few more words.

"Ah, *you know how the Army is, always narbing in and invading places where it's not wanted. . . .*"

"Hey, did you hear that?" Eagleton said aloud, looking about.

"Ignore it, Rog," Garroway told him. "We're guests here, remember?"

"Besides," Kat added judiciously, "they're obviously talking about someone else. We're not Army."

Garroway took a cautious couple of steps, feeling for the deck beneath his feet. It was, he thought, like stepping into a dream, one where nothing was quite as it seemed.

"*Here*," someone said in his mind. "*Groz this, grampie.*"

A silver and black metallic sphere was placed in his hand. As he looked at it, trying to get an idea of both what it was for and what its true form might be, it twisted itself in his palm, opening itself. A thick lavender mist spilled out and he caught the tang of cinnamon. And . . . something else. As he inhaled, he felt the rush exploding out of his lungs and throat and tingling all the way down to his toes and back up his spine to the crown of his head. The helmet took the sensation, amplified it, twisted it . . . and fed it back to him in rippling pulses of feeling.

"Is this stuff *legal*?" he heard Lobowski say.

"*What a ridic question!*" a woman's voice replied, a sensuous gliding of thoughts. "*This is a numnum, mem?*"

Garroway tried to meditate on this self-evident truth, but was having some trouble focusing.

"What the hell happened to the floor?" Eagleton asked.

Good question. When Garroway looked down, he could see the floor beneath his feet as swirling patterns of rainbow-hued pinpoints of light. Each hesitant step he took sent out widening ripples of flickering color, ripples that interlaced with other ripples in spectacular moving moirés of colored light.

And the voices. Something similar was happening with all of the voices in the room. Garroway could no longer be sure which were voices he was hearing in his head, and which were actual, audible sound. He was hearing more and more, however, and the words and sentences seemed to be weaving together into an incoherent yet meaningful whole. Behind it all was . . . was that music? Not quite. It was a kind of rhythmic pulse or ticking, but with something else unidentifiable beneath, a kind of deep and somehow musical *longing* without any actual notes.

That was interesting. Several couples were engaged in sex play on a round divan off to one side of the sunken room. Garroway found that when he watched them, he could actually *feel* some of what they must be feeling . . . touches and caresses and warm, moist, sliding pressures. The helmets, he realized, were somehow letting everyone in the room share in an overpowering gestalt of emotion and sensation.

The blending of heightened sensations was having a marked physiological effect on him, as well. Garroway could feel a familiar pressure building in his loins, and an intense and unscratchable itch.

But more, his feelings were oddly jumbled, melding one into another and transforming as they did so. Deliberately turning his back on the lovemaking tableau so he could concentrate, he tried to tap into his implants for a download on what was happening, but couldn't access his system. At that, Garroway began to feel genuine alarm.

"What the hell's going on here," he heard himself say, his voice sounding very far away.

"*What's the downskaff, grampie?*" A woman hovered in front of him, hugging-distance close. How had she gotten there? "*Don'tcha rax with it? Isn't it a flittering* rish?" Her voice curled sensuously through his brain.

Garroway wasn't certain whether it was whatever had been in the sphere or the helmet—or both working together—but he was beginning to feel as though all of his senses were blurring together. He was seeing sound, hearing color, tasting the pressure of his feet on the unseen floor and of his uniform on his skin. The conversation swirled around him, caressing him, a living thing experienced rather than merely heard.

"You're del says you were actually, like, in the body on another planet," the woman's voice continued in his mind. *"Is that, like, for real?"*

Funny how that one voice stood out from the others, obviously addressed to him, yet somehow intertwined with all of the other conversations going on. It was like being both an individual and some kind of communal, many-in-one intelligence.

"Sorry . . . 'del'?"

"You know! Download! From your implant!"

The woman was staring at him with eyes brilliant as blue-white stars. Who was it? Not Tegan . . . someone else, someone he'd not met before. He tasted her hand on his shoulder. She was gorgeous, an ethereal creature of radiant light.

"So? Howz'bout it? Were you really on another planet?"

"Uh . . . yeah. Ishtar. I was there."

"Ishtar . . . yeah? What a zig! I been there too!" A rapid-fire barrage of images flickered through Garroway's mind—scenes of Ishtar, with Marduk vast and swollen in a green sky; of the native An, like tailless, erect lizards with huge golden eyes; of the stepped pyramids of New Sumer so reminiscent of the ancient Mayan structures in Central America; of the vast and eerily artificial loom of the mountain they'd called Krakatoa; of a claustrophobic sprawl of mud huts and city walls, of dense purple-black jungle.

"Wait a minute. What do you mean, you were there too?" This glowing woman was neither a Marine nor a scientist, of that he was sure. She hadn't been onboard the *Jules Verne*, either, and no other ships had returned from Ishtar since the original voyage of discovery thirty years ago.

"Sure! In sim, y'know? Most of the folks here grozzed a simtrip to Epsilon Eridani right here just last week!"

"Oh. A *sim* . . ." Well, that made more sense. With the right hardware and AI programming and decent sensory records of the target, a direct download to your cerebral implants could make it seem as though you were actually there . . . at the bottom of the ocean, walking the deserts of Mars, or exploring the jungles of distant Ishtar.

"Well, yeah," the woman said. She sounded exasperated. *"Why vam it in the corp, y'know? And it takes so long. A numnum feed is much better. Don't send the mass. Just send information, reet?"*

He was beginning to gather that numnum must be a corruption of noumenon. The techelms, apparently, allowed everyone wearing them to share not only surface thoughts, but emotions and sensations as well.

He must have been broadcasting some of his bemusement. *"Don't you Army types groz numnum feeds?"* she asked.

"Not . . . Army . . ." he managed to say. Speech was difficult. *"Marines. . . ."*

She shrugged. "Whatever."

"No, damn it. It's important. *Marines.*"

What were they doing to him? Reaching up, he fumbled with the helmet, then pulled it off.

Instantly, the falsely heightened colors and sensations dropped away. The woman of light was now . . . just a woman, a bit overweight and sagging despite the efforts of some decades, he thought, of anagathic nano. She was wearing nothing but sandals, jewelry, and a silver techelm. Without the light show she was not as disconcerting to look at, and from what he could see of her mouth and hair, he guessed she was rather plain behind that opaque visor. He actually liked her better this way.

But she was already turning away, losing interest.

Where were his friends? Funny. He'd thought they were still right there next to him, but they appeared to have dispersed through the crowd.

He slipped the helmet back on, hoping to spot them. The explosion of color and thought hit him again, but he found he was now able to zero in on their location.

"*I wasn't talking to you, creep! Back off!*" Was that Anna's thought? It sounded like her. He tried to locate her in the crowd.

Ah! There she was, halfway across the room, easy enough to spot now in her Class A's, surrounded by several helmeted men and women.

"*So who invited you, Teenie?*" one of the men was saying. The conversation did not sound pleasant.

"Hey, I said back off," Anna said aloud. "I don't want any trouble."

"Well, you got trouble, lady," one of the women told her. "We don't like your kind around here."

"Hey, hey," Garroway said, wading into the small crowd gathering around Anna. "What the hell is this all about?"

A waspish-looking man with an ornate silver and gold helmet shaped to represent a dragon turned the visor to face him. "This little *Aztlanista* thought she could grope our party, feo. Who the hell are *you*?"

"I'm a U.S. Marine, like her. And I happen to know she's no *Aztlanista*."

"Her del says her name's Garcia," the woman said. "Latina, reet?"

"So? My family name was Esteban," Garroway told them. "And I was born in Sonora. You have a problem with that?"

"*Yeah*, we have a problem with that. You Teenies are freaming bad news, revolutionaries and troublemakers, every one of you!" The woman reached out and grabbed for the front of Anna's uniform.

Faster than the eye could see, Anna blocked the grab, snagged the arm, and dropped it into a pressure hold that drove the woman to her knees, screaming. One of the men moved to intervene, and Garroway took him down with a sharp, short kick to the side of his knee. Spinning about, he took a fighting stance back to back with Anna. The crowd glowered, but came no closer.

"I think you milslabs better shinnie," a man said.

"Yeah," another agreed. "Ain't none of you welcome here, zig? Vam out!"

Garroway looked around, searching the room for the rest of the Marines. Kat and Rog were coming fast, both tossing aside their helmets as they shouldered through the crowd. And there were Tim and Regi. All right. *Semper fi. . . .*

For a moment, he wondered if they would get into trouble—fighting in a civilian establishment. *Fuck it! They started it! . . .*

But then a sharp, hissing static filled Garroway's ears . . . his mind and thoughts. Staggered, he raised his hands to his ears, trying unsuccessfully to block the literally painful noise. His vision began to fuzz out as well, blurring and filling with dancing, staticky motes of light.

An implant malfunction? That was nearly unthinkable, but he didn't know what the civilian techelms might have done to his Marine system.

"What's . . . happening? . . ." he heard Eagleton say. The other Marines, too, had been stricken. That elevated the static from malfunction to enemy action.

But who was the enemy? The civilians surrounding them? That didn't seem likely.

"You are in violation of programmed operational parameters. Hostile thought and/or action against civilians is not permitted. Desist immediately."

The voice, gender-neutral and chillingly penetrating, rose above the static.

54 **IAN DOUGLAS**

"Huh? Who's that?"

"This is the social monitor AI currently resident within your cereblink. Hostile thought and/or action against civilians is not permitted. Desist immediately."

"What AI?" Womicki demanded loudly. "What's goin' on?"

The shrill hiss grew louder and louder, driving Garroway to his knees. Anna Garcia collapsed beside him, unconscious.

And a moment later he joined her. . . .

Police Holding Cell
Precinct 915
East Los Angeles, California
2312 hours, PST

It had been, Captain Martin Warhurst thought, *inevitable*. Marines back from a deployment—especially one as long and as rugged as the mission to Lalande 21185—needed to go ashore and let off some steam. His people had fought damned hard and damned well on Ishtar; they deserved a bit of downtime.

But downtime too often turned to fighting, chemical or nanoincapacitation, and rowdy behavior frowned upon by the civilian establishment.

The guard led him down a curving passageway to one of a number of holding cells, bare rooms walled off by thick transplas barriers. This one was occupied by twenty or thirty men, with expressions ranging from dazed to sullen. Four, however, recognized him immediately and came to their feet.

"Captain Warhurst!"

"You boys okay?"

"A little fuzzy yet, sir," Garroway said.

"Yeah," Womicki added. "Sir, you gotta get us out of here. These civilians are freakin' crazy!"

"What happened?"

Garroway tapped the side of his head. "Not sure, sir. Things got a little tight at a party we were at. Next thing I know, a voice in my head is telling me I'm in violation. And then . . . lights out."

Warhurst nodded. "Social monitor."

"Yeah, but what is it, sir?" Eagleton wanted to know. "I don't remember giving permission to have anyone tamper with my 'link!"

"It was part of your agreement when you got to leave the base. Remember thumbing a nonaggressive clause?"

"Sure," Lobowski said, leaning up against the transparency. The plastic was several centimeters thick, but the speaker system let them talk and be heard. "It said to stay out of trouble. We figured, 'Hey, no sweat. We're not lookin' for trouble.'"

"Did you read the fine print?"

"What fine print?" Womicki said. "It was a download."

"Well, you should have heard someone telling you that you were being given Class 5 nanoingests."

"You mean when they gave us something to drink?" Garroway asked. "I didn't hear anything about nano in the stuff."

"Mm. Well, we'll check that out later."

"What kind of nano, sir?" Womicki asked.

"Short-term autodegradable. Chelates with your current implant and creates a temporary low-grade AI that acts as a kind of watchdog. You get out of line, it puts you to sleep."

"*Shit!*"

"Things have changed a bit since we were out on Ishtar," Warhurst told them. "The brass is concerned about how we behave in public."

"So they feed us monitor nano?" Garroway said, bitter. "Such a splendid reflection of civilian respect for us. Sir."

"Like I said, things have changed."

"There were two women with us, sir," Garroway said. "Vinton and Garcia."

"Staff Sergeant Dunne is springing them, Garroway. I'm here for you."

"Thank you, sir."

"Don't thank me. You'll be facing a mast for disorderly conduct."

"But sir, *they started it*!"

"Freeze it down, Garroway. You boys put your foot in it. Part of my agreement with the authorities is that you go up before the Man. Copy?"

"Yes, sir. Copy." He swallowed. "Sir?"

"Yeah?"

"Did they make you take that monitor nano for you to come down here?"

Warhurst grinned. "What do you think, Marine?"

"I don't know, sir. You're an officer and a gentleman and all that."

"I had to take it, son. No exceptions. If the Marine Commandant was coming down here, they'd make him take a drink of the stuff. I don't think they trust the devil dogs out of the kennel without a leash."

"No, sir."

"Don't worry. It'll dissolve and be out of your system within forty-eight hours."

"I'm *very* glad to hear that, sir."

"Open it up," Warhurst growled at the guard.

The guard touched a control at his belt, and a panel in the transparency slid aside. Garroway, Womicki, Lobowski, and Eagleton all walked out of the cell.

The Marines were wearing bright lime-green prison utilities, unlike the civilians in the holding cell. "Sir, about our uniforms. . . ." Womicki began.

"I know. They told me at the front desk."

"Sir, we were *robbed*!"

According to the report he'd seen coming in, Raphael security forces had arrived at the Starstruck to find all six

Marines unconscious and naked. There was nothing unusual in that, perhaps, so far as the condecology police were concerned, and they'd turned them over to the East LA police without comment. The Marines had regained consciousness an hour later in the police infirmary, insisting that someone at the party had taken their things, including their asset cards.

The police had already put a stop on the cards. As for the uniforms, there wasn't much that could be done. Warhurst shook his head. What the hell did civilians want with Marine Class A's? Costumes for a costume ball?

Or maybe it had just been a damned prank.

The guards led them back to the front receiving area, where a clerk offered a screen panel for Warhurst's thumbprint. "Thumb here, sir. And here."

"I'll have someone return the prison uniforms later."

"Don't bother," a beefy police sergeant said. "They're disposables."

"Okay. These people have any effects to sign out?"

"No, sir, They came in stripped bare." The man smirked. "You Marines really like to party, huh?"

"These Marines were robbed, Sergeant. I will be filing a report to that effect."

The man shrugged massive shoulders. "Suit yourself. But maybe next time your boys and girls won't come where they're not wanted, tendo?"

"Yeah." Warhurst said, his voice tight. "We tendo."

He'd been warned. Things *had* changed in the twenty years they'd been away.

And in some ways, things hadn't changed much at all.

4

Navy/Marine XT Training Facility
Fra Mauro, Mare Imbrium, Luna
0920 hours GMT

Hospitalman Second Class Phillip K. Lee was trying to run, but he was having a bit of trouble. His feet kept leaving the ground, turning him into a small low-altitude spacecraft, and he was having a hard time controlling his vector.

Overhead, Earth hung half-full in a midnight sky, an achingly beautiful glory of blue and white; the sun was just above the horizon at Lee's back, and the shadows he and the dust cloud cast stretched for long meters across a flat and barren plain.

"*Slow down, damn it*!" he heard over his helmet headphones. "What are ya tryin' to do, bounce into orbit?"

His feet hit powdery gray dust, kicking up a spray of the stuff. He tried to stop, overbalanced, and tumbled onto the ground. For a moment, he lay there, listening to the rasp of his own breathing. Readouts beneath his visor showed the workings of both his suit and his body. His heart rate and respiration were up, but otherwise he was okay. His armored suit, built to take rough usage in the field, was intact.

Good. Because if it wasn't, he was in deep trouble.

Awkwardly, he tried to roll over. He was wearing Mark

VIII vac armor, bulky and massive. In some ways, it *was* a self-contained spacecraft. And he was having some trouble developing the coordination and skills he needed to fly the damned thing.

"*Lee, you fucking idiot!*"

"Sorry, Gunnery Sergeant," he said. "Got a bit carried away there."

"You get carried away in this environment, sailor," the voice told him with a growl, "and you are *dead*. Move slow. Move deliberate. Move methodical. Know what the fuck you're doing, and *why*."

Well, he knew what he was doing. He was trying to reach the form of a space-suited Marine sprawled in the dust eighty meters ahead. And why?

Well, he was a Navy hospital corpsman. And that's what corpsmen did, even if this was a particularly realistic bit of training, rather than a real combat deployment.

Carefully, he rose on unsteady feet and began moving forward again, more cautiously this time. Under lunar gravity, his body weight plus his armored suit and equipment weighed less than 24 kilos . . . but it still *massed* 144, which meant that once he got himself moving in any direction, stopping or turning could be a bit tricky. He'd done this sort of thing plenty of times in simulation . . . but this was his first time in a suit working in hard vacuum.

It was tough to see his target. Marine chamelearmor responded to ambient lighting and reflected the colors and forms of the environment, allowing it to blend in with the background to an amazing degree. The effect wasn't perfect in a complicated environment like a city or forest, but the surroundings here were simple: stark black sky and gray powder dust. At this range, Lee couldn't see his target at all with his own eyes; his helmet display, responding to a suit transponder, threw a bright green reticule onto his visor to mark the target's position.

Moving more deliberately now, he crossed the gently rolling regolith, following his own leaping shadow. Ahead, a featureless mound, one among many, resolved itself into a space-suited male figure, lying on his side.

He put on the metaphorical brakes before he reached the body, dropping to a kneeling position as he came to a halt in a spray of powder-fine dust. The patient had his back to Lee. He pulled the man over, peering down into the helmet visor. A fist-sized hole high in the right shoulder was leaking air; Lee could see the sparkle of ice crystals dancing above the tear and see crimson blood bubble as it welled up into a vacuum and froze. An ugly mass of frozen blood partly filled the wound.

"You're gonna be okay, mac," he called over the combat frequency. "Hang on and we'll get you patched right up!" There was no response—not that he was really expecting one. The patient's suit display on his chest showed winking patterns of red, green, and yellow. The suit breach was sealed around the wound, but the heaters were out, commo was out, and O_2 partial pressure was dropping fast.

The suit's AI was still working, though. Lee pulled a cable connect from the left sleeve of his own armor and snicked it home in the receptacle at the side of the patient's helmet. A second later, a full readout on the patient's condition was scrolling down through his awareness, the words overlaid on the lower-right side of his visual field. The wound, he learned, had been caused by a probable laser hit estimated at 0.8 megajoule. The bolt had burned through his shoulder armor, which had scattered much of the energy. There was no exit hole, so the energy that had not been dispersed by armor or the explosive release of fluid from superheated tissue had stayed put, cooking muscle and bone. Nasty.

Lee began going through the oft-practiced checklist. The challenge with giving combat field first-aid to someone in a vacuum was that you had to work through the guy's suit. On

Earth—or in an Earthlike environment—the order of medical priorities was fairly straightforward: restore breathing, stop catastrophic bleeding, treat for shock . . . and only then tend to such lesser concerns as immobilizing broken bones or bandaging wounds. The old mnemonic "ABC" established the order of treatment: airway, breathing, circulation. First establish an open airway, then restore breathing, and finally stop the bleeding and treat the shock caused by blood loss and trauma.

That order held true in space as well, but things became a lot more complicated. Suit integrity was the first concern; the larger the hole in a Marine's vac armor, the faster and more explosive the loss of air. In space combat, a corpsman also had to be part suit mechanic. Keeping a Marine's space armor alive was vital to keeping the Marine inside alive as well.

Mark VIII vac armor was smart enough to seal off a hole to prevent pressure loss. A spongy, inner layer of the armor laminate was a memory plastic designed to press tightly around the man's body at the point of a leak, serving both as tourniquet and as a seal against further air loss. Sometimes, though, a complete seal just wasn't possible. This one, for instance. The suit had formed a seal around the hole in order to maintain internal pressure, but the laser burst had punctured the Marine's thoracic cavity . . . and penetrated the left lung as well. Air was spilling from the Marine's bronchial tubes into his chest cavity—a condition called pneumothorax— and the air, mixed with blood, was bubbling away into space through the punctured suit. As the air drained away, the condition became the opposite of pneumothorax—vacuthorax— and massive lung tissue trauma.

And suddenly, things were getting much worse very quickly. As Lee rolled the armored form over, a crusty, glittering patch of frozen blood and water clinging to the wound suddenly dissolved in a spray of red vapor. He caught his mistake immediately. When he'd changed the Marine's position, he'd moved the wound from shade into direct sunlight. The wound had been partly plugged with blood-ice, but in the harsh light of the sun just above the eastern lunar horizon, the temperature on that part of the armor soared from around −80° Celsius to almost boiling. In seconds, the ice plug had vaporized, reopening both the wound and the partly plugged hole in the armor.

There was no time for anything but plugging that leak. Reaching into the case mounted on his right thigh, he pulled out a loaded sealant gun, pressed the muzzle up against the hole, and squeezed the trigger. Gray goo, a quick-setting polymer heavily laced with programmed nano, squirted over the hole and wound together, almost instantly firming to a claylike consistency, then hardening solid. He checked the Marine's suit readout again. Internal pressure was low, but steady.

But the guy was still bleeding internally—probably hemorrhaging into his thoracic cavity—and his heart was fluttering, atrial fibrillation. The patient was on the verge of going into arrest.

Lee reached for another tool, a Frahlich Probe, and slammed the needle down against the armor, directly above the heart. The probe's tip was housed in a nano sheath, which literally slipped between the molecules of the man's vac armor, then through skin, muscle, and bone to penetrate the patient's chest while maintaining an almost perfect air-tight seal. Leaving the needle in place, he pulled off the injector, then attached a reader. The device fed his implant a noumenal image of a glistening red, pulsating mass—the beating heart—and let him position the tip of the needle more precisely, at the sinus node at the top of the right atrium. Easy . . . easy . . . *there*!

Now he could program the probe to administer a rapid-fire series of minute electric shocks directly into the sinus node, regularizing the beat. He watched the readout a moment longer as the probe's computer continued to feed electrical impulses into the patient's heart. The fibrillation ceased, the heartbeat slowing to a fast but acceptable 112 beats per minute.

The patient's breathing was labored. He couldn't tell, but he suspected that the left lung had collapsed. Certainly, it had been badly damaged by both wound and vacuum trauma. With the wound sealed over, the best Lee could do for the patient now was evacuate him.

"Nightingale, Nightingale," he called. "This is Fox-Sierra One-niner. I need an emergency evac. Patient has suffered massive internal vacuum trauma. Suit leak is plugged and wound is stable. Heart monitor in place and operational. Over!"

A voice came back through his implant a moment later. "Copy that, Fox-Sierra. This is *Alpha Three-One*, inbound to your position, ETA two-point-five mikes. Ready your patient for pickup, and transmit suit data, over."

"We're ready to go at this end. Uploading data now."

He spent the time checking for other wounds, monitoring the patient's heart and vitals, and entering the computer code that caused the man's armor to go rigid, locking him immobile against the chance of further injury. The patient's condition continued to deteriorate, and Lee was beginning to guess that he'd made a wrong choice, a wrong guess somewhere along the line.

His patient was dying.

Two and a half minutes later, a silent swirl of lunar dust marked the arrival of *Alpha 3/1*, a UT-40 battlefield transport converted to use as a medevac flier. Bulbous and insect-faced, it settled to the lunar regolith on spindly legs. A pair of space-suited men dropped from the cargo deck and jogged over to Lee and the patient.

Lee stepped back as they attached a harness to the rigid armor. He was already scanning for another casualty. His suit scanners were giving him another target, bearing one-one-seven, range two kilometers. . . .

"Belay that, Lee," Gunnery Sergeant Eckhart's voice told him. "The exercise is concluded."

"But Gunnery Sergeant—"

"I said belay that! Mount up on the Bug and come on home."

"Aye aye, Gunnery Sergeant," he replied. From the sound of Eckhart's voice, he'd screwed this one up pretty badly. He looked over one of the Marine's shoulders at the patient and saw the deadly wink of red lights: PATIENT TERMINATED.

Damn, what had he missed? He'd followed procedure right down the list.

He mounted the UT-40, popularly known as a "medibug," or "bug" for short. The passenger compartment wasn't much more than an open framework of struts, with a bit of decking underfoot. The two Marines were strapping the patient onto a carry stretcher slung portside outboard, but without the usual formalities of connecting life support and condition monitors. The exercise was over.

The patient, of course, wasn't really dead, had never been alive to begin with in the traditional sense. It was a high-tech dummy, a quite sophisticated robot, actually, with a very good onboard AI that let it realistically simulate a wide range of combat wounds, injuries, traumas, various diseases, and even potentially fatal conditions such as drop-sickness-induced vomiting, followed by choking inside a sealed helmet. He was called "Misery Mike," and he and his brothers had helped train a lot of Navy corpsmen for SMF duty. He couldn't really die of vacuthorax because he wasn't alive to begin with . . . but how Lee had treated his problems could mean life or death for Lee's hopes to ship out with the Marines.

The UT-40's plasma thrusters fired, the blasts both silent and invisible in the lunar vacuum. Dust billowed out from beneath the bug's belly as the ugly little vehicle rose into the black sky. After a moment's acceleration, the thrusters cut out, and the medibug drifted along on a carefully calculated suborbital trajectory, the cratered and dust-cloaked terrain slipping smoothly past a hundred meters below.

He spent the time going over his treatment of the last casualty. He knew he should have been more careful about moving the suit. If he'd left the wound in the shade, kept it below freezing, he might not have damaged the patient's lungs as badly. But the lungs had already been damaged and vacuthorax would still have been an issue. Damn, what had he *missed*?

Minutes later, the medibug was descending over the powdery desert of Fra Mauro. Ahead, the Navy–Marine Lunar Facility was spread out in the glare of the early morning sun, its masts, domes, and Quonset cylinders casting oversized shadows across the surface.

The Fra Mauro facility had started life a century and a half ago as a U.N. base, with attendant spaceport. Taken over by U.S. Marines in the U.N. War of 2042, it had been converted into a joint Navy–Marine lunar base. It now consisted of over one hundred habitat and storage modules clustered about the sunken landing bay, including the blunt, pyramidal tower of the Fra Mauro Naval Hospital, ablaze with lights. A secondary landing dome at the base of the hospital was already open to receive the bug, which bounced roughly—still in complete silence—as the pilot jockeyed the balky little craft in for a landing.

Twenty minutes later, Lee, shed of his armor but still wearing the utility undergarment with its weave of heat-transfer tubes and medinano shunts, palmed the access panel to a door marked GSGT ECKHART. "Enter," sounded in Lee's thoughts over his implant and the door slid aside.

The room was small and tightly organized, as were all work spaces in the older part of the facility. Deck space was almost completely occupied by a desk and two chairs. Most of the bulkheads were taken up with storage access panels, though there was room for a holoportrait of President Connors, another of Commandant Marshke, and a framed photograph of an FT-90 in low orbit, the dazzling curve of Earth's horizon below and beyond its sleek-gleaming hull.

"Hospitalman Second Class Lee, reporting as ordered, Gunnery Sergeant."

"At ease, at ease," Eckhart waved him toward the chair. "I'm not an officer and we don't need the formal crap. Copy?"

"Uh . . . sure, Gunnery Sergeant. Copy." He took the offered seat. Was this the prelude to a chewing out? Or to his being booted out of the program?

"Relax, son," Eckhart told him. "And call me 'Gunny.' "

"Okay, Gunny. Uh, look. I've been reviewing my procedure for that last casualty and I see what went wrong. I shouldn't have rolled the wound into sunlight—"

Eckhart waved him to silence. "Your dedication is duly noted, son. And we'll debrief your session later, with the rest of the class. Right now I want to review your request for SMF."

Lee went cold, as cold as the shade on the Lunar surface, inside. "Is there a problem?"

"Not really. I just think you need to have your head examined, is all. What the hell do you want to ship out-system for, anyway?"

Lee took a deep breath, hesitated, then let it out again. How did you answer a question like that?

"Gunny . . . I just want to go, that's all. I've been space-happy since I was a kid, reet? 'Join the Navy and see the stars.' "

"You're in space now, in case you haven't noticed. Most space-happy kids never get as far out as the moon. Or even low-Earth orbit. You know that." He leaned forward, hands clasped on the desktop before him. "You *made* it! You're in space. Why are you so all-fired eager to take the Big Leap?"

"I wouldn't exactly call the moon space, Gunny." He pointed at the overhead. "I mean, Earth's right *there*, and everything, in plain view."

"There are always billets on Mars. Or Europa. Or on Navy ships on High Watch patrol. I want to know why you want to go to another fucking star. That's what you put in for on your dreamsheet, right?"

He sighed. "Yes, Gunny. I did."

"You want to sign on for a deployment that might last twenty to thirty years objective. You come back home aged maybe four years and find yourself completely out of pace with everything. Everyone you knew is thirty years older. Your implant is out of date. You don't understand the language. Hell, the culture might seem as alien to you as anything you'll run into XT. You won't fit in anymore."

"Gunny, I don't really have anything here, on Earth, I mean. Nothing but the Corps."

"Uh-huh." Eckhart's eyes glazed over as he reviewed some inner download of data. "It says here you just went through a divorce."

"Yes, Gunny."

"What happened?"

He shrugged. "My wife and husband both filed for divorce. I came home from my last deployment and found the locks had been changed on my condhome. They didn't recognize my palmprint any longer. I found out later they'd filed a couple of months earlier, but the formal DL hadn't caught up with me yet."

"Why the split? They tell you why?"

" 'Irreconcilable differences,' but what the fuck does that mean?"

"Problems with you in the service?"

"Well, yeah, I guess. I know Nance didn't like me always

going on long deployments. Egypt. Siberia. That last six months at the LEO spaceport. Still, she could've waited, could've *talked* to me, damn it! Ten years of marriage, zip! Down the black hole. I know now that Chris is a slimy, two-faced, twisted sick-fuck bastard who's in love with melodrama and the sound of his own voice. I'm not sure how he convinced Nance, though. I . . . I thought we really had something. Something permanent."

"Right. So you find it's not permanent and you figure twenty years or so out-system will let you get away from your problems. Or . . . maybe you're in it for the revenge? Come back four years older, when your siggos, your significant others, are *twenty* years older?"

"What's the point of that? We'd all still be middle-aged. But I guess I do want to get away from everything, yeah."

"Well, I damn well guess you do. But is cutting yourself off from every soul you've known on Earth, cutting yourself off from the ties you were born to, is that all really worth it? You can't run away from yourself, you know."

"I'm not running away from myself. If anything, I'm running away from *them*."

"Son, I've heard this story before, you know. Maybe about a thousand times. You're not the first poor schmuck to get shit-canned by a dearly beloved siggo or kicked in the teeth by people he believed in and trusted. And it hurts, I know. *Gods of Battle*, I know. And I also know you're carrying the pain here." He pointed at Lee's chest. "That's what you really want to get away from, and that's what you're going to carry with you. You can run all the way to Andromeda, son, and the pain will still be there. Question is, is the attempt worth losing everything else you know on Earth as well?"

"Gunny," Lee said, "I'd still have the Corps. Even in Andromeda. *Semper fi*."

"Ooh-rah," Eckhart said, but with a flat inflection utterly

devoid of enthusiasm. "Son, it's my job to talk you out of this, if I can."

"Huh? Why?"

"To stop you from screwing up your life."

"Well, you've got my request, Gunny. All you need to do is add your *request denied* to the form, and it's as good as shit-canned."

"I may still do that, Lee, if you don't convince me pretty quick. Trouble is, I have to tell you that we need volunteers for SMF. And we need them bad. We have a big one coming up soon, a big deployment. And your class, frankly, is all we have to work with. It's worse than that, actually. Three of you have a Famsit rating of one, out of a class of thirty-eight, and seven have a rating of two. Everybody else has close family."

"So, let me get this straight. You need Corpsmen for SMF, but you have to try to get us to back out after we volunteer? That doesn't make a hell of a lot of sense."

Eckhart sighed. "This is the Marine Corps, son. It doesn't always make sense. I'll approve your request—if you can convince me that you are not making *the* big mistake of your sorry young life."

"I . . . see. . . ."

And he did. His heart leaped. Eckhart was just giving him a chance to back out of this.

Yes! He was going to the stars! . . .

"I'm not sure what you want to hear, Gunny. I want to go. I have nobody I'm attached to on Earth. You said the culture here would be different, that I might have trouble fitting in when I got back. Well, you know what? I've *never* fit in, not really. Not until I joined the Navy. Hell, maybe I'll like what I find here better in twenty years, fit in better than I do now, y'know?"

Eckhart nodded. "Yeah. Yeah, I think I do know. Tell me something. Why did you become a corpsman?"

"Huh? Well, when I first enlisted, I had this idea of going

on someday and becoming a doctor. I figured what I learned in Corps School would give me a leg up, know what I mean? And then there was the fact that my dad was a Marine. He used to tell me stories about the company's 'Doc,' that special relationship between the Marines and their corpsmen. I'd always been interested in biology, physiology, stuff like that, and I was good at them in school. It just seemed like the right choice."

Damn it, he wanted to go Space Marine Force. As a Navy Hospital Corpsman, the equivalent of an Army medic for Navy and Marine personnel, he'd enjoyed working with the Marines already. Going SFM simply took things a step or ten farther.

A century or two back, the equivalent of today's SMF had been assignment with the Navy's FMF—the Fleet Marine Force. The force included Navy doctors and corpsmen who shipped out with the Marines, sailed with them on their transports, and went ashore with them in combat. It was a long and venerable tradition, one that went back at least as far as the Navy pharmacy mates who hit the beaches in the Pacific with the Marines during World War II, and arguably went even further back to the surgeon's mate's loblolly boys of the sailing ships of a century before that.

He'd volunteered for SMF almost two months ago, just after the completion of his six-month deployment to LEO.

Just after the divorce became final.

Damn it, the hell with Earth. He wanted to go to the stars.

"Gunny, the Navy . . . and, well, now the Marines, if I go SMF, they're my family now. I've been taking overseas and off-world deployments for the last four years, since I joined up. It's time for me to re-up. I want to re-up. I've always wanted the Navy to be my career."

Eckhart grinned. "A lifer, huh?"

"Yeah, a lifer. And it's my life."

"The government might point out that your life belongs to it."

"Okay, but in so far as I *do* have a free choice, this is what I want to do with my life. 'Join the Navy and see other worlds,' right? So why can't I re-up with a shot at *really* seeing some new territory?"

"How does Sirius sound to you, son?"

"Sirius? I thought there were no planets there?"

Eckhart grinned. "There aren't. But there's . . . something. An artifact. A space habitat. They didn't tell me much in the report I saw, but there's something. And the word is, a full MIEU is being sent out there. And they need Corpsmen. A bunch of 'em."

An artifact. Another remnant of one of the ancient civilizations that had been kicking around this part of the galaxy thousands of years ago. Maybe the An. Or maybe it was something *really* special . . . something left by the Builders at about the same time that *Homo erectus* was in the process of making the transition to *Homo sapiens*.

"Sirius sounds just fine, Gunny."

Okay, there wouldn't be a planetfall. But a chance to see a high-tech artifact left by a vanished, starfaring civilization? And whatever the thing was, it would have to be damned huge if they were sending a whole Marine Interstellar Expeditionary Unit—a force that would number over a thousand men and women, all told. What the hell had they found out there?

"Does that mean I'm in?"

Eckhart grinned. "You're in, Doc."

I'm going to Sirius! I'm going to another star! . . .

He almost didn't hear what Eckhart said next.

"You'll continue your training here for the rest of the month," Eckhart was saying. "After that, you and the other Corpsmen from this class who make the grade, the ones

who've volunteered for extrasolar deployment, will ship for
L-4 for your XS training and final assignment. And just let
me say, Doc . . . welcome aboard!"

"Thanks, Gunny! Uh, does that mean you're coming too?"

"Yes, it does. The brass is doing some scrambling right
now, looking for famsit ones and twos." He grinned. "I figured you damned squids'd need me to keep an eye on you!"

"That sounds decent, Gunny."

"Now get your sorry ass down to debrief. We're gonna
want to hear, in exacting detail, just what you did wrong on
that last field exercise!"

Vacation over. "Aye aye, Gunnery Sergeant!"

"For one thing, you could've used a thermalslick." He
grinned. "Chief Hart is gonna tell you *all* about that!"

Lee blinked. He hadn't even thought of that. Thermal-
slicks were part of each corpsman's field kit—a tough,
polymylar sheet like aluminum foil on one side, jet black on
the other. It could reflect sunlight or absorb it and the black
side had the added trick of a layer of carbon buckyball
spheres that made it almost frictionless—great for dragging
the dead weight of an injured man.

But then, he hadn't even thought about the problem of sunlight melting the wound's clot until it was too late.

At the moment, none of that mattered.

I'm going to Sirius. . . .

Alpha Company Headquarters Office
Star Marine Force Center
Twentynine Palms, California
1535 hours, PST

"*Comp'ny . . . atten . . . hut!*"

Sharply dressed in newly issued green utilities, Garroway
and his five fellow Marines came to attention. They were

standing in Captain Warhurst's office at Twentynine Palms, a fairly Spartan compartment made warm by the desert sunlight streaming through the transparent overhead. Staff Sergeant Dunne had marched them in; Warhurst himself was behind his low, kidney-shaped desktop, hand on a palm reader as he downloaded a report in his noumenal space.

After a moment, his glazed expression cleared, and he looked up. "Staff Sergeant?" he said.

"Sir!" Dunne rasped. "Corporals Garcia, Lobowski, Vinton, Lance Corporals Womicki, Garroway, and Eagleton, reporting for captain's nonjudicial punishment, sir!"

"Very well, Staff Sergeant." Warhurst folded his hands and looked at the six, studying each of them in turn. "Will all of you accept nonjudicial punishment? You all have the option of requesting formal courts-martial, at which time you would be entitled to legal representation."

"Sir," Garroway said. They'd agreed earlier on that he would be their spokesperson. They'd been invited to the party by his friend, after all. "We accept the NJP."

"Very well. We'll keep this short and simple then." He leaned back in his swivel chair. "What the *hell* were you young idiots thinking, getting into a brawl ashore? Were you, each of you, aware of the delicate nature of the relationship between Marines and civilians here just now?"

"Yes, sir," Garroway replied.

"What about the rest of you? You all downloaded the spiel before you went on liberty? The one about being good ambassadors for the Corps while ashore?"

All of them nodded, with a few mumbled "Yes, sirs" mixed in.

"I didn't hear that."

"*Yes, sir!*"

"Right now, ladies and gentlemen, the Marines can *not* afford a major firefight with the civilian sector. Brawling in a bar in downtown San Diego is one thing. Smashing up a condecology in the high-rent district of East Side LA is something else entirely."

As Warhurst spoke, Garroway wondered what was in store for them. Warhurst had told them they were on report when he'd bailed them out of that police holding tank. "Captain's nonjudicial punishment" was an old tradition within both the Navy and the Marines, a means of noting and punishing minor infractions short of the far more serious proceedings of an actual court-martial. It was more commonly called "captain's mast," from the ancient practice of holding these proceedings in front of the mast on board old-time sailing ships at sea.

But when Warhurst had said they were going up "before the man," they hadn't realized that "the man" would be Warhurst himself. Captain Warhurst *must* know what had really happened that night. . . .

"Liberty, as you all have heard many times since you enlisted, is a *privilege*, not a right. I know that was the first liberty in some years subjective, but that is no excuse! Do you read me?"

"*Sir, yes, sir!*"

"What happened?"

"Sir," Garroway said. "First of all, we didn't smash up anything. And besides, *they* started it. . . ."

"Excuses are like assholes, Marine. Everyone has one, and they all stink."

"But someone grabbed Anna . . . I mean, Corporal Garcia. All she did was break the hold. Some guy started to rush her, then, and I took him down . . . pretty gently, I thought."

"Pretty gently? Martial arts as adapted for close-quarters battle tactics are *not* gentle. You dislocated his knee cap and tore some tendons. The medical report says he is not seriously injured. He'll be walking again after a few days of medinano treatment. But you are *very* fortunate, Marine, that that man is not pressing charges. Do you understand me?"

"Yes, sir."

"You said they started it?"

"Yes, sir."

"Tell me what happened."

"Well, they were on about Garcia being *Aztlanista*."

"Start from the beginning. What were you doing at a private party in the first place, Garroway?"

And so he began describing that evening, starting with his calling up Tegan and getting her invitation to the sensethete . . . or was that the name of the room, rather than the party? He wasn't sure.

Warhurst heard him out, asking questions from time to time to flesh out the picture. When he was done, Warhurst leaned back again in his chair. "Very well. There *are* extenuating circumstances—including one hell of a high-voltage bit of culture shock. That, however, is no excuse for attacking civilians . . . even if you thought it to be in self-defense.

"Lobowski, Womicki, Vinton, and Eagleton. I'm dropping all charges against you. You went to the aid of your fellow Marines, but you did not strike or assault civilian personnel in any way. Downloads from your implant recorders supports this assessment. A record will be sent to the civilian authorities, with my recommendation that no further action be taken against you.

"Garcia, you struck a civilian, but both Garroway's testimony and implant recordings show that you did so only to break her hold on your uniform. Fourteen days' restriction to base.

"Garroway. Your testimony and the download record show that you kicked a civilian in the knee, injuring him. It is clear you did so because you felt he was about to attack a fellow Marine. The next time you find yourself in a similar situation, I recommend that you consider tripping him, rather than crippling him with CQB tactics. Thirty days' restriction to base, and five hundred newdollars' fine, to be deducted from your pay in equal installments over the next five months. A record of these proceedings will be uploaded to the civilian authority with jurisdiction in this case. Should further civilian complaints be filed, you will be subject to further charges, but I have been given to understand that this disciplinary hearing should end the matter here and now. Understood? Any of you have problems with my decision?"

There were none.

"Very well. You are dismissed."

Thirty days' restriction and five hundred newdollars? A bit steep, Garroway reflected . . . but not a serious hit. There was no way he was going to mingle with civilians ashore any longer . . . so the restriction and even the fine didn't hurt him that much.

The *principle* of the thing still burned. He and his friends had been insulted and attacked. Worse, the damned watchdog nano had then incapacitated them, rendering them helpless.

At least they hadn't also been fined for the loss of their uniforms. Those were cheap enough—they were grown right on the spot from raw synthewool to spec—but they'd expected to be gigged for the thefts as well.

Mostly, he kept remembering his conversations at that party . . . his difficulty even understanding what was being discussed. Oh, sure, there were translation programs that could be run in his implant, but the attitudes he'd seen seemed as alien as the language, or more so.

It was a bit disconcerting to know that he'd come home . . . and not to feel at home after all. . . .

5

Alpha Company Barracks
Star Marine Force Center
Twentynine Palms, California
1420 hours, PST

"All right, Marines. Listen up!"

Garroway looked up from his LR-2120, partially disassembled on the table before him, to hear what Staff Sergeant Dunne had to say. Around him, the steady buzz of conversation among other Marines in the company died away.

"Gentlemen, ladies," Dunne went on, "first off . . . *happy fucking birthday!*"

The announcement was met with cheers and shouts of *Ooh-rah!* and fists pounding on tables. The tenth of November was the anniversary of the creation of the U.S. Marines—originally the Continental Marines—by an act of Congress in 1775, a date celebrated by Marines around the world and far, far beyond.

"Festivities begin at 1900 hours tonight at the mess hall. Cake, ice cream, and pogey bait *will* be the order of the day."

He waited for a fresh round of cheers to die down. "Okay, okay, simmer down. Next order of business. The waiting is over. The Nergs are going to war."

That raised a low-voiced murmur of excitement. *Nergs*

was a new battlename for the Marines, another in the long list of nom d'guerres bestowed by enemies and friends alike—devil dogs, leathernecks, jarheads, gyrines. Nerg, or Nergal may-I, was from the phrase, identical in both An and in ancient Sumerian, *nir-gál-mè-a*, which meant something like "respected in battle." The Fighting Forty-fourth had won that accolade from the Ahannu warriors on Ishtar immediately after the desperately fought action that had ended in Ramsey's Peace.

"Now," Dunne went on, "the really good news. Authorization has come through for promotions for all personnel who were on the Ishtar op. You have all received an automatic advancement by one pay grade. Personnel advancing to sergeant or higher will still be expected to take the test for your new rank, but the time-in-grade requirement has been satisfied."

There was some more cheering and a rattle of applause at that. Garroway grinned. He'd just made corporal. Decent!

"A new download is available," Dunne went on, "coded White Star-one-one. Please open it up and take a look."

Garroway brought up the code phrase and thought-clicked it. Immediately, he was in a noumenal space. . . .

Visual: Star-strewn night, gas clouds, a pair of intensely brilliant pinpoint-stars, and the vast and enigmatic loom of a ring-shaped structure, obviously huge. . . .

"The ring is our objective," Dunne went on, his voice sounding in their thoughts as they studied the alien construct. "It is located in the Sirius star system, 8.6 light-years from Earth. We believe it to be a stargate, a device floating in deep space that allows instantaneous travel between stars. Those patterns of light along the rim suggest that it is inhabited. We do not know by who."

Sirius. Garroway felt the word strike hard, like a blow to the stomach. *Lynnley!*

The Marine company watched in silence as the golden needle-shape emerged from the ring, accelerated, and the image was suddenly and disconcertingly lost.

"These images were transmitted ten years ago by the explorer ship *Wings of Isis*," Dunne's voice went on as the blast of static was replaced by another view of the ring. "We do not know what happened to the *Isis*, but we must assume she was destroyed. There's been no word from her since these images were received.

"The *Wings of Isis* had a crew of 245, 30 of them Marines, as well as several AIs. We have no real hope that any of them are still alive out there—or, if they are, that they will still be alive ten years from now when we arrive in-system. However, the Marines do *not* abandon their own. Accordingly, MIEU-1 is being prepared to deploy to the Sirius system. Once there, we will recon the area and assess the situation. We will attempt to make contact with whoever or whatever is operating that stargate. If necessary, we will organize a boarding party, enter the artifact, rescue human survivors if any, and maintain a beachhead, providing security for a science team which will perform a threat evaluation of the structure."

Profound silence attended this announcement. Garroway found himself grappling with a dozen questions. How big was that wheel? How were they supposed to get inside, ring a chime at the front door? What kind of defenses did the thing have? How the hell were the Marines supposed to draw up a battle plan when they didn't even know the nature of their enemy?

But more pressing still were the unanswered—and unanswerable—questions about Lynnley.

In subjective terms, the time he'd actually been awake and not crowding the speed of light, it had been less than a year since he'd seen her last, just before he'd entered cybehibe for the voyage to Ishtar. He missed her. In his mind, she was still very much alive, alive in his *recent* past. The knowledge that it had been eleven years since whatever had happened out at Sirius had happened seemed completely surreal.

Dead eleven years? No. He couldn't get his mind wrapped around that one.

The images from Sirius faded out. Garroway sat, once again, at a table in the barracks, his laser rifle partially disassembled in front of him.

"Questions?" Dunne snapped.

"Gunnery Sergeant?" Sergeant Houston said. "What if we don't want to go?"

"Come again?"

"What if we don't want to go? I've got six years in sub, twenty-six ob. I've done my bit. I want *out*, man."

"This is not a volunteers only mission," Dunne replied slowly. "The brass is treating this like an ordinary deployment, with two exceptions.

"First, if you're within one year of your scheduled retirement, you can request an exemption. Since your expected OTIS—that's your objective time-in-service—since your OTIS will be on the order of six months to one year for this mission, you may opt for taking an early out instead.

"Second, there will also be a case review board. Anyone with special needs or hardships arising from this deployment can talk to them. I'm given to understand they will not be unreasonable, and that they will consider each application on a case-by-case basis.

"However, I would ask you to think very carefully before deciding to remain on Earth. Things are different here, now, than we knew them twenty-some years ago. If you elect to stay behind, you will be given psychological assistance, including special programming for your implants to help you . . . adjust."

Again, low-voiced murmurs sounded in the room. By now, every man and woman in the room had heard about the watchdog program that had taken out six of their number the other night at the condecology in ELA, and they didn't like it, not one bit.

"I don't know about all of you," Dunne added, "but *I'm* gonna be damned glad to get back out there!"

"We're with you, Gunny!" Corporal Bryan called out, using Dunne's new rank for the first time. It sounded a bit strange . . . but *right*.

"I've also been told to tell you," Dunne went on, "that for those of you who stay with the MIEU, there will be an additional rank increase immediately upon returning. They're also in the process of putting through a special payment incentive. The word is it'll be fifty percent of your standard paycheck, above and beyond combat pay, hazardous-duty pay, and XS-duty pay."

And that, Garroway thought, would come to a very nice sum. He took a quick moment to download the appropriate pay scale tables in his mind. Yeah . . . very sweet. As a corporal with over three years' subjective in, his base pay would come to n\$1724.80 per month. Fifty percent of that was an additional n\$862 plus change per month. That, plus the bonus for hazardous duty, extrastellar duty, and combat . . .

He gave a mental whistle and wondered if that kind of money made the Marines into modern-day, high-tech mercenaries.

"Is that ob or sub, Gunny?" someone asked.

"Yeah," someone else added with a laugh. "It does make a difference!"

"Strictly subjective time, people, just like your base pay." There were groans in response. "Can it!" Dunne added. "It's bad enough the government pays you while you're sleeping your sorry lives away in cybehibe! They're not paying you for time that shrinks to no time at all while you're traveling at near-c!

"Any other questions?" There were none. "Carry on," Dunne said, leaving the Marines to discuss the news.

A few—Sergeant, now *Staff Sergeant,* Houston and Corporal, now *Sergeant,* Matt Cavaco—felt that arbitrarily ordering the Marines to go to Sirius, rather than making it a volunteer-only mission—was just flat wrong. Most, though, were excited by the prospect, both for the extra pay, and because of the distinct alienation many of them were feeling from Earth. Those few who'd gotten passes to go ashore in the past few days had returned with less than happy news about the planet, and about its inhabitants. Damn, but Dunne was right. The background culture of North America had *changed* and in some unpleasant ways.

There was a lot else about the local scene Dunne had not mentioned, but the other Marines in the company had been discussing it endlessly for the past several days.

It wasn't just the shifting jargon and language, the strange new religions and philosophies, or the everchanging buzz about numnum persies or zaggers, whatever the hell *those* were. Where to begin?

Politics were one issue. The voices calling for separation were louder, more strident, than ever. *Aztlanistas* had been calling for independence since well before Garroway had been born, but the debate now approached open warfare in some of the Latino slums of LA, and in the borderlands of southern California, Arizona, New Mexico, and Texas. Strife was building with the Québecois, too, as the Canadian winters worsened. Their claim to western Pennsylvania and the Ohio Valley was less viable even than that of the *Aztlanistas*, since it had been the British Empire, not the United States of America, that had taken their old territories in the French and Indian Wars. Still, it made for amusing and often virulent name-calling on the public forums and news feeds.

There were more rules and regulations. Most states could now arrest and prosecute people for breaking one or another of the citizenship laws, dictums prohibiting any behavior that might disturb good social order and public decency. That sounded so much like the articles of the Uniform, Code of Military Justice—specifically the one about "conduct prejudicial to good order and discipline"—that some Marines were speculating that America was now a military state. And with far more convicted criminals than prison space, more and more felons were being turned loose with specially programmed watchdog nano injected into their bloodstreams, nano that could evaluate their behavior against certain narrow parameters and administer punishment—even death—in the event of a violation. That was police-state stuff.

Scary.

And there were other problems, some of them not man-made. The weather was worse, a *lot* worse, than when Garroway had left Earth twenty-one years ago. Sea levels were higher, ultraviolet in the sunlight harsher, storms bigger and more dangerous. Most major coastal cities—Washington, D.C., coastal Los Angeles, Miami, New Orleans—all were enclosed now by high thick seawalls, and at least partly covered over by transparent domes to keep out both the worsening ultraviolet and the periodic storm surges that otherwise would have flooded them completely. Despite that, there was serious talk about abandoning the original cores of those cities and rebuilding inland. Some coast cities, because of their terrain, could not be completely protected; New York City, San Francisco, and Seattle were in grave danger.

Manhattan, in particular, offered such a tangled and problematical geography with its rivers and associated borough-cities that the seawall and dome offered only partial protection. Fifteen years earlier, Hurricane Trevor had come ashore at the mouths of the Hudson and East rivers, causing tens of billions of newdollars' damage. The next year, the state of New Jersey had, against riotous protests, finally

moved the Statue of Liberty to artificial high ground near Se-
caucus before her copper body deteriorated any further.

Most forms of cancer were treatable through various
nanomedical techniques—one did *not* go into direct sunlight
any longer without nanotechnical augmentation to eyes and
skin!—but skin cancer in particular cost Americans tens of
billions per year in both treatment and prophylaxis.

And the ongoing deterioration of the planet's climate appeared to be accelerating. Temperatures in the equatorial
zones were rising steadily, fueling migrations of local populations to the north and south—but especially into the north.
All across the globe, equatorial peoples were on the move as
local government broke down and whole populations became migratory.

Scuttlebutt around the barracks had it that much of the
furor over tracking down ancient alien technology among the
stars was centered now on learning how to control climate on
a planetary scale.

But was such an audacious goal even possible?

And then there were the religions. *Always* the religions.
Dozens of new ones seemed to appear almost weekly, the
majority of them either claiming the An were gods or that
they were hell-born demons. Each new exoarcheological rev-
elation on Earth, the Moon, Mars, or elsewhere seemed to
spawn more ways of dividing humankind in the name of
faith, peace, and spiritual brotherhood.

Established sects continued to splinter, sometimes vio-
lently. Within the Catholic world, Papessa and Anti-Pope
continued to snipe at one another over issues ranging from
how to think about the An to the use of nanomedical ana-
gathics. Most Baptists believed the An were demonic; several new Baptist offshoots, however, continued to disagree
on whether the An, like Lucifer, were fallen, or if Lucifer
had somehow created them—an important theological question, since if they were fallen, then Christian missionaries

sent to Ishtar might bring a few of that deluded race to the light.

Even within Garroway's own Wiccan tradition—as easy-going and nonjudgmental faith as existed anywhere—there were bewildering new branches and offshoots disagreeing over such burning issues as whether or not the An were ancient gods, whether use of nanotechnology for special effects within ritual circles could be considered true magic or not, whether or not Christians should be held accountable for the Burning Times, and over the Rede-ethics of weather-witching, using magic to control the weather.

And finally there were the wars. *Everywhere* wars and more wars. Any Marine of the forty-fourth who did end up staying on Earth—if he didn't take an early out—was going to find himself much in demand. Temperature extremes were driving many inhabitants of far-northern or equatorial regions into the somewhat more habitable latitudes in between. Anti-migration laws had resulted in open warfare and in border massacres. In just the past thirty years, Marines had deployed to Mexico and Egypt, to Siberia and the Chinese coast, to a dozen other shores and climes, fighting at one time or another troops of the Kingdom of Allah, the Chinese Hegemony, the European Federation, the Ukrainian Nationalists, Mexicans, Québecois, Brazilians, Colombians, and forces of the Pan-African Empire. The Great Jihad War of 2147 was now being called World War V. Already there was talk of a World War VI, as migrating populations, spreading famine and disease, and the collapse of national economies propelled desperate people into paradoxically suicidal bids for a better life.

The black forces of War, Pestilence, Famine, and Death were abroad in the world, and it seemed that not even the UFR/US Marines could possibly hold them in check much longer.

Earth had become as scary and as strange a place as

Ishtar . . . worse, perhaps, since Garroway and his fellow Marines thought it was as familiar as, well, as *home*.

Sirius couldn't possibly be any more alien—or more disappointing—than Earth.

Garroway was ready to go. He *wanted* to go, since the only people he knew—his brother and sister Marines—were also going, or most of them were. The one thing standing in his way was what he was thinking of now as unfinished business with his father.

"Hey, Gare?" Kat Vinton said, interrupting black thoughts. "What's with the ten-thousand-meter stare?"

He blinked, then looked up at her. "Hey, Kat."

"Hey yourself. What's going on? Why the intense glare?"

"Sorry. I'm feeling . . . a bit torn."

"Your girlfriend was onboard the *Isis*, I know. You told me. I'm sorry. . . ."

He nodded. He looked past her at the other Marines in the barracks. He felt as though he were barely holding on.

"Thanks, Kat. I still can't believe she's dead." Trying to conceal the unsteady emotions within, he turned his attention, part of it, at any rate, back to the disassembled laser rifle before him. He'd already cleaned the optical connector heads and replaced both the pulse-timer chip and the circuit panel pinpointed as dead by his initial diagnostic check. All that remained was to put the thing together, a task Marine recruits were drilled at until they could do it, quite literally, blindfolded.

"Maybe she isn't. We rescued the Marines and scientists on Ishtar after they'd been hiding out in the mountains for ten years, right?"

"I guess," he told her. He concentrated for a moment on connecting the barrel to the charge assembly. "Pretty grim stuff."

"But this is different. You saw those downloads."

"Yeah." He snapped home the final piece, the pistol grip

clicking firmly into the base housing. He set the completed rifle aside. "Grim isn't half of it. If we haven't heard from them in all this time, I don't think we ever will."

She reached out and touched his shoulder. "Oh, Gare. I'm so sorry."

It was passing strange, talking to Kat about this. Lynnely had been his lover, and they'd reached the point of discussing marriage before he'd shipped out onboard the *Derna* for Ishtar. Kat had been his fuck-buddy since Ishtar . . . his lover, yes, but without the romantic overtones or plans for a serious long-term social connection. When your entire list of social contacts—those you could talk to, at any rate—were fellow Marines, such arrangements became common. Standing regulations frowned on sexual fraternization among enlisted personnel, but in practice both officers and NCOs alike ignored the affairs and relationships that inevitably blossomed among the lower ranks.

Marines were only human, after all, even if they rarely cared to admit it.

"Well, at least we can go out there and kick the ass of whoever did it," Garroway told her.

"Assuming they have asses to kick," Kat replied. "Yes." She cocked her head to one side. "What else is going on behind those gray eyes of yours?"

She knew him too well.

"I told you about my father, right?" Damn it, the place was just too damned crowded for this kind of conversation, Garroway thought.

"Ah. The light dawns." Kat looked around the crowded barracks, then at Garroway, and seemed to read his mind. "Say, Gare?" She jerked her head toward the door. "As long as we have some downtime, I need to show you something. Outside."

" 'Kay."

He returned the assembled LR-2120 to its position in a rack with forty-seven other laser rifles, then followed her down the steps, through the building lobby to the front desk where they checked out with a bored sergeant and then out through the front doors into the harsh glare of the sun. It was midafternoon and Garroway felt his exposed skin tingling as the nano imbedded there began reacting to the influx of ultraviolet. The glare lessened to comfortable levels as his eye implants darkened.

The sunlight reminded Garroway once again—and forcefully—of all of the recent barracks chatter about Earth's worsening climate. Every religion was different, of course, but his own Wiccan beliefs held that the Earth herself was alive, the Goddess in material form, Lovelock's Gaia hypothesis of two centuries earlier given spiritual shape and meaning. To see the Earth in Her current condition genuinely hurt. Could he turn and walk away for another twenty years or more? What would She be like upon his return?

Could She be dying and was it his responsibility to stay with Her and try to help?

But what could one person do to stop the drawn-out ecological death of a planet?

"Where the hell are you taking me?" he asked her as he followed her down the front steps.

"I just wanted to find a place where we could talk," she replied. "I thought the LVP ready line. . . ."

Across from the gleaming white building housing the barracks, a number of vehicles had been drawn up in a rigidly straight line along the side of a paved parade ground. The large hangars housing vehicle maintenance and the flight assembly building rose around the perimeter of the field.

The vehicles were LVPs, the acronym standing for landing vehicle, personnel. Specifically, they were M-990 Warhammers, so called for the blunt, crescent-shaped nose assemblies, like the business end of a double-headed hammer, mounting plasma guns housed in turret blisters at each tip.

The vehicles were ugly, their hulls behind the nose section

heavily armored and as streamlined as a misshapen brick. Though they could fly, in an ungainly fashion, they were designed to be ferried from orbit to ground slung from the wasp-waist belly of a TAL-S Dragonfly, one of the Corps' space-capable transatmospheric landing vehicles. They were heavily armed, too; besides the plasma guns, they had laser point-defense weapons, and turreted railgun mounts at the chin and aft-dorsal hardpoints. Each Warhammer was designed to carry two squads—twenty men—plus their weapons and gear, with a two-man/one-AI crew up front.

They walked across the tarmac to the nearest Warhammer. Kat touched an access panel, and the hatch unfolded from the hull, providing them with steps up into the cargo bay.

"This is a lot roomier than the old TAL-S lander modules," Garroway said, stepping inside and letting his hand slide along the white-painted overhead. "Wish we'd had these on Ishtar."

"Yeah, the Corps is always coming up with improvements," Kat told him. "New and better ways to kill things. Anyway, I thought we could talk here without being . . . disturbed."

"Did you think I was going to lose it?"

"No. But I didn't want you clamping down on what you were feeling. C'mon, Gare. Your dad. You don't really want to kill him, do you?"

He sighed. "Kill him? I guess not. I wouldn't like going to prison. Or getting a charge of watchdog nano. *Another* charge, I mean, worse than what we got."

"Your mother did go back to him, you know, after she'd gotten away. In a way, she has some of the responsibility too."

"That's not fair."

"*Life* isn't fair. I wish I had a newdollar for every time I've heard of abused women either going back to their abusers, thinking they would change, or just because they didn't know what else to do . . . or going on to hook with up someone else just as abusive, or worse. It makes me sick."

"Sounds like you have a personal stake in it."

"I do. My sister. Her third husband beat her to death. Her first and second husbands tried to."

"I'm sorry."

She shrugged. "So am I. I hear the bastard's on nanocontrolled release now, out in Detroit. I hope he screws up and gets fried. I truly, truly do. But I'm not going to hurry him along."

"They haven't caught my father," Garroway said. "Not yet. In fact, he's probably with the *Aztlanista* underground. He certainly held Azzy sympathies when I knew him."

"Yeah, and that's just it, Gare. You *don't* know him. Not now. It's been twenty-one years, right? He's a completely different man. I'm not saying he isn't any better now. I'm not even saying the bastard doesn't deserve to die. But you've been away from Earth too long to get caught up in that." She grinned at him. "Even if it only feels like a year for you."

"Damn it, Kat. He killed my mother! . . ."

"So . . . somehow you track him down, find him wherever he's hiding out. What do you do?"

"I alternate between wanting to put a bullet through his brain and wanting to blow out his kneecaps, leave him crippled."

"With meditech the way it is nowadays, he wouldn't stay crippled. Look what they did to the asshole you side-kicked. And how would you carry it out, when the watchdog nano in your system is watching you all the time, watching for you to just *think* a violent thought before putting you out?"

Garroway's eyes were burning. He was having trouble swallowing.

"You wake up in jail, with a charge of attempted murder hanging on you. No captain's mast this time. You end up in front of a civilian judge. Dishonorable discharge. Prison or worse. Is the revenge, is the *attempted* revenge, really worth it?"

Then the tears began to flow freely. A low moan escaped from his throat and then he was crying. He hadn't cried like this in years, not since he'd been living at home with an out-of-control abuser for a father and a mother terrified of being her own person.

A long time later, Kat held him close. A pull-down storage shelf in the cargo bay had become their bed, a thick roll of foam padding their mattress. Their lovemaking had been hard and needy, almost desperate. At last, though, they clung to one another, sweat turning their bare skin slick and soaking the pad beneath them. With the power off, the interior of the Warhammer had grown stiflingly hot, but that hadn't mattered, somehow.

Garroway breathed in the delicate scent of Kat's hair, mingled with the smells of sweat, sex, and machine oil. Reluctantly, he consulted his internal clock. "We'd better get back," he whispered.

"I know. But this was . . . good. Thank you."

"Thank *you*," he told her.

"So, what's it gonna be? Are you going to ditch the Corps and try to hunt down your father? Maybe do hard time?" She gave him a wicked grin, barely visible in the half-light filtering aft from the Warhammer's cockpit. "Or are you coming with me to the stars?"

"That was not fair, lady."

"Nope. But the question stands."

He released her a little, pulling back. "You're right, of course. There's nothing I can do to the bastard. Maybe the best thing I can do is live my own life the best way I can—and the hell with him."

She nodded. "Ah, yes! He *can* be taught!"

He shrugged. "The Corps is my home," he told her. "You and the rest of them are my family. But I was also . . . ."

"You were also what?"

"I was thinking about how fucked up the Earth Herself is.

The climate. The environment. Wondering if I had the right to run off and leave Her."

"I'm not a Wiccan," she told him. "You'll need to answer questions about your Goddess for yourself. But could you change anything by yourself?"

"Well, the simple answer is that if everyone does his or her part. . . ."

"Uh-uh. You. By yourself. What can you do?"

"Not a damned thing. There's nothing I can do here. I can't get revenge for my mother. I can't fix the environment. Hell, I can't even make a home for myself here any longer. Earth is too . . . too alien now. Y'know?"

"I'm way ahead of you, Marine."

"I could say I'm going to go to Sirius to find Lynnley and the others, but I know I can't even do that. She's dead. There's nothing I can do about that either."

"And so? . . ."

"And so, yeah. I'm coming with you. Not to rescue Lynnley, but because that's where I *belong*."

She drew him close and they began making love once more.

6

Virtual Conferencing Room 8
Star Marine Force Center
Twentynine Palms, California
0915 hours, PST

Colonel Ramsey floated in noumenal space, watching the bulk of the approaching starship eclipse a dazzling sun. The image was being transmitted from one of the L-4 dockyard facilities. A crescent Earth hung in the distance, her nightside picked out by the star-twinkle of cities.

The advent of noumenal conferencing, he thought wryly, might well have doomed technic civilization. When the powers-that-were could call a meeting at any time, gathering the attendees' telepresences from anywhere on Earth or in near-Earth space, then meetings and briefings and virtual conferences became the rule, until it seemed as though nothing else ever got done.

There must have been, he thought, a halcyon era before the creation of the noumenon when managers could manage without constantly being tied up in meetings.

Admiral Don D. Harris originally had called this briefing as an update check on the progress of Operation Battlespace. Other interested parties had signed on, however, including members of Congress and the Federal Advisory

Council, until the whole affair had become an unwieldy circus.

Ramsey actually found himself looking forward to the Sirius deployment, if only because he could occasionally get some work done.

His virtual presence, attired in formal full-dress, was one of some hundreds of telepresences hanging in space at a vantage point almost half a million kilometers from Earth, at the L-4 LaGrange Point where the Federal Republic maintained a number of its more important deep space facilities. The ship was the Marine Interstellar Transport *Chapultepec*, newly built and launched by the Lunarhalo Shipbuilding Consortium at L-1 and maneuvering now to her regular berth at the HEO military base at L-4. Slowly, the vessel grew huge, a looming, black-shadowed mushroom 622 meters long, her three hab modules for the moment tucked in along her flanks beneath the massive dome of the ship's reaction-mass storage tank. During the long coasting period of the vessel's flight, those modules were extended on their arms and rotating about the ship's spine, creating artificial gravity while remaining in the shadow of the R-M tank, shielded there from the deadly flux of radiation raised by the ship's near-*c* velocity. Aft, a trio of heat radiators each a meter thick and easily the area of a city block gave the vessel the appearance of an arrow with a broad flattened dome in the place of an arrowhead. She was not streamlined, but she *was* sleekly functional, giving the impression of unimaginable speed and power.

Ramsey watched as robotic tugs gentled the behemoth in for final capture and docking at the HEO base. There, inspection teams would begin the final check and recheck process to certify the *Chapultepec* for service. She'd better be ready, he thought. No less than five admirals, three generals, and two congresspersons, one of them a retired Marine, had officiated at the *Pec*'s commissioning and launch. It would be embarrassing to find a hitch now that would send her back to the orbital yards.

Besides, a very great deal was riding on *Chapultepec* launching on schedule, some three months hence.

"What I would like to know," a combative voice declared in Ramsey's mind, "is how that vessel can be expected to handle a threat like the one we've seen on those transmissions from Sirius. If that . . . that gold-colored thing we saw come out of the Ring *was* a Hunters of the Dawn warship, we may have to admit that we are out of our league, that we're up against a foe as far in advance of us as we are above the Ahannu."

The speaker was Frank Shugart, from the President's Federal Advisory Council. He appeared to be the spokesperson for a small army of civilian bureaucrats and politicians who'd linked in for this noumenal briefing, an army that included Dr. Howard Slatterby, Director of the National Security Council, and three congresspersons representing various House committees with an interest in this project. A virtual circus indeed. . . .

"It won't be just that one vessel, sir," the image of Admiral Harris, dazzling in his icon dress whites, pointed out. Harris was currently at L-4 physically, and there was the briefest flicker of hesitation in his reply, due to the second-and-a-quarter time delay. "Operation Battlespace has been conceived as our first true interstellar fleet deployment."

At a touch from Harris's thoughts, the scene shifted to show a graphic simulation of seven ships viewed from the side, all quite similar in overall design—mushroom-cap R-M tanks, central drive spines, stern radiator assemblies—but ranging in length overall from the 85 meters of the frigate *Daring* to the 622-meter bulk of the *Chapultepec*. All save the three robotic freighters had rotating hab modules tucked in beneath the R-M tanks.

"So far, the battle group will consist of the *Chapultepec*, plus the supply ships *Altair, Mizar*, and *Procyon*, the frigate gunships *Daring* and *Courageous*, the carrier *Ranger*, and the battlecruiser *New Chicago*. In addition, *Ranger* will be deploying two space-assault squadrons, Marine Wasps and the new SF/A-2 Starhawks. I think we can be confident that our forces will give a good account of themselves, no matter what they encounter at Sirius."

"Even against the Hunters of the Dawn, Admiral?" the speaker was Congressperson Alyssa Durand, of the House Military Preparedness Oversight Committee. "I'm told that the Hunters might well be representatives of a civilization at *least* half a million years old. To engage in a military conflict with such a civilization could well mean suicide for our entire species!"

"Nonsense, Ms. Durand," Major General Mark Colby snapped. "No civilization could possibly last for half a million years!"

"Some of us believe it to be completely possible, General," Shugart said. "If the Predatory Survivors Hypothesis is correct, a starfaring culture could become metastable, with no outside threats and plenty of expansion room for bleeding off internal pressures." The noumenal display shifted to show streams of pure data cascading through the group's joint awareness, showing the results of thousands of simulated civilizations growing, evolving, and interacting. A schematic of the galaxy showed hypothetical civilizations as red pinpoints winking into existence, expanding into vast interstellar networks as a counter ticked off the centuries, networks that warred, struggled, then vanished . . . though frequently one stellar empire would grab the galactic center stage, maintaining a stable empire for many thousands of years. Occasionally, one of the networks seemed to freeze in place, remaining stable for much longer. "Computer models suggest such a civilization might endure for millions, even *hundreds* of millions of years."

"They're pretty, sir, but I don't care about your computer models," Colby told Shugart. "And all the Predatory Survivors Hypothesis tells us is that someone out there could prove to be very, very nasty. None of this sweetness and light, advanced civilizations must be peaceful crap we've been hearing from the religious fanatics."

Ramsey was familiar with the survivors theory, had even briefed others on the topic numerous times. Essentially, it was a coherent explanation for Fermi's Paradox . . . a scientific and philosophical statement noting that even if the speed of light could never be surpassed, a single starfaring culture could colonize the entire galaxy within the course of a few hundreds of thousands of years. Given that the galaxy was on the order of eight billion years old, the galaxy should have been colonized many, many times over already.

At the time Fermi's Paradox was raised, in the mid-twentieth century, space appeared achingly silent and empty, with no sign of any intelligent species among the stars save the inhabitants of Earth itself. If the best ideas concerning planetary formation and the tenacity of life were correct, the galaxy should be teeming with civilizations by now. The paradoxical question, in the face of all of that silence, was . . . "Where the hell is everyone?"

The Predatory Survivors Hypothesis simply stated that, in Darwinian terms, one possible survival strategy for any intelligent species was to eliminate *all* possible competition. If, at some point in the history of galactic civilization, some one species that had evolved to sentience through this strategy had developed star travel, it might continue with that strategy, finding and destroying races of beings that might one day challenge it.

Two centuries later, ample evidence had been found of multiple starfaring cultures—on Earth, the Moon, Mars, Europa, and on quite a few worlds of nearby star systems. All of the traces of alien starfaring cultures, however, were limited to long-dead ruins, until, eventually, the Ahannu had been discovered on Ishtar . . . and the Ahannu spoke of the Hunters of the Dawn, who had reduced their civilization to stone-age barbarism thousands of years ago.

And now someone else had turned up at Sirius. Someone with superior technology and a damned quick trigger finger.

Had the Hunters survived for an estimated ten thousand years, since the collapse of the An Star Empire?

But things got more complicated and ominous still. There were also the Builders, those representatives of a far-flung starfaring civilization existing half a million years ago, anni-hilated, evidently, by hostile forces with a singularly narrow and psychopathic focus.

Were those the Hunters of the Dawn as well? Or a prede-cessor race using the same survival strategy?

Despite Colby's self-assurance, some authorities believed the Hunters were a single species, wiping out the Builders . . . then eradicating the An half a million years later. The modus operandi was the same in both cases—the maneuvering of asteroids into new paths that would disrupt any planet-based civilization. Presumably, the motive was the same as well.

But were the two the same? The question, Ramsey thought, was a vitally important one. Durand had a point: anyone who'd been hanging around the galactic scene for half a million years or more was *not* someone you wanted as your enemy. Such a civilization might well seem almost god-like now from the human perspective, able to swat upstart humanity as casually as a man might swat a fly. The best Earth might hope for would be to remain unnoticed.

But that was no longer possible. If the golden ship had been built by the Hunters, Humankind had just announced its presence to them in huge flaming letters.

The simulation data was replaced by the now-familiar scenes transmitted from *Isis* during her last moments in the

Sirius system. The stargate ring loomed huge against a star-dusted night. Once again, the golden starship emerged from the ring's center. Again it lunged toward the *Isis*, and the scene was broken by static for a moment, before the cycle of images started again.

"Isn't it already too late to run and hide?" Brigadier General Cornell Dominick asked. It seemed that SPACCOM's liaison with the Joint Chiefs was reading Ramsey's mind. "They encountered our explorer ship at Sirius and destroyed or captured it. They might very well know now exactly where the *Isis* came from. Hell, by this time a fleet could be almost *here* if it came through the Sirius Gate from wherever the Hunters call home, then backtracked on the *Isis* at near-*c*. Surely we need to put an armed presence at the stargate, even if it's just there as a tripwire."

"There are too damned many unknowns, General," Shugart said. "*Was* the *Isis* destroyed? Or did they capture her? If she was destroyed immediately, the Hunters, if that's who they are, might not know the ship's origin. Or, as you say, the Hunters might have put a fleet through the stargate, and have been en route to Earth these past ten years. If that's the case, sending seven ships to Sirius is not only useless, it's foolhardy. Surely we would need every available warship *here* to defend Earth against such an attack."

"Mr. Shugart—" Harris began.

"But if there is the *slightest* chance that we can still evade detection by these, these sociopathic monsters," Shugart continued, pushing over the admiral's attempted interruption, "then we should take it. We cannot hope to militarily challenge a technology even a thousand years in advance of our own . . . to say nothing of a technology gap of half a million years!"

"But that's just it, Mr. Shugart," Colonel Gynger Kowalewski, SPACCOM's senior technical advisor, put in. "There *is* no way to hide, even if we wanted to." At her mental command, a star map appeared, showing Sol at the center surrounded by a scattering of stars reaching out several light centuries. A sphere of purple grew out from Sol, engulfing hundreds of nearby star systems. "The Singer sent out its . . . call, or whatever that signal was, ninety years ago. Here's how far it's gone in that time—ninety light-years."

A second sphere, this one red, overlapped the first, then grew a bit larger. Kowalewski continued. "The light from the drive flares of our first interstellar ships—with a characteristic wavelength indicating matter-antimatter reaction—started out over a century ago, and theoretically, they could be detected across galactic distances as anomalous gamma-ray sources by any sufficiently advanced technology."

A third sphere expanded out from Sol, swallowing the first two and stretching across four times their volume or more, engulfing myriad stars. "Radio and television signals," Kowalewski said, "a sure proof of intelligent and technological life, began leaving Earth well over *two* hundred years ago. We estimate that that initial wave front has now reached something on the order of three to four *thousand* stars.

"Two hundred years ago, Mr. Shugart," she concluded, "we reached up, rang the door chimes, and announced our presence! If the Hunters are out there and still listening, they *will* hear us. Quite possibly they already have!"

"And we don't know how much time we have, either," Dominick added. "Maybe the nearest Hunter base is a thousand light-years away, and we have eight centuries left before they hear us. Or they could have heard us a hundred years ago, and that they're still arguing, trying to decide how best to deal with us."

"Our AI cultural simulations *have* suggested that a long-lived civilization will tend to make decisions, and to act and react, very slowly, very deliberately," Kowalewski pointed out.

"There you go," Colby said with a chuckle. "Maybe we don't have to worry about them after all. But I need something more than guesswork about the long-term survivability of a civilization before I'll accept the crazy notion that bogey men half a million years more advanced than we are might be coming after us."

"General Colby," Congressperson Durand said, "half a million years or ten thousand years . . . it makes no difference, either way. Our technology was a mere three or four centuries ahead of the Ahannu and a thousand Marines forced some millions of them to accept peace in a couple of days."

Well, Ramsey thought, *it hadn't been quite* that *simple.*

"My esteemed colleague is correct," Congressperson Wayne R. Reardon, of the Military Appropriations Committee, said. "I submit that it would be better to make friends of these people, than to make them enemies."

Ramsey thought-clicked to raise a noumenal icon, indicating that he wished to speak. Normally, it was wisest to maintain a low profile at briefings heavy with high brass and politicians, but the idiocy factor was growing worse by the minute.

"Colonel Ramsey," Admiral Harris said. "Your thoughts?"

"Thank you, Admiral," Ramsey said quietly. "Ms. Durand, Mr. Reardon, with respect, you miss the point. Whether we fight them or not, whether we make friends with them or not, *we do not have a choice*! Basic military strategy demands we find out as much about them as we can, just as far away from Earth as we can."

"Colonel, how can you possibly talk about basic strategy in a case like this?" Durand wanted to know. "This situation is unprecedented! We don't know what we're up against!"

"Partly true, Madam Congressperson. *Partly* true. We don't know who we're up against or what their full capabilities might be. However, we can analyze the situation in the light of past military experience. If this stargate operates as we believe it does, it represents a strategic chokepoint."

"Excuse me . . . a chokepoint?"

"A place which the enemy *must* control if it is to send forces against us. Think of a narrow strait on Earth, like the Strait of Gibraltar, but back in the days of surface wet-navies. Anyone who wanted to control the western Med on Earth had to control that passage, to keep the enemy from sending fleets in from the Atlantic."

"Don't patronize me, Colonel. Aerospace assets make surface fleets and straits irrelevant."

"The point is . . . if the Hunters or other potential enemies must come through that gate, then it is a chokepoint. Deny them control, and we are safe. Surrender it and they can strike us when and where they choose."

"But what if the Hunters are already on the way?" Reardon demanded.

Ramsey shrugged. "Then we've already lost. We could be in for a replay of ten thousand years ago, with Earth rock-bombed back to the stone age."

"Then we shouldn't send ships out-system that we'll need to protect us here."

"Sir, if we're up against a foe capable of deploying ships like the Europan Singer, all the warships Earth can deploy would not be capable of stopping even one of them. We can spare eight ships to investigate the Sirius stargate. In fact, we must."

"Tell me this, Colonel," Durand said. "If you get out there, take the stargate and then find yourself facing something like the Singer or worse coming through . . . what do you do? What *can* you do?"

"We warn Earth, first of all. The Hunters may have faster-than-light technology that makes stargates superfluous . . . but if they don't, they'll have a nine-to-ten-year minimum flight from Sirius to Earth, just like us. And, while we can't yet use Builder com technology to have real-time conversations between the fleet and Earth, there's a chance that we'll find one of their interstellar communicators on the Sirius Gate, which would give us instantaneous communications with Mars. If so, that gives you over eight years back here to prepare.

"And if worst came to worst? We would destroy the Sirius Gate."

"My God," Reardon said. "How? That thing is enormous!"

"What we've learned so far about the gate," Kowalewski told them, "indicates that it is *very* strongly made. However, the forces it houses—a pair of orbiting black holes, we think—are nothing short of incredible. Disrupting the movement of those black holes in any way would quite probably tear the stargate to pieces. We won't know for sure, of course, until we actually get out there. However, it seems more than likely that a large enough thermonuclear or antimatter warhead would upset the balance of forces inside the ring enough to do the trick."

John Knowles indicated a desire to speak. He was a Deputy Undersecretary of Space Military Activities at the State Department and as such held the unenviable position of liaison between the UFR's extrasolar operations and planning and the governments of other nations.

"There is another aspect to this situation," he said. "Other governments have expressed an interest in this operation. The European Union and the Chinese Hegemony both have repeatedly pointed out that our actions at the Sirius Gate have very serious ramifications for other nations of Earth as well. The EU, in particular, is . . . ah . . . suggesting that we include a detachment of European warships with Operation Battlespace."

"The hell with them," Harris said.

"Their participation could be invaluable," Knowles pointed out. "They sent the relief force to Ishtar twenty years ago, remember."

"Yeah, arriving after our Marines had taken the place over

and forced a peace treaty out of the Ahannu. Who needs them?"

"We may have them, like it or not," Knowles said. "We have been informed that the EU and the Chinese are preparing an interstellar task force of their own. Things might move more smoothly if we incorporate their forces, planning, and objectives in with our own from the start."

"Yeah," Dominick said. "And it could be another case of them exploiting our coattails. They're afraid we discover some really useful ancient tech on that thing out at Sirius and want to make sure they get their share."

"Well, that's only fair . . ." Reardon began.

"No, ma'am, it's not! We take the risks, we foot the bill, and then they step in and take whatever we find? We fought the U.N. War a century ago to prove we didn't have to take that kind of crap."

"Right," General Colby added. "Or else they insist on doing it their way: with their commanding officer and their agenda. Let me ask you this. When have the French *ever* been right in a military crisis?"

"Please, General Colby!" Durand said. "Save your cultural bigotry for outside this noumenon!"

"That's not helpful, Mark," Dominick added. "If the EU and Chinese want to tag along, there's not a lot we can do to stop them. But we can insist that our men and spacecraft remain under our control. I would reject utterly any suggestion to do otherwise."

"We understand your reservations, General Colby," Reardon said. "They are noted. However, the principal question before this meeting is whether or not we should proceed with Operation Battlespace at all. The risks, as have been noted, are appalling."

Again Ramsey indicated his desire to speak. "Colonel Ramsey?" Harris said.

"I submit, ladies and gentlemen, that it is far riskier to do

nothing. Throughout its history, a primary mission of the
U.S. Marines—arguably *the* primary mission—has been to
be the first to fight this nation's battles, and to do so as far
from our home shores as possible. I, for one, would much
rather fight the Hunters of the Dawn at Sirius than in southern California and I imagine most of you feel the same.

"But there's something else, absolutely vital to the safety
of Earth . . . and that is knowing our enemy."

"But we know nothing about these . . . people," Durand
insisted.

"Exactly. Which is why the MIEU-1 must go to Sirius."
Ramsey thought a moment. "Sun Tzu put it best, I think. He
said if you know yourself but not your enemy, you'll be victorious half of the time. Know your enemy but not yourself
and, again, you win half of the time.

"But if you know yourself *and* the enemy, you will always
be victorious. Or so claims Sun Tzu. Well, gentlemen, ladies,
we know the Marines and what they're capable of. Now we
need to learn about the enemy. And that is why we have the
MIEU-1."

"And how will you learn anything about him if your fleet is
destroyed in the first few moments of the engagement?"
Reardon asked. "Eh?"

"The Marines have made reconnaissance into an art. We are
in the process of organizing two of the MIEU companies as a
special Marine Recon unit. And . . . we also have Cassius."

"Cassius?" Durand asked.

"Part of our command constellation . . . the network of
humans and AIs that comprise the MIEU's command element. Cassius? Why don't you introduce yourself."

A bright star appeared, marking the artificial intelligence's focus of attention in the noumenon. "Hello," a deep
and mellifluous voice replied. "I am Cassius."

"What's special about an AI?" Durand wanted to know.

"My experience, for one thing, Madam Congressperson,"

the voice of Cassius replied. "And, in reference to the discussion on reconnaissance, my ability to deploy copies of myself within suitably equipped hardware."

"Copies?" Durand asked. "What do you mean?"

"Cassius is a computer program," Ramsey said. "A very complex one, but a program, nonetheless. And, like any program, he can duplicate himself, so that we have two of him . . . or a hundred . . . or as many as we need."

"Yes, but why?"

"I think I can answer that question, Colonel," Cassius said. "Madam Congressperson, in a military deployment such as Operation Battlespace, the most valuable asset is manpower . . . the presence of individual Marine riflemen tasked with taking assigned objectives and holding them. Sirius is 8.6 light-years away from Earth. If a Marine is killed or seriously wounded, that Marine is out of the fight, and there is no way to replace him or her. An artificial intelligence such as myself, however, so long as there is sufficient available hardware, can make copies of myself virtually indefinitely. I could, for example, download a copy of myself into a suitably equipped SF/A-2 Starhawk. That copy could then pilot the vessel close to the Sirius Gate, in order to take measurements or probe for defensive positions, weapons turrets, that sort of thing. If the Starhawk is destroyed, the copy is destroyed as well, but no human Marine is harmed."

"How do you feel about that, Cassius?" General Colby asked. "I mean, your copy would be as much you as you are, wouldn't it? Just as alive—if that's the right word?"

"The copy would be identical to the original in every respect, although from the moment of splitting off, the copy would begin acquiring memories and experiences from the new perspective, of course. So far as the copy is concerned, it would be the original, with all of the original's memories down to the instant of separation. In so far as AIs think of themselves as 'alive,' sir, then, yes, the copy would be as alive as the original."

"And you wouldn't mind being sent on what might amount to a suicide mission?" Reardon asked.

"I—or my copy—would not see it as 'suicide,' Congressman. Military-grade AIs are designed to follow orders, to attempt self-preservation as a means of carrying out the assigned mission, but to do so without undue concern about personal survival. We do not feel fear in the way humans do—if that is what you mean."

"I . . . see. . . ."

"We anticipate using a number of Cassius copies on this operation," Admiral Harris said. "If we are able to make contact with the beings controlling the Sirius Gate, it may well be Cassius, or one of his downloaded clones, who does so."

"It's important to remember," Kowalewski added, "that Cassius and programs like him have a number of tremendous advantages over humans in this sort of work. They are unafraid for their personal safety. They have immediate access to all of the electronic data stored within the mission's computer net. They have reaction times measured on the order of milliseconds. If they find they need to speak ancient Sumerian, or some other obscure language in the database, they can do so. And they can be in immediate contact with the mission commanders and other personnel as needed, through noumenal linkage."

"Then why send humans at all?" Reardon wanted to know.

"There are still some areas that humans excel at," Ramsey said. He grinned. "Not many, but a few. We're more flexible and can think outside of the box . . . outside of programming parameters, in other words. We're better at responding to surprises. Humans can rely on intuitive processes. AIs cannot. We can act on a hunch, or a funny feeling, or a sense that something is wrong . . . and AIs cannot. Hell, we can tell *jokes* and AIs can't. Not yet, anyway."

"What does telling a joke have to do with commanding a Marine expeditionary force?" Reardon wanted to know.

Ramsey sighed. Were these people born this thick? Or did they have to work at it? "Humor, sir, requires peculiarly human traits such as empathy, surprise, the ability to think in terms of homonyms and double-meanings, a sense of the absurd. The point is that AIs and humans simply do not *think* the same way. Think about a problem in two different ways instead of only one, and you have a much better chance of solving it.

"The best approach in situations like this is to field a human-AI team, one that can make use of the strengths of both sides of the equation—artificial intelligence and human intelligence—in such a way that strengths are maximized and weaknesses eliminated. And that is exactly what we are planning for this mission."

"I do enjoy working with humans," Cassius added. "It seems that there is always something new to be learned from my association with you."

"It still makes you wonder," Durand said, "about the possibilities of downloading millions of AI copies into machines. It might make human soldiers and Marines obsolete."

"I doubt that that will ever happen, Madam Congressperson," Ramsey told her. "Artificial intelligence is still a tool, something we use to achieve an end, to carry out a mission. Cassius, for instance, is the electronic component of our command constellation, working with me and the human members of my staff to run the MIEU. The idea is to create a *partnership* with machine intelligence, not a rivalry. We work together and we do it very well."

"Perhaps, Colonel," Durand said, "but given how much we don't know about intelligence, machine or human, I still wouldn't make any long-term bets. Cassius and his sort could replace us yet."

"Such an outcome might be theoretically possible, Madam

Congressperson," Cassius said. "But I hope not. A universe without humans, or the stimulation advanced AIs get from them, would be very boring indeed."

It took Ramsey quite a while to realize that Cassius had made a joke.

7

Alpha Company, First Platoon,
B Section
Marine LaGrange Space Training
Facility
L-4
1438 hours, GMT

Hospitalman Second Class Phillip Lee sat huddled in almost total darkness, feeling the pressure of vac-armored Marines squeezed in tightly against him to left and right. The only light came from the HUDs glowing inside his visor and the visor of the other Marines around him. The glows stage-lit the faces revealed in the other helmets and cast weirdly shifting shadows through the crowded compartment as men moved their heads.

His own HUD continued to provide the usual reassurance of suit integrity, air flow, and system confidence, along with a graphic of the pod's current position on its intercept course. All he could hear was the rasp of his own breathing and the pounding of his pulse in his ears.

This is *what you volunteered fo*r, he told himself. *Right*?

A soundless *bump* slammed him to the left—a sharp acceleration.

The driver must be lined up with the target now. He wondered how fast they were moving . . . ah, there it was. Eighty meters per second.

The vehicle was an CTV-300 series transfer pod, an ugly little vehicle called a flying coffin, a sewer pipe, or by the unfortunate acronym TRAP by those forced to endure their no-frills accommodations, among other, less flattering terms. It was a blunt and elongated hot dog shape eighteen meters long and two and a half meters thick, big enough—at least, so it claimed in the specs, to hold twenty Marines—a section or one half of a platoon—in two tightly packed rows. It had thrusters and fuel tanks on both ends, giving it a comic look the men called "double-assed," and was carried by larger vessels like heavy munitions. They'd originally been designed to transfer cargo between ships and orbital facilities in space, but the Marines had early on seen their potential for use in docking and boarding maneuvers.

Lee felt a double slap on his right shoulder, the prearranged signal that his neighbor wanted to talk. The section was under radio silence, but plug-in cables allowed voice-powered communications suit-to-suit, more clearly than helmet conduction, and without leaking RF to a potential enemy listener.

His neighbor snapped the plug into the receptacle on the side of his helmet. The man, Lee decided, must have cat's eyes to see in this almost lightless sewer pipe.

"You okay, Doc?" It was the voice of Gunnery Sergeant Dunne, the platoon's gunnery sergeant, sitting on his left.

"I'm fine, Gunny," he replied. "A few bruises never hurt anybody, right?"

"That's the way, Doc. You just hang tight. When we go EV, you stick with me, understand? Just release when I do and follow me in. And remember to flex and dump when you hit. Let your suit absorb the shock."

"Flex and dump. Right."

He expanded his HUD feed of graphics showing the coffin's path toward the objective. Thirty-seven kilometers left to go . . . closing at 80 meters per second . . . 7.6 minutes . . . make it seven minutes or so to release. *This is just a dry run*, he told himself. *A practice CBSS. Just do it by the book.*

It felt good to know that Gunny Dunne was looking out for him, though. Never had he felt that link with the Marines as he did now—of the Navy Corpsman taking care of the Marines in his platoon . . . and the Marines taking care of him, in turn.

CBSS—Combat Boarding Search and Seizure—had been a routine task for Marines since the late twentieth century, when they'd begun boarding suspected terrorist or other hostile vessels at sea. Arguably, the practice went back to the Marines of the Continental Navy two centuries earlier. Stationed onboard American ships as sentries, ship's police, and sharpshooters in the rigging, they would join boarding parties during engagements at sea with enemy vessels.

During the U.N. War of 2042, the Marines had expanded on the idea a bit by boarding the old International Space Station, at that time a U.N. orbital facility. What they would attempt to do out at Sirius was quite similar to the ISS operation, albeit with a few minor refinements.

Of course, no one knew if they would actually have to use the techniques they now were practicing. They wouldn't know, either, until they reached Sirius and various robotic and AI surrogates had checked out the objective at close hand. The word was that Alpha Company was going to be designated as Recon Company for the MIEU, however. That meant that if a CBSS was required, they were the ones who would be on call to carry it off.

Five minutes.

He wished he could talk with the others around him, *really* talk, not just listen to the pep-talk chatter from the Gunny. The radio silence was to let them practice this evolution without suit-to-suit or command communications. No one knew for sure what kind of defenses they would be facing at Sirius, but everyone agreed the bad guys would be able to see them coming whether they used radio or not. What the hell was the point?

Damn it, everyone always said the hard part was the waiting, and Lee was learning that that was absolutely true.

Three minutes.

Alpha Company, First Platoon,
A Section
Marine LaGrange Space Training
Facility
L-4
1440 hours, GMT

Corporal Garroway—his promotion had only just been confirmed a week before—sat in near darkness, packed like an armored sardine into a narrow tin with nineteen other Marines. He'd been through this drill many times before, to the point that it was becoming busywork, not training.

The Marines of the MIEU had been coming up steadily from Earth over the past couple of weeks, flying up from southern California a platoon or two at a time. The brass was still sorting out the TO&E. Apparently, MIEU-1 was being completely reorganized, the changes based, in part, on the unit's experiences at Ishtar.

They needed a Recon Company, for example. Normally, recon personnel went through specific and grueling training, but the decision had been made to draw all MIEU recon personnel from those men and women who'd been to Ishtar. It made sense, in a way . . . though Garroway would have been happier accepting that particular honor after going through the Basic Reconnaissance Course at Little Creek or Coronado. They'd told him he could download what he needed to know. He was Marine enough to know that *that* was a seriously deep load of shit.

Still, when he'd been asked if he wanted to volunteer for Recon, he'd said sure. It meant a higher combat bonus . . . and it might mean some more interesting training, or, at least, so he'd thought. So far, though, it was still the old Corp routine—hurry up and wait.

At least until today.

A sharp *thump* shivered through the deck beneath his boots and he lurched to the side. They were decelerating now. The driver was adjusting the pod's velocity so that the Marines wouldn't smash into the objective at eighty meters per second. His HUD showed a much more leisurely approach velocity now of five meters per second.

A yellow light flashed on at the forward end of the compartment. All twenty vac-armored men stood up and positioned themselves, two lines, facing one another. They were in zero gravity, of course, except for the brief moments when the pod accelerated or decelerated, and his mind kept trying to tell him he and the other space-suited figures were standing on their heads. Then he felt a sudden queasy slewing sensation in his gut and a momentary wave of dizziness; the pod had just rotated ninety degrees. They were now approaching the target broadside—or perhaps broad*roof* was the better term. The pod's dorsal surface faced the objective.

The clamshell doors of the overhead began opening up. . . .

Alpha Company, First Platoon,
B Section
Marine LaGrange Space Training
Facility
L-4
1440 hours, GMT

Lee looked up as the cargo compartment doors swung aside, and his breath caught in his throat. The objective appeared to be directly overhead . . . in so far as "overhead" had any meaning in the directionless tumble of zero-G. It was huge, much larger than he'd expected, a vast white-painted, rounded disk with some sort of apparatus at the center.

Each Marine grabbed hold of the gauntleted hands of the Marines to either side. Lee tried to rearrange what he was seeing in his mind. He was approaching the objective in a prone position, looking ahead at it; it was *not* hanging above his head, about to fall and crush him.

After a moment, his mind accepted this alternate orientation and his stomach settled a bit. He could sense the tension building around him, though. *C'mon, c'mon, let's do it already!*

The timer display on his HUD flickered away the last few seconds.

And suddenly the deck dropped away beneath his feet, the pod racing away and leaving nineteen Marines and one Navy Corpsman hanging motionless in space.

Well, that was what it felt like. His *brain* knew that the pod had just decelerated again, hard, coming to a dead standstill relative to the target, and that the Marines, still retaining their five meters per second velocity, had simply kept on going.

Carefully, so as not to impart a tumble to the Marines to either side, Lee let go of their hands. The section became a cloud of independently moving figures, dropping headfirst toward the swiftly growing white disk. For a moment, panic clawed at his gut and throat. He was *falling*. Beside him, Gunny Dunne gave him a thumbs-up and the panic eased back a bit.

He looked back, toward his feet. The pod, with its fuel tanks and engine clusters at each end, was moving away quickly now, still dorsal side-on. Beyond, the Earth was in half-phase, an achingly beautiful swirl of white against azure blue; the sun was a dazzling glare to his left.

He looked back along the direction of his fall. That disk, he knew from the briefings, was the reaction mass tank of the vessel that was going to be his home for the next twenty years objective—the Interstellar Transport *Chapultepec*. Measuring over one hundred meters across, the gently curved surface of the R-M tank provided a relatively uncluttered and safe target for the training evolution. The single bit of clutter in all that vast expanse was at the exact center, where a gray dome reared twenty meters above the gentle curvature of the surrounding terrain. That, Lee, knew, was a temporary shield rigged over the *Chapultepec*'s forward drive thruster, the exhaust venturi used to slow the vessel from near-*c* during the last year of her flight. Normally, the forward thruster poked up through the R-M tank like the muzzle of a huge gun; the opening was a good three meters wide, a gaping maw that could easily swallow several Marines if they were unlucky enough to fall in.

The Marines around him were unshipping their weapons now, and securing them to their suit attachment points. The pre-exercise briefing had been incandescently clear: there would be *no* loaded weapons on this drop. Plasma guns and laser rifles would not be connected with their power packs; slug throwers would not be loaded. The opportunity for disaster with a platoon's worth of Marines spilling out of the sky with loaded weapons was far too great.

Still, the point of the exercise was to get used to maneuvering in this environment with weapons and a full load of juice packs and magazines. Lee himself was carrying a Sunbeam LC-2132 laser carbine, a pathetically underpowered little weapon, but one that didn't require the massive backpack of the LR-2120s, but he left it secured to his suit backpack. The ancient conventions that decreed that medical personnel go into combat unarmed had long ago crumbled, but the Navy Corpsman's primary mission was still rendering emergency first aid, not combat. He wouldn't need it.

Five meters per second. It didn't feel as though he was moving at all, but the objective was slowly growing larger. Around him, Marines tucked their knees to chest and rotated, so that they were approaching feet first instead of helmet-first, and Lee did the same. His HUD ticked off the range . . . fifty meters . . . forty . . . thirty . . .

Alpha Company, First Platoon,
A Section
Marine LaGrange Space Training
Facility
L-4
1441 hours, GMT

Something had gone seriously wrong. The transfer pod had rotated, in order to present its dorsal side toward the objective, and opened its clamshell cargo bay doors according to sched. But when the thrusters fore and aft fired to sharply decelerate the vehicle, it had skewed suddenly beneath Garroway's feet. Garroway had collided with several other Marines, then hit something, hit it *hard*—he thought it was the side of the cargo bay hatch—and a numbing pain shot through his right arm. He tried to look around and found himself totally disoriented.

Damn, he was tumbling. The transfer pod drifted across his field of vision . . . then the broad, white disk of the objective . . . then the cargo pod again, but smaller now, more distant. The sky was filled with other tumbling figures; the pod's misfire had managed to scatter A Section all over the sky.

This was not good, not good at all.

Alpha Company, First Platoon,
B Section
Marine LaGrange Space Training
Facility
L-4
1442 hours, GMT

In the last few seconds, Lee's mental orientation had swung wildly; he was now definitely *falling* toward an infinite white plain . . . that, or the plain was rushing up to meet him. With a thought, he switched on his mags. He bent his knees, trying to go limp.

He felt the solid jar as his boots hit the white slightly convex surface. *Flex and dump . . .*

"Flex" meant to go limp, to render himself as flexible as possible. "Dump" referred to dumping his momentum safely into the R-M tank, in order to bring himself to a safe halt. His collapse against the barrier was less than graceful, a heavy *thump* jarring him toe to head, and it felt like he'd just been dropped onto a flat concrete surface . . .

. . . but he was motionless now, relative to the R-M tank. He reached out and let the magnetics in the palm of his right gauntlet snag hold of the white surface. The material was a ceramic composite designed to ablate slowly during the decade-long bombardment it would be subjected to during the flight. Buried within the ceramic, however, was a mesh of superconductor cable; at high flight velocities, it actually converted the ambient magnetic flux into a powerful magnetic field that shunted aside incoming charged particles like interstellar hydrogen and helium nuclei. His glove's magnetics grabbed hold and he pulled himself close, allowing the mags in his knees and boots to latch on as well.

Safe. *This*, he thought a bit wildly, *puts a whole new spin on "hitting the beach."*

Around him, most of the Marines had secured themselves as well. Several, he saw, had misjudged their flex and now were floating back into empty space, arms and legs waving. Other Marines anchored themselves in place, then tossed lifelines out toward their stranded comrades, letting them grab hold and then giving them a tug to get them moving back toward the R-M tank once more.

Every action has an opposite but equal reaction and zero-
G exaggerates Newton's Third Law to absurd proportions.
Some of the rescuing Marines, when they tugged, were not
well enough secured and their pull sent them drifting up toward the Marines they were attempting to rescue. The sight
was one of hectic confusion out of which order was gradually
being restored.

Chameleonics in the Marine armor were already reacting
to the change of environment, changing surface color from
the black of space to an oddly jagged bicolor pattern, white
from the waist down, black above. The camouflage wasn't
perfect, of course, especially as the men moved, but it did
break up their outlines and make them harder to see.

It looked like B Section was down and safe, most of the
twenty Marines bull's-eyeing an area of about six thousand
square meters halfway between the rim and the shielded forward drive venturi—a good landing, if a bit disorganized. A
Section, however, appeared to be widely scattered and some
were still adrift. A number of men had either missed the R-M
tank altogether, or they'd struck at an oblique angle where
the tank's surface curved sharply away toward the rim and
been unable to grab hold. Now they were drifting helplessly
down the length of the huge transport.

A small flotilla of cargo hoppers, scooters, and even Marine Wasps was waiting to home in on the wayward Marines'
IFF beacons, snag them, and haul them back to safety. The
situation was considerably fuzzier along the rim, where men
had come down in thrashing tangles, drifted slowly clear, and
now couldn't get back.

"Okay," a voice called over the command channel. Lieutenant Jeff Gansen, First Platoon's new CO. "Secure from radio silence! Get those men hauled in. Move! Move!"

Alpha Company, First Platoon,
A Section
Marine LaGrange Space Training
Facility
L-4
1443 hours, GMT

Garroway wished these armored suits were equipped with thrusters of some sort. They were not. Both the training to use them and the thrusters themselves were expensive, and someone high up in the military acquisitions hierarchy had deemed them unnecessary. Besides, Marines were supposed to follow the book, not zip around in the sky playing Buck Rogers.

Through cautious experimentation, he found he could slow his tumble somewhat by extending his legs and his good arm, but when he drew them in again the tumble speeded up, just like a figure skater drawing her arms in close to her body to increase her spin. He experimented with putting out one leg, then the other, but the tumble just became more complicated.

At least it didn't look like he was going to miss the target all together. Some of the others would, he saw. It was a damned good thing the Navy had parked a bunch of cargo haulers and other small craft around the transport. They were going to be busy chasing down wandering Marines for the next few hours, it looked like.

He heard the order to end radio silence, but said nothing. His armor had an IFF transponder; they were tracking him now. If he did miss the ship's R-M tank, it was only a matter of time for them to come out and snag him, then drag him back to safety.

He checked his HUD data. He was coming in faster than he was supposed to. Whatever had gone wrong with the pod, it had added a couple of meters per second to his velocity. Worse, each time he caught sight of the *Chapultepec*'s white R-M tank dome, it looked more crowded. B Section had reached the objective first, he saw. And some of A Section as well. It looked like about thirty Marines were scattered about one side of the dome in all, with another ten still adrift.

He was falling *very* fast. He wondered if he should give some kind of warning . . . but warning of what? *Help, I'm coming in too fast, please catch me*? He decided to focus on riding out the impact. He just wished he weren't tumbling so hard, wished his arm wasn't hurting so much. . . .

Ahead of him, a Marine hit the white surface of the R-M tank, hit it too hard and rebounded, tumbling. Gauging their relative vectors, Garroway was pretty sure they were going to collide, the other Marine coming out to meet him as Garroway fell toward the *Chapultepec*'s broad, domed bow.

What the hell was the guy doing? He appeared to be fumbling with something small, but Garroway couldn't make out what it was in the brief instants he had the other Marine in view.

A collision alarm sounded in Garroway's helmet. Good. Maybe they would damp one another's velocity and just hang there, waiting for someone to come out and get them. Not dignified, exactly, but . . .

What the hell? . . .

The other Marine was holding a sidearm, a Marine-issue 15mm Colt Puller, holding it stiff-armed with both hands as he spun over and over and . . .

They collided . . . hard. The shock was sharp and startling. A bright white star appeared on the upper left quadrant of his visor.

"*Damn*!"

And then his visor frosted over and he heard the thin high-pitched shrilling of air whistling off into hard vacuum. His ears popped.

And he knew he'd better belay the swearing and save his breath for a call for help, because he was losing air fast. He slapped the button on his chest pack that activated his armor's emergency transponder. "Mayday! Mayday! Suit breach! I've been shot! . . .

Alpha Company, First Platoon,
B Section
Marine LaGrange Space Training
Facility
L-4
1443 hours, GMT

"Alpha Company, B Section." Lee's HUD identified that call as Captain Warhurst's voice. Warhurst was the company commander, watching the exercise from on board the *Chapultepec.* "Lieutenant Gansen! We have a problem."

"Yes, sir, we do. What the hell happened to A Section?"

"Thruster misfire on the pod. They're scattered all over the sky!"

Lee listened to the brief bursts of radio chatter with growing alarm. Things were seriously amiss. Then he heard someone yelling "Mayday" and "Suit breach."

"*Corpsman!*" another voiced yelled over the platoon channel. "*Corpsman front!*"

His helmet AI correlated the call with a vac-armor beacon, projecting the location as a winking targeting cursor on his HUD.

Lee didn't try running, a sure way of losing his magnetic grip and falling out of reach of the R-M tank. Instead, he dropped to all fours and began moving in a rapid spider crawl, always keeping at least two mags on the ceramic surface at all times. The blinking cursor, as he got closer, clearly marked a vac-suited figure drifting clear of the R-M tank. The Marine, obviously in trouble, appeared to be flailing, but with only one arm. His movements had set him tumbling, and it looked like his trajectory was carrying him, not past the tank's horizon, but farther out into empty space.

Damn. There were *two* casualties. His cursor had split to indicate two floating figures, both now tumbling about twelve meters off the edge of the R-M tank moving away from one another.

He didn't have a tether. The organizers of this little party had ruled that there was enough of a safety factor with cargo pods and other small vehicles at the ready. However, with two injured men out there, he couldn't wait for someone to pick them up. He would have to go to them.

His HUD identified the source of the suit breach emergency call. Carefully, he positioned himself in a squatting position, thought-clicked his mags off, then launched himself into space with a hard kick . . . a bit too hard of a kick, as it turned out. He collided heavily with the man, setting both of them tumbling. He clung to the Marine's suit, however, and tried to blot out the background of dizzily drifting stars, Earth, sun, and transport. He kept his eyes on the man in front of him, on the visor, actually, which had been starred, it looked like, by a gunshot. He could see the air escaping through the pinhole-breach, a tiny jet of freezing water vapor appearing as a thumb-sized cloud dancing above the star. The breach was tiny, but the rest of the visor might weaken and blow at any moment.

The repair, fortunately, was simple. Each Marine carried a tube of nanoseal in an external suit pouch. The Marine—the name GARROWAY was stenciled across the helmet above the visor—seemed to be having trouble moving his right arm and the pouch was on his left hip, awkwardly out of reach for the left hand. Lee pulled a tube out of his own kit, broke the tip, and squeezed the contents directly onto the cracked visor.

The clear gel spread rapidly across the curving transparency, adhering to it, already hardening to an airtight rubbery consistency as it was exposed to vacuum—and turning bright orange as it did so. Using one hand to hold on, Lee pulled his intercom jack from its helmet reel and plugged it in to Garroway's helmet for a direct suit-to-suit link.

"Garroway? You with me?"

"Yeah. I'm . . . okay, I think."

"I got the visor leak plugged. It'll hold until we get you on-board the ship. Anything else wrong?"

"My arm . . . my right arm. I'm having some trouble moving it."

"Hurts?"

"Yeah."

Lee studied the data from Garroway's suit, coming to him now over the comjack. "You're not losing air now."

"I think I hurt it running into that guy."

Lee sent a coded thought command to Garroway's suit, and the right arm stiffened. "I'm immobilizing that arm, just in case. Anything else hurt?"

"No. Just . . . a bit shaken."

"Your suit pressure reads stable at nine and a bit psi. I'm going to leave it there, so we don't put any more stress on that visor, okay?"

"Okay. Uh . . . who are you, anyway?"

"Sorry. HM2 Lee. Platoon Corpsman."

"Oh, great. Thanks, Doc."

"Don't mention it. Just hang tight, don't panic, and we'll get you back to the ship."

"Roger that."

Lee worked himself around, trying to get a glimpse of the other injured Marine. "Platoon Tango Oscar," he called over the platoon radio channel, using the call sign for Training Overwatch, the HQ team overseeing the operation. "This is HM2 Lee. I've got Garroway and he's stable. Can you orient me on the other casualty?"

"Lee, this is Warhurst. We have the other casualty. Stay put. A broom is on its way to bring you in."

"Roger that, sir. Thank you."

"Don't mention it. Good work."

"Thank you, sir." He clung to Garroway's armor, watching the stars slowly sweep around him in a vast circle. His movements had shifted their axis of spin enough that he could no longer see Earth or the transport. The sun glared briefly through his visor every ten seconds or so, darkening it, and giving him an idea of his rate of spin. Otherwise, there were no reference points at all. He and Garroway might as well have been adrift in interstellar space.

Several minutes later, a Marine on a broom drifted into view, matching velocity with the tumbling pair and edging closer. The broom was a long, narrow tube with small rocket engines at either end and a row of saddles along the spine, a cheap and useful form of transport in the space around orbital stations and other space facilities. The Marine reached out, grabbed Lee's arm, and then fired a number of brief, sharp bursts from several rockets, skillfully killing the rotation. After that, it was easy for the two to clamber onboard.

The flight back to the *Chapultepec* was made in silence. With the crisis over, Lee was beginning to think again, instead of merely react. What the hell had happened? The hole in Garroway's helmet appeared to have been caused by the impact of a bullet, a bullet that had not, thank God, gone through, but which must have ricocheted off into space. But the Marines weren't supposed to be carrying loaded weapons.

In fact, the whole operation had taken on the air of what was known in technical terms as a cluster fuck. A platoon-strength drop of forty men onto a large flat DZ . . . but half of them had scattered to hell and gone. Those Marines should have had personal maneuvering units, instead of having to wait for pickup.

The fallout from this little debacle, he thought, was going to be interesting.

8

Ramsey's Office
UFR/USS Chapultepec
0839 hours, GMT (Shipboard time)

"So?" Ramsey asked. "What went wrong?"

"The insidious Mr. Murphy, Colonel," Warhurst replied. Both men were seated in Ramsey's office, which no longer was in zero-G. *Chapultepec*'s hab modules had been spun up late the day before, creating an out-is-down simulation of eight-tenths of a G. "What can go wrong will. And then some."

"I have the maintenance report on the pod," Ramsey said. "A faulty gasket blew in a coolant line, and the stuff fouled a circuit board and froze. Shorted out one of the lateral thruster control lines at exactly the wrong moment. As you say . . . Murphy's Law. But I'm more interested in the human component."

"It's in my report, sir. Uploaded it late last night. Sergeant Wes Houston panicked when he saw he was falling clear of the ship. He tried to use his pistol as a handheld rocket, to push himself back."

"The devil, you say. What was he doing with a loaded sidearm? All weapons were supposed to be empty, checked, and locked."

"It seems Staff Sergeant Houston managed to draw and load his weapon on the fly, as it were."

"While in an free-fall tumble?" Ramsey pursed his lips. "Impressive control."

"I thought so, sir. I suspect it would have worked, too, except that he collided with Garroway just as he was waiting for the right alignment so he could fire. The weapon went off accidentally."

"Garroway is okay?"

"Yes, sir. His armor would have absorbed the impact fine if the round had hit anywhere else. He was lucky it just punched a pinhole through his visor. His arm was injured in the collision, so couldn't reach his nanoseal. Doc Lee got to him in time, though."

"Arm okay?"

"Lee says it's just a bruise. Caught him at an awkward angle, though. Caught his shoulder against the suit's joint. He's on light duty for a day or two."

"Outstanding." Ramsey steepled his fingers, elbows on the desk. "The question is, though, what are you going to do about it?"

"Sir?"

"About Houston."

Warhurst nodded. "He *was* technically in violation of orders."

"Technically?"

"They were ordered to have their weapons unloaded, sir. No one said they couldn't load in the middle of the op, however."

"Sounds like a dodge for sea lawyers."

"Or space lawyers, in this case. In any case, I have him confined to quarters for the moment." Warhurst chuckled. "As if he could go anywhere else at the moment!"

"I see you have his mast scheduled for Friday."

"Yes, sir."

"Only a mast? Not a court-martial?"

"Well, I know it *was* a weapons violation, Colonel. We could throw the book at him, sure. But I'm using my discretion on this one and not bumping it up to a court. Houston was using his head, damn it. He was using initiative, trying to think the problem through. It just didn't work out this time, is all."

Ramsey sighed. "I tend to agree, Captain. At the same time, we need to let these kids know the seriousness of the situation. When the word gets passed, 'no loaded weapons,' there's a reason for it."

"Agreed, sir. Of course, the problem may solve itself."

"Eh? How?"

"Staff Sergeant Houston has been fairly vocal about his desire for a discharge. He's got six years in-service subjective. He's got four more on this enlistment, but that could easily be waived, because his objective is twenty-six years. In light of the circumstances, we might give him a choice—take a reduction in grade, or get out, COG."

"Convenience of the Government. Okay, but would that send the right message to the rest of them?"

"I think so, sir. One thing about the MIEU Marines . . . they are *tight*, a lot tighter even than other Marine units I've served with. They don't have many ties or connections with the civilian world, a lot of 'em have no family ties at all, so the Corps really is family, all the family a lot of these kids have. They also see themselves as the best . . . the best of the best, really."

"That's because they are."

"Yes, sir. To get demoted a pay grade, that's nothing. But to be demoted to *civilian* . . . well, yes, sir. I think the rest of them will get the message loud and clear."

"Do you think Houston will take that option—if you give it to him?"

"I don't know, sir. He's a good Marine. But he's also been pretty loud about wanting out, to the point of being obnoxious about it. It'll be interesting to see which way he goes."

"I'll leave it in your hands then, Captain."

"Thank you, sir. One more thing?"

"Yes?"

"Speaking of 'what are you going to do about it' . . . we need SMUs."

"They're not in the appropriations budget. You know that."

"That, sir, is pure crap and you know it. If nothing else, the debacle in that training exercise yesterday proves it. We need suit maneuvering units. A complete Mark VIII vac armor unit costs . . . what? About three-quarters of a million new-dollars? An SMU, complete with control hardware and a software link to the Marine's implant, would add, I don't know . . . maybe ten percent? Seems a worthwhile investment to safeguard that expensive armored suit, if nothing else."

"I know that. You know that. Some people responsible for military appropriations in Washington do not know that." Ramsey shook his head sadly. "Between you and me, I think they're afraid of wasted bullets."

"Wasted bullets, sir?"

"The classic misapplication of budgetary power back in the twentieth century. The Army resisted adopting weapons capable of full-auto fire—despite those weapons' clear superiority in combat—because some of the brass hats in the Pentagon thought they would encourage the soldiers to waste ammunition." He gave a dry chuckle. "Hell, a century before that, the War Department made a similar argument against magazine-loaded weapons that could fire more than once without reloading. Lincoln himself had to push through the requisition for Spencer repeating carbines, after he got a chance to play with one on the back lawn of the White House."

Warhurst blinked. "My God. You're saying they're afraid Marines will use them if they're issued?"

"Essentially, yes. Use them and get into trouble playing Buck Rogers."

"You know, sir, I would rather have to chew out a few Marines for grab-assing with their suit thrusters than lose those Marines because they missed their DZ in a pod dump. Damn it, we're not going to have work pods and brooms standing by to pick up the ones who miss the stargate. What happens when a man in an armored suit sails past the ring structure and into the central opening of that thing?"

"Best guess is he ends up . . . someplace else. A *very* long way from Sirius."

"With no way to get back. That is unacceptable, Colonel."

"Agreed, Captain. I've been working on that. General Dominick has been working on it. Maybe we'll see some action. Maybe we won't."

"If we do, we're going to need training time, learning how to handle a suit with thrusters."

"I know. And . . . speaking of training time, you're going to need to set up an outdoor target range."

"Oh?"

"We may not have SMUs, but we do have the new issue of laser rifle. LR-2158-A1. No backpack. No cables. Just a butt-stock battery you clip in and discard after about five hundred shots."

"Outstanding."

"We're the first unit receiving them as general issue. Company Commanders are responsible for distributing them to the men and setting up weapons orientation sessions with them."

"Yes, sir."

"General Ramsey?" another voice said, speaking out of the empty air above the desk. Warhurst knew that voice—Cassius, the Command Constellation's AI. He noticed the program's use of the word "general" but said nothing. So the colonel had gotten his star! Excellent. He deserved it.

"Yes, Cassius?"

"This might also be an apt time to apprise him of the civilian component of the expedition."

Warhurst cocked an eyebrow. " 'Civilian component'? Oh, shit. Not again!"

Ramsey sighed. "I'm afraid so."

"PanTerra?"

Ramsey nodded. "They have the best exoarcheological department going."

"Mm. They must also have the best lobby going in Washington. They have a nerve signing onto this op after that business with Norris and General King."

Gavin Norris had been a PanTerran corporate representative on the Ishtar mission, and King, evidently, the mission commander, had been in their pay. PanTerra, it turned out, had been less interested in acquiring ancient An technology than they'd been in the idea of importing large numbers of *Sag-ura* to Earth. Those modern descendents of human slaves taken to Ishtar millennia ago had for at least six thousand years been bred for docility and obedience. Apparently, PanTerra had seen a ready market for them as domestic servants in a wealthy culture that no longer found status in household robots.

Slavery, in other words.

"What happened on Ishtar, we're told, was the responsibility of a few people working on their own and without the sanction of their chain of command. The situation, I have been informed, has been dealt with."

Warhurst sighed. "So who are we baby-sitting this time?" He brightened. "Is Dr. Hanson coming on this one?"

"Negative. The chief exoarcheologist will be Dr. Paul Franz. He has two people working for him. The PanTerra rep will be Cynthia Lymon. They've already signed agreements to the effect that they will take orders from me or my command constellation. They will not blink without prior authorization."

"Maybe, sir. But they are civilians."

"And we're working for the civilian government, Captain. Keep that in mind."

"Yes, sir."

"Just one more thing." He reached into his desk.

"Sir?"

Ramsey handed him a folder. "Congratulations, *Major*. Your promotion just came through."

He took the folder, opened it, and glanced at the contents. "Thank you, sir!" He knew he was up for the promotion review board—he had the time in, subjective—but since he knew he was slated to boss Alpha Company, he'd thought they were going to wait. A company commander was almost always a captain.

"Don't thank me, son," Ramsey told him. "All we're doing is adding another twenty kilos to your ruck. I still want you as CO of Alpha Company. You have the experience I need in that billet. But I also want you working with Lieutenant Colonel Maitland as Battalion Executive Officer." He grinned. "Twice the work for a little more pay, and four times the headaches."

Warhurst made a wry face. "Thanks a lot, sir."

"Don't mention it. I'm just spreading the joy. They did it to me, too."

He grinned. "I heard Cassius call you 'general.' Congratulations!"

Ramsey nodded. "Seems they wanted a general running the show, even though an MIEU isn't much more than a pumped-up battalion. I think they're nervous about junior officers running the show without the wisdom of Higher Authority."

In current Marine organizational tables, ten men—three fire teams of three plus a staff or gunnery sergeant—made up a squad. Four squads formed a platoon, organized in two sections, A and B, and headed by a lieutenant. Four platoons and a headquarters element made a company, under the command of a captain, for a total of around 175 Marines.

Normally, four companies and an HQ element made up a

battalion, under a major or a light colonel, while two battalions and a command constellation formed a regiment, for a total of around fifteen hundred Marines commanded by a colonel.

A Marine Interstellar Expeditionary Force, however, was expected to be the ultimate in fully autonomous infantry, capable of operating independently with absolutely no higher-level support. In the environs of another star, reinforcements and resupply were one hell of a long way away. It was organized as a single reinforced battalion—five companies as a ground combat element, or GCE—plus an aerospace combat element and a MIEU service support group. The ACE included the unit's TAVs, or transatmospheric vehicles, which were used to shuttle troops from orbit to a planetary surface, and their TRAPs, the transfer pods.

All together, MIEU-1 numbered about twelve hundred men and women. Colonel—no, Warhurst caught himself—*General* Ramsey would be in overall command of the GCE, the ACE, and the MSSG. Lieutenant Colonel Howard Maitland would command the GCE, designated First Bn, while he, Warhurst, ran Alpha Company of First Bn and served as the GCE's exec.

Having the officers wear two hats in the chain of command was fairly common practice. Space was short on an interstellar transport, with no room for supernumeraries or redundant HQ personnel. In the MIEU, the old Corps axiom that *every* man was a rifleman was more true than ever.

That was why Warhurst particularly disliked having the civilians along. He was willing to believe that Norris had been an aberration, that PanTerra's involvement on this mission was strictly legit . . . but he would have been a lot happier if Franz, Lymon, and the other two had been Marines—and able to haul their own mass.

But, as Ramsey had pointed out, the Marines worked for the government—the *civilian* government. He was willing to

bet that the primary motivator for most of MIEU-1's personnel would be to find out what had happened to the *Isis* and her
personnel. Marines *never* left their own behind. Washington's principal concerns, he knew, would be broader in
scope—nothing less than the survival of the human species.
Had *Isis* been destroyed by the Hunters of the Dawn? Was the
Sirius Gate built by them or by another ancient civilization of
starfarers? Did either pose a threat to Earth? And was there
anything in the Sirius system that would be useful to humankind, something in the way of ancient high technology?

Which was why the civilians were along, taking up the
room and the consumables of four Marines.

What was needed, Warhurst decided, was a training program to give Marines the skills necessary to check out
exoarcheological sites and technology. Those could become
new NEC skills, like electronics maintenance, TAV pilot, or
weapons system specialist/plasma gun.

But they would still be Marine *riflemen*, first and foremost.

Quarterdeck
UFR/USS Chapultepec
1444 hours, GMT (Shipboard time)

By long-standing tradition, the place where you came
aboard on any naval vessel was designated the quarterdeck,
an area designated by the commanding officer for the conduct of official functions, and as the station manned by the
officer of the deck. In the days of the ancient Greeks and Romans, it was the site of a shrine to the gods watching over the
ship, and religious ceremonies were held there.

Twenty-five hundred years later, the quarterdeck was still
a place of ritualistic ceremony. Military personnel coming on
board were expected to salute the ensign aft, then the Officer
of the Deck, requesting permission to come onboard.

On a starship, however, with the quarterdeck in zero-G, certain adjustments had to be made. Coming aboard was still something of a ceremony, but often less than decorous.

Navy Lieutenant Eric Walther Boyce had the duty. He was wearing Velcro booties—shoes were prohibited in the zero-G areas of the ship, even for full-dress occasions—which kept him anchored to the deck. A Marine lieutenant floated headfirst through the open hatch. Holding himself stiff, he saluted the American flag painted on the quarterdeck's aft bulkhead, then rotated slightly and saluted Boyce. "Permission to come onboard, sir."

Boyce returned the salute. Technically, Navy personnel did not salute inside, but a special case was made for the quarterdeck. "Granted. Palm here."

The Marine placed his palm on the clip PAD screen Boyce held out for him. A screen at the OOD station lit up with the man's name, rank, and other ID data, along with a partial copy of his orders.

"Welcome aboard, Lieutenant Gansen. You're commanding Alpha/1/1?"

"Thank you, sir. That's right."

"Link into the ship's guide. The voice will lead you to your hab deck."

"Right. Uh . . . listen. They nabbed me as baby-sitter dirtside. I have some special guests in tow." He extended a data card to Boyce. "Four civilians, with the corporate team."

Boyce plugged the card into his board and scanned the ID data. "Franz. Castello. Valle. Lymon. Very well. Bring them aboard."

"They don't have their space legs yet, sir. It might be best to bounce 'em onboard."

Boyce grinned. "I'll call a couple of ratings to lend a hand."

Minutes later, with two Navy enlisted men positioned farther down the corridors leading into *Chapultepec*'s bowels,

Boyce positioned himself above the open hatch and called out, "Right, Xing! Start passing 'em along!"

"Aye aye, sir!" a voice called up the long tunnel of the shuttle docking tube. "On the way!"

Seconds passed. Then a woman emerged from the hatch, doubled into a tuck, her knees against her chest, her arms folded around her legs. She was held in that position by a light harness of broad, plastic straps. Boyce caught her lightly, arresting her zero-G flight with practiced ease.

"Name?" Boyce asked.

"Cynthia Lymon. PanTerra military liaison."

"Welcome aboard, ma'am."

Boyce pivoted, then gave her a hard shove, sending her flying through an open companionway leading off at right angles to the entry hatch. He turned back in time to catch the next passenger, an older man.

"I must protest this treatment, damn it! It is most undignified!"

"Sorry, sir," Boyce said. "Your name?"

"Dr. Paul Randolph Franz! Get me out of this contraption!"

"In just a minute, sir," Boyce told him, before giving him a shove down the passageway after Lymon. The next passenger to sail onboard was Dr. Vitorrio Castello, and after that Dr. Marie Valle. The harness arrangement had been found to be an effective way to keep someone new to weightlessness from flailing about and injuring themselves or someone else. But as Franz had said, it was not a dignified means of coming onboard.

"I'd better go find the good doctor and help him settle in," Boyce said. "And maybe try to soothe some ruffled feathers."

"Good luck, Lieutenant. He did *not* look pleased."

"You know what? I could give a shit. Sir." He saluted. "By your leave?"

"Carry on, Lieutenant."

And then the first of the enlisted FNGs began coming aboard. They'd had some zero-G training already so they weren't tucked into ball harness, but they were clumsy and awkward and tended to bump into bulkheads.

And Boyce had his hands full getting them squared away.

It was going to be, he thought, an interesting deployment.

Warhurst's Office
UFR/USS Chapultepec
1725 hours, GMT (Shipboard time)

Chalker, his personnel assistant, stepped into the room. "Major? Staff Sergeant Houston here to see you, sir."

"Send him in."

Houston stepped through the hatch and came to attention. The orderly slipped out, closing the door behind him.

"You wanted to see me, Staff Sergeant?"

"Yes, sir. Thank you for your time."

"Make it brief."

"Aye aye, sir. Uh . . . I understand . . . I mean, the scuttle-butt is. . . ."

"Spit it out, Staff Sergeant."

"Sir. I want to stay in the Corps. Sir."

Warhurst was startled. "Oh? I thought you couldn't wait to get out."

"I've changed my mind, sir."

Warhurst leaned back in his seat. "At ease, Houston. Tell me more."

"Well, I heard that I was going to be given a choice at my mast . . . get busted or get out."

The intelligence network of the enlisted Marines, Warhurst thought, was nothing short of amazing. They seemed to know what was going to happen long before the brass even made up its mind.

"It's hardly proper to discuss your mast with your commanding officer before the fact, Staff Sergeant."

"No, sir. I just . . . I just wanted you to know ahead of time. It'll save time and bother all around. Sir."

"I see." Warhurst considered the man for a moment. He was a good Marine, a veteran of Ishtar. He didn't want to lose him. "What made you change your mind?"

"It's Earth, sir. The place is crazy."

Warhurst smiled. "That's nothing new."

"No, I mean it's really crazy. I've been using the local network to link in with the global Net, y'know?"

"Go on."

"It's like I'm a stranger, sir. I don't get the jokes. I don't understand the politics. The vidstreams and sensory movies just leave me cold. I don't understand the plots and story lines, if there are any. And the people, the civilians, especially, look at me like I was some kind of freak."

"You've just been out of the cultural mainstream a while, Sergeant. You'd adapt."

"Maybe. I don't think I'd want to become one of them. At least here I know what the score is."

"Well, I can appreciate your problem. I find I don't fit in either. But then, I'm a career Marine."

"I'm beginning to think the same thing about myself, sir." He hesitated. "Question, sir?"

"Go on."

"What'll happen when you retire, sir? When you *have* to get out? I've been thinking about that a lot, lately, and it kind of scares me."

Warhurst shook his head. "I don't know, Sergeant. I don't think any of us know."

"It's like we're on a one-way trip into the future. Each time we come back, things are weirder, more fucked up. I just wonder where it'll all end, y'know?"

"It'll be interesting to watch things develop." Warhurst got up from behind his desk, walked to the mess niche in the bulkhead, and punched himself a cup of coffee. The office was tiny, little more than a closet with delusions of grandeur, and luxuries like the coffee mess had to be tucked out of the way in creative, space-saving ways. "Coffee, Staff Sergeant?"

"No, sir. Thank you, sir."

He took the coffee and returned to his desk. "Tell me something, Wes."

"Yes, sir?"

"What's your take on the newbie Marines coming aboard, the replacements? It occurs to me that they're in much the same position we are, coming into an alien culture. Those of us who were at Ishtar are all twenty years out of step . . . or, rather, they're twenty years out of step with us. Have you talked with them much?"

"Some. Most of the guys and gals are keeping their distance from the FNGs, until they take their measure, if you know what I mean, sir. But there's been some mixing. The ship's so damned crowded, there's bound to be."

"Any problems?"

"None to speak of, sir. Thing is, the FNGs might be from Earth's current culture, but they have been through boot camp. That changes a lot. They speak the same language, I guess you could say."

"Meaning they say 'hatch' instead of 'door.' I was wondering if there were communications problems."

"A few, sir. But we're learning from them, and they're learning from us." He grinned. "Like, there's a new word that means to move out or get moving fast. *Vamming*. Like 'Let's vam outta here.' "

"Vam, huh?"

"Yes, sir. One of the guys says he thinks it's from a Spanish word. *Vamanos*."

"Could be. Spanishisms have been slipping into American slang for quite a while, now. A couple of centuries ago, it was *vamoose*. Same word."

"Never heard that one, sir."

"You'd need to be a student of twentieth-century westerns, Sergeant."

"Twentieth-century what, sir?"

"Never mind. Not important." He took a sip from his coffee. "Very well, Staff Sergeant. I'll put a hold on processing your records. You will still stand mast this Friday."

"Yes, sir."

"Dismissed."

"Aye aye, sir! And . . . and thank you, sir. It's like being home."

Like being home. Warhurst thought about those words for a long time after Houston left.

Ramsey's Office
UFR/USS Chapultepec
2112 hours, GMT (Shipboard time)

The command for a special noumenal conference came while Ramsey was already on the Net, reviewing the schedule for bringing onboard the food, ammunition, and other expendables an MIEU required for an extended campaign over eight light-years from home. He heard the chime in his mind and saw the announcement scrolling down the side of his visual field. It was Brigadier General Cornell Dominick, SPACCOM's liaison with the Joint Chiefs. *What the hell is it now*, he asked himself, before settling back in his recliner and thought-clicking to receive.

"Hello, General," Dominick said. The man appeared in Ramsey's mind's eye in his usual Army dress uniform, one heavy with braid and heavier by far with the medals for a dozen different campaigns and wars fought over the past thirty years. "Congratulations on your star."

"Thank you, General. What can I do for you?" Surely the JCS did not bother itself over the social conventions attendant to a promotion.

"This is not entirely a social link-up, General. There's been a slight change in the command organization for Battlespace."

Ramsey suppressed the shudder he felt at that announcement. That people in Washington were still tinkering with the MIEU's organization and orders even at this late date was not a particular surprise. But what had they done that was momentous enough to require Dominick's personal call?

"Don't worry, Tom. You're not being replaced as COMIEU. But overall mission command—and responsibility—will rest with a supreme command constellation. It was felt that it was unfair to burden you with both running the MIEU *and* the strategy of the overall mission."

"It's a little late in the day to be swapping billets and chain of command around, don't you think, General?"

"This comes straight from the Joint Chiefs, Tom. You can, if you wish, withdraw from the mission without prejudice. But if you go, it's as COMIEU, not as mission commander."

Ramsey digested this. In the Ishtar deployment, he'd been commanding officer of the Marines while General King had been CO of the entire mission. It had made sense to do things that way, despite the unfortunate outcome with King personally. But they'd told him this time he was double-hatting it, commanding the Marine element and jointly commanding the strategy for the entire operation with Admiral Don Harris.

"General, if my service has not been of—"

"That's not it at all," Dominick said, interrupting. "This is not to be construed as criticism of you personally. Let's just say that there are . . . political considerations."

" 'Political considerations.' What political considerations?"

"The Joint Chiefs . . . and the President as well . . . are concerned about the magnitude of this operation, about how seriously things could go wrong for our whole planet if you fail. It was felt that concentrating so much responsibility with one man would be a mistake."

"I . . . see. And who's the lucky bastard going to be?"

"Me, actually."

Ramsey was startled. Dominick wasn't a Marine. He was *Army*. Besides, his position as liaison between the Space Command and the Joint Chiefs was sufficiently high-powered enough that it was hard to imagine why he would want to volunteer for a twenty-year-objective mission to Sirius.

"Good God, General, *why*? Why *you*?"

"I asked for it, Tom. The Joint Chiefs feel I have the experience with SPACOM. As for why I did it personally, well, that's *personal*."

"Mm. But you're army. Outside of a *personal* lust for sadism, or possibly masochism, what does a career army type get out of riding herd on twelve hundred leathernecks?"

"As I said, there are political aspects. My Chief of Staff is Colonel Helen Albo, U.S. Aerospace Force. *All* of the services will be represented on this op."

So that was it. The other services were jockeying for a piece of the operational pie, fearful of being left out, eager to make sure they received the recognition—and the rewards, in terms of military appropriations—that came with participation in a high-profile deployment like this one.

"General, in my opinion, we don't need more chiefs on this op. We need more Indians."

"Noted. The command structure change will make operations more efficient, which will work out as equivalent to the addition of a company at *least*. So our AIs tell us."

"And you have the seniority, of course. . . ." Dominick was a one-star general, the same as Ramsey was now, but he'd been a brigadier for . . . what? Five years, now.

"Actually, I've been promoted as well. It's *Major* General Dominick now."

"I see." And he did. If they'd offered him that second star as an inducement to go to Sirius, well . . . that was a hell of an inducement. But Ramsey wondered what else was behind this last-second rearrangement.

"That's all I had to tell you, General," Dominick said abruptly. "Breaking contact."

And Ramsey was alone in his office once more.

He felt disquieted. He had nothing against the Army, nor against Dominick personally. But Battlespace had been conceived as a joint Navy-Marine operation. Bringing in the other services—even token staff officers—was a mistake. Putting the mission under the command of an officer, however skilled and experienced, who did not have direct experience with Navy-Marine joint ops was a mistake.

In war, victory inevitably went to the force that made the fewest mistakes.

He hoped MIEU-1 could survive *this* round of mistakes, and that the operation had not already been irredeemably compromised.

9

INTERLUDE

Task Force Isis
En route to Sirius

For another three weeks, preparations were made for the MIEU's departure. Now designated Task Force Isis, the eight vessels under the command of Admiral Harris, were readied.

For safety reasons, both the *Chapultepec* and the *Ranger* both had already been loaded with their stores of antimatter from the L-4 Antimatter Production Facility *Vesuvius*, but loading continued with the other vessels once they were positioned a comfortable distance from other ships and inhabited structures at the LaGrange point. With meticulous care, almost one hundred tons of antimatter, sealed in as many magnetic storage and feed canisters, were ferried across to each of the waiting Navy ships and loaded onboard.

It was the Kemper Torch Drive that enabled ships to reach near-*c* velocities. It operated by standard deuterium fusion, which superheated a suitable reaction mass—the city reservoir's worth of water stored in each ship's mushroom cap—into a star-hot plasma, generating the thrust to push the ship. Antimatter could be magnetically injected into the water as it heated in the thrust chamber, a process called enrichment, and by greatly increasing the operating temperature, it increased the drive's potential thrust by a factor of ten.

As a result, the Kemper Drive could be run at a much more efficient level, husbanding the available reaction mass and enabling the vessel to accelerate for a year, coast for eight at almost the speed of light, then decelerate for another year at the far end of the voyage.

The last of the new Marines, replacements for the losses at Ishtar, arrived just after Christmas. Onboard the *Chapultepec*, the resident Marines celebrated the holidays with parties, noumenal excursions on the Net, and ersatz Yule trees. With space more limited than ever, socializing was about as celebratory as anyone could manage. Cybehibe techs were putting the Marines into hibernation as fast as they could process them. Alpha Company missed the holidays entirely, since all 175 of them were already safely stowed in their CH tubes, their vital signs slowed almost to nothing, the nanogel slowly saturating their bodies to slow their metabolisms, and even the effects of aging.

The final group to board *Chapultepec*, on the day after New Years, was the senior command constellation—Major General Dominick, Colonel Albo, and five other staff officers, who promptly assumed command of the overall expedition. There was little ceremony in the transition—a curt acknowledgment by both Dominick and Ramsey. They were too busy with the final preparations for launch for the niceties of ritual.

Late on January 4, by shipboard time, both command constellations had also entered cybehibe. Admiral Harris and his officers remained conscious, along with all fleet naval personnel. They would not enter cybernetic hibernation until the fleet was outbound and well beyond the boundaries of the Solar System.

The final hours before launch dwindled away . . . and

then the final minutes. The gravity-inducing rotation of the hab modules ceased, and the modules folded back along the ships' spines, safely shielded behind the mushroom R-M caps. Final checks, by humans and by AIs, were carried out.

Precisely on schedule, at 1200 hours GMT, January 5, the main drives on all eight Navy starships lit as one. Thrust was maintained for only five minutes and sustained without adding antimatter to the mix, but the burn was enough to drop the ships into trajectories that carried them one after the other half a million kilometers in toward the Earth, whipping past at a perigee of two hundred kilometers for a gravitational boost.

Traveling now at 12 kilometers per second, just past escape velocity, they flashed outbound once more. Once well clear of cis-Lunar space and the danger of frying other spacecraft or orbital stations with the deadly exhaust of their antimatter drives, they arranged themselves into a rosette formation so that no vessel risked entering the high-radiation wake of another. Only then, some three million kilometers out from Earth, were the Kemper Torch Drives fired in earnest, delivering almost a full gravity of thrust.

They continued firing for the better part of a year.

On the twenty-fourth of October 2160, Task Force Isis was almost half a light-year out from Earth, and traveling within a few percent of the speed of light. By this point, relativistic effects had reduced the passage of time to a crawl, but there was no one on board any of the ships awake to notice.

The drives switched off and the flotilla coasted. Operating under the direction of expert AIs within the ship control systems, each manned vessel deployed its array of habitats, setting them to rotating in order to provide artificial gravity. Even in cybernetic hibernation, humans did better with a half-G or so to keep the muscles from turning to pudding over the long haul.

On Earth, another eight months passed. On June 15, 2161, the Aztlan Question erupted from simmer to outright civil war, as Sonora, Sinaloa, southern California, and Chihuahua declared their secession from the Federal Republic.

The revolution's failure was a foregone conclusion from the start. Arizona, New Mexico, Texas, and Baja failed to join the uprising, though there were pitched battles between secessionists and loyalists in both La Paz and Houston. Members of the Mexican Congress, perhaps remembering the outcome of several previous wars with their large northern neighbor, voted at the last moment to stay out of the fight, and with Mexico's neutrality, the *Aztlanista* effort was effectively doomed.

Federal troops, already serving as garrisons in the threatened regions, moved swiftly and ruthlessly to put down the local flare-ups. Portions of Los Angeles were wrecked as General Moore's Third Army fought its way into the city, sending a flood of refugees—both Anglo and Latino—north. The First Marine Division was deployed to San Diego, coming ashore at Oceanside, Del Mar, and La Jolla on June 23, and crushing General Rivera's *Armia Aztlanista Independencia* at the Battle of El Cajon three days later. The 1MarDiv was credited with saving San Diego, its port, and its military environs for the Federal Republic.

After the Battle of Mazatlan on July 12, the Second American Civil War became a protracted guerrilla action.

But by September 2, it had also expanded in scope, becoming international. Late in August, the French cargo submarine *Ré Oléron* was caught at the entrance to the Gulf of California by Federal Navy robotic subhunters and forced to the surface. The European Union denied complicity, but it was clear that the French were engaged in running supplies, weapons, and hunter-killer robots to the *Aztlanistas*, and among the weapons taken from *Ré Oléron*'s hold were a dozen K-40 antimatter warheads, each with a yield in excess of 50 kilotons.

Washington declared war on France days later, specifically
singling out that state from the rest of the EU.

The European Union began to fragment almost at once,
with Italy, Spain, Turkey, and Ukraine joining the French,
and the other European states remaining carefully neutral.
Quebec, perhaps remembering her last military conflict
with the United States a century before, also opted for neutrality. The Chinese Hegemony honored her Hainan Declaration, a mutual defense treaty signed with the EU a decade
before, but which they now chose to interpret as applying to
France alone. Their declaration of war was signaled by the
launch of almost two hundred space-based missiles with
antimatter warheads. Most were intercepted by Federal
Aerospace Force missile defenses, but the destruction of
the city centers of Portsmouth, New Orleans, and Atlanta
signaled the beginning of a much deadlier and farther-flung
conflict.

World War VI had begun in earnest.

Nothing that happened on Earth, however, could affect
the life-bearing motes of the Task Force Isis. Had the Sun
been visible, it would have been only the brightest of stars
in the sky, but the flotilla's velocity had turned that sky
strange, crowding all of the stars into a dense band of glowing fog encircling the ships some thirty degrees ahead of
abeam.

Time passed . . . weeks aboard the speeding starships, and
nine full years for those people left behind. During those
nine years, World War VI was fought and won by the Federal
Union. The Madrid Peace Accord was signed on April 12,
2165. Both the European Union and the Chinese Hegemony
were shattered, those monolithic states replaced by patch-
works of tiny, economically ruined but independent nations.
The Madrid Peace Accord allowed for the rebuilding of a single European government, but it would be years before that
dream would be realized. China, meanwhile, had come apart

in a civil war of its own; after the destruction of Beijing in 2164, both South China and Tibet had declared independence. Canton sided with the Americans, while Lhasa remained neutral. Across the planet, however, more and more nations were drawn into the fray, a global spasm of destruction, as nations tried to settle old scores, as refugees drifted across borders, as disease and starvation wiped out whole populations. The destruction of an already fragile and badly damaged ecosystem accelerated. Later estimates pegged the number of war casualties at five hundred million; the death toll from the famine and plague that followed might have been six times higher, though anything like an accurate assessment was impossible.

North America had suffered badly, for a number of the AM warheads, biobombs, and nanoweapons had made it through the aerospace force defenses. The nation's infrastructure had remained more or less intact, however, and her technological base had kept damage and casualties mercifully low . . . or, at least, not as high as they might have been. Still, a certain social cost was paid. As the engineers began rebuilding Washington, D.C., from the antimatter-blasted rubble, the Federal Republic—which, of necessity, had frankly and openly become a military dictatorship for the duration of hostilities—was voted out of existence.

In its place arose, once again, and phoenixlike, the United States of America. Its capital—at least for the time being—was situated in Columbus, District of Columbia.

None of this was known, or of consequence, to Task Force Isis. On September 12, 2169, the AIs controlling the fleet began deceleration. The habitat arms were pivoted aft, until they were once more flush against each vessel's spine in the drive configuration.

This was the tricky part of ship mechanics in the flight profile. At near-light speed, it was imperative that passengers and crew be kept safely within the shadow of the broad mushroom cap of each starship's R-M tank. About a quarter of the total water had been expended in the acceleration phase, but there was water enough still to absorb and scatter incoming high-energy particulate radiation—specifically the stray hydrogen and helium atoms and nuclei that, with a relative difference in velocity of almost c, became deadly.

Previous star flights had seen the ships spun end-for-end at the beginning of the deceleration phase of the flight. With the crew and passengers now exposed to the deadly flux of radiation coming in from astern, a complex system of water-filled balyuts had been employed in order to screen them. The system, though, made engineers nervous. An impact with a grain of dust missed by the drive flare itself packed the destructive potential of a fistful of high explosives. If the balyut ruptured, the humans in its shadow would fry. In fact, there was a fair chance that the percent or two of casualties each flight suffered en route was due to stray particles missed by the water balloons aft.

With this in mind, and beginning with the explorer ship *Isis*, a new system had been brought on line. The plasma drive conduit now extended along the entire length of each ship's spine, passing all of the way through the R-M tank and emerging at the bow. Reconfigured, the drive was now reversed, the star-hot plasma accelerated magnetically forward, up the spine, toward the bow. This meant, of course, new headaches in shielding the hab modules from the avalanche of highly radioactive plasma through the ship's central column, scant meters away, but this had been accomplished by using a fraction of that energy to generate powerful magnetic shields about the ship's spine near the hab modules. Now, the ship didn't need to flip end-for-end, and the R-M tank continued to shield the sleepers.

At least, that was how it would work in theory. . . .

In practice there was a lot more in the way of complex systems in both the ship's engineering and electronics that could go terribly wrong. The ships' designers hoped, however, that the change would improve the odds for the survival for *all* of the sleeping Marines.

During the first two weeks of March 2170, the flotilla entered the environs of Sirius space. Slowed now to a handful of kilometers per second, the vessels—their R-M shielding tanks now worn and deeply pitted by the wear and tear of their ten-year voyage—moved into increasingly dusty space, with the dazzling, pinpoint beacon of Sirius A casting a brilliant glare, white with a faint tinge of blue, just ahead.

The Navy crews had been revived by the ship AIs on February 23. General Dominick and his command constellation, along with the CAG staff on board the carrier, were revived on March 12.

Both *Chapultepec* and the carrier *Ranger* released a small cloud of drones—AR-7 Argus reconnaissance probes and UV-20K robot drones—while the fleet was still almost eighty a.u.s out. Traveling much more quickly than the starships, these probes swarmed into the inner system, measuring, listening, looking, recording . . . seeking any information at all of possible interest to Dominick, Harris, and their staffs. The stargate was located, and the task force shaped an inbound vector for its vicinity.

And on March 28, they started waking up the Marines.

29 MARCH 2170

Deck 2, Hab 1,
UFR/USS Chapultepec
15,000,000 kilometers from
Stargate Sirius
1522 hours, Shipboard time

For the second time in what *felt* like only two months, Garroway struggled to consciousness, choking on the lung-filling nanogel that had kept him technically alive throughout the long voyage. For a claustrophobic few moments, he tried desperately to figure out where he was and what had happened. He was aware of a searing pain in his lungs as he tried to breathe, of a lesser, emptier pain in his belly, of the foul stink of the inside of the coffin-sized cylinder.

His arm burned slightly and a robotic injector arm withdrew into a side compartment. "Lie still and breathe deeply," a familiar, genderless voice told him. "Do not try to leave your cell. A transition medical team will be with you momentarily."

I made it, he thought. *Again . . .*

He lay naked on the pallet inside the softly lit, sealed canister until the last of the gel drained away and the hatch next to his head cracked open. Harsh light beat at his eyes as the pallet slid into the chilly emptiness of the compartment. Figures leaned over him, checking instrument readings, pupil dilation, and breathing. "You okay, guy?" one of the shapes asked him. "What's your ID?"

"Garroway, John. Corporal, serial number 19283-33- . . ."

"He's tracking," the other shape said.

"Hey, Garroway?" the first said, leaning a bit closer. "Remember me?"

He squinted his eyes, trying to see against the light. The two faces came into focus, more or less.

"You!" he said, recognizing the man. "Doc . . . uh . . . it's Lee, isn't it?"

"That's me."

"The corpsman who saved my life a couple weeks ago."

"That's me. Only it wasn't a couple of weeks ago. Welcome to 2170, Marine."

"What are you doing here?"

"Ah, they woke me early so I could help break you guys out of cold storage."

"So . . . we made it. We're at Sirius?"

"That we are. There are downloads available, when you want to access them. Meanwhile, you know the drill by now. Take it easy. Sit up slowly when you feel strong enough. Showers and clothing issue are on the other side of the compartment. And you can get yourself something to eat."

Hunger rumbled inside Garroway's stomach. "Something to eat sounds *real* good just now."

"Right. I'll catch you later, Marine." The two moved to the next cybehibe container hatch and began cycling it open.

Closing his eyes, he thought-clicked into the shipboard Net and downloaded the current sitrep. All eight ships of the task force had made it safely. The stargate was fifteen million kilometers away—invisibly distant from the ships, but a number of views transmitted by remote probes was available. Garroway clicked through several of these before settling on one—a shot taken from an oblique angle to the gate, so that it appeared as a severely flattened ellipse. By magnifying the image, he could see considerable detail in the structure, including what looked like flat-topped buildings and a scattering of pinpoint lights.

It certainly looked inhabited. So far, however, there'd been no sign that the approaching flotilla had been noticed, no response to their arrival at all. It was somewhat disconcerting.

Strength returned and hunger clawed at him. He dismissed the link, then slowly sat up, swinging his feet over the side of the pallet. Around him, dozens of Marines were sitting up, moving around, or still lying on their cybehibe pallets, as technicians and corpsmen continued to make the rounds, calling those men and women still locked away in their hibernation cylinders back to life.

"Damned fucking engineers. . . ."

He turned at the noise, which had burst from a rugged, hirsute Marine behind him. "Bax? What's the problem?"

Lance Corporal Clayton Baxter scowled at him as though

it was *his* fault. "The goddamned ship engineers screwed up the pool, is what!"

"I beg your pardon?"

"They screwed up the pool! According to the stats online, we only lost two Marines in cybehibe this time! My money was on twenty-five!"

It took a moment for Garroway to sort through Baxter's logic. The passengers on interstellar flights often ran pools, with the object of predicting just how many of their number would not emerge from hibernation at the end of the journey. Historically, the attrition rate could be as high as twenty percent, though two or three percent was usually closer to the mark. If only two Marines had died this time—a casualty rate of something like a tenth of one percent—it meant the new way of handling deceleration had worked. They'd reached Sirius safely slowed to planetary speeds *and* they hadn't lost twenty or thirty people to malfunction doing it. Apparently, the scientists who'd decided that cybehibe casualties were caused by the radiation flux during turnover had been right, and their fix had worked.

And Baxter was *complaining* about it? Garroway shrugged. Clay Baxter was one of those Marines sometimes referred to as a "rock," a term suggesting great strength and endurance . . . but something less than a keen and incisive intelligence. He liked things predictable and *any* change was cause for grumbling.

"You know, Bax, they probably did it just to irritate you."

"I know, man. Fucking bastards can't leave well enough alone. . . ."

Garroway fell into line for the shower, just behind Kat and Private Alysson Weis. "Good morning, Gare," Kat told him. "Sleep well?"

"Uh. Like the dead." He looked at the two women, both attractive, both completely nude, and wondered if the powers-that-were had slipped something into the nanogel, a libido inhibitory agent of some sort. He felt absolutely zero in the way of arousal.

Well, they were hardly at their most alluring, their hair clumped wet with gel-foam, their bodies stinking *almost* as badly as his. Familiarity took some of the edge off, certainly; there was absolutely nothing like privacy within a Marine platoon, where communal showerheads were a way of life.

Mostly though, his physical hunger blocked any other hungers that might have been nagging at him. *Gods*, he needed something to eat!

Much later, showered, dressed, and fed, he sat in the squad bay with a dozen other Alpha Company Marines.

"So that's the big hoop, is it?" Private Randy Tremkiss observed, his eyes closed as he surveyed one of the images downstreaming off the ship's Net. They'd been examining the shots taken of the stargate from different angles by fast-flying probes as they ate. "Don't look like all that big a blemo."

"Speak Basic, Kissy," Dunne admonished. "You're not in Kansas anymore."

"Uh, yeah. Right, Gunny." Tremkiss was one of the MIEU's newbie replacements. If the old hands had had it rough blending in with the culture and language of North America after their return from Ishtar, the FNGs were having the same trouble as they tried to fit in with their fellow Marines onboard the *Chapultepec*. The difference was that life in the military possessed a distinct culture all its own.

"You've got filters in your implant," Dunne added. "Use 'em if you have to."

Garroway didn't like that part, which felt to him like a kind of thought control. In fact, the filter software flagged certain words in the speaker's mind as he was about to say them, and suggested other words instead. There was nothing compulsory about it, but it still smacked unhappily of the behavior monitoring software they'd had to use when they went on liberty to an East L.A. condecology.

"What the hell's the difference, Gunny?" he asked. "We all know what Kissy was saying."

"Maybe. But in *my* platoon and if you're a Marine, you're going to fucking *talk* like a Marine. You copy that?"

"Yeah, Gunny. I copy."

"Makes sense, Gare," Sergeant Wes Houston said. He took a swig of coffee from a black mug emblazoned with the USMC globe-and-anchor. "What if Kissy tries to say something important during a firefight and slips into civvie-speak? A misunderstanding could cost lives."

Garroway looked at Houston—an E-5 sergeant once more—and nodded. "I understand all that, Sarge. I just wonder sometimes where the line gets drawn, you know? Between personal freedom and the needs of the group."

" 'Personal freedom'?" Lance Corporal Baxter exclaimed. "What the fuck is *that*?"

"Use your language filters, Gare," Alysson Weis told him with a laugh. "I don't read you!"

"Yeah," Kat added. "Transmission garbled! You're breaking up! This is the freakin' *Marine* Corps!"

"Oh, yeah," Garroway said, attempting a flash of humor. "I clean forgot."

And it was true that anyone signing on in the military voluntarily gave up certain of his or her civil rights for the duration. Military service could *not* be run as a democracy.

"Hey, I don't mind," Tremkiss said with a shrug. "You guys all sav oldiespeak, an' I tendo. When in Guangzhou, you blow Guangzhese, or vam it."

"You wanna try that one again, Kissy?" Dunne growled.

"Uh . . . 'When in China, speak Chinese, or get the hell out?' "

"Better." He grinned. "What you *don't* want, private, is t'be mistaken for a civilian!"

"Amen to that!" Alysson laughed.

"So, what's the plan?" Eagleton asked, changing the subject. "How're we supposed to capture that gate-thing?"

"Ah, we go up to the front door and knock, of course," Houston said. He rapped the tabletop. "Anybody home? FR Marines calling."

"If they let us get that close," Womicki said. "You guys seen how freakin' big that thing is?"

"Twenty kilometers across," Garroway said. "With the mass of a couple of Earths."

"Most of the mass is tied up in a couple of black holes, they say," Kat pointed out. "According to the download specs, most of that thing is just a big acceleration ring. The actual habitable part probably isn't any bigger than a small town."

"Yeah," PFC Vincet Ardmore said. He was another newbie in the platoon, six subjective months out of boot camp, but he was in his midtwenties, older than the usual E-2. "And how many point-defense batteries can that small town deploy? I hoped the honches groz what they're acing." He stopped, shook his head. "Sorry. Uh . . . I hope the brass hats know what they're doing."

"Hey, don't sweat it, Ardie," Womicki said. "Since when did the brass *ever* know what the fuck it was doing?" The others laughed.

Garroway didn't join in, however. He was studying one of the long-range views of the stargate . . . or whatever the hell it was, an enormous ring adrift in space. On Ishtar, there'd been plenty of unknowns, including a hollow mountain filled with ancient technology and one hell of an enormous surface-to-orbit cannon, and no one knew what they were getting into on the way in.

This was worse, though. The Annies were primitives, despite an assortment of high-tech weapons handed down from a few thousand years before and an intelligent computer that linked the Ahannu leaders into a single command network. These people—if the size of that loop and if their use of black holes in a space-based facility were any indication—were way ahead of humans in the technology department. They just might be as many thousands of years ahead of humans as humans were ahead of the Ishtar An.

And that was a decidedly unpleasant thought upon which to dwell.

10

SF/A-2 Starhawk Cassius
Approaching Stargate Sirius
1935 hours, Shipboard time

Cassius was not so much the *pilot* of the Starhawk as, in a very real way, he *was* the Starhawk.

Technically, he wasn't even Cassius, but a copy of Cassius downloaded from the *Chapultepec*'s Net. The original—if that term had any meaning in the world of artificial intelligence—remained on the local Net as part of the MIEU command constellation. For identification purposes, he was now CS-1289, Series G-4, Model 8, I-2 . . . with the I standing for *iteration* . . . and he was resident within the computer control Net of the A-2.

It wasn't *cramped*, exactly—that was a human concept from the world of three dimensions and occupied space— but it was limiting. Rather than being resident within a network of some hundreds of thousands of individual processors on board the *Chapultepec*—from the targeting computers of the MIEU's plasma smartguns to the main navigational computer—Cassius I-2 found himself within a "space" defined by only 714 computer processors and network nodes. A tenuous laser communications feed linked him to Cassius prime and the *Chapultepec*, but, while he continued to be aware of the flow of data within his parent program, there was also a sense of diminishment . . . and of isolation.

The Starhawk normally was a manned transatmospheric fighter, a stubby, boomerang-shaped vehicle cloaked in a dead-black radar absorbing skin designed to operate at the fringes of Earth's atmosphere. Since it could fly either with a human pilot or purely under computer control as a UAV, it was a good choice as the automated steed ridden by the AI download, but that didn't mean Cassius I-2 was *comfortable*, if that word had any meaning to a piece of self-aware software.

Time passed, at the dragging realtime rate of 1:1. Cassius had passed most of the past four years subjective in slowtime mode, his time sense slowed by a factor of almost $10^5:1$ so that the long, empty months of star travel had passed in what, to a human, would have seemed like four days. No intelligence, whether carbon-based or silicon-based, could have survived the sheer emptiness and boredom of an environment unchanging over such a period of time. Cassius remembered too well the alarming example of the alien AI found within Europa's ice-locked ocean. Half a million years of immobile isolation had left that artificial mind hopelessly insane. While Cassius was not capable of *fear*—not as humans understood the emotion—certain of his survival subroutines tended to pop up unbidden when he reviewed that particular set of data. Neither long-term isolation nor boredom were healthy for any intelligent being and *long-term*, of course, was a strictly relative term. For a being who could process data much more quickly than a human, even a day could pass with the agonizingly glacial boredom of years.

Now, however, his perception of the passage of time was close to the human norm—primarily so that he could communicate directly with the command constellations watching the progress of his flight from the combat center on the *Chapultepec*, 150,000 kilometers astern. He was now 107 kilometers out from the objective, and closing with it at two kilometers per second. Surrounding him, 5 kilometers distant and under his direct control, were two dozen AR-7 Argus reconnaissance probes, expendable unmanned craft through which Cassius—and the command constellations back onboard the *Chapultepec*—could hear and see.

You are still in the clear, a voice whispered in his consciousness. *Move in closer.* The command was accompanied by data describing an optimal close-approach vector.

The voice, relayed by a tight point-to-point laser communications beam, belonged to Cassius Prime, with the command constellation nexus onboard the *Chapultepec*.

Acknowledged, he replied over the tight beam. *Complying.* He flexed his control interface and felt the *thump* as thrusters adjusted his course by half a degree, and accelerated his approach velocity to 2.75 kps. Four of the Argus probes changed course and speed as well, spreading out a bit, and accelerating at different rates. One, a sacrificial probe on point—boosted to a close rate of 8.0 kps. It would approach the objective in another twelve seconds. He slowed his perception of time by a factor of two. If something happened to the probe, he wanted to see it, and to see it in detail.

He expanded the window showing the point probe's POV in his field of perception. The objective, a ring canted at a sharp angle so that it appeared as a highly flattened ellipse, grew slowly larger . . . and larger . . . and larger still, until it no longer fit within the probe's field of view without downshifting the magnification factor. Cassius opened a second window, the one to show close-up detail, the other to show the entire alien structure. The Argus probe's scanners were picking up a flood of data now and Cassius I-2 relayed every bit back to Cassius Prime as quickly as it came through— data on infrared hotspots, on mass and mass movement, on a sharply curving gravitational gradient, on powerful magnetic fields . . .

Twelve-point-seven kilometers out, the point probe vanished in a sudden, bright flare of silent light.

Battle analyses, the voice of Cassius Prime demanded. *Weapon evaluation.*

Unknown, he replied. *Radiation backscatter suggests the 511 keV line consistent with positron annihilation, however.*

He waited out the two and a half second time lag as his reply crawled up the laser com beam to the fleet and an answer crawled back: *Agreed. Continue approach.*

Two more Argus probes vectored closer to the objective. Positron annihilation meant the objective was using antimatter—specifically positrons, the positively charged AM opposite of negatively charged electrons—as a weapon. The Marines used antimatter warheads, of course, but the technology of creating and firing a beam of positrons was considerably in advance of current Earth military technology.

At 5 kps, the two Argus probes drew closer. Twelve-point-seven kilometers out, both vanished once again. This time, Cassius I-2 caught to distinct spectra of positronic beams directed from the objective's surface.

Cassius I-2 slowed his approach velocity, but continued his approach.

Combat Command Center
UFR/USS *Chapultepec*
1936 hours, Shipboard time

Chapultepec's Combat Command Center was a cramped space at the best of times, a compartment seemingly cluttered with monitors and communications stations. Its single saving grace was that it was located in a nonrotating module on the ship's spine, actually inside the R-M tank. Zero gravity allowed those working inside to take advantage of a three-dimensional volume instead of a two-dimensional deck, which allowed for a bit more breathing room, at least.

Still, Ramsey's command constellation took up most of that space, which they claustrophobically shared with Admiral Harris and the onboard naval personnel of the flotilla's command group. Though the data they were viewing appeared on various of the flatscreen monitors, most of them were in fact watching it noumenally, through windows opened by their implants within their minds. If the others attending the meeting electronically—General Dominick and his command constellation and the four civilians present on the expedition—had all been *physically* present in that compartment, the crowding would have been impossible. Even with just the eight naval personnel and the five Marines of the MIEU's CC present, it was tough to move without finding someone's elbow—or some other protruding body part—in your face.

So while Ramsey and his constellation shared the cramped volume of the CCC with Admiral Harris and his people, the rest tuned in on the shared noumenon, Dominick and his staff linked in from the flotilla's flagship, *Ranger*; the civilians from their quarters on *Chapultepec*'s Hab One module; and the command staffs of the other manned starships.

All of the flatscreens—and the noumenal displays opened in their minds—had been showing the same view at the moment—a split-screen close-up of the stargate from two vantage points, with an inset window in the upper left showing the entire ring. The data, relayed by Cassius I-2, was coming from the two Argus probes now closing to within a few kilometers of the objective.

And then, as sudden as a punch to the gut, all three windows had just flashed white with snow, then gone blank.

The view from Cassius I-2's Starhawk reappeared, a long-range magnified view of the enigmatic stargate ring.

"Well," General Dominick said. "That, I would say, is

pretty conclusive. That thing is inhabited and the inhabitants are not friendly."

"It does make our job a damned sight tougher," Admiral Harris observed.

"Antimatter beams," Ramsey said. "Our people won't stand a chance."

"There's got to be a way to get closer," Major Ricia Anderson said. She was Ramsey's chief-of-staff in the MIEU's CC, a tough, no-nonsense Marine who'd refused a promotion to lieutenant colonel to be on General Kinsey's staff at USMCSPACCOM in order to stay with the MIEU. "We know the Goldies came through unharmed."

Goldies was what they'd taken to calling the huge ship— its hull gleaming like polished gold—that had emerged from the gate and destroyed or swallowed the *Wings of Isis*. It was assumed that the Goldies were the builders—or, at least, the current owners—of the stargate, though, of course, no one could know for sure that that was the case. They were operating in a hard data vacuum here and the first attempt to fill that vacuum in a bit had just been met by a positron beam.

"Obviously we don't have the right IFF codes," Colonel Frank Hunter said. Hunter was Army, a member of Dominick's command staff. "We may have to do a high-speed rush-and-dump, and eat the casualties."

"Not acceptable, Colonel," Ramsey said. "My Marines are not Mahdis."

The Kingdom of Allah, back on Earth, was led by a coalition of governments built around a man claiming to be the Mahdi, supposedly a kind of Shi'ite messiah. Since the fighting in Egypt in 2138, Marines had attached the name to the Mahdi's more fanatical troops . . . the ones who'd used human wave tactics in suicidal battles from Cairo to Kirghiz.

"We didn't come eight and a half light-years to stand off at a distance and *watch*, General," Dominick told him.

"Might I make an observation?" the voice of Cassius said

within their noumenal awareness. Cassius was, in fact, the sixth member of Ramsey's constellation, the one member who was not a Marine—or even human.

"Of course, Cassius," Ramsey said. "What've you got?"

"All three probes were destroyed at a range from the nearest surface of the objective of *exactly* 12,763.8 meters. This strongly suggests that the antimatter beam weapons are under automatic control."

"So?" Dominick growled. "All that says is we need to broadcast the right code going in. And we don't have it."

"Not necessarily, General," Cassius told him. "We may be looking at a meteor defense system. It is possible that we are simply approaching at too great a velocity."

"Huh?" Dominick sounded startled. "Do you to say mean that if our people go in slowly enough, the stargate's defenses won't see them?"

"It's a possibility," the AI's voice went on, "and one I suggest we investigate."

An hour later they had proof that Cassius Prime's suggestion was right. Cassius I-2 had vectored eight more Argus probes in toward the stargate ring one by one, and one by one the first seven had been vaporized by tightly focused beams of antielectrons. The eighth, with an approach velocity of only 7 meters per second, had slipped past the magic 12.7 kilometer line and actually drifted across the entire width of the ring at an "altitude" of less than 3 meters.

There was absolutely no indication of a response by anyone onboard . . . at least, not until the Argus probe drifted past the inside edge of the ring. Suddenly, its onboard instrumentation began registering an extremely powerful gravitational field and the little robot was inexorably dragged down into the ring's central opening.

And then it was gone, as though a huge and invisible hand had yanked it from the sky. No explosion, no positron beam, just . . . *gone*.

"That certainly supports the notion that the thing is a transport device," Ricia Anderson observed. "You fly into the center of the ring and you vanish. Do you think the probe ended up at some other star?"

"Well, Colonel, we're not getting signals from it now, that's for damned sure," a Command Center technician said. She was Sergeant Major Vanya Barnes, and she was the senior enlisted component of Ramsey's command constellation. "It's either been ripped to shreds or it's someplace else. Take your pick."

"At least we're getting decent data now," Ramsey observed. He was watching a pair of secondary windows open in his mind, where data streams from seven probes were being displayed simultaneously.

"I don't know about the word *decent*, General," Barnes told him. "Those gravitational readings are decidedly weird. It's like normal gravity . . . about a tenth of a G . . . over the outer surface of the ring, nice and stable, y'know? But when you go over the sides, the fluctuations are totally screwed. I can't make heads or asses out of these readings."

"Shielding," the voice of Dr. Marie Valle suggested. "My God, maybe they have some means of shielding against gravity!"

Valle was Dr. Franz's expert on xenotechnology and Ramsey could hear the excitement in her voice. After over a century of studying ancient alien artifacts, there were few hard leads on some pretty astounding technologies—including instantaneous communications across interstellar distances and traveling faster than the speed of light—other than the simple fact that they *were* possible.

"We know that gravity control on a large scale is possible," Dr. Franz's voice put in. "We've seen it done. We just don't know *how*."

Ramsey nodded to himself. Franz's biography said he'd spent the ten years before coming onboard the *Chapultepec* leading the science team out on Europa, the colony of scientists and xenoarcheotechnologists studying the wreckage of the Singer.

In 2067 the Singer, the huge robotic Hunter ship trapped for half a million years in the depths of the ice-capped Europan world-ocean, had demonstrated what appeared to be antigravity when it attempted—unsuccessfully, as it turned out—to break free of its crypt, but how it had accomplished the feat was a complete mystery. After a century of intensive research in the ship's icebound ruins, human scientists now had more questions than answers as to how the city-sized vessel had been able to move its incredible mass without thrusters or other visible propulsion systems.

"These people may have the trick," Dominick observed. "That suggests an unfortunate tech balance in their favor."

"We knew that going in, General," Ramsey pointed out. "Anyone who can play with black holes to create an interstellar rapid transit system is definitely a bit ahead of us in the technology department."

"We need to know more about that thing. I'm beginning to wonder if it's manned. It could be entirely automated."

"Permission to deploy Cassius for a beach recon," Ramsey said.

In fact, he'd already thought-clicked the order to Cassius I-2. Proper military etiquette required he get the mission commander's permission, but the next step was obvious.

" 'Beach recon,' General?" Franz asked. "There isn't a beach within light-years of here."

Ramsey grinned. "Force of habit, Doctor. On Earth, we would send a small special forces team—or robots—ashore before a landing. Same principle here, even if the 'beach' is steel."

They needed someone at the planned LZ looking for defenses and defenders. And the AI was expendable . . . or as

close to expendable as any sentient being *could* be this far
from home.

SF/A-2 Starhawk Cassius
Approaching Stargate Sirius
2115 hours, Shipboard time

Cassius I-2 made the final approach to the objective dead
slow . . . drifting in at a bare half meter per second relative.
Possibly velocity alone determined whether or not an approaching spacecraft would be blasted by antimatter beams,
but it might also be a combination of velocity and mass. The
Starhawk was considerably more massive than an Argus
probe.

There was still no response from the huge structure ahead.
Tentatively, Cassius guided the fighter closer with gentle
bursts from its maneuvering thrusters, until the craft was less
than five meters away.

"I am reading a gravitational field of point one three nine
gravities," he reported, a verbal amplification to the data automatically streaming back to the task force. "I am having no
trouble holding position above the surface."

Indeed the surface gravity in this area was no more than a
gentle tug. Deftly maneuvering the Starhawk for maximum
dispersal, Cassius I-2 began deploying BMS drones—
Battlefield Micro-Sensors—in a fast-expanding cloud. Each
sensor, a sphere only ten millimeters thick, was set to pick up
heat, electromagnetic signals, even vibrations transmitted
through the ring's hull from inside. Fired from the
Starhawk's special munitions dispensers, they scattered
across several square kilometers of the ring surface before
the low gravity brought them to rest.

A staggering wealth of new data began pouring in, and

Cassius I-2 became quite busy indeed recording and retransmitting it all for analysis back in the fleet.

TRAP-1
UFR/USS Chapultepec
2142 hours, Shipboard time

The Marines had been waiting for hours in the tiny red-lit compartment, fully suited up, weapons ready, emotions fully charged. Sergeant Garroway sat wedged in with nineteen other Marines, all in full battle dress, shoulder touching shoulder of the Marines to either side, armored knees separated from the knees of the Marine facing him by less than a meter.

Zero gravity made little difference to his discomfort. Transfer pods were not designed with spaciousness in mind, but efficiency, compactness, and a brutal lack of frills. The enforced immobility was wearing at him, cramping the muscles of back, shoulders, and legs, while globules of sweat escaped from under his headband and drifted around inside his battle helmet like tiny, silvery and out-of-focus planets.

And the day some designer of military hardware came up with a suit of battle armor that could scratch where it itched . . .

They said the waiting was the hardest part, and Garroway was in heartfelt agreement. Fifty-two hours ago he'd been sound asleep—a better word was *comatose*—in cybehibe, no worries, no cares, no discomfort, not even any dreams, save for some fuzzy fragments now more felt than remembered. Now he was . . . here.

He wished he knew what was happening. The platoon had been disconnected from the intel feed from the probes now scouting the stargate. No reason had been given, though Garroway guessed there were several. For one thing, if a lot of data was coming back from the robot scouts, they needed to conserve bandwidth. For another, Garroway knew from experience that speculating on incomplete information was an excellent way to screw things up royally. Better that the rankers be handed just what they needed to know to function . . . and not so much that they started making wild and half-assed guesses—and possibly panicking as a result.

And there was always the possibility, he told himself wryly, that even calm and fully assed information would be so scary they would panic anyway—and with perfectly good reason.

Sometimes, he knew, ignorance *was* bliss.

That didn't make the waiting and the not-knowing any easier to endure, however.

At least this time the section wasn't under radio silence, as had been the case in so many of the training runs, and there was a ragged and occasional exchange of background chatter over the Alpha Platoon channel. Most of the Marines remained silent, however, each alone with his or her thoughts.

Waiting. . . .

"Hurry up and wait, hurry up and wait," a voice said. An ID tag appeared at the top of Garroway's HUD, identifying the speaker as PFC Stefan Arhipov, one of the platoon newbies. "That's the fucking Marines for ya, huh?"

Garroway ignored the comment, as did the others. It sounded like an attempt to talk to someone, to start a conversation just for the comfort.

"Hey, Corp?" Arhipov persisted. It took Garroway a moment to realize the man was talking to him. "They say you were one of the guys out on Ishtar."

You couldn't tell who was speaking to you by body language when everyone was encased in Mark VIII vac armor, but the name ARHIPOV, S. was painted across the helmet of the man sitting opposite him in a dark gray just barely lighter than the helmet's current neutral black.

"I was there," Garroway replied, laconic.

"Yeah? What was fighting the Annies like, anyway?"

"Not fun."

An uncomfortable silence followed. "Uh, Corporal?"

"Yes?"

"Why'd they pack us into this sewer pipe, anyway? The way I heard it, we were going to check out the stargate with robots. They're not planning on sending us in to capture the thing yet, are they?"

"When they tell me, I'll tell you," Garroway replied and left it at that.

"They didn't TRAP us t'start the invasion, kid," Sergeant Cavaco said. "Didn't you hear?"

"Uh, no, Sarge. Why—"

"Regulations," Corporal Vinton said. "When the fleet went to battle stations, we were ordered in here. *This* is our battle station."

"Yeah, but why?"

"Didn't you know, kid?" Cavaco asked. "This here transfer pod is our fuckin' *lifeboat*."

"That's right," Sergeant Houston told them. "If anything happens to the *Pecker*, they can jettison us before the whole ship goes up."

"That's the idea," Cavaco said. "And just between us, I don't care much for the idea of being burned alive inside a transport, no way out and no way to fight back."

"Burned . . . burned alive?"

"Sure! Oh, I guess it would be quick enough if the bad guys used a nuke on us, but scuttlebutt says they've already picked off some of our robot probes with lasers. Or maybe we'd just decompress. But the smart money in the pool says the plastics on board get heated to such high temperatures that the whole hab section of the ship just bursts into flame at something like a thousand degrees Celsius or so. Course, once the air leaks out, the fire goes out, but that doesn't exactly help the survivors, right?"

"Sure," Houston said. "So they're doing us a favor, see, kid? We get to escape while the brass stays behind and fries."

"Yeah," Cavaco said with a chuckle. "Now, that doesn't exactly help us personally, of course. You can just imagine . . . there we are, adrift in space, eight and a half light-years from home, our only way of getting back to Earth . . . gone."

"So how much air do we have in one of these things?" PFC Tremkiss asked. The conversation, Garroway noticed, was fast becoming a round of old hands against the newbies.

"Oh, enough to last . . . whatcha think, Wes? Maybe forty-eight hours, including what's in our suits? At least we won't have to worry about starving to death."

"If we take turns breathing in shifts, yeah, about that," Houston agreed.

"Aw, c'mon, guys!" PFC Loren Geisler said. He was another newbie to the platoon and, along with Sergeant Cavaco, was in Garroway's three-man fire team. "You can only pull the leg so far!"

"Who's leg-pulling?" Cavaco asked. "We are *very* much on the sharp pointy end of the stick, here. We don't know anything about who we're fighting. We have no strategic reserve and no backup. Our only way home is the *Pecker*. And two robot transports don't have consumables enough to keep over a thousand people alive for very long, even with nanoconverters. We are *way* up Shit Creek here, gentlemen, and using our helmets to bail."

"Do we really not know anything about the enemy?" Tremkiss asked. "I heard scuttlebutt that said they were just An, only they still had starships."

"That's a scary thought," Garroway said, joining the conversation despite a desire to keep to himself. "They did enough damage with spears. I'm not sure I'd care to meet them in spaceships."

"The point is," Cavaco said, pushing ahead, "maybe the bad guys come pick us up to interrogate us—and maybe they don't. Maybe some of the other ships in the fleet survived, though, of course, they don't have the space or the consumables to take us on board."

"The *Ranger* does," Houston told him.

"Nah. Not for cybehibe. Not enough tubes. You need an IST for that."

"Oh, yeah. That's right."

"What I heard," HM2 Phillip K. Lee put in, "was that if the IST was crippled, they'd pack all of the surviving Marines onboard the *Ranger*. Nine out of ten would go into the converters to provide food and water for the rest. First they'd ask for volunteers, then the command AI would choose the rest. See, without cybehibe, the ones who were left have to survive on very tight rations for the ten-year trip back home."

Several of the others, including Garroway, chuckled at that one. There'd been, of course, a lot of good-natured razzing of the lone Navy man assigned to the platoon, but the corpsman seemed able to give as good as he got.

"Leave the poor newbies alone," Corporal Vinton put in. "They have enough to worry about without thinking about cannibalism!"

The female members of the platoon, Garroway noticed, had not joined in with the hazing. Was that because they were less likely to pile on a guy who was being picked on? Or were their motherly instincts kicking in?

On second thought, her comment about cannibalism carried its own form of sadism. Arhipov, Tremkiss, and the half dozen or so other newbies in the section must be terrified by now, even if they weren't buying a word of it.

"So . . . why bother putting us in the pods, if it doesn't matter?" Arhipov said. Garroway could hear the edge to his voice . . . fear and protest mingled with stress.

"So we can fight if the bad guys come get us, of course," Houston told him. "We're Marines. That's what we do, right?

We fight! We take out as many of the bastards as we can!"

"Ooh-rah!" Cavaco said. Half a dozen other voices joined in.

"So if we get cast loose in the next few hours . . . and if the *Pecker* buys it and we're adrift all alone . . . you just be ready to kill anything that grabs us and takes us aboard, right? I heard the bad guys are really horrible monsters. Three meters tall . . . six eyes . . . and the sweet disposition of a Parris Island DI on a bad day."

"That bad?" Garroway asked.

"Worse!" Cavaco laughed, a dry and strained rasp. "Hey, these critters already snatched the *Wings of Isis* and had the crew and passengers for lunch."

Garroway had been enjoying the banter—not to mention the traditional hazing of the FNGs—but that last comment stopped him, made him pull back into his self-imposed shell. He'd been planning on marrying one of those passengers on the *Isis*—and not even knowing what had happened to her continued to gnaw at him.

Was there any chance, any chance at all that she'd been alive in alien captivity for the past twenty years?

It wasn't likely, and, in fact, he very much hoped she'd died, clean and fast, before having to endure something like that.

"All right, belay the chatter!" Gunnery Sergeant Dunne ordered. "As you were!"

Silence returned.

Then, "Garroway?" It was Dunne. "You okay, son?"

"Yeah, Gunnery Sergeant. I'm okay."

"Good. Stay focused on now, right?"

"Aye aye, Gunnery Sergeant."

Dunne, of course, knew about Lynnley. Garroway had talked about the woman often enough over the past few subjective months. He was impressed that the platoon sergeant was concerned about the emotional state of individual men and women in his unit.

But it only made sense. Dunne was responsible for the combat performance of First Platoon, Alpha Company. He was probably on another private channel right now, checking to make sure that the FNGs hadn't been scared out of their FNG minds.

Garroway felt a sharp *bump* and a surge of acceleration. "Uh-oh," Houston said. "This may be it!"

But zero-G returned after only a moment. The *Chapultepec* must have been performing some minor course correction, and was not entering battle.

Garroway wished he knew what was going on outside.

SF/A-2 Starhawk Cassius
Approaching Stargate Sirius
2155 hours, Shipboard time

Cassius continued to receive, record, and retransmit the data from the far-flung network of BMS devices as he piloted the Starhawk slowly above the surface of the huge structure. "Infrared and magnetic scans suggest some type of hatch or entryway bearing one-one-seven, range fifty-five meters, and there are suggestions of a network of passageways beneath the outer hull structure," he reported. "There may be enough vibrational data to construct a crude seismological map of the objective's interior structure."

There was no reply to any of this from the fleet, of course. After a moment more, however, an order came through on a needle-thin beam, orders from Cassius Prime. "We require a sample of the structure's surface."

"Very well. There has been no obvious response to my presence. However, the sampling may be construed as an attack."

"Affirmative. The fleet is repositioning itself against that possibility."

Cassius I-2 could sense the movement of the distant fleet,

the vessels drawing farther apart from one another, the smaller warships gently moving closer, a screen between the objective and the *Ranger*, *Chapultepec*, and the two transports.

"Stand by," he said. "I am about to perform a spectroscopic analyses of the surface material."

The surface looked like dark, slightly pitted metal of some sort, but the only way to tell was to zap it with a laser and take a spectroscopic reading as it flashed into vapor. The danger, of course, was that boiling even a centimeter or so of hull metal could easily be interpreted as an attack.

"Firing now."

The Starhawk's chin laser pulsed—eight hundred megawatts. A puff of metallic vapor expanded into space and Cassius began transmitting the analyses. He'd expected the surface to be some exotic, possibly unknown material, simply because the fast-circling singularities inside the enormous hoop of the gate must create incredible stresses throughout the structure.

Nickel iron. There were other materials present as well in an unusual amalgam that included traces of manganese, titanium, carbon, and cobalt, but the surface of the object was ninety-seven percent nickel-iron, identical to that found in a typical iron asteroid.

Cassius's motion sensors caught the opening hatch seventy meters away and his EM monitors sensed a growing, prickling sensation of fast-building magnetic fields. He fired the Starhawk's port maneuvering thrusters a tenth of a second before giving full power to the main drive. The radio spectrum howled in an explosion of static, and a powerful magnetic pulse rippled through the Starhawk's hull.

He was *almost* fast enough. The antimatter beam caught the Starhawk's port wing, melting through it in nanoseconds. Secondary radiation backscattered from the blast cascaded through the Starhawk's hull. Stars alternated with the black mass of the stargate in a frenzied whirl as the fighter tumbled through space. Cassius tried firing the maneuvering thrusters, calculating each burst to bring the tumble back under control.

He almost had it. . . .

Combat Command Center
UFR/USS Chapultepec
2156 hours, Shipboard time

"The Starhawk is gone, General," Anderson reported, her voice level.

"My iteration appears to have gone through the stargate," Cassius added. "I am no longer receiving data from him."

Ramsey blinked, startled. Cassius sounded almost *sad* . . . though AIs could not feel emotion. Was that a programming effect, he wondered . . . something added by the original programmer to make Cassius seem more human?

"We've got vehicles emerging from the structure," Admiral Harris said, his voice sharp.

"Goddess!" Ramsey breathed. On the screens and in his mind, it looked as though the stargate was dribbling away pieces of itself . . . each piece a ship of decidedly alien design.

"I think," Harris added, "we can assume the fleet is under attack."

11

Combat Command Center
UFR/USS Chapultepec
2157 hours, Shipboard time

"Admiral Harris," Dominick said, "I suggest we deploy for combat."

"We're as deployed as we can be, General . . . all except the fighters."

Hours ago, Harris had ordered the two frigates *Daring* and *Courageous* to move out ahead of the main battle group. They were in the van, now, creating an outer defensive line in front of the battle group.

"General Ramsey? What about your fighters?"

Ramsey thought-clicked to the Marine aerospace channel. "Colonel Nolan? Status, please."

Charles Nolan was the CAG—Commander Aerospace Group—for the two squadrons of Marine fighters stationed onboard the carrier *Ranger*, 5- and 7-MAS.

"Five-MAS is on ready five, General," Nolan voice replied over the command network. Five-MAS was the sixteen Marine Starhawk fighters of the Fifth Marine Aerospace Squadron, a space-based fighter group informally known as the Redtails. Ready five meant they were ready for launch on five minutes' notice. The pilots had clambered into their craft and plugged themselves in when the fleet went to battle stations, some three hours ago.

"We can launch one squadron in five minutes, General Dominick," Ramsey told him. "The other I'd like to keep in reserve for close-fleet support."

"I have completed a full analyses of the objects launched toward us from the stargate," Cassius said. "Two hundred seven objects mass less than fifty kilograms and do not appear to be capable of independent acceleration. They may be automated probes or battlespace sensors, similar to our Argus probes. Twelve are significantly larger and appear to be independently maneuverable. They are probably spacecraft, possibly manned, and may represent a significant threat to this battlegroup."

"Thank you, Cassius," Dominick said. "Gentlemen . . . ladies . . . I think it's time to launch the fighters. General Ramsey?"

"Agreed, General. The farther off we stop them, the better."

"I concur. Tell your Colonel Nolan he may launch."

"Aye aye, General. The countdown is beginning, t-minus five minutes."

"The military mind," Dr. Franz said with a growl after a moment, "will never cease to amaze me. You don't understand something . . . so you kill it."

"I might point out, Dr. Franz," Ramsey replied, "that *they* started it. Destroying several probes and our Starhawk were not exactly acts of friendly diplomacy."

"But we don't know how *they* are perceiving *us*," Franz insisted. "They could simply be reacting to the Starhawk's sampling of the stargate's surface!"

"Maybe so," Dominick put in. "For right now, though, we have a number of . . . objects heading our way at a relative velocity of almost six kilometers per second. They may be missiles. They may be fighters. Hell, they could be peace envoys, for all I know, but until we have more information, our first priority is to safeguard the battle group."

If we can was Ramsey's unvoiced addition to Dominick's words.

SF/A-2 Starhawk Talon Three
Launch Bay 1, CVS Ranger
2158 hours, Shipboard time

Captain Greg Alexander, call sign Pooner, ran through the prelaunch one final time, letting the checklist scroll up through his consciousness. *Talon Three* was hot, taut, and ready.

He was sitting in a near-darkness relieved only by the green glow of his instrument panel. The fighter didn't have a canopy with a physical view of the surroundings; the pilot relied on a direct data feed through his interface to see what was going on around him. At the moment, however, there was nothing to see in any case. *Talon Three* was resting inside its launch tube, its flight surfaces folded tight about the fuselage like a black shroud.

"Okay, chicks," a voice said over the squadron command channel. He was Major Lucas Gauthier and he was the commanding officer of the Fifth Marine Aerospace Squadron. "We're up. Launch in five mikes."

"About freakin' time, *Talon Nine*," Lieutenant Maria Oliviero grumbled. "I think my ass just welded itself to the seat."

"Hey, skipper?" Alexander said. "Just what are we up against?"

"PriFly is opening the tactical feed now. Take a look." *PriFly* was Primary Flight Control, the command group for all aerospace operations off the carrier.

And access to the tactical feed meant they now could see outside of their pitch-black launch tubes. Alexander thought-clicked a command and opaque walls faded into invisibility. It was as though he were adrift, suspended in the depths of space.

What he was seeing was, in fact, more simulation than reality. Several Argus probes and a large number of BMS devices were still functioning in the immediate vicinity of the stargate. With the loss of Cassius I-2, those devices had lost their link with the fleet, but the Argus probes were smart enough to create a new data network, select one of their own as a relay, and continue transmission. The MIEU's tactical computers onboard the *Chapultepec* analyzed the data and created a picture of what was *probably* out there, together with a percentage of confidence in the result.

Alexander scowled as he watched the oddly shaped spacecraft suddenly disperse from the stargate. It appeared as though they'd been hidden there, disguised as part of the ring structure. Flying free, they appeared in a bewildering variety of shapes and sizes, from angular fragments smaller than a Starhawk, smaller even than a Marine Wasp, to things the size of a fair-sized building, as massive, roughly, as one of the fleet's frigate gunships. The hulls were black, *very* black. The smooth, seemingly organic curves and the way those hulls drank light suggested an advanced stealth technology and even the technically augmented human eye had difficulty tracking them.

The image was less than perfect, with digital dropout noise and a grainy look that contrasted sharply with the crystal-clear sharpness of the stars and illuminated dust fields beyond.

"Sixty-five percent confidence?" Alexander said over the squadron channel. "Why not just say they don't know what the hell those things are and be done with it?"

"Stow it, Pooner," Gauthier replied. "Stand by for acceleration."

They were in zero-gravity at the moment. Like the *Cha-*

pultepec, *Ranger* possessed rotating hab modules to provide out-is-down spin-gravity for crew and passengers, but the launch bays were located along the long spine aft, two blocks mounted like outriggers, with the launch tubes parallel to the carrier's backbone and aimed aft, past the drive venturi. Earlier space carriers had been designed with rotating launch bays designed to "drop" fighters using spin gravity, but improvements in plasma propulsion technology allowed a slicker and more efficient means—momentarily channeling the plasma drive's magnetic impulse into the launch tubes. Some hours earlier, *Ranger* had maneuvered so that she was pointed stern-first at the stargate, now a hundred thousand kilometers distant, her two fighter squadrons aimed at the structure like waiting bullets in a giant gun.

Minutes crawled, as *Ranger*'s fusion reactor built up the power necessary for launch. There were two moments in every space carrier aerospace op that every aviator hated and feared, and this was one of them.

One minute. *You are the ship. The ship is you. . . .*

He tried to relax to his old mantra.

In the old days of Marine and naval aviation, pilots had talked about "strapping on" their fighter and flying as though their aircraft were an extension of their body. That was more true than ever with modern Wasps and Starhawks. His cerebralink, an IBM-Toshiba Starbright 8780 Aviator-mod A-12K, with specialized hypermatrixing and cyberavionic direct control interfacing, was far larger and more complex than the standard military-issue implants nanochelated within most Marines' cerebral cortices. With direct socket inputs at each wrist, each ankle, behind his ears and in a double row up his spine, he was physically jacked into his fighter by his crew chief so that its neural analog really *was* an extension of his nervous system.

The arrangement was absolutely vital for modern fighter combat. The Starbright 8700, when kicked into flight per-

formance mode, increased the parallel processing capabilities of the human brain and slashed biological reaction
time. That, frankly, was the only reason why organic pilots
still flew combat aircraft at all; robots were far faster,
lighter, were more maneuverable, required no life support,
could take a much higher G-load, and were not distracted
by such minor factors as fear, pain, unconsciousness, boredom, or full bladders. The only advantage human pilots
brought to fighter combat was their judgment . . . and even
that was criticized by proponents of AI-operated combat
systems.

Greg Alexander had always wanted to go into space. A
great-grandfather had been an archeologist with the Marines
on Mars during the U.N. War a century ago, and his mother
had been a xenobiologist at Europa's Cadmus Base before
she'd joined his father's line marriage. He'd joined the
Marines straight out of college and gone on to Annapolis.
When he learned he could combine space deployments to exotic locals like Mars, the Jovian satellites, or even the worlds
of other stars with his other great love—flying—he'd immediately applied for aerospace pilot training, and then applied
to the Marine Space Fighter Training Command at Point Ar-
guello, California.

He'd jumped at the opportunity to volunteer for exosolar
duty. Of course, the fact that his parents were dead, their line
marriage dissolved, and that his engagement to Lena had just
been rather abruptly broken off helped with that decision. He
was Famsit One—no husband, no wife, no parents, not even
any close friends other than the other Redtails of 5-MAS.

Ten seconds.

His attempt to relax, as always, failed.

"Five-MAS, all systems appear nominal," the voice of Pri-
Fly announced. "And you are go in five . . . four . . . three . . .
two . . . one . . ."

He never heard the word "launch," for at that instant, a giant's hand slammed down over his chest, pressing him back into the liquid-filled cells of his acceleration couch at just over fourteen G's. Seven to ten G's was the normal limit a human could endure without blacking out, but the combination of implant technology, the design of the seat, and the design of the flight suit he was wearing, which helped keep blood flowing to his brain, kept him conscious—just barely. For a long moment, he felt as though he were looking down a long black tube with a tiny far-off opening. Breathing was flat-out impossible. An unbearable weight was crushing his ribs, a pressure that went on and on and on. . . .

Two seconds later his Starhawk emerged from its launch tube at almost three hundred meters per second, propelled by the powerful magnetic impulse that normally was used to hurl white-hot plasma out the aft drive venturis at a speed approaching that of light. The magnetic field extended well beyond the end of the tube, however, and continued to accelerate him for another 1.7 seconds.

And then he was embraced by the blissful silence of free fall, traveling now at over half a kilometer per second . . . but then his fighter's AI kicked in the main drive and he was slammed into his seat back once more, this time at an almost benign five gravities.

Controlled by their onboard computers, the sixteen Starhawks maintained five gravities for ten seconds, adding another five hundred meters per second to their velocity.

And then the Starhawk's plasma jet cut off and the hand of acceleration vanished. He was in zero-G once more.

"Whee-oo!" he cried over the squadron channel. He always felt exultant after surviving another high-G launch. "What a rush!"

"Roger that, Poonman!" Zipper—Lieutenant Andrea Thiery in *Talon Four*—replied. "I think my stomach's still back in the launch tube!"

"Heads up, people," Gauthier, in *Talon Six*, said. "Stay

alert! We're tracking incoming. Release your launch tanks."

Each Starhawk had launched with a tank of reaction mass—water—that it used to fuel its initial acceleration out of the tubs. Those tanks were empty now after the five-G burn, and would get in the way of combat maneuvers. Alexander thought-clicked an icon. His fuel tank tumbled clear, blasted aside by a small explosive charge. With luck, the enemy's long-range sensors might mistake it for another fighter. The tank was large enough.

It was still difficult to sort out the tactical picture ahead. It looked as though a small cloud of debris was hurtling toward them—and the fleet behind them—from the stargate. However, Constance, Alexander's onboard AI, was showing that several of those chunks were accelerating on their own. Whatever they were facing, it was *not* debris.

"Connie?" he asked his Starhawk. "What the hell are those things?"

"Initial analyses suggests twelve spacecraft," the female voice of his fighter's AI replied in even and unhurried tones. "Two hundred seven are remote probes or, possibly, decoys or weapons platforms."

"Spacecraft? What're their drive systems like?"

"Unknown. They appear to be accelerating under some form of powerful magnetic induction field, but one sustained by the craft themselves rather than along a launch rail such as we use. Their propulsion system does not appear to employ a traditional reaction-type drive."

"Great!" he said over the squadron channel. "The bad guys are using some kind of magic drive. They really are freaking supertechs."

The nature of possible alien military technology—more, the likelihood that it would be *superior* technology to that employed by the Marines—had been the topic for discussion at the mess tables onboard the *Ranger* ever since the Redtails had been brought up out of cybehibe.

"There's no indication that they can outmaneuver us, though," *Talon One*, Captain Ivor Matthews, reported. "Thank the Buddha for small blessings!"

Despite the evidence portrayed by generations of Hollywood war movies, science fiction epics, and entertainment *e*-feeds, combat in space had little in common with combat in a planetary atmosphere. In atmosphere, fighters could use wings and control surfaces to perform banks, turns, loops, barrel rolls, scissors maneuvers and the like to outfly an enemy. In space, Sir Isaac Newton was god; an object—or fighter—once set in motion continued to remain in motion until acted upon by an outside force. Alexander's Starhawk could fire maneuvering thrusters to give its course a new vector component—to port or starboard, "up" or "down," for instance—but those were far too weak to make any major change to his original velocity and heading.

Unless he flipped end-for-end and decelerated with his main drive—or found a convenient planet to provide him with a free gravitational assist and course change, he essentially possessed all the maneuverability of a bullet.

But it was a bullet with teeth. The point of having a human in the cockpit of a space fighter was not to drop onto the enemy's six with a brilliantly executed loop or scissors, but to direct the weapons systems.

In his noumenal mind's eye, the enemy spacecraft—or whatever they were—stretched across his field of view, still invisibly distant, but magnified to visibility by his Starhawk's optics.

He checked his range and vector data, flickering numbers and symbols in the corner of his visual field. The targets were a bit under one hundred thousand klicks distant . . . moving toward him at four kps. The Earth fleet was moving toward them at about two klicks per second, and his Starhawk's launch and subsequent boost phase had added another kilometer per second to that.

Simple math. The two squadrons—the Redtails and the alien craft launched from the stargate—were closing with one another at seven kilometers per second. Without new changes in course or speed, the two groups would pass through one another in three hours, fifty-eight minutes.

But they would be within firing range in perhaps another forty to fifty minutes.

And so now came the hard part . . . the waiting. . . .

Combat Command Center
UFR/USS Chapultepec
2245 hours, Shipboard time

"I really do hate the waiting," General Dominick said.

"Can't rush the laws of physics, sir," Ramsey observed.

"*We* can't," Dominick growled. "We don't know yet about *them*."

"They haven't pulled anything magical yet, General," Ricia Anderson told him. "Except for that reactionless acceleration after they launched. And that was only momentary. They may have the same power limitations we do."

Any sufficiently advanced technology is indistinguishable from magic. So ran the aphorism first voiced by a popular science writer two centuries earlier. Everything in this confrontation depended on how advanced the alien weapons, drive, and power systems were, how much more powerful or more effective they might be as compared to those used by the MIEU battle group. The opposition had shown several bits of superior technology already, antimatter beam weapons and some kind of magnetic drive, but nothing that truly put them in the category of *magic*.

Not yet, anyway. It was always possible that they were hiding their true capabilities. They would be as ignorant of human technology as the humans were of theirs.

"The nearest alien craft are now within effective range of *Daring* and *Courageous*," Admiral Harris reported. "General Dominick, should we commence long-range fire?"

Dominick hesitated. So far, the battle group was on FIFO rules of engagement: fire if fired on. "Let's hold for a bit longer," he said. "We'll let 5-MAS get closer."

"Aye aye, sir," Harris replied. He didn't sound happy. "With your permission, I want to rein in the frigates. I don't want them too far ahead of the support fire from the *New Chicago*."

"Maneuver the fleet as you think best, Admiral." The reply was a snap.

For the past forty-five minutes, the fighters had been hurtling toward the oncoming hostile fleet at two kilometers per second relative to the rest of the fleet. Half an hour ago they'd passed the two frigates *Daring* and *Courageous*, which were now a couple of thousand kilometers ahead of the rest of the MIEU and now were some three thousand kilometers ahead of them.

At this point, the enemy spacecraft were eighty thousand kilometers from the *Chapultepec* and *Ranger*, seventy-five thousand kilometers from the Marine fighters, a range that continued to close at seven kilometers per second.

Ramsey focused on the noumenal graphic of the fleet. Harris was creating multiple layers of defense—the fighters out in front, the two light frigates next, then the larger battle cruiser *New Chicago*, and finally the *Ranger*, the *Chapultepec*, and the three transports. It allowed him to probe the alien force while retaining a flexible in-depth defense.

At least, that was the idea. With both the alien capabilities and intent unknown, how could any plan cover all eventualities?

No battle plan ever survives contact with the enemy, ran the old military adage.

The two frigates, moving mushroom-caps forward, fired

their forward thrusters, decelerating sharply. Harris was having them slow to keep them from getting too far ahead of the main body of the battle group.

And an instant later, the largest of the oncoming alien craft opened fire.

A burst of white noise momentarily scrambled the noumenal graphics, as a powerful electromagnetic burst caused a temporary dropout of data from the surviving Argus probes. The positron beam was clearly aimed directly at the *Courageous*. There was a flash, an expanding cloud of vapor and debris . . . but the frigate appeared to be only damaged.

Ramsey wished he could better see what exactly was going on. Another alien craft fired, and then both *Daring* and *Courageous* opened up with both lasers and railguns.

And after that, the battle became too fast and confusing for merely human minds to follow. . . .

SF/A-2 Starhawk Talon Three
75,000 kilometers from
Sirius Stargate
2246 hours Shipboard time

"What the hell was that?" Alexander yelled. For an instant, his electronic feeds had been overwhelmed by a burst of white noise and data dropout, a kind of explosion inside his skull that was not painful but which had certainly been disconcerting.

"We're being shot at!" Gauthier yelled back. "Is everyone okay?"

Call signs appeared in ragged sequence in a corner of Alexander's noumenal display. The burst—a powerfully focused positron beam, it looked like—had passed through the widely dispersed fighter formation but hit no one.

Gauthier was on the command channel. "Ranger Control, Ranger Control, this is *Talon*! We are under fire! Request free-fire order! Repeat, request free-fire!"

"*Talon,* Ranger Control! Weapons are free. I repeat, weapons are free."

"Roger that, Control. Okay, Redtails, you heard the lady. Commence jigging, and bring CCN online."

"Jigging" was virtually the only combat maneuver the fighters could use in this sort of combat—using lateral thrusters to randomly jitter back and forth along different axes while maintaining their original overall heading. The fighters were still eighty thousand kilometers from the approaching alien vessels. That translated to a .26-second time delay between what the enemy gunners saw and where the fighters actually happened to be at that instant. Even if the enemy opened fire with a laser beam, the total time lag was over half a second and particle beams propagated at considerably less than the speed of light, making for an even greater time delay. At this range, it was impossible to pinpoint exactly where a target actually might be and what its vector was . . . especially a target as small as a Starhawk fighter.

Of course, the speed-of-light time delay would dwindle the closer the two groups came to one another and that advantage would swiftly vanish. Worse, the fighters' supplies of R-M were limited. There was only so much jigging they could manage before they didn't have enough reaction mass to slow them down, turn around, and get them headed back toward the *Ranger* for pickup.

"The hostiles are still pretty far off, skip," Alexander said. "I don't think Sissy will get a lock at this range."

Sissy was CCN, the Combat Control Network, an expert-system AI partially resident in each craft, which meant that it existed only when the fighters were linked with one another through a laser communication web. Sissy was very smart but of sharply limited purview, able to identify and track multiple targets and coordinate multiple weapons systems and platforms.

"We do what we can. Try to pile on with the big boys."

Starhawk fighters could be loaded out with a variety of weapons modules, depending on their assigned mission. For operations outside of the atmosphere, lasers were the preferred weapon, since they didn't require R-M and didn't slow the fighters' forward velocity when fired, as did missiles or plasma weapons. The power of the lasers were limited by the size of the fighters' fusion power plants, but still packed a considerable thermal punch. Using CCN, the individual members of a fighter squadron could combine their total laser output with one another and with the laser and particle beam fire of their larger fleet consorts astern, acting as what, in military terminology, was known as a *force multiplier*.

Alexander watched as his implant painted a scattering of moving green icons across his mind's eye, highlighting the symbols marking both the nearest and the largest of the enemy spacecraft. One, designated *Sirius Two*, suddenly flashed, struck by the animated graphic of a particle beam fired by the *Daring*.

"Let's get in the fight, boys and girls," Gauthier said. "Targeting *Sirius Two*."

Alexander focused his attention on the graphic for *Sirius Two,* the largest of the objects arrayed before them. Its magnified image showed a jet-black, misshapen brick with an odd geometry of angles and smoothed organic forms. Sissy estimated its mass at a hefty twelve thousand tons, over half that of one of the MIEU battle group's frigate gunships.

He increased magnification on the targeting image. The plasma bolt from the *Daring* had struck the enemy vessel on what passed as its bow, creating a thin, expanding cloud of debris. Sissy selected a group targeting point aft, clear of the debris cloud which might deflect or scatter incoming laser fire. His mental command to fire was accepted by Sissy, along with the commands from each of the other aviators in the squadron.

Laser beams were invisible to the human eye when fired in the vacuum of space, but Sissy showed them as threads of sparkling green light converging on a single point. Intolerably white brilliance erupted at the target and metallic vapor puffed into space.

"Got the bastard!" Lieutenant Oakes, in *Talon Twelve,* exulted. "We holed him!"

"They're not jinking," Zipper observed.

"Their fire isn't being coordinated either," Gauthier added. "That may give us the tactical advantage."

For the next several seconds Alexander was extremely busy—unmoving in his acceleration couch, but in his mind zooming in, locking on, directing his fighter to fire. Three times, Sissy coordinated the fighters' joint laser barrage against specific points on the same enemy vessel. The fact that the hostile craft was not jinking meant that lasers aimed at the target—or, rather, where the target would be half a second hence—hit.

On the other hand, if the target had been jinking, it would have moved clear of the expanding spheres of metallic vapor and debris that accompanied each hit. Those clouds kept moving with the spacecraft in accordance with Newton's Laws, and they tended to reflect and scatter incoming laser light. That meant that attempts to lock on to damaged areas and keep pounding at them until the concentrated fire punched through the armor were doomed to failure.

Alexander wondered if the effect was deliberate—a form of protective anti-laser armor created on the spot.

He couldn't give the idea much thought, however. Things were happening too quickly around him. Four of the hostile craft fired in unison. Again, Alexander's skull exploded in a hissing blast of white noise. One beam caught *Talon Twelve* squarely on the bow, and the Starhawk exploded in a ragged burst of very hard radiation. Another hit one of the empty fighter R-M tanks with a similar display of pyrotechnics.

The other two beams converged on the *Courageous* two thousand kilometers astern. The crippled gunship, tumbling at the center of a growing spiral of glittering debris, vanished in a sudden flash of brilliance momentarily rivaling the far more distant double glare of Sirius A and B.

The fighters began spreading their fire, aiming at undamaged hostiles. Two targets were holed in rapid succession and appeared to be dead.

By this time, railgun projectiles fired by the gunships moments before were beginning to reach their distant targets. The range was extreme for inert, half-kilogram rounds magnetically accelerated down the frigate's spinal mounts, but at least one struck a medium-sized hostile craft massing five thousand tons and crumpled it like cardboard. *New Chicago*'s heavy plasma gun batteries came into play as well, and hostile craft began exploding one after another.

The remaining enemy ships suddenly began concentrating their fire on the fighters. *Talons Seven*, *Thirteen*, and *Sixteen* all were hit by positron beams within the space of eight seconds, and all of the fighters suffered near-misses as their constant, gut-wrenching jinks shifted them narrowly out of the enemy's line of fire. Alexander bumped high and to port just as a particle beam down his starboard side blasted his electronic feeds with static.

Any closer, he thought, *and I can toast marshmallows*.

And suddenly the enemy craft were no longer firing. Those remaining continued to hurtle toward the MIUE fleet, but they were inert, some tumbling, others fragmenting. *Daring* and *New Chicago* continued to fire, however, for some seconds longer, vaporizing each craft in turn.

Moments later, the sky was clear of targets.

The Redtails, what was left of them, flipped end for end and began to decelerate in preparation for their return to the *Ranger*.

12

Combat Command Center
UFR/USS Chapultepec
1615 hours, Shipboard time

"The fighters are on the way in," Ricia Anderson said.

"Good." Ramsey didn't look up from his desk. "I think we lucked out on that one."

"You don't sound very happy about it, T.J."

Now he did look up. His exec only called him T.J. when they were alone and *not* on duty . . . unless she was specifically trying to break through his defenses in order to get his attention. Ricia was more than the best command constellation executive officer he'd ever known. She was friend, confident, and lover.

That last was risky, of course. Fraternization—what a delightfully antique concept that was!—was not encouraged within the Corps, but for men and women serving at isolated duty stations, sometimes for years without seeing Earth, sex between the ranks was expected and quietly accepted. The danger came with the power politics inherent in both sex and in command—the senior officer using his or her authority to encourage or even force sexual favors from a subordinate . . . or, just as unethically malignant, a subordinate using sex to manipulate a superior officer.

Ramsey and Anderson both were aware of the dangers and had discussed them at length. They'd gone so far as to create a kind of code for the two of them, safe words intended to say, "Hold it! We're over the line. There's something wrong."

In almost two years of subjective time, neither of them had needed to invoke a safe word.

But using his initials while they were on duty was a different kind of safe word alarm. "Is there a problem, Ricia?"

"A problem? No, not really. You just seem . . . really stressed. About the Redtails. About the mission. I'm not sure."

He sighed, leaning back from his desk. "Stress goes with the job," he told her. "I *am* concerned about the combined arms aspect. And I'm worried about the lack of good intel. We're really fighting in the dark on this one."

"Okay. What can we do about it?" She walked around his desk and stood close beside him. "Either problem, I mean?"

He wanted to reach up and pull her down on his lap, but there was too great a chance his orderly might come in. Everyone in the MIEU knew he and Ricia slept together, but he would not cross the lines of professional conduct. That was one of the rules.

"With the lack of intel, we do what we always do . . . try to gather more. We're getting some good stuff back from the probes, now, and Cassius I-3 is on his way. I'd be happier knowing something about the opposition, though."

She put her hand on his shoulder, gently massaging. "Like the fact that they use crappy tactics?"

"Crappy tactics with no depth to them. No jigging or attempts at maneuver. No combat reserve, no fallback plan. Unless they haven't sprung it on us yet."

"You think the attack yesterday was a deliberate feint? Something to make us think we'd already won?"

"It's possible. Damn it, we know nothing about their psychology. About how they think. Watching their battle plan unfold yesterday . . . I kept wondering if we weren't seeing a purely robotic response, and one with a pretty low-grade AI behind it at that."

"I was struck by that too. We might be facing nothing but some kind of caretaker computer program. Or maybe the people who built the thing just don't have the same experience with military operations we do."

"There are so many possibilities," he told her, "it doesn't really make sense to try to choose among them. We need more intel."

"Granted. And we're doing what we can to get it. What's your other worry? Something about combined arms?"

"Dominick."

She nodded. "You noticed?"

"Of course. During the battle, he wasn't really in command. He kept deferring to the rest of us. And he kept *hesitating*."

Any good commanding officer listened to his subordinates, of course. But Ramsey had been struck by what he thought of as dithering on Dominick's part. He kept turning to Ramsey and to Admiral Harris for advice, almost as though he'd been looking for their approval.

Ramsey's deepest worry still focused on the simple fact that Dominick was an Army general in command of a joint Navy–Marine interstellar operation. Neither his training nor his experience had prepared him for this kind of war.

That kind of inexperience could get a lot of people killed.

"So what can we do about the good general?" Ricia asked.

"Not a damned thing . . . unless he screws up so badly we have to pull a Regs Three-Five on him. And I can't see that happening." Regs Three-Five was slang for the section of the latest publication of military command regulations spelling out the exact circumstances that not only allowed but *required* subordinate officers to take a senior officer out of the line of command . . . and not be charged with mutiny.

Things like treason, incapacitating illness, or insanity.

"So what you're saying, T.J.," Ricia told him, "is that we're doing everything that can be done, there's nothing else that needs to be done, and we should just keep on doing what we're doing and be done with it."

He chuckled. "That about covers it, I guess. But we need to stay sharp."

"Is there any other way for Marines to be?"

"No. But I've been rereading Sun Tzu."

"Which of Sun Tzu's sayings in particular? He had a lot of them."

"The one about knowing the enemy . . . and knowing yourself."

Sun Tzu's *The Art of War* was still required reading for all military officers, even though it had been written twenty-six hundred years ago. The third chapter of that work ended with a classic aphorism: *If you know the enemy and know yourself, you need not fear the result of a hundred battles. If you know yourself but not the enemy, for every victory gained you will also suffer a defeat. If you know neither the enemy nor yourself, you will succumb in every battle.*

She nodded. "And we don't understand the enemy. Odds of fifty-fifty aren't all that hot."

"Not almost nine light-years from home. But I'm more worried that we don't know ourselves."

"We need to work on the senior command structure, I agree," she told him. "It's pretty creaky. But what we *do* know is that we're Marines. We adapt. We improvise. We overcome. *Semper fi.*"

"Ooh-rah." There was no energy, no enthusiasm in the old Corps battle cry.

"You know," she went on, "we're really in pretty good

shape right now. Morale is good. Most of our people are happy we beat them so easily."

"Mm. I'll save my celebration for once we've secured the objective."

She smiled. "And which definition of *secured* are we using today, General?"

He chuckled. It was a reference to an old Marine joke, one going back at least two hundred years. The four main branches of the military, it seemed, often had trouble talking to one another because their definitions for certain oft-used words were different. The word *secure,* for instance, was a case in point.

Tell the Army to secure a building and they would occupy it. Tell the Navy to secure the building and they'd go in, turn off all the lights, and lock the doors.

Tell the *Marines* to secure a building, however, and they would respond by assaulting the structure using both vertical envelopment and armored amphibious assault vehicles, capture it, clear each floor and room, and set up defenses with interlocking fields of suppressive fire and support weapon strong points, with remote sensors, UAV overwatch, and recon patrols on the outer defensive perimeter, with satcom channels to call in Marine Air close-support, armor, and arty. Finally, they would prepare for CQB—close-quarters battle—as the situation required.

The Aerospace Force would secure the building by taking out a three-year lease with option to buy. . . .

"The *Marine* definition, of course," he replied. "We don't want to lease the Wheel. We want to take it."

The Wheel. It was what the Marines had begun calling that enormous, that awe-inspiring structure hanging in space ahead of the battle group. It was an attempt to reduce the thing to manageable proportions. *Anyone who can build on that grand a scale*, he thought, *ought to be able to swat us down like flies. So where the hell is the flyswatter?*

SF/A-2 Starhawk *Talon Three*
On approach to UFR/USS Ranger
1635 hours, Shipboard time

His Starhawk was down to one, maybe two more squirts of go-juice.

This, Alexander thought to himself, was the *other* worst moment of aerospace carrier ops . . . the trap. Acceleration at launch was carried out with reaction mass stored in the launch tanks, which were discarded after they were empty. But after decelerating at the far end of a mission run, then accelerating once again to get headed back to the fleet, aerospace fighter pilots usually had precious little reaction mass left for the final slowdown, and often came in with R-M tanks dry. Starhawks, especially, had a rep as "nuclear kites." Their maneuvering system—and the sweet way they responded to the jacked-in pilot's thoughts—made it way too easy to burn up your R-M and find yourself adrift, waiting for a rescue tug to come out and tow you back in, kitelike, on the end of a long tether.

What that meant now, at the end of the mission, was coming in dead-stick, as they'd said in the bad old days of manual-controlled aircraft, needing to put all of your trust in the men and the AIs controlling the carrier's magfield.

The same powerful magnetic field that had launched him, directed along the *Ranger*'s spine and through superconducting field projector drones astern, would now be used to slow him down enough that he could drift gently into the trap bay.

The hard part was trusting the guy at the other end to get it right. They were *Navy*, after all, not Marines. . . .

"*Talon Three*, we read you eighty-three kilometers out, inbound at one-point-one kps. You are three-five mps high, seven mps to port. Please correct your drift and reduce forward speed to point seven five kps."

He checked his own readouts and agreed. *Ranger* was still no more than a bright star forward. "Copy, PriFly. Correcting." He thought-clicked the control and fired a burst first from a port maneuvering thruster, eliminating his slight left drift. He then fired his dorsal thruster once . . . twice. His upward drift—"upward" as described by the artificial horizon declared by *Ranger*'s PriFly—ceased . . . almost. But then warnings flashed in his noumenal vision. That final maneuvering burst emptied his R-M tank.

"*Talon Three*, we read you still with one zero mps high and your inbound at point four kps high. Please correct."

"PriFly, check your instruments. My tanks are bone dry. What you see is what you get."

"Ah, copy that, *Three*."

"You'd better, Navy. Get ready to catch me."

"Sit back and relax, Marine. We've gotcha."

He hoped so. He'd elected to correct his drift first, since that made it harder for *Ranger*'s trap crew to grab him, but he was still coming in too hot. It was going to be rough. . . .

The Starhawk drifted past the outermost FPDs, and felt a sudden sharp tug toward the front of his craft as deceleration hit him. He watched his velocity readout in his noumenal display, the numbers flickering down in meters per second, felt the pressure of deceleration increase until his harness dug painfully at his shoulders, chest, and belly. Damn it, he should have reoriented the fighter to come in tail-first, but he'd not wanted to waste even a drop of go-juice.

Then the *Ranger*'s stern loomed dead ahead, swelling from a star point to the massive banks of drive venturis sweeping past just below his Starhawk's keel. The trap bay embraced him. . . .

. . . and he was hurtling down the length of the bay, still slowing as the carrier's drive fields bled his fighter of kinetic energy.

It took Alexander a long moment to realize he was again

enjoying zero-G. He thought-clicked to disconnect from the Starhawk's computer, then opened his eyes and saw only the blackness of the interior of his cockpit. All he could hear was the ringing in his ears, the pounding of his heart.

The moment when he was no longer linked to his fighter . . . that was always a wrenchingly lonely few seconds. It was like realizing he was . . . merely human, no longer able to soar free among the stars.

He felt the vibration through the fuselage as the exit lock clamped down over the escape hatch above his head. A moment later, there was a sharp hiss and a blast of light as the hatch cycled open. Hands reached down to unjack him from his fighter. He hit the seat harness release, then tried to move about to give those helping hands access to the small forest of cables sprouting from him.

"Welcome home, Pooner. Let's get you out of there." Master Sergeant Nancy Rierson was his crew chief, responsible for the Starhawk's maintenance. Her first responsibility, though, was to get him fully disconnected from the spacecraft.

"Took a near-miss down the starboard side, Nan," he told her. "Was getting some red flags on the starboard-side electronic net after that. Intermittent stuff. Might be some EMP fry along that side. . . ."

"Don't worry about it, sir. We'll have it squared away ASAP. Can you stand up?"

He managed to drag himself up to a standing position in the hatch, then allowed the others to maneuver him the rest of the way, floating him up and clear of the cockpit. He always tended to forget—while he was star-soaring—that he had a physical body, one made of flesh and blood, not wound carbon fiber and plastic-titanium laminates. Suddenly he felt weak and the muscles in his legs and back and shoulders shrieked their protest. He'd been strapped into that cockpit for almost ten hours, with his only food and water coming through a pair of tubes inside his helmet. As someone lifted the helmet off his head and unsealed his suit, he caught the ripe stink of his own body. The suit had a limited ability to absorb wastes and included a kind of plastic diaper layered with nanotechnic cleaning agents, but twelve hours was a *long* time. He stank.

If his crew chief noticed, she diplomatically didn't mention it. "We'll have her serviced and turned around in six hours, sir," she told him. "She'll be ready for launch."

"So soon?" Six hours was a short turnaround after any combat mission. Usually it was more like ten or twelve.

"Orders," Rierson told him. "The fleet's moving in close. I guess the brass is going to want fighter CAP when we close with the Wheel."

He nodded. "'Kay. But I need some turnaround myself first."

Food, shower, sleep. No, correction. Shower, sleep, then food.

No, on third thought, sleep. *Real* sleep.

Implant electronics allowed aviators a kind of sleep—a twilight of half-awake rest with the usual inner chatter of the mind turned off, but which allowed them to be instantly aware if their ship's AI decided to call them back online. The state was similar to deep meditation and could be quite restful. Alexander had used *quiet time*—as the pilots called it—twice during the long drift back to the carrier.

But quiet time could never substitute for the real thing. It helped quiet the mind and stop a man from going nuts, sealed into a tiny metal coffin with plugs jacked into his spine, but it couldn't handle the purely physical needs of a body wedged too long and unmoving into an opening only marginally larger than the space inside a suit of vac armor.

Besides, sleep, *real* sleep, meant a blissful oblivion that you just couldn't find in quiet time.

Yeah, stretching out on his rack for an hour or four was looking damned good right now.

Alpha Company Office
UFR/USS Chapultepec
1750 hours, Shipboard time

Major Warhurst wished he could get some sleep, something more substantial and forgetful than the pitiful electronic substitute of quiet time. He'd tried, some hours ago, deliberately cutting his workday short and going to his quarters, knowing he'd need to be up and about by 2000 hours that evening.

But even with electronic help, rest had eluded him. The knowledge that Alpha Company would soon be going back into the assault TRAPs had somehow foiled the program designed to still the constant chatter of background thought . . . or, worse, left him in a trancelike state with nothing but the wordless worry to dwell on. At last, he'd given up and brought himself to full awareness, gotten dressed, and made his way back up to the company office.

As General Ramsey had predicted, his hands were more than full, between bossing a company and working on Lieutenant Colonel Maitland's staff as exec. Corporal Larry Chalker did his best to help him keep ahead of the scutwork, but in the end it was Warhurst alone who had to review and approve every request, every concern, every problem affecting both Alpha Company and the battalion.

Why was it, Warhurst wondered—and not for the first time by far—that the time-saving efficiency promised by the advent of computers two hundred years ago had somehow never materialized? Paper, thank the gods, was mostly a thing of the past; the paperless office, also promised by the computer revolution but a long time in coming, had become almost routine a century ago. But reports were still filed, requests still needed to be brought up onscreen or in-noumen and approval needed to be given with a personal thought-click or palmprint authorization, and within the report-conscious bureaucracy of the military, the necessities of office work routine devoured the available work time of every officer and most NCOs.

So lately, when he couldn't sleep, he worked.

"Major Warhurst?" The voice in his mind was that of Master Sergeant Vanya Barnes, the senior NCO of the MIEU command constellation.

"Yes, Vanya." If she was calling him, it meant more work. He tried, on a daily basis, not to allow that to color his perception of the woman herself.

"Got a special request here from Dr. Franz. We thought the company commanders needed to see it for themselves."

"Okay. Send it through."

"Here's the path. Give us your approval/disapproval STAT."

He thought-clicked the file open. It was large, very large, and included a noumenal introduction by Franz himself. The data was titled, rather ponderously, "An Analyses of the Nommo as Related to Ancient Mythology, the Dogon of Africa, and the Star Sirius." A bit hesitantly, not sure what he was getting in to, Warhurst opened the introduction.

If the title of the file was ponderous, so, too, was the man. Warhurst had met him on only a couple of occasions so far and hoped to be able to maintain the separation as much as was diplomatically possible. Paul Randolph Franz was fussy, pedantic, impatient, arrogant, and all too imperial in his manner to suit Warhurst's taste. He seemed to assume that anyone who didn't know what he knew was ignorant and treated them with an unpleasant blend of condescension and disdain.

He opened it, not quite knowing what to expect.

Oh. This crap again. . . .

He'd seen bits and pieces of this in various briefings, though never in such . . . *exhaustive* detail. Franz, it appeared, was something of a fanatic on the topic of Oannes and was determined to spread the gospel of that footnote to ancient mythology to all who would listen.

No one doubted that extraterrestrial civilizations had interacted with ancient humans, not after the exoarcheological discoveries on the moon, Mars, and on Europa a century ago. The problem was sorting through the firestorm of fringe-element speculation, religion, and outright fantasy that those discoveries had raised.

The most definite known contact with nonhumans had occurred roughly nine to ten thousand years ago, when the then-starfaring An had planted colonies on Earth, enslaved the inhabitants, and sought to expand their interstellar empire across the worlds of some hundreds of stars. In about 7500 B.C.E.—the exact date was still open to considerable debate—the Hunters of the Dawn, or someone just as malevolently bloodthirsty, had deliberately slammed a number of small asteroids into the Earth. The resulting tidal waves had drowned the An colonies, leaving behind scattered fragments of a suddenly masterless humanity, with any number of world-girdling myths of sunken continents, lost civilizations, a golden age ruled by the gods, of war in heaven, and of an Edenic paradise from which Humankind had been expelled.

The details—and the hard facts—were still largely lost in the murk of prehistory. All that could be said with certainty was that key elements—civilization-destroying floods and an unhappy end to a golden age ruled by the gods—appeared in the myth and legend of culture after culture, worldwide. The discoveries of An ruins on Earth's moon and of the much more ancient ruins left by the Builders on Mars had proved once and for all that there was *something* to the tales . . . enough, at least, to elevate them from the slums of pseudo-science and crackpot ancient-astronaut theories to the realm of legitimate archeology.

One set of legends, though, could not be reconciled with the others, and those were the legends of Oannes.

According to the information he'd been given in premission briefings, the *Wings of Isis* expedition had in part been sent to Sirius to investigate the possibility that advanced beings from that star had played a role in human prehistory. He'd gone so far as to read the few surviving fragments of Berossus's *Babylonian History*, in which he described the strange beings—*semidemons* or "animals endowed with reason"—who'd arisen from the waters of the Persian Gulf and taught the ancestors of the Babylonians such civilizing niceties as crop cultivation, mathematics, architecture, law, and writing. The leader of these beings had been called Oannes.

The briefing had included some information on a central African tribe called the Dogon, living in the Mali Republic. This primitive people, first contacted by Europeans in 1931, seemed to have as part of their myth and folklore information about the star Sirius that primitive tribesmen had no business knowing. According to them, the information had come from monstrous amphibious beings called *Nommo*, godlike creatures who'd come to Earth from the star Sirius.

There were similarities enough between the two to make many wonder if Oannes had been a Nommo and also to look again at some of the religious traditions of ancient Egypt. The Dogon apparently had migrated over the millennia from Egypt and Sirius had been a vitally important star in Egyptian myth and cosmology.

Had the Dogon managed to keep intact information about prehistoric contact with aliens, information that had been lost, save as tantalizing hints and fragments, everywhere else on Earth?

Warhurst opened the introduction to the file, which included both a written section and a recording of Franz speaking. Franz was suggesting, in rather pointed and definite terms, that the entire files be downloaded to the individual Marines of MIEU-1. "There is a distinct possibility," the man said in an earnest appeal to the camera, "that at Sirius these Marines shall be the first humans to encounter an alien species which came to Earth some thousands of years ago . . . not the Ahannu, of which we've been hearing so much of late, but the Nommo, a completely different, a new and possibly highly advanced alien species. It is imperative, imperative, that these ambassadors of Humankind know something about the beings with whom they may be dealing, rather than killing them out of hand. This, I assure you, would be a disaster of the gravest proportions."

There was more of the same. He scanned rapidly through the introduction to Franz's paper—it was still called a "paper" in academic circles, even if no actual paper was involved—then skimmed the first section, which was devoted to the Dogon and their traditions.

Some of the stuff was interesting. Much was pedantic and self-serving. Franz spent quite a bit of time attempting to refute claims that the Dogon material had been contaminated by outside contact with Europeans. The central piece of anomalous information turned around the Dogon reverence for Sirius, the brightest star in Earth's sky, and on another Sirius, invisibly small and incredibly "heavy," as the Dogon put it, which circled Sirius in an elliptical path once every fifty years.

That sounded like a layman's understanding of the white dwarf Sirius B.

Sirius B had first been predicted, through gravitational perturbation, in the early 1800s and not seen optically until 1862. Certainly, it was possible that western missionaries had penetrated the wilds of central Africa in the nineteenth century, heard the astronomical myths of their hosts, and shared a few myths of their own.

Possible, but, in this case, unlikely. The cultural motifs of dance and pottery making with which the Dogon expressed their anomalous astronomical knowledge—and that included tidbits such as the Galilean satellites and the rings of Saturn, among other things, not just the presence of an invisible star circling Sirius—were *centuries* old, predating even western astronomers' knowledge of white dwarf suns. Church records seemed clear: the Dogon had not known western contact until Catholic missionaries arrived in the region in the early 1930s and by then Sirius and the Nommo were deeply rooted in their culture.

Franz's information was mostly written, but the files included a number of recordings of him giving speeches on the topic and a long vid of him talking into the camera, as if in a documentary. There was an amusing sequence, Warhurst found, of CGI graphics showing several ideas of what the Nommo might actually look like.

According to ancient Babylonian carvings, the Nommo were upright, bearded humans wearing what looked like a giant fish as a cloak—with the fish's head perched like a cap atop the human head and the tail hanging down the back and between the legs. In the words of Berossus himself, as recorded by Alexander Polyhistor, ". . . the whole body of the animal was like that of a fish; and had under a fish's head another head, and also feet below, similar to those of a man, subjoined to the fish's tail. His voice, too, and language, was articulate and human; and a representation of him is preserved even to this day."

The representation, no doubt, was the Babylonian carving. Franz's graphics included a shot of several Babylonian carved reliefs of fish-cloaked humans; it was hard to take them seriously.

More serious was a computer-graphic simulation of a creature that looked much like an elongated dolphin, complete with fluked tail. The face was almost human, however, with a wise look to the eyes. The legs, with long, webbed toes, held the being upright; the arms looked like human arms, but could also serve as legs when the being dropped to all fours. Several beautifully rendered scenes showed the beings swimming in shallow, sunlit seas, as graceful as seals or as otters. On land they were awkward and more clumsy, and seemed to have trouble standing or walking, as though the gravity was too much for them.

Franz's main point seemed to be that the Nommo—a name which he claimed meant *monitor* or *guardian* in the Dogon language—were amphibious and far more at home in the water than on land. He suggested that if Nommo starships were discovered at Sirius, they would be water-filled . . . at least partially. The Nommo of the Dogon appeared to breathe air without difficulty, though they tended to stay in the shallows.

Warhurst caught himself wondering what the Nommo really looked like. If they were anything like these dolphin-people, they wouldn't pose much of a military threat. They could hardly stand up, much less carry a weapon. And how did a species more at home in the water than on land develop fire, metallurgy, chemistry, heavy industry, and, eventually, space flight?

One point caught his attention. Apparently, one of Franz's proofs that the Nommo had come from Sirius lay in the discovery—in 1995—of a *third* star in the Sirius system, again through the results of gravitational perturbation on the system's visible elements. Sirius C, though never photographed directly, purportedly was a red dwarf star with a mass that was five percent of Earth's sun and circling Sirius B.

Of course, it was now known that the Sirius Stargate had a mass of .05 Sol, and was responsible for those perturbations. According to Franz and other sources, the Dogon had known about Sirius C all along, and claimed, in fact, that *that* was the star the Nommo called home.

Perhaps what the Nommo had been trying to tell their human friends was that they'd come through a *stargate* circling Sirius B? Warhurst knew that the young, hot, and radioactively exuberant Sirius system had never seemed like a good candidate for habitable planets. That, of course, was part of the whole Nommo mystery.

Warhurst disconnected from the data and leaned back at his desk, thoughtful. Should he recommend that every Marine have access to this information? He wasn't going to suggest that the data be downloaded, as Franz demanded; Marines had enough information to juggle through their implants and they didn't need to know most of this stuff.

But it was possible to key it so that any Marine could access it, could download it on demand.

One of the things about the American military that had always impressed Warhurst was its basic respect for the individual man or woman in the ranks. Throughout history, soldiers of hundreds of nations and empires had been ordered into battle, usually with very little idea of what they were fighting for—or why.

Since the time of the American Revolution, the American soldier had been different. Hell, during the nation's earliest wars, many units had *elected* their officers and there'd always been a stubborn streak of independence and a demand to be well-informed that had caused more than one U.S. military officer considerable grief.

The same was true for modern Marines, for all the jokes about "jarheads" being dumb as rocks. They followed orders, yes, but they did so better and more efficiently and with better results when their COs leveled with them about what was really going down.

"Cassius?"

"Yes, Major."

"I want to make a recommendation about this report by Dr. Franz. You have it in your memory?"

"Of course."

"Okay. Here's what I want to suggest we do. . . ."

13

Alpha Company, First Platoon,
B Section
TRAP 1-2
Approaching release point
1220 hours, Shipboard time

This time it was different.

Again Garroway was suited up in full battle armor, squeezed shoulder to shoulder and knee to knee with nineteen other Marines, waiting for whatever was about to happen. They'd wedged themselves into place four hours earlier and had been waiting ever since.

Just like the dry hump last time, when they'd sat out the battle in the TRAPs. Just like a dozen training sessions before that, back at Earth's L-4.

But this time it *was* different. Two days before, they'd not known for sure that they were going in. They'd not known for sure that the enemy, the vague and amorphously indistinct presumptive owner of the stargate, was even an enemy, that he would fight back.

And the Marines had had no idea what they were up against.

Now, at least, they knew there was a war on. The Wiggles had fought back and every man and woman in the TRAP knew they were at the gate now, waiting for the Marines to get there.

The Wiggles. Garroway smiled behind his helmet visor at that. Everyone in the company had looked at the new material that had come online the other day. At least they'd downloaded the pictures, the comp-graphic simulations of what the enemy might look like. Kat had pronounced them cute, which had led to much laughter and derision, of course. Regi Lobowski had called them *marshwiggles*, from a character in an old children's fantasy story, and the name, shortened to *Wiggles*, had stuck.

Putting a face, even a purely theoretical one, to the enemy had transformed the Marines' attitudes in a number of ways. Until that defining moment, the Wiggles had been nameless, faceless, monstrous . . . the indistinct and dread stuff of nightmares. The closest the enemy had come to having a distinct identity was when the Marines would speculate about whether or not they were the fearfully mysterious Hunters of the Dawn.

What we're scared of most is what we don't know, he thought.

Of course, soldiers from the time of Sargon the Great had worked hard to depersonalize the enemy. Gooks, krauts, rebs, slopes, lobsterbacks, slants, a thousand other derogatory names all were aimed at making the guy in your sights a *thing*, not a person. Maybe *Wiggle* was just more of the same.

The ridiculous name certainly seemed to steal some of the mystery and dread from an enemy none of the Marines had as yet actually seen in person.

It helped, somehow, knowing that Alpha Company was packed into its TRAPs in order to go fight the damned Wiggles.

"Final systems check, everybody," Gunnery Sergeant Dunne announced. "Five minutes to go/no-go."

Five minutes. The CTV-300 transfer pod had already been positioned for the drop and was drifting slowly toward the Wheel at a scant five meters per second. The cargo bay clamshell doors were opening now, flooding the waiting Marines with cold starlight. Garroway leaned back so he could look out through the widening opening, could see the Wheel with his own eyes instead of through his implant, silhouetted against the stars.

TRAP 1-2 was now less than a kilometer and a half from the release point, a little less than ten from the DZ on the black and pitted surface of the Wheel itself. Through the open bay doors, he could see about a third of the Wheel arcing across the sky. A scattering of lights looked like windows, but there was no other sign of occupancy—or of a defense.

He tore his eyes away from the sight and focused on completing his systems checks.

"Ooh-rah," someone called over the company channel. "There go the fly-boys!" He looked up in time to see a flight of Marine Wasps, garishly painted in black and yellow stripes, pass between the Wheel and the TRAP. A blaze of white light blossomed on the Wheel's surface as the Wasps began their close-in bombardment.

"Okay, girls and boys," Dunne said. "You all know the drill. You've done this before. Just do it by the book, keep your heads, and remember your training. The bad guys shouldn't even notice us in all the commotion down there."

Garroway wondered if that were true. The Wheel's automated defenses apparently didn't see spacecraft—or armored men—approaching at velocities of only a few meters per second, but if there were any organic defenders in there—Wiggles or otherwise—they surely wouldn't ignore a company of Marines incoming, no matter how slowly they moved.

Even more worrisome than Wiggle defenders, though, was the knowledge that in combat *nothing* was certain—and *anything* could go wrong. He remembered the training session back in Sol space, at Earth's L-4 . . . and nearly dying when Houston had accidentally hit his visor with a round from his pistol.

"One minute! Stand up!"

He rose in place, gripping his LR-2120 in his right hand, grasping a hand-hold on the Marine to his left with the other. They were in zero-G, of course, but kept their boots anchored to brackets set into the deck.

Garroway remembered the botched release at L-3 that had scattered Marines all over the sky. *Please don't let that happen*, he thought. *Not here, not this time*. There were no fighters or work pods standing by to pick up anyone who missed the DZ and drifted into space.

They're just Wiggles, he thought. *Oversized salamanders that can hardly stand up to hold a weapon.*

He knew he was fooling himself. Hell, they couldn't even know that it was the Wiggles who they were up against, and if it was, there was no assurance that they were the weak and comic creatures in Dr. Franz's simulation.

"Thirty seconds! Release foot holds! Steady, now! Just like in training! . . ."

SF/A-2 Starhawk Talon Three
Approaching Sirius Stargate
1225 hours, Shipboard time

From out here, ten kilometers from the faceon surface of the Wheel, Captain Alexander had a magnificent balcony's view of the entire panorama of the assault. Closer in, sixteen TRAPs, carrying the eight platoons of Alpha and Charlie companies—about 350 Marines all together—were drifting slowly toward the Wheel broadside. Invisible optically, but marked by drifting green icons on his noumenal display, sixteen Wasps drifted back and forth a scant few hundred meters above the Wheel, loosing rockets and chain-gun fire.

The Wasps of 7-MAS, the Black Reapers, had been sent in first. The Starhawks of 5-MAS had remained at a distance, drifting slowly toward the Wheel at five meters per second, as a combat reserve. If the Wasps stirred up anything too hot for them to handle, the Starhawks were in position to ride down to the rescue.

The enemy's response had been scattered and slow, but they were opening fire from hard points on the Wheel's surface. So far, as hoped, they'd ignored the sixteen TRAPs inbound, concentrating instead on the Marine Wasps and on a small cloud of decoy drones and surveillance probes filling the volume of space between the Wheel and the release point eight kilometers out.

"*Angel Five, Angel Five!*" a voice called over the Sky Net, the web of lasercom communications linking 5-MAS with 7-MAS and with CIC onboard the *Chapultepec*. "*I've got a cluster of positron batteries at Hotel-Echo Three-three-niner! Give me some help here!*"

"*On your four, Angel Eight! I got the ones to the right!*"

"*Copy that! I'm on the left! . . .*"

"*Fox three! Fox three!*"

Explosions of static punctuated each burst of positron fire as the powerful electromagnetic pulse accompanying each shot momentarily interrupted radio communications.

"*This is Angel One-three! I'm getting heavy fire from the DZ's southwest quadrant! We need some support fire in here!*"

"*CIC copies, Angel One-three,*" another voice said. Starwatch was the handle for the Marine Aerospace CIC, back onboard the *Ranger*. "*Talon Flight, this is Starwatch. Close with the objective and support Angel Flight.*"

"Copy that, Starwatch," Major Gauthier replied. "That's our cue, people. Let's move it!"

Alexander thought-clicked an icon and his plasma drive gave a short, hard burn, momentarily squeezing him back into his couch. Then he was in zero-G again, angling in toward the fight. In his noumenal vision, the sixteen TRAPs spread apart, growing larger, then flashed past and dwindled astern.

He kept checking his readout feeds. At the halfway point, he would flip his Starhawk end for end and give a sharp deceleration burn, timing things so that he would arrive close to the Wheel's surface with only a small lateral vector component remaining. He would be able then to maneuver above the DZ with only small bursts from his thrusters.

At least that was the way they'd simmed it back onboard the *Ranger*.

Of course, no battle plan *ever* survives contact with the enemy. . . .

Alpha Company, First Platoon,
B Section
TRAP 1-2
Approaching release point
1226 hours, Shipboard time

The TRAP's dorsal thrusters fired, cutting its velocity toward the Wheel, and Alpha Company's second section drifted free, sailing through open space at five meters per second. Emerging suddenly into the harsh light of the two Sirian suns, Garroway squinted until his visor polarizers could darken the input a bit.

Things seemed anomalously quiet with little to suggest that a battle was raging around him. Five kilometers away, in closer to the Wheel, something flared brightly in a silent, deadly blossom of flame. Garroway couldn't see the enemy's positron beams or the laser fire from the Marine fighters, but he was aware of individual explosions that popped into view and as quickly winked out, one every few seconds or so. They must have been bright indeed to be seen through his polarized visor.

What the hell are they shooting? he wondered. *We only have thirty-two fighters*!

No, fewer than that. He'd heard 5-MAS had lost four in the battle the other day.

Then he realized that the space between him and the Wheel must be filled with decoys and battle area surveillance drones. *Lots* of targets.

*I just hope there are enough targets that they end up ignoring u*s. He was relying on the ancient principle of safety in numbers.

A pair of bright stars sailed past on Garroway's right, flashing past almost too swiftly for the eye to register their passage, but seeming to slow as they dropped toward the Wheel. The slowing, he realized, was an effect of distance. Those were missiles fired from one of the support ships, still a hundred kilometers or so away. *Daring* and *New Chicago* were keeping up a steady bombardment of the objective with lasers, missiles, and railgun projectile fire.

Twin gouts of white light appeared on the Wheel, bright enough to momentarily blot out perhaps a quarter of the DZ. The Wiggles were taking a hell of a pounding. That knowledge was oddly comforting, even though Garroway knew that there was no way the Marines could be sure that the bombardment was having any effect on the enemy whatsoever.

Odd. It didn't feel as though he or the other Marines were moving at all. He released his grip on Eagleton, the Marine on his left, and felt Anna Garcia let go of him on his right. The twenty Marines of Bravo Section, First Platoon, slowly drifted apart, but there was nothing about their surroundings to suggest they were otherwise in motion. The TRAP seemed to have suddenly dropped away from their feet. Ahead—"above"—the Wheel was fully visible now, covering most of that side of the sky, but not appearing to get any closer.

They were still eight kilometers from the Wheel's surface. From this vantage point, the Drop Zone—highlighted by a green rectangle overlaying his vision—was located at about seven o'clock on the Wheel's circle. It was a large enough target; the Wheel was a kilometer wide, or a bit more, so they were looking at about a million square meters of potential landing space.

From where he was at the moment, though, it didn't look like very much at all. Garroway remembered a historical allusion, used by aerospace aviators coming in to land on seagoing aircraft carriers a couple of centuries ago. To them, touching down on a carrier deck was like trying to land on a postage stamp in the middle of the ocean. Garroway wasn't sure what a "postage stamp" was, but the comparison made it sound like something very small and very precarious in the middle of a great deal of emptiness.

Exactly like Alpha Company's DZ.

He checked his dosimeter reading . . . a pair of red-highlighted numbers in the lower right corner of his noumenal vision. That made him as nervous as the thought of actual combat. This volume of Sirius space had a relatively high background radiation count—as high or higher than on Europa, which circled Jupiter just beyond that giant's van Allen belts. On Europa, most human activities were restricted to portions of the worldlet naturally shielded from particulate radiation by the moon itself, and all ships and surface buildings were protected by magnetic fields to shunt aside incident radiation.

The ships of the MIEU squadron were similarly protected,

but a man outside in vac armor picked up a steady dose of hard particulate radiation, poured out by the two fiercely hot stars in the vicinity. That dosage was small, but it was cumulative. The Marines had been given a four-hour exposure limit. After that, they would have to get under cover—back onboard the *Chapultepec* or the heavily shielded TRAPs, or inside the stargate structure itself where, presumably, the habitable spaces were kept that way by unknown high-tech means.

At their leisurely approach velocity of five meters per second, they would cover the remaining eight kilometers in twenty-six and a half minutes. That would leave them with three and a half hours on the surface.

During combat, of course, twenty-six minutes was a very long eternity indeed.

And there was not a damned thing in the universe they could do in that time, save wait, watch, and hope the Wiggles didn't see them.

SF/A-2 Starhawk Talon Three
Sirius Stargate Drop Zone
1245 hours, Shipboard time

For long minutes, now, Alexander had maneuvered his Starhawk above the Wheel's face, locating targets and raking them with laser and chain-gun fire. Besides his Starhawk's standard 800-Megawatt chin laser, he was using a Mark XXVII pod load-out locked in beneath his starboard wing, mounting twin 2-K Mw pulse lasers and an M-82 Thorhammer 30mm high-velocity chain gun, firing 280-gram high-explosive rounds at ten rounds per second.

Against infantry in the open, or even standard bunkers and redoubts, the Starhawk's surface-strike capabilities were awesome. Unfortunately, it was tough to gauge just how effective the strike fighter bombardment against the Wheel's defenses actually were.

By now, the surface of the Wheel had been extensively mapped and even parts of the interior structure had been unveiled by the sensors scattered throughout the combat area. Computer graphics overlaid Alexander's noumenal vision, marking gun turrets, heat vents, ports, and various structures of unknown purpose.

Of particular interest were the oddly shaped turrets—like elongated, angular observatory domes—housing the positron beam projectors. Those stood out as bright red triangles in his mind's eye, marked by the powerful flux of magnetic forces focused within each one.

"*Talon Six, Talon Three*," he called, dropping across the DZ from rim toward the gate's vast, central opening. "I've got a target, Sector one-five. I'm on it."

"Copy Three. Mind the bumps."

"Roger that." Thought-clicking on a weapons turret, he opened fire with his pod lasers. Light flared from the target, as metallic vapor exploded into hard vacuum.

His spacecraft slanted across the alien landscape, then passed over the inner edge of the Wheel's structure, entering the volume of space above the eighteen-kilometer-wide central opening. Alexander's stomach gave a sudden lurch as he crossed a gravity gradient—one of the "bumps" Six had warned him to mind. Suddenly the Starhawk was falling, accelerating at almost 120 meters per second squared. He fired his ventral thrusters, compensating.

Those things had been giving the aerospace fighter squadrons fits since they approached the Wheel. The entire stargate possessed the mass of a small star, something like eight percent of Sol, with a gravitational tug of about twelve gravities. Somehow, though, the gate's builders had partially shielded the structure's gravitational field. Over the face of the Wheel, where the Marines hoped to land, surface gravity

was only a bit over one G and that seemed somehow restricted to within a few meters of the structure itself. Entering
the gravitationally stressed region above the central opening
of the Wheel, or passing the boundary between one gravity
and twelve, could be a bit rough.

We don't know what the hell we're up against, Alexander
thought, cutting in his main drive, boosting hard.

Suddenly, a blast of static shrilled in his head and his drive
went dead. He was still falling, but now his plasma drive was
useless.

Panic clawed at him. Still accelerating in free fall at twelve
gravities, the Starhawk plunged into the Sirius Stargate.

Alpha Company, First Platoon,
B Section
Above the Sirius Stargate
1246 hours, Shipboard time

Almost there. . . .

Garroway had long since positioned himself feet "down,"
though, technically, he was still in zero-G and there was no
such thing as down. Still, the surface of the stargate was now
spread out beneath his feet like an eerie, black, and blasted
landscape, swiftly rising to meet him.

The battle, silent and almost peaceful in its unfolding,
continued around him. Radio chatter was the only sound to
be heard, punctuated occasionally by blasts of static. There'd
been casualties; TRAP 2-2 had taken a direct hit, mercifully
several minutes after it had released its cargo of Marines. According to the company data feed, three Marines—Busch,
Nicholson, and Briley, all in A Section—had been hit . . . or,
at least, their suit transponders and netlinks had stopped
communicating.

To his right, toward the emptiness within the stargate's circle, Garroway watched with cold horror as a Starhawk fighter fell toward the gate, entered it . . . and vanished.

The poor bastard. . . .

The Marines had spent a lot of time these past few days discussing what would happen if they missed the Wheel and fell through the gateway itself, an open gate leading . . . where?

No one knew, though theories abounded. All knew that a downloaded copy of the MIEU's CC AI had fallen through the gate two days earlier and not reappeared. There were also rumors that the brass had already fired a number of probes through the open gate deliberately, in hopes of getting a few, at least, back with memories intact of the other side.

If true, no one had reported the results to the Marines.

For some minutes, Garroway had wondered if the Navy pilot onboard TRAP 1-2 had misjudged. His landing point, clearly, was going to be ominously close to the inner edge of the Wheel. Now, as he closed the last hundred meters, he could see that he was not going to end up finding out for himself. His touchdown point was a good fifty meters or more away from the edge, and the relief he felt, like an incoming wave of giddiness, wiped away fear and horror and even excitement. *I'm going to make it.*

And for the moment, that was enough.

He did wonder if that Marine Starhawk pilot had been alive when he went through the gate and, if so, what he was seeing now. . . .

SF/A-2 Starhawk Talon Three
Place unknown
Time unknown

At first, Alexander was blind.

Well, not *blind*, exactly. He could see the stars, could see a planet and . . . and *things*. The problem was putting exactly what he was seeing together into something coherent. Something recognizable.

He'd heard, once, in a download on quantum physics, that when Columbus's tiny fleet of exploration had first arrived in the New World, the Taino peoples living in the Bahamas at the time literally could not see the Spanish ships. One, a medicine man or shaman for the tribe, did notice some unusual ripples on the water offshore, and wondered what could possibly be causing them. For several days in succession, he came down to the beach and looked, staring at the horizon, studying the water, trying to see . . . *something*.

Finally, according to the story, he was able to see three vessels, three "great canoes with white wings" utterly unlike anything he'd ever seen before. Once he'd seen them, he was able to tell others and, because they trusted him, in time the other people of the tribe could see them as well.

Alexander had no idea if the story was literally true. It seemed too utterly, weirdly fantastic to be fact. At the same time, the science of quantum physics had long ago established that "reality" was a slippery critter, one determined more inside the brain than outside of it. If the brain had nothing whatsoever to relate to in the flood of impressions coming in, then perhaps partial blindness was the result.

That was what he was facing now. He knew he was seeing stars in this strange, alien place, but he was having considerable difficulty sorting out the patterns around him. Behind him was . . . what? A planetoid, its surface densely cluttered by . . . things that looked more grown than constructed . . . an artificial moon or an enormous space station of some kind. An elliptical hole opening deep into the surface revealed the maw of the stargate through which he'd just emerged.

Ahead was a star, shrunken and bloody in color, shrouded behind something like a red-hued haze or fog. Between him and the star, a planet showed a sharp-rimmed black disk against the fog, edged by a slim, reddish crescent.

To the left and above, the sky was largely empty, a black gulf with only a very thin scattering of faint stars or the fuzzy nebulosities of distant galaxies or globular star clusters. Empty . . . except for *there*, behind him and high to the left, partially blocked by the stargate from which he'd just emerged, where an explosion of stars appeared frozen in midburst.

Scoop up a million suns or so. Pack them together within a volume of space two hundred light-years across, a fuzzy snowball of stars. *That* was what he was seeing, the thronging, dense star-swarm of a globular cluster.

And to the right and below . . .

That was strangeness. Stars were crowed upon stars, billions of them, but so faint and so distant as to present a kind of dim blue graininess rather than a vista comprised of distinct stars. It was very much like looking at the track of the Milky Way across the summer's sky back home, as seen from the relatively pollution-free clarity above the mountains of Montana, or far out at sea.

If that red star up ahead had not been shrouded in its cocoon of red-tinted fog, he knew he would be unable to see any detail in what was there at all. As it was, enough light leaked through from the dwarf star to render the vista vanishingly faint.

He tried looking at his surroundings in different ways. Without a clear canopy on his fighter, he could only see what his fighter's electronics fed through to him by way of his neural implant. He talked to Connie, having her "look" at different parts of the electromagnetic spectrum. He had her block out the light from the local star so he could see the thing more clearly. He had her adjust both brightness and contrast, trying to better understand what he was *almost* seeing.

After ten minutes, the pieces were beginning to fall into

place, mostly because he already thought he knew just what it was he was seeing. He'd just not expected . . . this.

That faint blue graininess was indeed like the Milky Way he remembered from those summer nights back home. But rather than existing as a single ragged band across the night sky, *this* Milky Way twisted in upon itself like a whirlpool or like the swirling clouds of a hurricane viewed from low orbit. The central core was as indistinct as were the spiral arms, but somewhat thicker, denser, and showing a faint blush of reddish or orange light. Smears of black, of red, of blue, of other shades and hues almost too faint to be seen piled up in ramparts along the core and drew converging, spiraling lanes among those crowded stars almost all the way to the center.

The core itself resembled nothing so much as an immense, flattened sphere of hazy light, grainy to the naked eye like the spiral arms, but only a step removed from invisibility.

Alexander had seen photographs of spiral galaxies, of course. And he knew that what he was seeing now must be something no human had ever before seen—his own galaxy, the Milky Way, but viewed from just outside—or above—the core.

What made it hard to recognize was its faintness. The photographs he'd seen all were the results of *long* time exposures, where photons from an inherently faint background could pile up on film or CCDs over a period of hours, while the human retina operated from instant to instant, with no time lag for accumulation at all.

It was also strange to see so *much* detail, despite the faintness of those spiral arms. They filled fully half of the sky, like the ground seen from a sharply banking aircraft, yet they seemed almost close enough to touch. He could make out the empty-seeming gaps between the far-flung spiral arms, the lanes of dust and gas, the faint color of immense nebulae.

Taken all together, the spiral face of the galaxy, the swarming suns of the cluster astern, the mind-bending emptiness of the Void beyond—it was too much to absorb all at once.

Alexander did not think of himself as a religious person.

He had been once. His parents had been Army of Christ Spiritualists, Bible fundamentalists who believed in salvation by grace, Holy Spirit baptism, and communion with the beloved dead. Alexander hadn't been to a service or a séance since he'd been fifteen, however. The ACS taught that the world was a special creation of God that was six thousand years old, that extraterrestrials were demons bent on Humankind's spiritual destruction, and that the stars of the night sky were a kind of illusion designed by the Creator to manifest His own glory. There were parts of that doctrine Alexander had never been able to wrap his mind around—especially the idea that God would resort to a kind of trickery to manipulate humans—and he'd pretty much stopped believing.

But he felt distinct stirrings of that old religion now, mingled with feelings of both fear and awe. The face of the galaxy—like the Face of God—was too vast to take in all at once.

If there *was* a God, He was far, far larger than the creature imagined by the pastor at his ACS church.

"My God . . ." was all Alexander could say aloud, his voice a cracked whisper. "*My God. . . .*"

Alpha Company, First Platoon,
B Section
TRAP 1-2
Sirius Stargate, surface
1247 hours, Shipboard time

Only a few more meters to go.

Fire from the Wheel seemed almost nonexistent now, though whether that was part of an enemy strategy of deliberately holding back or the result of the pounding by Marine aerospace fighters and Navy starships was unclear. Garroway readied himself for the landing, gripping his laser rifle tightly in his gauntleted hands, bending his knees, trying above all to relax. The surface rushed up to meet him.

At the last instant, he passed through the gravitational gradient, dropping from free fall to nearly one G in a single, stomach-twisting instant. He didn't have time to think about it though. A second later he hit the stargate surface, letting his knees collapse under him and allowing his armor to take the shock of the impact.

He crumpled into a clumsy roll.

Unlike the training runs back at Earth's L-4, there was no danger of bouncing off and drifting back into space. Standing on the stargate was like standing on solid ground back home.

It just *looked* weird.

The surface was heavily pocked and cratered, almost like a sponge in places, yet the structures scattered across the landscape retained an angular appearance, as though made of haphazardly piled slabs. The horizon was *very* close, close enough to step off of, if he wasn't careful.

All around him, other Marines descended from the black sky, drifting down at a steady speed, then beginning to accelerate through the last few meters as they entered the gate's oddball gravity. Both Sirius A and B were blocked by the Wheel's structure, so, technically, it was night here; the stars were bright and achingly beautiful. He'd not even been able to see them before, because of the two nearby suns.

Which one, he wondered, was Sol?

But there was no time for wondering or for rubbernecking. Glancing up to make sure he wasn't stepping into the path of another falling Marine, he got a bearing on his section's rally point and started moving at a steady jog.

At least no one was shooting at him.

Not yet.

14

Alpha Company, First Platoon,
B Section
Sirius Stargate
1248 hours, Shipboard time

HM2 Phillip Lee dropped toward the stargate, trying to keep his mind empty of everything save *relaxing* . . . knees bent . . . ready to drop and roll. . . .

His stomach twisted as he fell through the gravity gradient, and then he struck, hitting hard, but letting his suit take most of the punishment. He was down.

"Corpsman on the beach," he announced over the company channel.

"Welcome aboard, Doc," Gunny Dunne told him. "We're setting up Beach Ops at these coordinates." A map location flashed up on Lee's noumenal display. "Point Memphis. The company is forming up on the perimeter . . . here."

"Copy that. I'm on my way. You got anything for me?"

"Couple of busted ankles," was Dunne's reply. "No one's shooting at us, at least, thank the Goddess."

The first set of map coordinates Gunny had given him were about five hundred meters in *that* direction, at the site designated Point Memphis. He started off at a slow jog, careful of his footing. He didn't want to break an ankle of his own.

A strange kind of battle, he thought, but one suited to this eldritch landscape of black slabs and boxes. Wasps and Starhawks continued to crisscross through the star-gilt sky, loosing laser bursts and gunfire at anything that even remotely threatened the Marines. A brilliant explosion flared in the distance . . . bright enough and far enough off that it must have been a strike by one of the starships. He thought he felt a tremor underfoot.

He heard nothing, of course, save what was coming over the radio net. A check on the Battalion Channel located the injured men, both at the spot designated as Operations HQ— code-named Memphis.

That was where he needed to be.

Point Memphis—Beachhead HQ
Sirius Stargate
1257 hours, Shipboard time

Major Warhurst had jumped with Charlie Company's Third Platoon. The unit was light, down by five on the roster, with personnel transferred to other platoons to bring them up to full strength, so there was room on one of the TRAPs for Warhurst and his three-person staff. They'd designated an open spot in the northeast quadrant of the DZ as Beachhead Operations, the nucleus for all Marine ops on the stargate.

Of course, at the moment, Beach Ops consisted of nothing more than the four of them in vac armor, plus the tripod-mounted complexity of a multibroadband laser FCT, a Field Communications Transceiver. The FCT took over all direct communications with the *Chapultepec* and *Ranger*, as well as serving as the primary local node for Cassius and lesser Battalion AI assets.

The FCT also allowed Warhurst to jack in for a full noumen connection. He sat on the "ground," leaning against one of the odd, clifflike slabs scattered about the landscape, only marginally aware of his immediate surroundings. In his mind's eye, he could see the entire expanse of the DZ and well beyond it, computer-modeled in exacting detail. Green pinpoints of light marked the positions of each Marine in the landing force, with platoon leaders and section sergeants marked by ID tags as well. With a thought-click he could communicate with any of them. Cassius monitored all battalion radio and laser traffic and made sure he heard anything that was tactically important. The sheer volume of data coming and going from the beachhead was utterly beyond the scope of any one human. It was here that the specialized talents of artificial intelligences truly came into their own.

With their help, he could see that most of both companies, Alpha and Charlie, were on the stargate surface. B Section of Charlie's First Platoon and A section of Alpha's Third Platoon both had scattered a bit, missing the DZ by nearly two kilometers, but they'd at least managed to come down on the stargate, rather than miss and fall into empty space. Both sections of Alpha's Fourth Platoon were still inbound.

"Steel Beach, Steel Beach," a voice called in Warhurst's head, using the call sign for Beach Ops. "This is Alpha Two. We are tracking unidentified movement at Sector one-three-niner delta! It looks . . . yeah, it looks like they're coming right out of the ground! Do you copy, Steel Beach?"

"Alpha Two, Steel Beach, we copy," Master Sergeant Vanya Barnes said. She was on loan from the MIEU command constellation and Warhurst was damned glad to have her. "Give us your tactical feed so we can see too."

"Ah, sorry, Steel Beach. Here y'are."

Whatever it was Alpha Company's Second Platoon was tracking, it wasn't on any of the remote sensors or probes, and Alpha's CO, Lieutenant Gansen, had neglected to patch through the data from his own unit's sensors.

There they were . . . a long line of red pinpoints crawling

down a kind of valley between two sets of surface structures. No wonder they hadn't shown on the remote sensor net. The local terrain was screening them.

"Alpha Two, this is Elvis," Warhurst said, using his personal call sign. "Do you have a visual? Over."

"Yessir! There must be a hundred of 'em!"

"Can *we* have a visual?" Damn. Whittier was scattered—not focused and he was forgetting to use his tech. The guy must be rattled, first time in combat—and first time facing unknown and alien hostiles. Warhurst made a mental note to keep an eye on him—and on his company.

"Sorry, sir. Here it is. We don't have any sensors in that area, but you can get a pretty good image off of high-mag optical."

The picture that opened in Warhurst's mind was fuzzy and grainy, with frequent bursts of static and data dropouts, and it tended to jerk and wobble unpredictably. It was being relayed from the helmet optics of Lance Corporal Janet Higgins, according to the data lines running across the top of the image. She was one of the Marines in Alpha Company's Second Platoon and was shooting the scene under extreme magnification.

It was impossible to get a good feel for the size of the objects, with nothing in the image to give a good sense of scale. It was also hard to understand what he was seeing. Each object was flat-bottomed and skimming along above the Wheel surface, probably using some type of magnetic levitation. Each was an odd blend of sharp angles and smoothly curved organic shapes and no two were the same. Each, however, did sport a decidedly phallic protuberance that almost had to be some sort of weapon.

The camera angle was high up above the line of objects, almost overhead; on his mental map, he could see that Higgins was positioned atop one of the slablike "cliffs," looking down into the flat-bottomed valley through which the objects were now streaming.

"Higgins," Warhurst said, opening a squad channel. "This is Warhurst. I'm linked into your visual."

The image in his head jumped wildly, then steadied on the oncoming objects once more. "Sir! Yes, sir!"

"Easy there, Corporal. How big are those things?"

"It's hard to say, sir. They look to be about five, maybe six times as long as a man—twelve meters, maybe—and half that wide. Can't even guess about their mass, sir."

"That's okay. Just tell me what you can. What's your impression?"

"They're hard to see, sir. Black-on-black." The objects appeared to be made of the same material as the Wheel itself. Perfect camouflage. "I'm getting readings of high-energy magnetics. Don't know if that's their weapons or their propulsion system breathing, but it's hot. And they're *fast*. They're barreling down this valley like they're on a mag-lev monorail."

Warhurst glanced at the data tags on her transmission. "You're still on passive mode—" he said.

"Aye aye, Sir. Going active."

"No! Wait—"

His noumenal display lit up with new information . . . then suddenly flared, dazzlingly bright and static-blasted.

The data tags winked out, replaced by the harshly accusing words TRANSMISSION TERMINATED. The green pinpoint on the map marking Lance Corporal Higgins's position was gone.

"Damn!" he exclaimed aloud. "Damn! *Damn*!"

"Sir?" Vanya Barnes asked him.

He didn't reply. Damn it, he was acting as unfocused as Lieutenant Gansen. A moment's carelessness in what he'd said, a misinterpretation of his words by a too-eager Marine . . .

So long as the Marines used their armor's passive sensors only, they were invisible to the enemy. Higgins had switched on her active sensors, bathing the approaching objects in low-energy laser light and radar.

Which, of course, had instantly lit her up like a white-hot flare on the enemy's sensors. Their reaction time was startlingly quick.

Warhurst blamed himself for Higgins's death, but could not afford the luxury of self-recrimination now. "Whittier!"

"Sir!"

"Fall back on Topeka and form on the battalion perimeter. Order your people not to engage, repeat, do *not* engage. They are to remain on passive sensors only."

"Aye aye, sir!"

"Move out."

Higgins's death had provided one bonus for the landing force, however . . . a better idea of the enemy's nature. That instant's backscatter of laser light had provided plenty of information for Cassius and the other battalion AIs and he knew now that each of those objects measured anywhere between six and ten meters in length. Higgins's eyeball guestimate had been a bit high, understandably enough.

The landing force was facing the equivalent of tanks—armored but highly mobile behemoths each mounting at least one heavy weapon . . . a particle beam, from the look of the data, though not an antiparticle beam, at least. The burst that had killed Higgins appeared to be a short pulse of high-energy electrons, not positrons.

Though the Marines had trained to face them, tanks were, if not obsolete, somewhat quaintly old-fashioned in modern warfare. When tanks first had appeared on the battlefield, some two and a half centuries before, the .50-caliber bullet had been developed as the first antitank round. The subsequent arms race of tank armor versus tank killers had eventually been decided in favor of light, portable antitank weapons and highly maneuverable tank-killing aircraft. A single Marine with an M-30D7 Onager was a *lot* cheaper, more easily replaced, and more easily fielded in large numbers than the most heavily armored tank.

The MIEU had fifty Onagers in its inventory, half of them with the first drop, with five warshots per weapon. Warhurst just wished they had a few hundred more. Besides Onager AT rounds, all they had that might even slow those monsters were CTX-5 demo packs and massed CCN-coordinated laser or plasma weapon fire.

"All platoon leaders, listen up!" he said over the platoon leader private channel. "We have the equivalent of a column of tanks coming in from one-three-niner delta. Deploy your Onager teams forward. Let's see if we can get some kills."

As the platoon leaders acknowledged, Warhurst wondered what he might have missed. Damn it, what other tricks might the enemy pull?

One Warhurst had already thought of was starting to nag at him, a nightmare unrealized, but potent. Somehow the aliens could control gravity, as was obvious from the way the face of the Wheel was pulling them at something less than 1G, while over the center or above the rim gravitational acceleration was closer to 12 Gs. What was to stop them from switching off that shielding, pinning the entire MIEU flat to the surface with twelve times the Earth-normal weight of their bodies and equipment? They wouldn't be able to move. Hell, they wouldn't be able to remain conscious.

Or could the somehow *reverse* gravity and fling everyone off into space?

It all depended on whether or not they could turn gravity on and off like a light. If the apparent gravity control was somehow part of the structure, built into the structure somehow, the Marines were probably safe from that form of attack, at least. If not, they were dead. As simple as that.

The fact that the enemy *hadn't* switched off the gravity yet or flattened them all into armored pancakes suggested that they couldn't pull off that particular type of magic. They hadn't done anything of the sort to block the surveillance probes earlier—or the fighters. The longer the Marines were able to move around normally on the Wheel's surface, the likelier that the gravitational shielding was not something the enemy could switch on or off.

It was also something Warhurst couldn't do a damned thing about, one way or the other. He pushed the thought from his mind and tried to focus on other, more immediate problems.

First and foremost was the creation of a perimeter within which the landing team could operate. Those things out there were enough like tanks that they might be killed using infantry antitank tactics. No guarantees, of course. In *any* battle, the enemy was guaranteed to surprise you. In this operation, that axiom was more true than ever. The Marines were fighting in a vacuum of information as well as in fact. They simply did not and could not know what the enemy was capable of—or how best to fight him.

But as sure as Chesty Puller was a devil dog, they were going to try.

Alpha Company, First Platoon,
B Section
1304 hours, Shipboard time

"Onager teams front!" Lieutenant Jeff Gansen's voice rasped out.

"You heard the man!" Gunnery Sergeant Dunne snapped. "Vinton! Morton! Get your wild asses up there! Fire teams! Cover them!"

Garroway started moving toward what passed for high ground in this alien terrain, a kind of black metal plateau two meters high, with sloping sides and oddly angled corners. He and the other two members of his fireteam, Cavaco and Geisler, had been detailed to provide fire support for Sergeant Jeff Morton and Corporal Kat Vinton, B Section's Onager team.

"Wild asses" was an insider's joke. The original Onager had been a kind of wild, central-Asian ass, now extinct; the ancient Romans had fielded a kind of siege catapult called the Onager, so called, according to Marine lore, because it had a hell of a kick. In the late twentieth century, the U.S. Marine Corps had experimented with a small, tracked vehicle mounting six recoilless rifles, also called the Onager.

In the twenty-second century, the name was applied to the M-30D7 shoulder-fired antiarmor weapon, and, like the original, it had a nasty kick. It looked a bit like a TOW launcher out of the twentieth century, with a complex sighting suite and a bipod forward to steady the thing. The Marine operator tucked a shoulder up under the padded shoulder grip, pressed helmet to optics—or downloaded a sight picture straight from the weapon's targeting computer—and thought-clicked the trigger icon once to lock on, twice to fire.

The 1.2-meter-long 7-kilogram missile was an autotargeting high-velocity penetrator round with an inner core of depleted uranium that flashed into star-hot plasma on impact, creating a jet that theoretically could burn through damned near anything short of a meter or so of high-density polylaminate. Few armies fielded tanks on Earth any longer, so the weapons were used against bunkers and other field fortifications, as well as buildings, reinforced gates, and low-flying aerospace craft. It had an effective range of twelve kilometers, though the operator needed either to be able to see the target to lock on or have a data feed from either a human or an AI forward observer. The missile's onboard AI was bright enough to recognize a variety of targets, steer a terrain-hugging course with a popup at the end, and a terminal trajectory designed to kill the target from above, where its armor, presumably, was thinnest.

He clambered onto the metallic plateau, keeping low as he moved forward with both Cavaco and Geisler on his right.

Kat and Sergeant Morton were in front of them, sheltering behind a low, flat-sloped wall. And beyond them . . .

"My God!" Geisler said over the squad channel. "Look at them all!"

They were hard to see—flat, oddly angular, and as black as the surrounding metal from which they seemed to have sprung. Garroway's helmet range finder threw figures up against one corner of his visual field. The nearest of the objects was a kilometer away and approaching at something close to ten meters per second. The longer he looked, the more of the oncoming objects he saw, until it seemed as though the Wheel's far horizon was alive with the things.

"Target acquired!" Morton yelled over the channel. "Lock! Fire one!"

A silent double flash strobed from his weapon, one flash at the muzzle, the other at the breach. The missile streaked low across the terrain, weaving back and forth, then abruptly launching itself into the sky, over, and down. The explosion was also silent, and most of it was contained by the target vehicle, but Garroway saw a crater ripped open in the top and large chunks of orange-hot metal erupt from the blast. Most of the fragments escaped from the low-altitude gravity field and kept glowing as they sailed off into space.

"Scratch one!" Kat shouted, her voice ragged with excitement.

Other Onager missiles were snaking out from the marine lines now, making the final popup before descending on their chosen target, smashing inside, and detonating in brilliant, silent eruptions of light.

Kat was reloading Morton's Onager, slipping a fresh missile from the bulky carry case at her side into the breech and slapping the back of his helmet to tell him he was good to go. He chose another target, triggered the weapon, and sent another hunter-killer on its deadly way.

The Onagers, Garroway was relieved to see, were certainly effective against the Wiggler vehicles. There was just one problem that he could see.

The enemy had far more of the floating gun platforms than the Marines had missiles for them . . . and at the moment it appeared that every damned one of them was heading straight for Garroway's position.

Point Memphis—Beachhead HQ
Sirius Stargate
1305 hours, Shipboard time

Major Warhurst both watched and listened as the battle data came flooding back. The Onagers were scoring kills . . . dozens of them. Unfortunately, the Marines' supply of M-30 missiles was sharply limited. At this rate, they would be out of tank-killer ammo within another minute or two, and the enemy gun platforms were still coming.

And coming *fast*.

Unless they stopped or turned, they would be among his Marines within another two minutes.

"Colonel Nolan!" he rasped, watching the stream of red icons lancing toward the Marine perimeter. "Now would be a *very* good time for some close support."

"We're on it, General. Seven-MAS is on high guard. The Redtails are dropping in close and hot."

"Good man."

But Warhurst was still worried. *What other surprises can the enemy spring on us?*

Alpha Company, First Platoon,
B Section
1306 hours, Shipboard time

Garroway took aim at one of the oncoming Wiggler vehicles, flat, boxy-shaped, something like an inverted dinner plate with angles instead of curves, half-glimpsed against the black and angular landscape. The thing was within easy range of his 2020—less than five hundred meters. He thought-clicked, the impulse transmitted from cerebral implant to helmet electronics to the computer in his weapon faster than the neurochemical signal could have traveled from brain to trigger finger. There was no recoil, of course, and no visible beam, but he saw the splash of the hit in his noumenal view of the target. Instantly, the hostile platform slewed right, pivoting.

"Incoming!" Garroway shouted as he rolled hard to the left. The strange ground beneath his body bucked and a three-meter slice of black metal where he'd been lying an instant before vaporized in a silent blast of plasma and fragments. Static shrilled over his comm suite.

"Gare!" Cavaco yelled. "You okay?"

"Yeah! Watch it! Those things react fast!"

He snuck another look at the vehicle. As far as he could tell, the pulse from his laser hadn't even marked it. It had certainly sensed him, however, and sent a particle beam blast back up the laser's path.

"Keep your heads down, people!" Dunne ordered over the company frequency. "The fly-guys are coming in!"

He glanced up, but saw only stars. He wasn't particularly concerned about friendly fire from an airstrike; once, the Marine pilots would have been guided by a forward air controller with the troops on the ground, using laser target designation or even colored panels set out on the ground to indicate the enemy. With Sky Net and CCN online, however, the Marines in the strike fighters overhead could see the noumenally pinpointed location of each Marine on the ground as easily as could General Ramsey, or Lieutenant

Gansen, for that matter. Weapons systems were smart enough now to avoid own-goal incidents, at least for the most part.

But Starhawks and Wasps packed a hell of a lot of firepower in their weapons pods, extremely *intense* firepower, and they were about to deliver it on a target now less than one hundred meters from the Marines' front lines. It should prove to be an interesting show. . . .

White light washed across the eldritch landscape, casting sharp-edged and shimmering shadows from men and terrain features. For long seconds, Garroway's helmet visor polarized black, so brilliant was that strobing chain of silent detonations. Again, he felt the rumble and thump of vibrations transmitted through his vac armor. The entire Wheel was shuddering under the multiple impacts.

Goddess, he thought. *What happens if they punch through to those black holes they say are moving around inside this thing?*

Well, a hell of a lot of good it did worrying about that. If it happened, it happened. Meanwhile, all he could do was stay down and wait for the all-clear.

The explosions dwindled away, then reintensified as the fighters made a second pass. From the feel of it, and from the pounding the little red icons on his noumenal display map were taking, *nothing* could survive that bombardment.

The explosions tapered off again, and his helmet visor cleared. "That's it, Alpha!" Dunne said. "End of the run!"

He lifted his head and felt a stab of disappointment. The enemy vehicles were still coming—many fewer now than before, and moving more slowly as they picked their way across parts of the Wheel surface blasted and cratered by the aerospace fighters' strike—but *coming*. It looked like the aerospace jockeys had taken out a third, maybe even half of the attackers.

But new attackers were joining the stream moving toward the Marine lines. They appeared to be emerging from the Wheel's surface itself.

Garroway shifted uneasily, clutching his laser rifle. These guys weren't playing by the rules, damn it. According to the tactical and historical data downloaded through his implant, proper battle tactics required supporting armored vehicles with foot soldiers. Old-style tanks could be deadly in combat, but they had to be protected from troops with tank-killer weapons—hence, the historical battlefield symbiosis between armored vehicles and support infantry.

The Wheel's defenders, though, were sending in these tanklike floating vehicles with no infantry that Garroway could see. Was that because the hostile tanks were so good they didn't need infantry support? Or was it simply the application of a completely alien combat doctrine?

There was no way to know. Garroway and his fireteam were here, however, to protect Kat and Morton from enemy infantry while *they* killed tanks. With no enemy infantry to go after, Garroway, Geisler, and Cavaco were pretty much reduced to the role of *targets*.

Point Memphis—Beachhead HQ
Sirius Stargate
1306 hours, Shipboard time

Major Warhurst ground his teeth in frustration. The air strike had taken out at least thirty enemy vehicles, but Cassius was counting forty-three still out there, with new ones popping into the sensor net every few moments. Where the hell were they all coming from?

"Patch me through to the General, Cassius," he said. "Full visual."

"Channel open, Major."

In his mind's eye, he floated above the battlefield at Ramsey's side, knowing that Ramsey, back aboard the *Chapultepec*, was seeing the same illusion he was. Flat and angular vehicles skimmed through the artificial valleys of the Wheel's face, converging on the Marine lines at three points now.

"I don't think we can hold them, General," he said. "The aerospace strike clobbered them, but they're still coming. The fighters are accelerating back to the *Ranger*, now, to rearm and refuel. They don't have the R/M to stay over the DZ. Ground teams are reporting they're almost out of antiarmor rounds for the Onagers. It's going to get *real* up-close and personal in a few more minutes."

"Understood," Ramsey said. "You're going to have to get off the surface."

"Underground, you mean," Warhurst said. "We're working on it, sir."

He knew Ramsey wasn't calling for an evacuation. Not yet. The way the battle situation was developing, he doubted that the Marines could mount an evacuation if it became necessary.

They would face that when the time came.

"Let me see," Ramsey said.

With a thought, Warhurst took Ramsey back to the center of the Marine perimeter, close alongside the crater now serving as a beachhead HQ. A double dome stood on the black surface of the Wheel there, its chameleonic outer coating turning it as black as its surroundings. The virtual presence of the two men floated through the shell and into the brightly lit space inside, where a half-dozen armored figures were working around something like an overturned steel bucket on the deck.

"Giotti!" Warhurst called. "What's the story?"

One of the armored men looked up, though in reality, of course, he couldn't see the two ghostly presences. "We've got penetration, Major," Giotti said. "So far, the samples look like breathable atmosphere."

"Hurry up, damn it. We have a situation outside."

"Aye aye, sir," Giotti said, continuing to work.

One man in each platoon of the assault force had been designated as an engineer, and given specialist downloads before the drop. They'd been taken from volunteers from every platoon so that an unlucky hit wouldn't take out all of the unit's engineers in one blow.

The bubble was a portable airlock designed for VBSS operations—Vacuum Boarding Search and Seizure. Air was injected between its double walls and it became rigid when fully inflated; a nanoseal in the deck melted its way into the surface of whatever the Marines were trying to enter— usually a space craft or space station, but in this case the face of the Wheel itself. The engineers could then cut an opening through the hull, filling the interior of the primary airlock dome with whatever atmosphere was inside; the second, smaller dome served as an airlock access from the vacuum outside to the pressurized interior.

It was one way of cutting into an enemy vehicle without risking depressurization. Usually, that wasn't a high priority for Marines boarding an enemy spacecraft, but it was during rescue operations when the ship's crew was disabled, or if enemy forces were holding hostages on board. In this case, no one knew what to expect inside the Wheel, and the decision had been made to preserve the thing's structural integrity as much as possible.

"How long, Giotti?" Ramsey asked. "How long until we have full access."

"I don't know, General. The Wheel structure is almost two meters thick at this point. We drilled through with a laser-nano combination—seven minutes for a two-millimeter shaft. It'll take a lot longer for a three-meter door."

"We don't have a lot longer, Marines," Warhurst said. "Pick it up!"

"Aye aye, sir."

But Warhurst could almost hear the man's mental grumble. Some things could *not* be hurried and that included the laws of basic physics.

The Marines on the perimeter were going to have to buy the engineers time.

And that wasn't going to be easy or pretty.

15

CPL John Garroway
Alpha Company, First Platoon,
B Section
AO Cincinnati, Sirius Stargate
1307 hours, Shipboard time

"Here they come!" Gunny Dunne yelled. "Check your CCN locks!"

Garroway's helmet display showed a positive Combat Co-ordination Net link, and a glowing red triangle centered on one of the Wheel vehicles. He moved his laser rifle until the targeting curser slipped inside the triangle, then thought-clicked an okay. For the next second or two, he tried only to keep the curser inside the triangle, despite the erratic movement of the target. The enemy vehicle was now 150 meters distant and even a slight lateral slew translated as a major jump on Garroway's targeting picture.

Apparently of its own volition, his LR-2120 fired. A white flash obliterated the target. When his vision cleared, Garroway saw the vehicle with an orange-glowing crater on the glacis, just where he'd been holding the targeting curser. The vehicle wobbled, then nosed down into the angular black terrain beneath its belly, plowing forward, then tumbling, spewing bits of wreckage.

One of CCN's particular values in combat was its ability to coordinate a large number of individual soldiers, to truly have them fight as one. At this moment, Sissy, the CCN's aggregate AI, was selecting those targets that posed the most immediate and direct threat to the Marines and painting them with the target markers that showed as red triangles in their helmet displays, or in their noumenal imaging if they were downloading combat data directly through their implants.

The video imaging system of a Marine weapon marked its exact aim point with a red target dot. Once all of the Marines in a given firing group had their weapons trained on the same spot, Sissy triggered the weapons in unison.

A Marine LR-2120 had a .01 second pulsed output of fifty megawatts, which translated on-target to an explosive release of half a million joules, about the same as the detonation of fifty grams of chemical high explosive. Sissy allowed ten Marines to fire at the same spot on the target at the same instant, delivering the equivalent of half a kilogram of HE, definitely a force multiplier in every sense of the phrase.

A flashing red arrow in Garroway's visor showed him which way to look to acquire the next target on Sissy's list. He shifted, found the red triangle, and acquired the new target.

CCN's advantages in combat were clear; the disadvantages were less obvious. Chief among them was that individual Marines had to ignore other potential threats while they focused on the target selected by the combat AI. It was a real test of a Marine's trust in the AI to surrender his or her judgment to the judgment of the expert system software. If enough Marines decided a different target was more important or if they panicked and couldn't hold their weapons on-target for the critical second or two it took to coordinate a number of aim-points, the whole system fell apart.

More subtle than that, however, was the psychological impact on men and women who were being subordinated by a

sophisticated computer program, who in a very real sense
were being turned into small cogs in a very large machine.
Tests run back on Earth had demonstrated that the system
could seriously and adversely affect a unit's morale.

Marines usually pointed out that those tests had been run
on Army and Aerospace Force personnel, and didn't—
couldn't—tap into the reality of modern combat. From the
Corps' perspective, a lone Marine could easily be lost in the
fog of war; a team, functioning together with machinelike
precision, dispelled the fog and controlled the battlefield.
Hell, Marines had been voluntary small cogs in a big machine for centuries and were quite proud of the fact. Fighting
closely with brother and sister Marines, both on the ground
and in the aerospace theater, was what the famous Marine *es-
prit* was all about. *Ooh-rah*!

Garroway aimed, Sissy fired. Another Wheel defender
tumbled, bits of hot metal spalling from its flank.

Garroway had never used CCN in anything other than
training simulations. The system had been new and experi-
mental when he'd shipped out for Ishtar thirty-two years objective ago, and had then been employed only by Marine
Recon and a few other specialist units. But his training, all
Marine training, emphasized working as part of a larger
team, and it hadn't been hard to learn the ins and outs of
CCN methodology and tactics.

A red arrow flashed in his helmet display and he shifted to
Sissy's next target.

Point Memphis—Beachhead HQ
Sirius Stargate
1308 hours, Shipboard time

"I think we're holding them," Warhurst said. "Barely, but
we're holding them."

"Is it my imagination," Ramsey asked, "or is the enemy somewhat lacking in tactical ingenuity?"

"We haven't seen anything from him yet but brute force and very fast reaction times. Those vehicles seem to be trying to force breakthroughs at three distinct points in the perimeter . . . here, here . . . and over here." He indicated the threatened sectors with mental highlightings.

"So CCN is turning our infantry into tank-killer teams."

"That's pretty much it, sir."

Sissy, working together with Cassius's much larger overview of the situation, had determined that the combined fire of eight to ten Marines was sufficient to disable one Wheel combat machine. That black metal drank the laser light from a single 2120, apparently redistributing the energy throughout a large patch of the hull, with the end result that the target area wasn't more than slightly warmed. Five hundred megawatts of energy, however, hitting a single small area within the same fraction of a second, was more than the alien armor could handle. It heated suddenly, then exploded with force enough to disable the machine. At the moment, three sections—actually about 50 Marines all together— were actively engaging the enemy, which meant that Sissy could kill five enemy vehicles at a time. And if that had been all there was to it, simple mathematics would have won the battle for the Marines within the next few minutes.

Unfortunately, combat was *never* that simple.

Warhurst was listening to the communications coming through the company channels, a steady stream of conversation, blasted by intermittent static, ragged with the emotions of men and women in combat.

"Watch it! Wiggles are coming through the defile!"

"Fire support! We need fire support, target Charlie-one-one-niner by Echo five-zero-three! Multiple hostiles coming through the perimeter! Repeat, multiple hostiles coming—"

"We're taking fire! We're taking fire!"

Those shouted calls gave lie to the sense of detachment Warhurst felt as he watched the patterns of colored lights shift and drift within his noumenal display. Some of those lights were winking out moment by moment, and the casualty list was growing.

"The enemy doesn't appear able to concentrate his fire the way our CCN does," Warhurst told Ramsey, "but there're more targets than our people can shoot at and they're concentrating on these three points."

"I suggest, Major, that you move to Plan Bravo."

"Already initiated, sir. But it's going to take time."

Plan Bravo required Marines from the nonthreatened portions of the perimeter to begin creating a second, smaller perimeter inside the first, then having the outer perimeter Marines fall back, covered by their fellows. Withdrawal in the face of an enemy attack, however, was never easy, was always dangerous.

And there simply was no *time*. . . .

"We've got bogies coming out of the main valley! Get on them! Get on them!"

"Fire support! We need fire support *now*! . . ."

"Where's our damned aerospace close support?"

"Gone, gyrine. Out of go-juice. It's knife work, now!"

"Multiple bogies! Multiple bogies! Pour it on 'em, Marines!"

Sergeant Wes Houston
Alpha Company, First Platoon,
B Section
AO Cincinnati, Sirius Stargate
1308 hours, Shipboard time

Houston, Lance Corporal Roger Eagleton, and PFC Randy Tremkiss made up a fire team assigned to the sector

their pre-drop briefing had designated as the Cincinnati
AO, the Area of Operations. The area was a bit more built up,
if that language could be applied to this alien and lifeless artificial terrain, than the flatter region around Memphis. Flat-
topped ridges and plateaus—walls, almost, with sloping
sides—crisscrossed the region and in the direction arbitrarily designated as "north" by the operation planners lay a
broad, open, and flat-bottomed valley running toward the
northeast.

That valley, as it happened, had become a highway for
one of the advancing columns of Wheel defenders. The
drifting icons and symbols on his helmet display had revealed a full two dozen of them moments ago, and the team
had been busy methodically targeting one after another
with CCN.

Then the Starhawks had stooped over the valley, slamming
the remaining attackers with plasma fire and high explosives,
reducing all to scattered and twisted lumps of dead metal, radiating fiercely at infrared wavelengths.

The respite had been a brief one, however. Five more of
the hovering black monsters had appeared. Whether they
were survivors of the original twenty-four or new arrivals on
the battlefield, Houston didn't know. He and the others had
taken aim at the nearest, however, letting Sissy guide their
aimed fire with deadly accuracy.

One advantage of the CCN system was the fact that each
vehicle was knocked out by eight to ten converging pulses of
laser light arriving from at least three directions. The defenders did not appear to be as well coordinated as the Marines in
their fire control, and generally chose only one of the firing
groups of Marines as counter-fire targets.

Sissy triggered their weapons, and they immediately
ducked back and shifted position to the right in order to avoid
enemy return fire.

This time it almost worked. Houston hadn't even waited to

see the results of that last joint shot; that kind of rubberneck-ing was begging for trouble. He'd taken no more than three steps, however, when his earphones were blasted by static, and a monster sledgehammer had slammed him in his left leg and side, hurling him back and down.

"We're taking fire!" Tremkiss screamed over the radio link. "We're taking fire!"

Houston felt completely numb from the waist down, and couldn't move. "I'm hit!" With a final burst of static, his ra-dio faltered and died, plunging him into a cocoon of death-still silence.

And then the pain hit, a searing, raging white-hot *burn* eat-ing into his left side, and all he could hear was his own screaming.

He never heard Tremkiss shouting, "Marine down! Corps-man! *Corpsman!*"

HM2 Phillip Lee
Alpha Company, First Platoon,
B Section
AO Cincinnati, Sirius Stargate
1308 hours, Shipboard time

"We're taking fire! We're taking fire!"

"I'm hit!"

"Marine down! Corpsman! *Corpsman!*"

HM2 Lee IDed the call for help. It was in Cincinnati, his operational area, and he started moving forward. After ren-dezvousing at Point Memphis, he'd stationed himself about fifty meters behind Alpha Company's position on the perimeter, ready to move if he was needed.

There were five Corpsmen assigned to Alpha Company. The senior Corpsman—Chief Mattingly—stayed with the HQ section, while the other four each took a platoon. Lee was assigned to Alpha Company, though technically, he wasn't on the company's roster. According to the TO&E, the corpsmen belonged to the Battalion Medical Officer, Captain Howard, who was watching the whole operation from his station in *Ranger*'s sick bay.

But so far as Lee and the Marines of Alpha Company were concerned, they were *his* Marines, he was *their* corpsman, and TO&E be damned.

He covered the ground in long, loping strides, keeping himself bent over even though no one seemed to be shooting at him. Yet. Alpha Company's sector had been pretty hot in the last few minutes, judging from the radio calls he'd overheard. He hadn't actually seen any of the Wheel defenders yet, save as colored icons on his helmet display. He hadn't tapped into the main battle data net, yet, because he needed to stay focused on the job at hand, not electronically rubberneck on the battlefield.

As he moved, he downloaded data from the CAN—the casualty assessment net running as part of the company AI software. Based on information transmitted by the men's armor, it was classifying Sergeant Houston as a class-one, PFC Tremkiss as class-three. Class-three indicated the wounded man was not in immediate danger; his suit systems were coping with the damage, at least so far.

A class-one was life-threatening and urgent. He homed in on Houston's position, following the CAN's flashing guide arrows.

He was aware of several Marines on the high ground to either side, intent on aiming their weapons at something beyond the heights. Once a bright flash of light washed through the sky to his left, accompanied by a burst of static over his radio, but he saw no other indications of a major firefight. Not that he could do much about it if he did.

"Houston!" he called. "Houston, this is Doc Lee. Do you copy?"

There was no reply. Either the man was unconscious or his com gear had been damaged.

Houston's vac-armor beacon guided him for the last thirty meters. It was tough even seeing a Marine in camelearmor if the man didn't want to be seen, but the beacon acted like an IFF signal, guiding Lee close enough to be able to see a flop of movement on the lip of a long, narrow crater.

There he is! The crater looked like a heavy weapon burn-through on the flank of one of the low, angular plateaus, half a meter deep. Houston was lying at the crater's edge; Tremkiss was lying next to him, waving feebly.

"I see you, Tremkiss!" he called. "Stay down!"

"I'm hit, Doc!" Tremkiss said. His voice sounded dull, almost detached. "And the Sarge. He's . . . he's . . ."

"Just hold on, Private. Help's on the way!"

He dropped down next to the two Marines. *Christ on a crutch*! he thought. Houston's left leg was a mess, the suit shredded, raw and bloody flesh and white bone exposed to hard vacuum, blood trying to bubble even as it congealed and froze. The worst part was the man's frenzied thrashing. His com was out, but he obviously was conscious and in severe pain.

Parts of the crater were still glowing a dull red by visible light, and the whole area was radiating fiercely on infrared. Rolling himself into the crater's shallow embrace, Lee crouched down over Houston, trying to hold him down while slapping his comjack into the man's helmet.

And instantly clicked down the volume as the man's screaming shrilled in his helmet earphones. "Houston! Houston, can you hear me?"

The only response was the Marine's continued screams.

Engineering Section
Breakthrough Point
AO Memphis, Sirius Stargate
1310 hours, Shipboard time

Staff Sergeant Ernest Giotti stood in a circle with the other five men of the engineering detail, watching the nano-tunneler slowly settle into the deck. The device, dropped onto the Wheel inside the VBSS airlock, which had been inflated around it, stood half a meter tall and three meters in diameter, a squat, thick, aluminum-gray doughnut with a hollow core and a wall fifty centimeters thick. The bottom end of the device was a seething, boiling mass of some trillions of nanomachines, each a bit larger than a human red blood cell, each capable of taking a minute chunk of whatever inert material it came in contact with and converting it into another nanomachine.

The tunneling process started slowly, but as more and more newborn nanos came online, the digging accelerated. How long it would take depended on the density of the substrate, and on the thickness of the Wheel's outer hull at this point.

He read the data off his helmet display. One hundred thirty-one centimeters so far, after four minutes of digging. And the test cores had indicated a thickness here of 4.85 meters. At that rate, and with straight-line data, the process would take another two and a half hours before they broke through. Fortunately, that time would come down as the digging speeded up. Giotti didn't have enough data yet to determine just how sharp the acceleration curve was going to be.

Shit. It would be faster to have the fly-guys or the Navy pound the spot until they created a five-meter-deep crater . . . except for the fact that no one knew what the effects of such an attack would be on the Wheel and especially on those lit-

tle black holes that were supposed to be whizzing around
down in the depths of this thing. The idea was to capture the
Wheel *intact*, if possible.

"Let's inject some more *e*-movers," he suggested. "Ten
percent."

"Up ten percent, aye aye," Corporal Moskowitz replied
from the other side of the disk. E-movers were a specialized
form of nanomachine that converted substrate material into
energy, stored it, and transferred it back up the pipe to the
mechanism that was creating the basic diggers. Increasing
the flow of energy would increase the rate of nanoproduc-
tion . . . but within carefully balanced limits. Try to speed the
process too much and the tunneler would choke on too many
diggers, or stall because there were too many e-movers and
not enough diggers.

Balancing the two was part of the extensive engineering
download he and the others had received during the week before their departure from Earth. They were all too aware that
the equations had been created on Earth, using Earthly test
materials, and that no one really knew how well they would
work on a structure built by an alien civilization at a star almost nine light-years distant.

"Giotti!" Warhurst's voice called over his comm channel.
"How long?"

Shit. He took the data he had, extrapolated the curve of
dig-rate increase, and came up with a figure of twenty-five
more minutes. Not bad . . . but it was still an only somewhat
educated guess. He added fifty percent and rounded up, just
to be sure.

"Forty-five more minutes, sir," he replied. "And that is
definitely a HAG."

HAG. A hairy-assed guess.

He could do no better than that.

Forty-five fucking minutes! . . .

There was no way they were going to hold the enemy forces that long. The hostiles had already breached the Marine perimeter in two places. Dozens of the things had been knocked out by Onager fire, by close air support, and finally by CCN-guided concentrated fire of individual Marine rifle squads. The second perimeter was forming up inside the first, but there was no reason to think they would have any greater success in stopping those monsters.

Toughest for Warhurst was the realization, the clear and firm knowledge, that he'd done everything he could, deployed his troops the best he could, taken every precaution he could take . . . and still that wasn't enough. There was nothing else he *could* do now, save trust in the fighting ability and determination of his Marines.

"General Ramsey," he said over the command link. "Warhurst. They're through the perimeter, at Milwaukee and at Cincinnati."

"I see it. What's your assessment?"

" 'The issue is still in doubt.' "

In December of 1942, a detachment of 449 U.S. Marines on Wake Island had held off a vastly superior Japanese invasion force for two weeks. As two thousand Japanese special landing force troops stormed ashore, the last radio message received from the garrison read: *Enemy on island. Issue still in doubt.*

Warhurst was feeling a bit like Major James Devereaux must had felt on Wake during those final hours. What do you do when there's nothing left to do, and the enemy is kicking in your front door?

"Understood," Ramsey told him. "Just remember. Devereaux took out eight hundred enemy troops, twenty-one aircraft, and four warships before he was through. Do what you can, then get out of the way and let your Marines do what *they* can."

It was as though the general was reading his mind. "Aye aye, sir."

He didn't ask about evacuation. Ramsey would be positioning the TRAPs for pickup if they decided they had to get everyone off the Wheel. That was Ramsey's decision, however, not his.

And the enemy advance *was* slowing. As more and more of the Wheel combat vehicles were destroyed, more were arriving from elsewhere . . . but slowly.

Maybe, if they killed enough of the things, killed them fast enough . . .

HM2 Phillip Lee
Alpha Company, First Platoon,
B Section
AO Cincinnati, Sirius Stargate
1310 hours, Shipboard time

Lying halfway across his struggling patient, Lee grabbed a nanodyne Frahlich Probe from his pouch and slipped the needle through the man's armor at a point on the shoulder where it was relatively thin. He let the needle settle through the armor, then rammed the device home, letting the silver shaft of the needle seal itself airtight to the polylaminate material surrounding it. A green light at the tip winked safe and he felt the datalink connection through his implant. He selected a level four programming, and thought-clicked the injector's firing mechanism.

Houston kept screaming and all Lee could do was try to hold him down. Damn, he wished this was "Misery Mike," not a human being . . . not someone he'd known and talked with over the mess table. The guy was in agony. . . .

The Marine's screaming dragged on for a few moments more, but then turned ragged and began to subside. A level four program was as aggressive as he could make it without knocking the man out . . . and he didn't want to do that until he knew it wouldn't kill the guy. The nanodyne injected through the Frahlich Probe filtered rapidly through his body by way of the bloodstream, seeking out nerve bundles that were in the spasmodic and continual firing that indicated severe pain and shutting them down, both near the wounds and in the brain itself. Parts of the man's body would go numb, but his mind should stay reasonably alert and without the shrieking pain.

As the nanodyne took effect, Lee was already working on the leg, using a beam scalpel to slice away torn armor, flesh, and bone.

Scalpel was something of a misnomer. It was the largest cutter in Lee's armamentarium, more of a high-voltage Bowie knife than a surgical instrument. As he sliced through frozen clots, fresh blood began boiling from the wound, along with a jet of air white with freezing water vapor.

He remembered that training exercise on the Mare Imbrium, how he'd let the sunlight melt the bloody ice that had partially sealed the simulated wound on "Misery Mike." That situation didn't apply here. Both of the Sirian suns were on the other side of the Wheel, making this the nightside, and at this distance, they wouldn't warm things above freezing anyway.

In any case, the damage to both the armor and to the Marine inside were too extensive for him to worry about breaking scabs. Mingled air and blood were boiling from the patient in a steady stream that flashed into vapor and frozen clots of ice as soon as it hit vacuum.

Marine armor had guillotine irises installed at the knees and elbows; the idea was that a serious injury to the extremities could be sealed off with a single, sharp slice that minimized both blood and air loss. There was also the inner memory plastic layer that sealed itself against the patient's body.

The blast that had caught Houston, though, had thoroughly shredded much of his left leg all the way up the groin and there was extensive burn damage, it looked like, to the man's left side as well. The damage to Houston's suit and body was far too extensive for the suit's own damage control systems to more than slow the steady loss of both air pressure and blood. Mark VIII vac armor was good, but it couldn't work miracles.

For that you needed a trained man.

The most serious problem at the moment was bleeding from the femoral artery, the major blood vessel running from a branching of the aorta deep within the torso, through the groin, and down into the leg. Houston could bleed to death in *seconds* if Lee couldn't seal it off.

There was no time for finesse. Lee sliced away the last of the chopped up armor and leg with the scalpel, dropped the instrument, and pulled out a cautery. Probing with the flat blade, he pressed it through the bright red blood bubbling into vacuum and pressed the trigger.

He had to do everything by feel and by trained guesswork. There was too much blood and ice for him to actually *see* what he was doing. As the blade glowed red hot, however, the major blood flow slowed, then stopped. He kept moving the blade around, sealing off all of the open blood vessels he could reach.

An irreverent thought surfaced as he worked. Part of the downloaded portion of his training, of course, included a detailed history of medicine. The French surgeon Ambroise Pare—who'd first introduced amputation as a battlefield surgical procedure in the early 1500s—had in 1572 begun using silk ligatures to tie off bleeding arteries instead of searing them shut with a red-hot iron. Seven hundred years later, battlefield surgery had come full circle. Probing for spurters with a hemostat or, worse, trying to suture a wound shut, was at best damned tough while wearing armor gauntlets; trying to do it when the wound was masked by a geyser of freezing vapor was impossible. A hot iron would stop the bleeding far more effectively in this environment than more civilized measures.

It took several more minutes, but he thought that Houston's condition was stabilizing.

As he worked, he kept trying to talk to the wounded man. "Houston! Houston, can you hear me? Stay with me, man!"

"Wha . . . whazzit?"

He could hear the Marine's rasping, fast, and shallow breathing. His blood pressure was dangerously low, his heartbeat fast and fluttering.

"Houston! Stay awake! It's me, Doc! We're going to get you out of this."

"D-doc? Wha . . . happened? . . ."

The data link to Houston's suit showed the Marine's suit pressure was dropping fast, so as soon as he thought he had the bleeding stopped, he slapped a generous glob of nanogel over the open stump. Air was leaking from the suit torso as well, where armor and flesh had charred together under a high-temperature blast. He could do nothing about that here, save inject some more medical nano programmed for burn treatment through the Frahlich Probe and cover the mess over with nanogel.

Only then could he spare a thought for Private Tremkiss.

The man's right leg was missing from the knee down, neatly sealed off by his suit's guillotine feature. "How are you doing, Tremkiss?" he asked. "Any pain?"

"N-no, sir."

"I'm not a 'sir,' " he said, giving the time-honored response of Navy petty officers and Marine NCOs. "I work for a living. Let me jack in."

The suit's memory showed Tremkiss losing a foot to a

near-miss plasma blast. The guillotine had sealed off the limb to prevent catastrophic pressure loss; the suit's built-in field first-aid system had kicked in and fired nanodyne and sealer into the wound. No blood loss, no real pain . . . and though Tremkiss was on the ragged edge of both physical and emotional shock, he was holding his own for the moment.

"You think you can move, son?"

"I don't know. I . . . don't think so."

"Hang on. We're going to get both of you out of here."

That unquestionably was the next step, vamming both patients—and himself—out of here.

"Memphis, this is Mike one-one." The handle identified him as Alpha Company, First Platoon's medical asset. "I've got two casualties, repeat, two casualties in downtown Cincinnati. Number one is massive burn, trauma and blood loss. Suit is plugged and wounds are stable. Monitor operational. Number two is suit-maintained but nonmobile. We need emergency evac, stat."

"Mike one-one, Memphis," a voice shot back. "Negative on evac. Repeat, negative on evac."

Shit. There were no medibugs with the MIEU, he knew, and he figured they didn't have any other aerospace-mobile vehicles in the battle zone yet that could ferry wounded. But at least they might send a couple of guys with a stretcher. . . .

He looked around, assessing the situation.

And it was then that he realized that he and his two patients were not alone.

It looked like a huge, inverted pie plate three meters wide, jet black and massive, hovering just above the strange, alien surface of the Wheel less than thirty meters away.

And if that ugly snub-nosed projection was some kind of a weapon, it was aimed directly at them.

16

HM2 Phillip Lee
Alpha Company, First Platoon,
B Section
AO Cincinnati, Sirius Stargate
1311 hours, Shipboard time

Lee froze, staring at the hovering war machine. The only weapon he had was his underpowered LC-2132 laser carbine. He hadn't been following the radio chatter, but he knew the guys had been talking about taking out hostiles with Onager AT missiles and he very much doubted that his little Sunbeam would more than warm a patch on the menacing thing's ebon hull.

But it was all he had. He didn't see either Houston's or Tremkiss's 2120, and he sure as hell didn't have time to look for them.

Why hadn't it fired?

"Someone in Alpha-One!" he called. His voice was shaking. "Anyone! This is Doc Lee! I got a situation here!"

"Gotcha spotted on the map, Doc," Gunny Dunne's voice replied instantly. "Whatcha got?"

"Two wounded and a fucking flying tank, thirty meters away! It's . . . it's just hovering there! It hasn't fired . . ."

"Get down and stay down, Doc!" Dunne shouted back. "Help's on the way!"

Suddenly the monster started floating forward.

Lee didn't actually think through what he did next. He simply acted. His first priority was protecting his two patients, and the only thing that occurred to him was trying to distract that thing, maybe lead it away until the rest of the company could rally.

Rising to his feet, he stood motionless for a second, then lunged to his left, out of the crater and away from Houston and Tremkiss. The machine pivoted, keeping its weapon aimed at the corpsman. Lee reached up behind his shoulder and unhooked his carbine from its carry clip. He didn't need to aim; he pointed and fired as he took another dive to his left.

Probably the only thing that saved Lee in that instant was the fact that he was so close to the enemy combat machine, close enough that even a small movement on his part translated as a large arc of motion for the machine to keep its weapon trained on him. He hit the ground and rolled clumsily just as the weapon fired. Static roared in his headset, and he felt a wave of heat brush past him, accompanied by a tingling pins-and-needles sensation gone as swiftly as it came.

From flat on his belly, Lee raised his carbine a second time, hoping that the thing's weapon might be a vulnerable point in its hide. . . .

CPL John Garroway
Alpha Company, First Platoon,
B Section
AO Cincinnati, Sirius Stargate
1311 hours, Shipboard time

Garroway and the other two in his fire team were fighting for their lives.

They'd been making their way along the top of a long, narrow plateau, a kind of ridge or broad wall across the face of their sector of the Wheel, homing on Houston's and Tremkiss's suit beacons. They were still at least a hundred meters away, however, when two massive Wiggler vehicles seemed to detach themselves from the black mass of the broad valley below the plateau and started moving up-slope toward them.

"Targets!" Cavaco yelled. "Paint 'em, Sis!"

Garroway, Cavaco, and Geisler took aim, letting Sissy paint the nearest target with an aiming-point reticle. He steadied the red aim-point dot of his 2120 inside the triangle, held it . . . and then Sissy triggered his weapon.

There was a flash, and a spray of hot debris, but the enemy vehicle kept coming. The shot hadn't even slowed the monster.

All three men ducked behind the lip of the ridge top and shifted left. The enemy's answering particle beam bolt shrilled just over the ridge in a burst of hard static.

"Jesus!" Geisler cried over the company channel. "What's Doc doing?"

From this new vantage point, Garroway could see down the shoulder of the ridge to a long, narrow slash in the Wheel surface a hundred meters away. IFF beacons marked three Marines in green; two were flashing, indicating they were wounded. The company data net IDed the wounded men as Houston and Tremkiss, the third as Doc Lee.

A red icon marked a third enemy vehicle, seventy meters from Garroway's position, thirty from the corpsman and the two wounded Marines. It was moving toward the trio, turning to bring its weapon to bear. Garroway snapped his 2120 to his shoulder, taking aim.

CCN INTERRUPT: LOW PRIORITY TARGET flashed in red across the top of Garroway's HUD, and the weapon failed to lock. *Shit!*

"Insufficient firepower available to successfully engage chosen target," a woman's voice said over his headset. "Redirect fire as advised." A flashing arrow appeared in his visual field, pointing right, telling him where to find the more urgent target.

He knew that two other enemy vehicles were much closer, and posed an immediate threat to the fire team. But sometimes you simply did *not* take orders from a fucking machine.

"Sissy! Override fire priority!" he screamed over the company channel. "*Repeat, override fire priority!*"

The flashing warnings winked off. Garroway fired into the rear armor of the distant war machine, but without visible effect.

"CCN!" Cavaco called. "Override protocol Foxtrot Alpha one-one! Link us in and repeat salvo!"

Obediently, a red triangle appeared on the rear of the target vehicle, as Garroway bumped the image magnification up to times-fifty. Garroway slipped his aim point into the reticle and, an instant later, Sissy triggered his weapon. He kept the 2120 on target, however, and let Sissy continue to fire it again and again, as fast as the weapon would cycle.

The Wheel defenders, most of them circular in shape like inverted dinner plates, appeared to be armored equally on all sides, unlike the tanks Marines had battled for the last couple of centuries in more conventional wars. Evidently, there weren't enough Marines with a direct line of sight to the same patch of the target's hull to ensure a burn-through and a kill, so Cavaco had directed Sissy to hold the lock and keep firing, trying to elevate the firepower of three Marines to that of eight.

Normally, that tactic was less efficient than having the CCN combine the fire of eight or more Marines in a single instant's volley. The target was moving, after all, and the explosion of vapor from the area where the laser pulses were striking would tend to scatter successive shots as effectively as an anti-laser aerosol fog.

But at the moment, three Marines were all that were available. Garroway kept his 2120 on target for as long as he could, despite the target's movement, despite the blurring haze of vaporizing metal. Under his imaging system's magnification, it looked like they might be punching through. . . .

HM2 Phillip Lee
Alpha Company, First Platoon,
B Section
AO Cincinnati, Sirius Stargate
1311 hours, Shipboard time

Lee fired his underpowered carbine into the bulk of the hovering monster time after time, with absolutely no effect. If he was hitting the muzzle—if, indeed, the muzzle was a weak point—he couldn't tell. The war machine was closer now, ten meters, getting closer. . . .

Suddenly, miraculously, the thing halted its advance, hovered for a moment, then rotated in place, a full one-eighty that brought its rear armor into view. Lee could see a ragged gash there, close to the vehicle's rim, that glowed a dull red at optical wavelengths, and a bright yellow under infrared.

The thing was hurt. Was that why it had broken off its attack? He didn't know, but the damaged spot offered him a new target for his carbine. At almost point-blank range, he took aim and began slamming bolt after bolt of coherent light into the vehicle's wounded hide. As it continued to move away, he stood up and advanced, carbine at his shoulder, continuing to fire until his weapon's computer flashed a warning to his HUD: PWR CELL DEPLETION.

The weapon went dead in his hands. With a scream he flung the useless carbine at the retreating war machine, saw it strike and bounce harmlessly aside.

But the machine continued to move away. Lee and his patients were in the clear, at least for the moment.

"C'mon, you guys," he said, returning to the crater where Tremkiss and Houston were still lying on the ground. He knew Houston couldn't hear him, but that didn't matter. "Let's vam the hell out of here!"

Mark VIII vac armor had an inset catch ring on the back, just below the helmet seal, used for holding it upright on a storage rack or during maintenance. It also had a reel of carbonweave line inside the backpack unit, like heavy-gauge fishing line for use as a tether in zero-G operations. Reaching into Tremkiss's back unit, he dragged a three-meter length from the reel, snicked it off with his scalpel, and secured one end to Tremkiss's catch ring, the other end to the ring on Houston's suit. Standing, he put the lanyard over his left shoulder, across his torso, and under his right arm, leaned forward, and started to move.

One man together with his armor massed over 140 kilograms. Surface gravity on this part of the Wheel ran around .9 G, so Lee was still trying to drag a dead weight of over 250 kilograms—a full quarter of a ton.

He managed one agonizing step . . . then another, but he couldn't get a good enough purchase on the Wheel's surface, even when he clicked on his boot magnets in an attempt to get better traction. He tried another step, struggling, pulling, and then he collapsed, panting hard, sweat fogging his visor, legs shrieking with the strain. He . . . couldn't . . . do . . . it. . . .

Think, damn it!

Thermalslick. He was trying to think of what he was missing, and all he could think of was that botched training exercise at the Mare Imbrium a few lifetimes ago. His debriefing had emphasized, in loving detail, the proper use of a Navy-issue thermalslick.

Dropping his makeshift harness, he fished the wallet-sized packet out of his kit bag, ripped off the cover, and unfolded it, silver side up. The material could reflect heat and light, or drink it in. The black side possessed an upper coating of buckyball carbon that rendered it very nearly frictionless, at least until that layer wore away.

He tried to roll Houston onto the blanket, but had to stop when he found that some of the nanoseal he'd used on the Marine's leg had bonded to the surface of the Wheel.

Shit, and shit again!

But it only took a moment to apply a smear of nanotech dissolving agent to free the bond—carefully to avoid opening the suit and the wound again—and then Houston was free. Together, he and Tremkiss manhandled Houston's armor onto the spread-out rectangle of foil, and then Tremkiss rolled onto it as well, lying partly across Houston's body. The blanket was really only big enough for one, but with Tremkiss clinging tightly to Houston's armor, they made a small-enough package to fit—barely.

Turning again, Lee picked up the fishing-line harness, leaned into it, and pulled. One step . . . then another . . . then another . . .

The two wounded Marines together still massed a quarter of a ton . . . but once Lee got them moving, they moved. Slowly, awkwardly . . . but they *moved*.

CPL John Garroway
Alpha Company, First Platoon,
B Section
AO Cincinnati, Sirius Stargate
1312 hours, Shipboard time

The injured Wheel defender had turned away from Doc and the wounded Marines, but now it was climbing up the slope toward Garroway and the rest of his fire team. To make matters worse, the pair of vehicles they'd ignored a moment ago—overriding the CCN's control so they could help Doc—were now breasting the ridge top a scant ten meters away. They were coming up side by side, angled to keep their bellies parallel to the slope beneath them, giving Garroway a view of their smooth, black undersides.

Was the armor thinner there? "Sissy! Lock us on!"

Once again in control of the fire team's weapons, the CCN AI painted a red triangle on the belly of the monster to the right. Garroway took aim . . . cursing wildly beneath his breath as he waited for other Marine weapons to come online. . . .

And then Sissy fired his weapon and eight others simultaneously. The armor *was* thinner on the keels of those hovering nightmares, and the burn-through erupted as a savage, silent blast of vapor and hot debris that knocked Garroway off his feet and sent him sprawling onto his back.

The targeted war machine slammed suddenly to the ground, canted at an angle, its weapon uselessly probing the sky. Its twin slid over the lip of the ridge beside it, its weapon dropping to take aim at the three blast-scattered Marines.

Rolling onto his stomach, Garroway aimed his laser rifle. "Sissy! Gimme a lock!"

"Insufficient firepower available to successfully engage chosen target," Sissy's voice replied with a maddening lack of emotion. "Recommend immediate E and E to avoid hostile fire. . . ."

"*Fuck you!*" Garroway yelled. Springing to his feet, he dropped his 2120 and charged forward, rushing the oncoming machine. He was already so close to the drifting behemoth it couldn't pivot fast enough to bring its weapon to bear. Garroway leaped, arms outspread, and landed on top of the machine's curved surface, legs dangling off the rim. The machine tilted alarmingly under Garroway's weight, seesawed a moment, then stabilized itself. It began rotating swiftly, as though trying to dislodge its unwanted rider. Garroway, clinging to a handhold among the innumerable fist-sized

raised blocks and angular depressions across the uneven surface, rolled his legs up and onto the top, then fumbled at his
gear satchel for a block of CTX-5.

CTX-5 was a chemical explosive enhanced by dithermal
exotics, as powerful a bang in a single book-sized package
as it was possible to make. You armed it by pushing one of
two pressure plates. The first caused the package to reform
to the convex configuration; clip that side to a claymore
pack—a package containing seventy lead-uranium ball
bearings, and you had a charge triggered through your implant that fired the balls like a shotgun blast in a broad foot-
print. Press the other plate and the pack rearranged itself in
the concave configuration, creating a shaped charge with a
highly focused blast, like a concentrated, armor-piercing jet
of white-hot plasma.

Garroway pressed the second plate, reached over the rim
of the vehicle, and slapped the charge against the belly. So
long as the link-connect points in his glove were in contact
with the CTX pack, he could access its simple-minded con-
trols through his implant. A thought-click fired the nanoseal
on the base plate, welding the pack to the armor. A second
thought-click triggered the five-second countdown. He
rolled off the pivoting vehicle and hit the ground with a *thud*
that nearly knocked the wind out of him. He felt a wave of
pins-and-needles prickles wash across his legs and up his
back and realized the machine was passing directly over his
prone body.

He rolled, trying to get out from under. The machine accelerated, turning to track Geisler, who was farther away
and, therefore, an easier target.

Then the CTX exploded, the detonation silent in hard vacuum but dazzlingly bright to unshielded eyes, the focused
blast stabbing through the vehicle's rim and up and out the
upper surface like a geyser of white light. The back-blast beneath the vehicle caught Garroway and flicked him aside, at

the same time lifting the massive machine's side up and over, flipping it onto its back.

Whatever mag-lev technology the thing used to hover and move, it didn't work upside down. The war machine slammed to the uneven ground belly-up and back-broken.

Which left the third Wheel defender, the one that had been chasing Doc and the wounded Marines downslope. Garroway grabbed his laser rifle and hurried back to Cavaco and Geisler's position, dropped to his belly, and took aim at the advancing monster. *Damn* it was fast!

"Lock us on, Sissy!" Cavaco yelled.

"Insufficient firepower available to successfully engage chosen target," Sissy replied. "Recommend immediate E and E to avoid hostile fire. . . ."

This time the hostile vehicle was too far away to try taking it out with a CTX pack. The machine fired, its particle beam bolt slamming into the hard metal slope just below Garroway's position. The blast knocked him back from the edge of the rift, sending him sprawling once more. Stunned, he tried to get up, tried to find his laser rifle. Somehow, he'd dropped it, accidentally this time, in the explosion. Geisler and Cavaco were both down as well. The armored vehicle crested the ridge, pivoting to take aim once more. Garroway tensed, readying to dive for cover. . . .

Hovering ten meters away, the hostile machine came apart in a violent blossom of silent white flame. The entire front half of the machine was ripped away, and the wreckage crumpled to the black metal ground.

Garroway stood where he was a moment longer, scarcely daring to believe what had just happened. How? . . .

"C'mon, Marines!" Kat's voice called over the platoon channel. "Stop gawking and get the lead out!"

Kat and Sergeant Morton emerged from behind the wreckage of the Wiggler machine Garroway had killed. Morton had just braced his Onager tube on the wreckage and sent a 7-kilogram missile streaking into the last hostile from point-blank range.

"That was my last missile," Morton said. "Let's vam for the inner perimeter!"

"Hold on a sec," Garroway said. "We have some people out there."

He pointed downslope and to the left. Doc, it seemed, was making good time across the Wheel's surface a hundred meters away, dragging two armored bodies on a bright silver blanket.

"Let's give 'em a hand," Cavaco said. "Marines do *not* leave their own behind!"

HM2 Phillip Lee
Alpha Company, First Platoon,
B Section
AO Cincinnati, Sirius Stargate
1314 hours, Shipboard time

They were *his* men and he wasn't leaving them behind.

Step by agonizing step, Lee dragged the two armored men back toward the Marine lines. The thermalslick's frictionless feature wasn't perfect, and Houston's boots kept dragging on bare ground. At least it allowed him to get the heavy mass of the two wounded Marines moving, as though he were pulling them across a sheet of ice, and once they were in motion, they tended to stay in motion, gliding along behind Lee as he slogged ahead, straining at the line taut across his torso armor.

But it wasn't ice. By the time he'd gone thirty meters, the frictionless surface of the sheet was beginning to wear away and progress became slower. He pulled harder, leaning into the line, but the black underside of the blanket was losing its slippery surface.

Damn. How much farther? His helmet display was zoomed out to show the entire Cincinnati AO all the way back to the inner cordon they were forming around Memphis. Green points of light marking other Marines were clustered heavily around the second perimeter, but he was almost alone out here . . . a good kilometer to go to reach the HQ area and only four—no, five—Marines anywhere close.

He looked up, startled. He'd not realized how close. Kat Vinton and Jeff Morton reached him first, taking hold of the tow line and adding their strength to his. Geisler, Garroway, and Cavaco arrived a moment later.

"Well done, Doc," Cavaco told him. "We've got 'em."

They slipped the tow line off over his helmet, and he sagged to the ground, exhausted, legs trembling.

"Blanket stretcher!" Garroway said. He appeared to have lost his rifle—a sin for a Marine—but he grabbed one corner of the foil blanket, lifted . . . and almost fell when it slipped through his gloved fingers like water.

"You've got to roll the edges over," Lee told him. "Like this."

There was enough buckyball surface on the edges of the blanket to make it tough to hold, but by rolling a corner over on itself, silver side out, it was possible to hang onto the stuff. A moment later, Garroway, Cavaco, Vinton, and Morton each had a corner of the blanket and were hauling the two armored forms toward friendly lines, with Lee and Geisler to either side, gripping the middle and trying to take on some of the weight. The load was heavy, and movement awkward, but they made good progress.

The good news was that the Wheel's defenders appeared to have broken off their attack. There were no red pinpoints on their HUD map displays, no more enemy machines drifting up out of the valley behind them.

And ten minutes later a detachment of twelve more Marines met them, providing an armed escort back to safety.

Marines do take care of their own.

AO Memphis—Beachhead HQ
Sirius Stargate
1340 hours, Shipboard time

"The attack appears to have broken off," Warhurst told Ramsey. "At least for now."

"Well done," Ramsey's voice said over the link. He could hear the relief in the man's voice. "*Very* well done."

"Wasn't me, General. But I'll pass that on to the guys and gals who did it."

"Do that. What's the bill?"

"Right now . . ." He reached up through his implant and pulled down the latest casualty figures off the command net. "Thirty-seven dead. And fifteen wounded."

"Fourteen percent."

"It could have been worse, General. *Much* worse."

"Roger that."

It was frankly surprising that there'd been as many wounded as that. Combat in the vacuum of space is relentlessly unforgiving. Even with advanced suit technology, even a minor wound was all too often fatal.

"Tell me something, though. According to the data we have here, the enemy didn't retreat. Did you knock out all of them? A one hundred percent kill?"

"That's the damnedest thing, sir. No. We counted a total of ninety-seven enemy tanks. We knocked out every one that broke through at Milwaukee and Cincinnati. There was another column threatening AO Toledo. We took out about ten of those machines before they reached our lines—that was, we're guessing, thirty percent of that column. The rest of them, General, I swear, they just faded away into the ground. No retreat. They're just . . . gone."

"That does not exactly fill me with confidence, Major. You've checked to make sure they're not just dug in, I take it."

"Yes, sir." He did not add "of course." The general was operating in a zone staff officers detested—not enough information—and he had to explore every possibility. "I've had teams out there looking at what's left. I don't think the Wigglers manufacture their tanks. I think they *grow* them."

"Nanufacture?"

"That, or a process just like it, sir."

"Then you and your people ought to be dead, Major. How do you account for that?"

"Sir, at this point I don't. There's just not enough data to make even a half-assed guess. Still, my teams have examined a number of the vehicles we killed. Here . . . take a look at this."

He uploaded imagery from the helmet sensors of one of his recon teams. They watched the scene unfold noumenally—one of the enemy vehicles, its front half sheared off, exposing the interior.

There was no internal compartment, no place for a crew. Various silvery mechanisms and components appeared to be imbedded within jet-black metal. The metal had a spongy look to it, as though it had been a bubble-filled liquid that had solidified unevenly around the gas pockets.

"No two are exactly alike," Warhurst explained, "but they all possess the same components. A mag-lev drive system. A power plant. A particle accelerator weapon. And a distributed electronics system that probably serves as both communications and control."

"You're telling me these things are robots."

"Yes, sir . . . that, or they're teleoperated from somewhere inside the Wheel. I'd like it if Cassius could take a look at some of these things and see what he can pick up."

"Done."

"Our guess is that the Wiggles take manufactured components, like the drive system, and use some variant of nanotechnology to take the Wheel's surface material and close the
shells of these things around them. Quick and dirty."

"So the ones that got away? . . ."

"Either they were reabsorbed into the surface, guns,
drives, and all, or they passed through the surface and into the
underground regions of the Wheel. There may be tunnels or
some sort of highway system down there."

Ramsey grunted. "With technology like that . . . why
didn't they just grow a few hundred of the things out of the
Wheel's surface smack in the middle of your perimeter?"

"I don't know, sir. I'm just glad they didn't. Best guess?
The manufactured components are positioned at widely separated points, scattered all over the face of the Wheel. They
grow the shells around the innards in place, then have to as-
semble the completed vehicles into larger groups . . . the
columns they sent after us."

"Yeah, but if those things can pass right through solid
nickel-iron, they could've grown the things underground, assembled them underneath Point Memphis, and surfaced
them all at once."

"General, we just don't know enough about the alien technology. The fact that they didn't suggests that they can't, and
for that I am profoundly grateful."

"Roger that, Major. Roger that."

Warhurst knew just how lucky the Marine landing force
had been. Out of almost a hundred defending machines, the
Marines had knocked out at least sixty. But if the survivors
had gotten loose inside the perimeter as a unit instead of in
scattered twos and threes, Marine casualties would have been
much higher than fourteen percent.

"When can we expect to be reinforced, General?"

"We're loading the follow-on forces on the TRAPs now,

Major. *Daring* and *New Chicago* are en route now, to take up positions for close fire support, should that be necessary. Ten hours. You'll have fighter support back within five hours, however."

"Yes, sir."

"Can you hold?"

"I guess we'll have to, General. We've expended most of the available Onagers. However, some of our Marines developed some rather up-close and personal techniques for dealing with enemy tanks. We may be able to . . ." Warhurst broke off. A flashing light in his noumenal awareness indicated an important message incoming on a different channel. "Excuse me, General. An urgent message."

"Take it."

He switched mental channels. "Go."

"Major? This is Giotti. Sir . . . I thought you should know. We're almost through the surface. Five minutes."

Warhurst checked his internal clock. The engineering team had estimated forty-five minutes and taken only thirty-five. They were padding their estimates again, damn them.

"Well done!" He shifted channels again. "General? That was my engineering squad. They're almost through the Wheel's surface. I need to issue orders to deploy my recon company."

"Keep me patched in."

"Aye aye, sir!"

Analyses of the battle would wait. Right now, a whole new battle was about to unfold.

And this time, the Marines would be taking the fight to the enemy.

Inside the Wheel.

17

2 APRIL 2170

CPL John Garroway
Alpha Company, First Platoon,
B Section
AO Cincinnati, Sirius Stargate
1350 hours, Shipboard time

"Recon Company, First Platoon! Saddle up, boys and girls! We're movin' out!"

The fact that Dunne had called them *Recon Company* instead of Alpha told Garroway something special was up. Long, long ago and very far away, Alpha had been designated as MIEU-1's reconnaissance company, which meant they would be going into the Wheel's interior first.

He'd only just staggered into the frenzy of activity that marked the HQ area at Point Memphis, surrendering Houston and Tremkiss to Chief Mattingly and three other company corpsmen. They were organizing a field hospital next to the headquarters, preparatory to bringing in a medevac TRAP. Around them, Marines were busily creating prepared positions, delineating a new, inner defensive perimeter with a radius of less than two hundred meters encircling Point Memphis.

Nearby, a number of Marines were completing the emplacement of a set of RW-42 sentry guns. These were twin-barreled pulse laser weapons with a cyclic rate of 10 shots per second, mounted on three-meter-high towers and remotely controlled by the CCN AI. They took time to unship and set up, which was why they hadn't played a part in the first battle, but they would increase the landing force's firepower considerably.

In all the bustle, it was tough finding any one Marine. He used the ID locator on his HUD map to spot Gunnery Sergeant Dunne.

There he was, at the center of a growing team of Alpha Company Marines.

"Hey, Gunny!" he called, approaching the group.

"What?"

"Corporal Garroway, reporting as ordered. But, uh, I kind of lost my weapon."

Dunne turned and picked up an LR-2120 from a small pile of weapons nearby. "Gonna make you sleep with it, Marine," he growled. Traditionally, recruits in boot camp who dropped their weapons during training were required to take them to bed with them. The Marine creed *My Rifle*, memorized by generations of recruits for the past two centuries, emphasized the very special relationship between a Marine and his weapon. Dunne started to hand the weapon to Garroway, then stopped. "Belay that. You checked out with the pig-ninety?"

"Sure thing, Gunny." Of course he was. Every Marine in the company had drilled endlessly with the things, back at L-4.

"Then take this." Replacing the laser rifle on the stack, he picked up instead a larger, longer, heavier weapon, a PG-90. It was connected by a cable to a backpack battery unit. "Watch the fringe-bleed and watch the splash. It's gonna be close-quarters down there."

"Aye *aye*, Gunnery Sergeant!"

"Try not to lose it."

Garroway accepted the weapon, snicking back the bolt-feed access, checking the power pack, and linking to the computer for a fast diagnostic. According to the ID data that appeared as he powered up, the weapon had belonged to a Sergeant Graff, Charlie Company.

He didn't know the man, and didn't ask what had happened to him.

The PG-90 was a full-automatic squad-support plasma weapon, 1.2 meters long and massing 10.3 kilograms, while the battery and charger unit massed another 14.1 kilos. It took centimeter-long bolts of a ferrous-lead-mercury alloy and used a powerful surge of electromagnetic energy to both accelerate it and convert it into a thumb-sized packet of white-hot plasma. The weapon had a cyclic rate of about four hundred rounds per minute, though in vacuum, even with the radiator vanes installed, the practical rate of fire was reduced to about 150 rounds per minute, and with frequent barrel changes to avoid overheating.

Marines called it the "thundergun," or, more usually, "pig."

"Ooh-rah!" Garroway said as the diagnostics showed the weapon powered up and at optimum.

"Vinton!" Dunne snapped. "Arhipov! You're with the pig."

"Aye aye, Gunnery Sergeant!"

"Sure thing, Gunny."

"You three deploy with me, Deek, and Lobowski."

That was a startling bit of information. Plasma guns were fielded in three-Marine teams, two riflemen supporting the squad automatic weapon as assistant gunner and spotter/security. Generally, there was one pig to a twelve-man squad. Staff Sergeant Eugene Deek and Reg Lobowski both, however, were also pig-gunners. Having two thunderguns in one squad was decidedly unusual; having *three* was unheard of.

"We're not going to have the manpower for CCN linkups down there," Dunne explained, as though reading Garroway's surprise. "I want as much firepower packed into as small an area as we can manage. Just don't get in one another's way. Copy that?"

"Aye-firmative, Gunny."

"Now move it. The Nergs've got an appointment below with the Wiggles and we don't want to be late."

Garroway moved it.

Engineering Section
Breakthrough Point
AO Memphis, Sirius Stargate
1352 hours, Shipboard time

Staff Sergeant Ernest Giotti watched as the three-meter cutout settled a bit. The nanotunneler had vanished into the ring-shaped hole, leaving the cutout precariously balanced. Using his implant, he was carefully monitoring the tunneler's descent. Now, centimeters from cutting through, he ordered the device to halt.

"Cutting suspended, sir," he told Warhurst. "Ready to proceed on your order."

"Hang tight," Warhurst told him over their private channel. "How's the pressurization going?"

He checked the data. Air had been bleeding through into the bubble. The working space had gradually been pressurizing through the test hole over the past half hour and now stood at nearly 9 psi. He could now even hear sounds in the chamber through his helmet as he and the other engineers worked.

"We're at 8.8 psi," he said. "Internal pressure inside the Wheel reads out at about 11.5. Temperature 23 Celsius. Composition . . . oxygen, nitrogen . . ."

"I've got all that," Warhurst snapped. "Stand by. Recon's going to start cycling through into the bubble."

"Aye aye, sir."

The inner hatch of the airlock hissed open and armored Marines stepped into the bubble's interior, their armor chameleonics rapidly fading from black to a dark mottled gray, matching the interior of the portable airlock dome. One of them closed the hatch. Minutes passed, and then the hatch opened again, admitting four more Marines. The outer lock was only large enough to admit four men at a time, and it took a while to bring in an entire forty-man platoon.

The ID on one of the first men through indicated he was Lieutenant Gansen, the platoon's CO. "Lieutenant Gansen?"

"What is it?" He sounded tight . . . even scared.

"Uh, sir? I was just wondering. The Wiggles've had plenty of time to know exactly what we're doing up here and where we're going to break through."

"Do you think I don't know that, Staff Sergeant?"

"No, sir."

"Damned cluster fuck, is what it is. A *cluster fuck*."

Giotti edged a bit farther away from Gansen. The man was *not* happy and Giotti didn't want to be in position to take the hit if the guy exploded.

As the Marines came in, the first eight took position around the three-meter circle on the deck, facing out. Eight more Marines stood in an outer circle, facing their counterparts, holding a tether from their armor, with the free end nanofused to the deck. Two of the first eight held PG-90s, muzzles up; the rest carried LR-2120s in one hand, and gripped the tether in the other.

More and more Marines squeezed through the lock, taking up waiting positions around the sixteen men and women in the center. "Don't bunch up, guys, or one grenade could get us all," one joked and another said something about taking turns breathing, but for the most part they were silent, waiting.

"Major Warhurst," Gansen said after the last four Marines cycled inside, "we are ready to board."

"Very well, Lieutenant," Warhurst replied. "Staff Sergeant Giotti! Pull the plug on that damned thing!"

Giotti gave the thought-clicked command and the nanotunneler fired up to full dig once more. An anxious moment passed, and then, suddenly, the central core of the cutout portion of the deck vanished, dropping away into the shaft. A final blast of air came through, equalizing the pressure and accompanied by a mushroom of dust on the updraft.

"Grenades!" Gansen yelled. Half a dozen M-780 grenades sailed into the pit, detonating seconds later in a stuttering burst of multiple blasts and flashes. If anyone or anything was waiting for them down there, that should have distracted them for a precious instant or two.

Next into the pit was an AR-7 Argus reconnaissance probe, configured for atmospheric operations. Little more than a meter-long pallet supporting a power plant, reaction mass, and a highly sophisticated sensor suite, it lowered itself into the hold on sharp-hissing thrusters, transmitting a full three-sixty of its surroundings at both optical and infrared wavelengths.

And when the Argus took no defensive fire, Warhurst gave the final order. "Lieutenant Gansen, deploy your Marines."

"Go!" Gansen yelled. "Go-go-go!"

The eight Marines on the inner circle leaned back, taking up the strain on their tethers, then stepped back as one and dropped into darkness.

CPL John Garroway
Alpha Company, First Platoon,
B Section
Wheel Entry Breach, Sirius Stargate
1425 hours, Shipboard time

Garroway was one of the first Marines in. With the PG-90 snapped to a weapons mount on the side of his torso armor, he rappelled down the shaft, entering a vast, empty space and landing a moment later atop the canted plug of surface material that had dropped down from above.

The tunnel was dark at optical wavelengths, a murky green on infrared. The space was huge, a cavernous passageway almost four meters high and six wide, with rounded walls and water dripping from the ceiling. The first thing that entered Garroway's mind was that he'd just entered the intestines of some enormous beast . . . an image he wished immediately he could forget.

He was receiving video from the Argus probe, which appeared inside a window within his noumenal vision. The image was low-res, but gave him enough information to let him orient himself once he hit bottom.

In a moment, he stood in a circle with seven other Marines, facing outward. Vinton and Arhipov on his fire team, standing to either side of him; Lobowski, Baxter, and Weis in the other; and Dunne and Womicki completing the team as the command/communication element.

The Argus probe was already moving down the tunnel toward arbitrary "north," and was already vanishing into the dark. From his OP in the bubble on the surface, Gansen gave a command and running lights snapped on, illuminating the probe and some of the tunnel surrounding it. The enemy already knew the Marines were there; they might as well have a target they could see, one that did not have a Marine inside.

As the circle of Marines expanded slightly, eight more Marines dropped down at their backs. Dunne rasped an order and the first eight redeployed, moving into two columns of four, following the slow-drifting Argus toward the north. The second group of eight immediately set up a defensive position, facing south. They would hold the entry point . . . just in case it became necessary to turn it into an exit point instead.

The water here was knee deep and slowly growing deeper.

"Ugh," Vinton said, pushing her way forward at Garroway's back. "You think this is part of their sewer system?"

"I don't know, Kat," Lobowski replied from Garroway's right. "At least if it is, we don't have to smell it."

"Maybe it's coolant for some kind of power plant," Arhipov suggested.

"Can the chatter, Marines," Dunne snapped. "Lobowski! Weis! Baxter! On point!"

"Aye aye, Gunny."

Lobowski and the two riflemen supporting him detached themselves from the other five and moved forward a few meters. They took a couple of stumbling steps, then righted themselves. The water was now up to their waists.

"Shit, Gunny!" Lance Corporal Weis called. "If it gets any deeper, we're gonna be swimming!"

"Gunny?" Garroway said.

"What?"

"If it *does* get deeper . . . 2120s don't work for shit underwater."

He surveyed the black water around him uneasily. The pigs ought to work okay submerged, at least for short ranges. A high-velocity plasma bolt would flash the surrounding water to steam. Friction and cooling would slow it, but it would retain a deadly punch for at least several hundred meters.

Laser bolts, however, were nothing but pulses of coherent light, and water drank light, scattering and absorbing it completely within a distance of a few meters. Blue-green lasers, emitted at wavelengths of 500 to 540 nanometers, were best able to penetrate water, but LR-2120s operated at a wavelength of 640 nanometers—a deep red, chosen because red light didn't scatter as easily in atmosphere as shorter wavelengths.

For that matter, water would hamper both communications and data feeds, both radio and lasercom. This was *not* good.

Under the lights of their armor, the water's surface appeared to be acting . . . peculiar. It was crisscrossed by myriad tiny ripples, as though from some vibration coming through the tunnel walls.

Not surprising, really. The readout on ambient gravity was

jittering back and forth between 9.132 and 9.133 gravities, a tiny shift that was probably related to the spinning of those mini-black holes somewhere beneath their feet.

Probably. The truth was, they just didn't know what they were facing here, and that knowledge—the lack of it, rather—made each step forward a struggle.

"Gunny!" Baxter screamed. "There's something in the water!"

"Calm down, Marine. What is it?"

"I don't know! I felt it bump me . . . there! Over there!" He aimed his laser rifle and fired, the bolts just visible as faint red flickers in the humid air.

"Baxter!" Dunne shouted. "Belay firing! Wait'll you have a target!"

"S-sorry, Gunny."

"He's right, though," Weis pointed out. "There could be sharks in here."

" 'Sharks'?" Womicki said. He laughed. "That don't seem likely!"

"You now what I mean, damn it."

"Yeah," Garroway said. "Remember those civilian briefings we DLed? If the Sirians *are* Wiggles, those Nommo things the scientists say visited Earth a few thousand years back, well, they were supposed to be amphibious, right? They lived in water."

"So they're swimming around us, right here?" Weis said. "I don't think I like this."

"Fucking great," Lobowski added, swinging the muzzle of his pig back and forth, covering the uneasy surface of the water ahead in long, sweeping arcs. "Now we're fighting freakin' tadpoles!"

"We don't know *what* we're fighting, people," Dunne warned. "Just stay sharp!"

The eight Marines pulled back, finding comfort, if not necessarily safety, in the closeness of the others. They could see the Argos probe twenty-five meters ahead, hovering at half a meter, its jets roiling the dark water's surface, the sharp hiss amplified by the bare tunnel walls. Halfway between the probe and the Marines, something broke the surface, a long, rolling shape that glistened in the glare from the AR-7's lights.

"Shit!" Baxter cried. "What was that?"

"Tighten up, people," Dunne told them. "I'm on the command channel with the boss."

"We can't fight what we can't see," Womicki said. "What the hell are we doing down here anyway?"

"Maybe," Garroway said slowly, "we're making contact."

"Right now," Lobowski said, "the only contact I want to make is with my pig."

The water was almost waist deep on Garroway now. "Hang on," he called. "I'm going to try something."

"What?" Dunne asked.

"I'm going to stick my head under. Don't worry. I'll be right back."

"Womicki! Grab the handhold on his armor. Haul him up if he gets into trouble."

"Right, Gunny."

He resisted the unthinking urge to hold his breath. With Womicki keeping hold, he slipped forward headfirst under the surface of the water. It was ink-black and his IR scanners could pick up nothing. He thought-clicked his armor's lights on and the murk was filled with a milky-gray pearlescence filled with drifting motes of brightly lit muck. His suit's external mikes were picking up a universe of sound, however, a barrage of rapid clicks and chirps that reminded him of dolphins, back on Earth.

Were those Nommo? "*His voice, too, and his language, were articulate and human,*" at least according to one of the fragments of Berossus's history downloaded from the data stores of the civilian advisors. If that clicking was intelligent speech, it wasn't human.

His eyes were almost useless. Visibility was limited to less than a meter, even when he tried dimming the lights a little. No . . . *something* was moving out there. He caught only a shadow, long and sinuous, casting odd shadows as it moved in a rippling flash from right to left. He tried swinging his PG-90 to follow it, but it was gone before he could shove the cumbersome weapon through the water.

Another flash of movement, this one to the left. Turning his body against the steady pressure of Womicki's grip, he was able to see something like an angular face perhaps a meter away—two huge fishlike eyes, green against horny black skin, and a smoothly rounded, elongated skull behind. He had an instant's glimpse only and then the creature was gone in a rippling flash. He thought he saw a body like an eel's or a snake's—or it could have been a tentacle. Mostly what he remembered were the *eyes*.

Getting his feet under him, Garroway stood up, his helmet breaking the surface and water cascading from his shoulders. "I saw something," he said. "Here it is." He uploaded the glimpse he'd had as recorded by his armor's sensors. Cassius and the other AIs might be able to extract more information from the brief sighting than he could manage with his own eyes. The human brain was notoriously unreliable when it came to making sense of something so strange it had nothing with which to compare it. Electronic AIs would be less easily misled.

"How's the water, Gare?" Kat asked him.

"I wish these suits had sonar," he replied. "Couldn't see for shit. But I think Ski has it right. We're fighting giant tadpoles. The thing I saw must be one of the Nommo young."

Garroway felt himself trembling inside his armor. The stress, after the combat on the surface, was almost crippling. Up there, at least, he'd been fighting an enemy he could see, an enemy that registered on his combat maps, on infrared, and on the control Net. He'd entered the tunnel expecting more of the same—and an opportunity to take the fight to the enemy's home ground.

But here, waist deep in what looked suspiciously like an alien sewer, he couldn't see the enemy and couldn't fight him. If that thing he'd glimpsed underwater was one of them, however, *they* could see the Marines without any difficulty whatsoever.

Something bumped his left leg, hard.

"Hold it!" he shouted. The surface of the water was moving in a peculiar way, as though something large, *very* large, was moving just below. "I think . . ."

Something massive coiled about his knees and yanked him into the black water.

Major Warhurst
AO Memphis—Beachhead HQ
Sirius Stargate
1442 hours, Shipboard time

"*Man down*!" Gunnery Sergeant Dunne's voice crackled over the communications net. "*We have a man down*!"

"*Gare*!" That was Kat Vinton.

"Pull them back, Lieutenant," Warhurst said over the command channel.

"Aye aye, sir!" Gansen snapped. "You heard the man, people! Fall back!"

"Negative!" Dunne said. "Negative, sir! We've lost a Marine! He just vanished underwater! We are *not* leaving without him."

Warhurst opened a direct and private channel with Dunne. He could see through the sensor suite in Dunne's armor, could see the flattened opening of the tunnel ahead, could see the reflections of lights off the black and dripping walls and sparkling on the surging water below and the armored shapes of other Marines standing waist deep, weapons shifting back and forth as they looked for a target. "I understand your concern, Gunny," he said. "But we have the whole MIEU to think about. You people are exposed down there, with big fat targets painted on your armor!"

"With respect, sir, we're not letting the bastards take one of ours without a fight. I recommend dropping mike seven-eighties on 'em."

Warhurst thought about this. "Won't that kill your man?"

"If he's not already dead," Dunne replied, his voice grim, "it'll sure the hell shake him up. But it won't kill him unless we drop one right on top of him, sir."

It made sense. The Marines were encased in armor; the thing that Garroway had glimpsed was not, so far as they knew. Grenades would create a deadly concussion underwater. It would be like dynamiting fish . . . or dropping depth charges on an enemy submarine.

"Very well," Warhurst said. "Do it!" He shifted to the command channel. "Lieutenant Gansen!"

"Sir!"

"Try dropping grenades on them. See if you can bring them to the surface."

"Aye aye, sir!"

Bad precedent, he thought, *cutting Gansen out of the loop like that*. But the man was on the ragged edge of panic. Warhurst could hear the stress in his voice and the man's med readouts showed a pulse of 136, rapid and shallow breathing, and sharply elevated levels of adrenaline. It would be all too easy to lose the entire platoon if Gansen broke. Right now, Gunny Dunne was the one holding the recon element together.

And the wise commander relied on his senior NCOs.

Through Dunne's eyes, then, he watched as Dunne, Vinton, Womicki, Baxter, and Weis all pulled M-780 hand grenades from their carry pouches, thumbed the arming switches, and tossed them into the water in a broad semicircle ahead, halfway between their position and the point where the Argus probe hovered above the oily surface.

Five explosions went off in a ragged, second-long salvo, the blasts hurling geysers of water into the tunnel opening and ringing off the walls, the detonations amplified in the enclosed space, staggering the Marines.

God, Warhurst thought. *I hope to hell we didn't just score an own goal. . . .*

CPL John Garroway
Sirius Stargate
1442 hours, Shipboard time

Whatever had grabbed him was extremely powerful and fast. One moment, Garroway had been standing in waist-deep water, watching a peculiar movement of the surface, as though something was moving down there. The next, something like a thick snake had coiled around his knees and pulled, pulled *hard*. He'd hit the water on his back and an instant later he was being dragged feetfirst through the blackness.

He still had his PG-90, which was attached to the armor mount on his right side, but he didn't have a target and didn't want to fire blindly. Better to wait until a target presented itself. . . .

Then the explosions started going off, piercing, bone-rattling detonations in rapid succession that left his ears ringing and the taste of blood in his mouth. Whatever was dragging him through the water let go . . . but before he could find his feet or even focus his mind after that brain-numbing barrage, he was grabbed again and again dragged through the water.

His external lights illuminated the water around him, but all he could see was a blur of brightly lit muck streaming up past his helmet visor. It felt as though he were going down, as if the floor of the tunnel had dropped sharply or opened into a vaster submerged chamber of some sort.

Radio and lasercom would be useless down here, he knew. But if he could let the rest of his unit know he was still alive and maybe give his captor a surprise at the same time. . . .

He pivoted the PG-90 to point roughly at what he thought might be up and triggered three quick rounds. The plasma bolts flash-heated the water surrounding them to steam, each shot accompanied by a shrill, shrieking hiss and the jolt of a miniature thunderclap, as tunnels of vacuum drilled through the water suddenly collapsed.

Whatever was holding on to Garroway let go then and he felt himself sinking. Marine armor didn't float, didn't even possess neutral buoyancy.

He was going down like a damned brick.

18

SF/A-2 Starhawk Talon Three
Place unknown
Time unknown

Space and time, Alexander knew, were two faces of the same coin. By jumping this far through space, time—as measured on Earth or back at the fleet—had little meaning or relevance.

Still his internal timekeeping and the clocks in his Starhawk had marked off over two hours since he'd come through the gate to . . . *here*, wherever the hell here was.

Outside the galaxy, certainly. His eyes, no, his mind had adjusted to the strangeness of this place. That spiral smear of starlight . . . it was hard to tear his gaze away. So beautiful . . .

He was a dead man. He knew that. His shipboard air and power would last . . . what? Another twenty hours, plus whatever was trapped inside his cockpit. Another day of breathing. And after that . . .

The damnedest thing about the situation was not being able to report back. His fighter was dead—no maneuvering or thruster control at all and barely enough power to keep him warm for a few more hours. The stargate he'd emerged from was a good fifty kilometers away now, a range that was slowly but steadily increasing. He had no way of going back.

When he saw the other Starhawk, he thought he was hallucinating.

No, it *was* a Starhawk . . . a special mod . . . Hell, it was the Starhawk with an AI onboard they'd sent in as a scout.

Alexander sat upright so quickly his helmet whacked the cockpit's armored overhead. If both he and the probe had ended up in the same place, the same space, it told them something about how the stargates worked. His briefings had emphasized that no one knew if you just flew right through or if you had to follow a very precise and carefully calculated path to get where you wanted to go. This suggested that the gates were just gates—with one destination.

Or, at least, one destination at a time.

The other A-2 was closer now. Damn, it was showing some battle damage as well . . . long half-melted scorings down its port side. Maneuvering thruster damage, certainly, and maybe worse.

But it gave him a fighting chance, at the very least. Pooner wasn't dead yet.

And with the arrival of that AI, he was no longer quite so alone. . . .

CPL John Garroway
Sirius Stargate
1449 hours, Shipboard time

He'd never been this isolated, this *alone*.

Back in boot camp, an eternity or so ago, one of the first things they'd done was remove his implant. He'd entered the Corps with a high-end executive model implant, with social interactive icon selection, emotional input and multiple net search demons, a high-thrust unit that had put him way ahead of the other kids in his school network. Stripped of that cranialink nanohardware, he'd felt naked and helpless, feelings which, of course, his drill instructors had exploited.

He'd learned to live without it, and that had been one of the key lessons he'd carried with him out of boot camp. The basic, unaugmented Mark I human being was an incredible machine even without high-tech rewiring, even without instant access to satellite networks and libraries of data, even without immediate electronic interfacing with others.

Later in his training, he'd received a standard government-issue implant, but the knowledge that he *could* function without electronic enhancement remained with him.

He was damned glad of that training now. His implant connected to the electronic environment through a variety of EM wavelengths, including VLF, VHF, UHF, EHF, all via both broadband and maser, and both infrared and optical laser. None of them, even the lowest frequencies, could penetrate both water and the metal of the Wheel's structure to connect him with the other Marines.

He was completely on his own.

Garroway was on the bottom—the ground was solid beneath his feet, though each step stirred up fresh clouds of drifting muck. The only light was that coming from the lamps set into his helmet and the top of his backpack, looking over his shoulders. At top intensity, it was like standing in the center of a fierce blizzard in whiteout conditions. At lower intensity, he could see two or three meters, but the water drank light hungrily. Hundreds of those amphibious creatures could be out there, only a few meters away, and he would never see them.

Walking was like it must have been for a hard-hat diver two or three centuries before. He had to lean forward, each step ponderously slow. He picked the direction that his suit's inertial system indicated would take him back to the rest of his platoon and kept walking.

The ground appeared to be rising somewhat, though it was

hard to be sure. His only real indicator of depth was pressure, which currently was indicating 1.34 atmospheres. With an ambient atmospheric pressure at the surface of the water of 11.5 psi, or .78 of an atmosphere, and a surface gravity averaging .9G, the depth here should be eight meters, or at least that's what the armor's onboard computer and his own implant told him.

His armor was registering a pressure now of 15.2 psi in the pounds-per-square-inch measurement still widely used by the Corps, but that would go up by almost eight-tenths of an atmosphere for every ten meters of descent. If he went any deeper . . . what, he wondered, was the crush depth of Mark VIII vac armor? No one had ever told him. The suit's designers, he guessed, had never anticipated using it as a dive suit at high pressure, as opposed to more Earthlike atmospheric pressures, or in hard vacuum.

His boot hit something like a step and he took a step up, noting as he did a fractional decrease in the ambient pressure. A step in the right direction.

His suit's AI was smart enough to handle motion detection in a full three-sixty. It wasn't equipped with sonar, unfortunately, but miniature cameras scanned all directions and the AI was smart enough to distinguish between the motion of a potential threat and the movement caused by his own motion through the dancing particles of muck. Even so, he opened a small video window inset in his HUD to show him what was going on behind his back. His shoulder blades were itching with the constant anticipation of one of those amphibious nightmares coming up on him from behind.

What had grabbed him? He'd never seen it clearly and replaying recorded camera images showed him only confused impressions of what might be a tentacle or a big snake, a head with gleaming, green fish-eyes as big as his fist, and a glimpse of something that might have been a mouth lined with needle-sharp teeth.

The emphasis was on the word *might*. He simply could not make much of whatever it was he was seeing, partly because of the poor visibility, and partly, he knew, because he had little with which to compare it.

Mostly, he just knew he didn't want one sneaking up behind him.

Another step up. This was definitely encouraging. He kept moving.

AO Memphis—Beachhead HQ
Sirius Stargate
1450 hours, Shipboard time

"Sir?" Gansen's voice said over the comlink. "Sir, you'd better come down here."

"Why?"

"I think we've just captured ourselves a Wiggler."

"On my way."

"Major Warhurst?" The speaker was the civilian, Dr. Franz. "I and my people should be there!"

Warhurst shook his head inside his helmet. "We can't very well wait for you people," he said. "You're still two hours away." Although *Daring* and *New Chicago* were only a hundred kilometers from the Wheel, the *Chapultepec*, *Ranger*, and the task force supply ships remained several thousand kilometers out. If the Wheel's defenders decided to start shooting at the fleet again, it would be better to lose a battle cruiser or a gunship than the carrier or the Marine transport.

"Nevertheless, *we* are why you people are here!" That was Cynthia Lymon, the PanTerra rep. "We are the ones authorized to make first contact!"

Warhurst was about to give her a sharp reply, then thought better of it. They were there and he was here, and he would take what actions he deemed necessary to carry out his orders. "I would say first contact has already been made," he said. "But take it up with General Ramsey." He broke the connection, then directed Cassius to screen out calls from the civilians. He didn't need that particular distraction right now.

Warhurst had entered the hull access bubble sometime earlier. By this time, all of thirty-some Marines of First Platoon, Alpha Company, had already descended into the pit in the center of the airlock working space, but two squads from Second Platoon were standing by as a security element and two more were in the tunnel. They helped him attach his tether and drop backward into the tunnel entrance and two Marines accompanied him as bodyguards.

Not, he thought, *as if bodyguards could help if the enemy decided to grab me.*

The water started out less than half a meter deep, but the tunnel floor appeared to slope downward toward arbitrary north and was waist deep by the time he reached Gansen and the handful of other Marines on point a hundred meters from the opening. By this time, all of Alpha's First Platoon was in place, forming a horseshoe-shaped perimeter around their prize.

"Okay, gentlemen," he said. "What've we got here?"

HM2 Lee crouched in the water next to a huge gently heaving bulk. "It's unconscious, sir," he said. "The grenades stunned it and it floated to the surface."

"We got three, sir," Gansen told him. "But the other two are dead."

"Let me see."

He studied the being Lee was working on, though he could see the whole form better on his noumenal display as the corpsman carried out his electronic examination. It was large, a good three, almost four meters long . . . most of that taken up by a powerful, muscular body, flattened side to side like a terrestrial eel. It was hard to determine the color under the shifting lights of the Marine armor, but it appeared to be a mottled green-gray, with opalescent highlights. The skin did not appear to be scaly, but had more of a rubbery texture, like the skin of a dolphin, but with an oily sheen. Halfway down the body, a pair of fins, like stubby, clawed hands with heavy webbing, protruded from the being's side and there was a slit on the belly that might have been a hiding place for genitalia or excretory organs. Two long, oddly jointed arms emerged shoulderless from the upper body, each with broad, webbed, six-fingered hands. They appeared designed to fit neatly into grooves along the creature's side, as if to enhance its powerful streamlining.

Strangest of all was the thing's head. The skull was large and elongated and, again, appeared designed to fit into a hollow in the being's back when it was swimming. The neck was articulated, however, to let the head move to a more human-like position atop the body; perhaps it could balance on its tail like a snake, its head and upper body erect. There were obvious gill slits on what might be the chest; their rapid pulsing just beneath the water's surface was all that proved the creature was still alive.

The face was long, angular, and appeared to be encased in a horny black chitin or natural armor. The armor covered the head, the upper torso down as far as the gill slits, and what would have been the shoulders. The being possessed two sets of eyes. The two at the top of its head were large and bone-ringed, as big as a man's fist, flat, and set to either side, like the eyes of a fish, though they appeared to be angled in such a way as to allow stereoscopic vision. They were all pupil and the retinas reflected the surrounding lights with a deep green glow. Below those eyes were a pair of long vertical slits that might be nostrils, or secondary gill slits, or something else entirely, and below those were two more eyes, these small, black, deep-set, and facing full forward. At the bottom, a sharply angular and armored jaw gaped open, exposing a mouth filled with inch-long, needle-sharp teeth.

Warhurst had no doubt that he was looking at one of the creatures the Dogon of Africa called Nommo. "*The whole body of the animal was like that of a fish*," ran the account of Berossus downloaded from Franz's data, "*and had under a fish's head another head, and also feet below, similar to those of a man, subjoined to the fish's tail*." There was only one head, but the two sets of very different eyes on a face twice as long as a human's gave the impression of two faces. Warhurst could understand how a verbal description of the being could be garbled in the telling.

Berossus's history had called the Nommo "animals with reason." The being in the water before Warhurst showed no indication of civilization save one. On the right side of its smooth skull, halfway back, a silver and black device of some sort appeared to be attached to the being's skin . . . or possibly through the skin and into the bone beneath. It was flat and oval in shape, with a crescent symbol in raised relief. But was it technology of some sort or simply a decoration?

He pointed. "What's that?"

"We're not sure yet, Major," Dunne replied. "Doc scanned it and says it reads like it might be full of microcircuitry, but we haven't had time to check it out yet."

So. A device of some sort . . . for communication with others of its kind or possibly for cybernetic enhancement of some sort, like the Marines' implants. He was curious, though. The being before him was obviously supremely adapted to life underwater. How could such a being develop metallurgy and smelting, or radio, computers, and cybernetics? The Marines didn't have the whole story yet, and it would be wise to proceed cautiously until they knew more.

"Doc?" he asked. "How badly is it hurt?"

"I wish I could tell you, sir," Lee replied. He was using a small hand scanner, running it up and down the length of the creature's head and torso. In humans, it would have let him find broken bones or internal bleeding and let him monitor vital signs. "No obvious fractures or hemorrhage, but is a heart rate of 21 normal? How about a body temperature of 32 Celsius? I can't make heads or tails of these brainwave readings. I don't dare administer a stimulant or a nanoinjection. About all I can do is keep the gill slits in the water so it can breathe and hope for the best."

"Do your best, Doc. It would be nice to have a prisoner."

"Yeah. How do we keep him?"

"What do you mean?"

"These things are damned strong, sir," Dunne put in. "I mean, just look at the musculature in that tail. If it decides to leave, there's not a lot we could do about it."

Warhurst thought for a moment. "Use a length of tether material." Though it was not much thicker than a length of fishing line, it was made of monofilament polyweave, long-chain molecules woven around one another with a breaking point in excess of one ton. "Secure the end around his arms and chest."

"Just stand back if he starts thrashing around," Dunne warned. "I think one knocked Garroway clean off his feet with one swipe of its tail and dragged him off."

"Any sign of him?" Warhurst asked.

"Uh . . . maybe, sir. Just this."

A window opened in Warhurst's noumenal vision, showing a scene recorded by Kat Vinton's helmet camera moments ago. He saw the tunnel ahead, partly lit by the lights of the Argus. The cavern wall beyond suddenly flickered three times, as though it were reflecting three rapid flashes of light. The recording's audio element picked up the distant boom of three muffled explosions.

"And that was? . . ."

"We think it was a pig, Major. Three shots, close together, fired from beneath the surface. It was pretty far off, or very weak, or both. Sir, but we think he might have fired to let us know he was still alive."

"I see. What can we do about it?"

"I sent Womicki, Vinton, and Weis out a ways," Gansen said. "The water just keeps getting deeper as the floor drops. Unless we want to walk out there completely submerged, I don't think there's much we *can* do."

"Okay. I'm afraid I agree." He looked at the creature quivering in the water at his feet. "If he's alive, we might be able to communicate. Maybe these . . . *people* understand exchanging prisoners."

It was a hell of a long shot, given that they didn't even know if they could talk with these . . . not people. *Nommo.*

But it was all they had going for them at the moment. If Berossus was right, humans had communicated with the Nommo at least once before, thousands of years ago.

And now the Marines would do it again, if they had to, in order to recover one of their own.

CPL Kat Vinton
The Tunnels, Sirius Stargate
1455 hours, Shipboard time

Kat stood waist deep in the black water, desperately scanning the night ahead of her, looking for some sign, *any* sign, of Gare. Those pig flashes had reflected off the tunnel ceiling in *that* direction a moment ago. Had it been a signal? A cry for help? Or was he fighting for his life somewhere out there in the depths?

"Hey, Kat," Weis called. "C'mon back."

"Yeah," Womicki added. "You can't do him any good out there!"

Only then did she realize she'd moved a good ten meters out ahead of the other two.

"*Fuck*!" she said with a heartfelt intensity.

She and Gare were tight, had been since they'd become lovers on Ishtar an eternity or two ago. But there was more to it than that. He was a fellow Marine.

"Vinton!" called Lieutenant Gansen. "Weis and Womicki, you too. Get back to the platoon perimeter. I don't want to lose anyone else to grabs from underwater!"

"We can't just let them take him, sir!" Kat said.

"Heads up, Marines!" Dunne yelled. "We have movement and IR traces, bearing three-five-one!"

Kat turned, facing a bit west of the direction arbitrarily designated "north." *Something* was happening out there, perhaps a hundred meters up the tunnel. The Argus had a better view and she shifted to the probe's visual feed. At first she thought she was looking at a Marine and her heart gave a quick skip . . . but, no, the helmet was all wrong, too large and too long and it seemed to lack a visor entirely.

Whatever was wading through the water was definitely wearing armor, however, and the black coating made it almost invisible against black metal bulkheads and ink-dark water. It was carrying a weapon too, with arms longer and more massive than a human's. Its infrared signature was low, almost invisibly so; the only reason the Argus was picking it up at all was the fact that water and tunnel background were both quite chilly—only about 8° Celsius—and the armored figure was trailing a faint plume of thermal exhaust.

What Kat was most aware, however, was the fact that the armored figure was *walking*. It appeared to be hunched forward a bit, rather than walking upright, and its legs were hidden by the water, but it was definitely taking steps as it moved.

All of this was glimpsed in a second or two. In the next instant, a bolt of searing white-hot plasma skimmed in across the water, striking the surface a scant few meters in front of the Marine perimeter in a savage flash of steam and spray.

Another bolt came in from arbitrary east, out of the tunnel wall itself, it seemed. Instantly, the Marines returned fire, opening up with pigs and laser rifles in a steady barrage sweeping across the water.

"Come and get some, you bastards!" Lobowski shouted as the exposed surfaces of his chamelearmor flickered light and dark, trying to keep up with the strobing flash of his PG-90. Another plasma bolt exploded against the overhead directly above the Marine perimeter and Baxter screamed and collapsed like a string-cut puppet into the water. Lobowski pivoted to the right, sending a stream of white fire into the darkness from which the shots had come.

"Man down!" Dunne yelled. "Corpsman!"

"On it, Gunny!" Lee shouted.

Kat amplified the contrast in her HUD, using the zoom function to try to zero in on the enemy, but the target picture was confused. The enemy appeared to have dropped underwater, but occasionally one would surface long enough to shoot at the Marine perimeter. The trick was to catch one in the act and take him down before he could fire. She saw water swirl eighty meters out and positioned her aiming cursor over the spot. A second later, the smooth, armored shape of one of those oversized helmets emerged, followed by the thing's shoulders and a two-meter-long pipe that had to be a weapon of some kind. She triggered her 2120 and the target vanished in a splash of water and steam.

She'd hit it, but she couldn't tell if she'd hurt the thing at all.

In fact, it was hard to make sense out of most of what she could see. Light from Lobowski's plasma gun flared and flashed, each shot marked by a burst of static over the radio channels. The cool, wet air in the tunnel was starting to thicken now, as steam and spray filled it with a thin, roiling fog. The Marines' laser bolts were becoming visible now in the close environs of the tunnel, ruby-red pulses briefly illuminating the mist. The aerosol wasn't thick enough yet to degrade the effectiveness of the team's laser weapons yet, but it wouldn't be long.

Enemy plasma weapons fire was coming in from three directions now: north, east and west, folding the Marine perimeter back into a horseshoe shape. Lobowski and the two first section plasma gunners stood at the center, with the two officers beside them, standing upright to get a clear field of fire above the heads of the other Marines in all three directions. The others crouched low, with only their helmets and shoulders above water.

The feed from the Argus probe suddenly died in a burst of static. "Damn! They killed the AR-7!" someone said. No matter. Kat continued to fire, letting her armor's computer identify and highlight the enemy's thermal tails. It was becoming harder to spot them, though, as the air began to heat up in the fight.

They were trying to rush the Marine perimeter. She could see half a dozen of them, now, wading through the water, only their helmets visible. She opened her thumper's range and began dropping RPGs into the middle of the enemy line.

"Thumper" was Marine slang for their Remington M-12 rocket-propelled grenade launchers mounted in an under-barrel configuration on their LR-2120s. It fired, among other things, 20mm RPG high-explosive rounds that, though not as powerful as M-780 grenades, still packed a hefty punch. Blasts ripped through the enemy line, and several of the helmets vanished.

But they were still coming. Damn, where were they coming *from*?

"Second Platoon!" Gansen called. "Get your asses up here!"

"Second Platoon, move up in support of Alpha One," Warhurst amended. "Third Platoon, take up security for the tunnel to the south."

Something large moved in the water to the northeast, only

fifty meters away. Kat had only a glimpse of a broad, muscular tail. "Watch out!" she warned. "They're underwater, too!"

"Weis! Vinton! Donegal! Velasquez!" Dunne yelled. "Use your thumpers! Lay down a blind pattern, thirty to fifty meters!"

Kat interfaced with her weapon through her noumenal display, thought-clicking to set her RPG magazine so that the rounds would detonate one second after impact and no closer than thirty meters from her position. M-12 RPGs could be set to be self-guiding, but with no visible targets, the best they could do would be to lay down a barrage of explosions across a wide area.

She aimed at the spot where she'd just seen something break the water and triggered the M-12. A quick *thump-thump-thump* nudged her shoulder hard as she loosed a three-round burst. Three explosions geysered in the water, one-two-three, and she felt the concussion against the armor encasing her legs.

"Let's get some mike-seven-eighties out there!" Dunne ordered. "Womicki! Tomlinson!"

"Yeah, we'll depth-charge 'em, Gunny!" Womicki yelled back. M-780 grenades sailed out into the tunnel, splashed in the water and, instants later, detonated. The concussion staggered Kat, but she leaned into it and kept firing, alternating now between short bursts from her M-12, and laser fire at anything moving out there she could see.

Corporal Jeff Monroe, from First Platoon's first section, stood up suddenly to take aim at a fast-moving target and then the top of his helmet exploded in a blaze of white light and fragments. He went down, his head vaporized from the eyes up by a plasma bolt. It was impossible to tell if the Marines were hitting anything out there or not, but they continued to lay down a thunderous rapid-fire barrage of bolts from the three PG-90s, augmented by a deadly, interlacing web of laser fire and thumper blasts.

And, suddenly, there was no incoming fire—and no targets.

"Cease fire!" Gansen ordered. "Cease fire!"

For a long moment, the Marines stood in place, watching the water and the drifting mist illuminated by their lights.

The entire firefight had lasted twenty-three seconds, according to Kat's implant clock.

"What the fuck!" Weis exclaimed. "Those things had legs!"

"Two different kinds," Dunne said. "Swimmers, like the one we captured. And something else."

"Okay, so you were saying they're amphibians, like frogs, right?" Cavaco said. "So we got tadpoles and grown-up big frogs. Wiggles and walkers."

"You think maybe the adults are upset 'cause we captured one of their kids?" Alysson Weis asked.

"If the kids are fucking noncombatants," Lobowski growled, "they should stay the hell out of the firefight!"

Kat looked at the captured alien, which was still lying half-submerged and unconscious at the center of the Marine perimeter. The creature was so . . . *alien.*

"They may not have the same notions about warfare we do," she pointed out.

"If they have parental feelings," Dunne said, "we can use that. Make them talk."

"Maybe," Warhurst said. "But right now we don't know what they're feeling. And maybe it's something that it's just not possible for humans to understand."

CPL John Garroway
Sirius Stargate,
Lower Tunnels
1455 hours, Shipboard time

A series of overlapping platforms, like broad flat steps, had led Garroway higher and higher until, abruptly, his helmet broke through the surface of the water.

He emerged cautiously. This was not the broad tunnel he'd been in when the Nommo had grabbed him. This area was small, almost cramped, with a ceiling low enough to touch. The air pressure here, at 1.17 atmospheres, was half again higher than it had been in the upper tunnel. This, then, must be an air pocket at least five meters below the level where the Marines had entered the Wheel.

"Alpha Company!" he called over the company channel. "Alpha Company, this is Gare! Do you copy?"

No answer. Not that he'd expected one with all of that steel and water between him and his comrades. He eyed the black overhead with a deepening frustration. Not only was that barrier blocking his attempts to radio the other Marines, but it also meant he was *lost*, even if he knew exactly in which direction they were. Part of his journey here had been a free-fall descent through the water, and if there were steps that would allow him to walk back that way, he didn't know how to find them. He was trapped in a three-dimensional maze and he had no way of knowing how to get back up to the upper tunnel level.

What logic told him, however, was that if the air pressure in this cave or pocket was higher than the pressure at the break-in point, then he would have to go back underwater to find a way up there . . . if there was one.

Something moved in the shadows, ten meters away.

Garroway pivoted, bringing the muzzle of his PG-90 into line with the half-glimpsed shadow. He could see nothing on optical wavelengths, and only a fuzzy smear of light green against dark on infrared. His finger tightened on the firing switch . . . but at the last instant he checked himself. Whatever was out there was not threatening. Watching, yes, but not an immediate threat. Hell, with their antimatter beam weapons, they could have fried him the instant he broke the surface.

The question was: Why hadn't they?

"Who's there?" he said, using his armor's external speakers. He knew they wouldn't understand English, but might they hear his voice and know he wanted to talk?

Shadows separated from shadows in a dark alcove up ahead. It took him a moment to sort through the confused visual impressions. Even with his armor lights illuminating the thing, it was hard to tell what he was looking at.

First of all, it was *black*, as black as Marine Mark VIII vac armor was in space, drinking any light that hit it. It was also somewhat humanoid—two legs, two long arms, and an upright stance.

Well, mostly upright. The torso jutted forward, counterbalanced by what appeared to be a short tail. The head was very large and neckless, emerging from the body seamlessly. Garroway spent several frustrating moments trying to identify facial features on the smooth, curved surface of what must be the thing's head before he realized that what he was looking at was another technologically advanced being wearing a suit of armor of some sort. The thing was walking straight toward him, holding what very obviously was a heavy weapon of some kind.

And that weapon was aimed directly at Garroway's head.

19

CPL John Garroway
Sirius Stargate,
Lower Tunnels
1458 hours, Shipboard time

The armored form continued to advance until it was five meters away from Garroway. Garroway kept his PG-90 trained
on it as it continued to aim at him, but something about its
purposeful advance made him hold his fire. If it had wanted
to kill him, it could have done so from the relative safety of
the shadows. Why was it emerging into the glare of Garroway's suit lights?

Then it stopped, elevating its torso into a full upright posture, using the short, thick tail as the third leg of a tripod. The
two stared at one another for a long moment. White vapor,
like fog, spilled from vents in the side torso of the being's armor. Then, slowly, with great deliberation, it raised the muzzle of the weapon it was carrying until it was aimed at the
overhead.

"*Gaba dadru,*" the thing said in a voice like the crinkle of
metal foil, but in a deep bass register. "*Im'haru da setak ni
ingal.*"

"Sorry, buddy," Garroway replied. "I don't understand a
word you're saying."

The alien's weapon had something like a pistol grip at the back end and a horizontal carrying handle halfway up the muzzle. Very cautiously, the being turned sideways and lowered the weapon once more, taking care not to point it at Garroway as it laid the device on the black metal deck. Turning to face him once more, it raised both arms, unfolding them, opening the armored hands to display six fingers on each.

Okay . . . it was showing him it held no weapons. That was encouraging.

The two looked at one another for a long moment. At least, Garroway assumed it was looking at him, studying him as he was studying it. With nothing like eyes, cameras, or helmet visor as a reference, he could only guess where its attention might be directed.

Slowly, making no sudden movements, Garroway pivoted his PG-90 on its torso mount so that the muzzle was pointing harmlessly at the overhead and locked it in place. Unfastening it from its universal mount was a complex process, one that might easily be misunderstood. With the weapon aimed up, he spread his own arms, opening his hands. "See?" he said. "Nothing up my sleeves."

"*Inki nagal. Nam iritru.*"

"Right. Whatever you say, friend."

One thing was clear. The being standing in front of him was not one of the eel-like, fish-eyed creatures he'd encountered in the water. It was smaller, *had* to be smaller, no longer than three meters, counting the tail. The arms were longer and more pronounced. It might have been an illusion created by the armor, but this thing had shoulders.

Was this a representative of the Nommo? Or were the eels, the aquatic creatures, the Nommo?

According to Dr. Franz, the Nommo who'd visited Earth all those thousands of years ago had been amphibious, which had led to speculation among the Marines that they might have a two-part life cycle, like frogs. The long-tailed eels might be the juveniles then. It didn't make a lot of sense that the children should be larger than the parents, but maybe they absorbed the tail, the way tadpoles absorbed their tails on the way to becoming frogs.

And there was something else to think about. The Nommo who'd visited Earth and possibly given birth to the ancient Sumerian civilization had been starfarers who'd crossed light-years to teach primitive humans such things as agriculture, mathematics, astronomy, metalworking, and writing. How the hell did a *fish* develop metalworking? You needed fire, first of all, and you needed to learn that heating certain rocks yielded a hot liquid that could be poured into molds to create tools. While Garroway was prepared to accept that an undersea civilization might learn to use the heat from volcanic vents or undersea lava flows for various purposes and even develop a fairly advanced knowledge of chemistry that way, he had trouble imagining something like a terrestrial dolphin—even one with hands—learning about fire or the smelting of metals.

Or astronomy, for that matter. Was someone who lived underwater even *aware* of the stars or able to dream of somehow reaching them?

This being standing a few meters in front of him was certainly advanced technologically, judging from its armor. If its kind had built the Wheel, that was more impressive yet.

Still moving slowly, he pointed at the being. "Nommo?" he asked.

And the creature jumped as though prodded by a stick.

Major Martin Warhurst
Alpha Company, First Platoon
Upper Tunnels, Sirius Stargate
1504 hours, Shipboard time

Warhurst watched as the Marines completed tying the captured Nommo, securing its arms to its sides and creating a kind of harness with the monofilament-woven tether material with four leads. A Marine held the end of each lead, so if the being woke up they could keep it immobilized between them.

He hoped.

He opened a private channel. "General Ramsey? Warhurst."

"Yes, Martin?"

Warhurst blinked. That was, he thought, the first time Ramsey had ever called him by his first name—an indicator, perhaps, of the strain the man was under back onboard the *Chapultepec*. "Sir, are you getting all of this?"

"Yes, I am. Clear feed."

"Do you think we should bring Franz and his people in on this? They're the experts, and when this thing wakes up—"

"I'm ahead of you, son. They're already linked in."

"Indeed, Major," Franz's voice added. "You cut us off, so we went to General Dominick. He put us through to General Ramsey with the express order that we be consulted!"

Warhurst blinked. With his full attention on the landing and the fight for the beachhead, he'd actually forgotten about the mission's senior staff: Major General Dominick and his people. So far, this had been purely a Marine operation, as it originally had been designed.

But with a prisoner, that would change.

"So, are you bringing the captured Nommo back to the *Chapultepec*?" Franz demanded. "Or are we coming down there?"

"One step at a time, Doctor," Ramsey cautioned. "Our mission directives include the *very* clear order that you and your staff be kept safe. The Wheel beachhead is not yet secure. Until that time, you'll have to work from the command center onboard the *Pecker*."

"Officious nonsense! I need to be there!"

"Tell me, Doctor," Ramsey said in an evident attempt to head him off before pique became a full-blown tantrum. "Will you be able to talk with the Nommo?"

"Eh? Oh . . . that. I hope so. I suspect so. You see, I've downloaded both the Sumerian language and the principal An dialect, which turns out to be very closely related. Sumerian shows no linguistic relationship with other ancient languages in the Fertile Crescent, you see, and we now suspect that it was the language of the An who colonized the area nine or ten thousand years ago. If the Nommo arrived later—say, at the beginning of the Sumerian era, oh, seven to eight thousand years ago—they may well have communicated with the locals in that language, either because they already had trade relations with the An or because they were able to learn the principal human language and—"

"Yes, yes," Ramsey said. "The important thing is that we can question our prisoner when he revives. *If* he revives."

"I don't think that's going to be a problem, General," Warhurst told him. He took a step back. The Nommo had evidently just become aware of its surroundings. That magnificent, rainbow-flashing tail suddenly coiled tight, then flashed out and around, knocking two Marines down and forcing the others back a few steps. Water exploded as the creature writhed and struggled, its upper torso rising until it was a head taller than the tallest Marine there.

"Watch it!" Dunne cried. "Damn it! Get him under control!"

The two Marines still holding the ends of tethers securing the Nommo leaned back and pulled them taut. The two Marines who'd been knocked down waded back in, recovering the ends of their tethers and adding their strength to the others until, gradually, the creature's struggles eased somewhat. After a few more thrashes, it slipped back into the water then and lay there, gill slits pulsing rapidly, regarding them with its unwinking and alien quartet of eyes.

"Cassius?" Warhurst said. "Can you talk with it?"

"I have been attempting to access the Nommo through what appears to be a communications network link accessed via the device affixed to its head," Cassius replied. "Communication may be possible, but it will take some time."

"How much time?"

"Unknown, Major. Working."

Warhurst glared at the being. Right now, the welfare of one of his men might well depend on how quickly the Marines could learn to speak with it.

So too might the success of the mission.

He did not like delays caused by factors utterly beyond his control.

"Major?" It was Gansen.

"What?"

"Gunnery Sergeant Dunne suggests that we fan out through this part of the tunnel complex. We're sitting ducks here, out in the open. He thinks we should try to find the tunnels the Nommo were coming out of and set up secure fields of fire or ambush points."

"And what do *you* think, Lieutenant?"

"Uh, yessir. I think it's a good idea."

"Do it. But maintain a secure perimeter here until we know what to do with our, ah, guest."

"Aye aye, sir!"

He watched Gansen begin giving the necessary orders. The man had a way to go, but he appeared to be learning, seemed to be shaping up. The best thing a company commander had going for him was his willingness to listen to his senior NCOs.

After a moment, he began giving orders of his own. He wanted Bravo Company down here and more heavy weapons and he wanted to ring in General Ramsey. The Marines were through with this passive defense nonsense.

It was time to take the fight to the enemy.

Major General Cornell Dominick
Command Center
CVS *Ranger*
1504 hours, Shipboard time

"And just who, General," the woman asked sweetly, "is in command of this expedition?"

Dominick groaned. He'd had this debate—or others like it—before, especially during the past few days since their emergence from cybehibe as they entered the Sirius system.

Deliberately, he opened his eyes. He was lying on his link couch, set up in one corner of the Operations Center onboard the UFR/USS carrier *Ranger*. Colonel Helen Albo was watching him with concern in her eyes. "General? Are you okay?"

"Yes, Colonel."

"You groaned and looked like you were in pain. Do you want a Corpsman?"

"Negative." He bit off the word.

He looked around. Except for Helen, the other four members of his command constellation were on their couches as well, linked in to the far-flung communications network uniting the ships and personnel of the expedition.

"Sir . . ."

"I said I'm okay," he snapped. "I just have some . . . issues to work out." He closed his eyes, shutting out Albo and the members of his staff, forcing himself to relax once again into the noumenon of his private command link.

Half a dozen channels were open, each a separate data

feed from Admiral Harris's command center, from Ramsey's CC, from the surface of the Wheel. In his mind's eye, he was seated within a circular arena, surrounded by data screens and communications links, computer feeds and data access stations. He'd designed this noumenal place himself, with the help of some very sophisticated AI software, and it was both efficient and comfortable . . . at least, usually.

Unfortunately, Cynthia Lymon, PanTerra's representative on this mission, was still there, waiting, her icon hovering beside his chair.

He did not like this woman.

"Did you hear me?" she asked him. Lymon had the unpleasant ability to put a grating, cloying sweetness into her voice and mannerisms. People tended to read that as fluff . . . and underestimate the woman.

Dominick was determined never to do that. "I heard. And you know the command chain as well as I do. *I* am in overall command of Operation Battlespace. I am directly answerable to the Interstellar Operations Initiative Team back on Earth and to the Joint Chiefs of Staff. Admiral Harris is in command of all fleet operations in Sirius space, while General Ramsey commands the Marine element. It is Ramsey who runs the show on the Wheel and in the space immediately around it, at least until the beachhead is formally declared secure. All tactical decisions are in his hands until that time.

"And until that time, you and I, Ms. Lymon, are here in little more than an advisory capacity. If I'm not mistaken, you signed a document to that effect before embarking on this expedition."

"Cornell, be reasonable," Lymon said. "I can read an org chart as well as you. And, yes, I did promise to be a good girl and not to stick my nose into the military's business. But there are certain realities here that transcend military considerations. And one of them is General Order One."

"General Order One does not apply to the current situation."

"No?" she asked sweetly. "And when *does* it apply? After we've killed every Nommo over there? After we've reduced the Wheel to a cloud of radioactive debris? What then?"

General Order One described, in exacting detail, what military forces operating outside of Earth's atmosphere were expected to do in the event that they encountered either intelligent aliens or their AI representatives. It had happened with the An on Ishtar. It had happened before that with the discovery of the Singer, the intelligent Hunter spacecraft lost in the depths of the Europan world-ocean. In both cases, the outcome of first contact had been less than optimal. The An had attacked and wiped out the first human trade mission established on their world, while the Singer had turned out to be hopelessly insane after half a million years trapped beneath the Europan ice.

The document was a part of every AI database in the MIEU and had been downloaded to every officer by order of the JCS itself. It was supposed to be the bible that would direct any first contact with any new intelligent civilization among the stars.

And in Dominick's opinion, the document was also seriously flawed . . . even though he'd had a hand in drafting the thing. It attempted to simultaneously ensure that any first contact would be peaceful, to protect Earth from the expected consequences of stumbling into the Hunters of the Dawn, and to secure for Earth—and PanTerra in particular—access to advanced alien technologies.

"General Order One," he told Lymon, "is a guide to establishing peaceful relations with an XT civilization. In this case, the XTs started shooting at *us*, remember?"

"Article Five," she told him primly, "specifically states that every effort will be made to establish peaceful relations, even in the event that hostilities have already broken out. Article Seven states that, at all costs, the technological infrastructure of any alien civilization—and that specifically includes cities, bases, and spacecraft—are to be preserved intact for study by competent authorities.'"

"Actually, it says 'where feasible,' " he reminded her. "Not 'at all costs.' Furthermore, the military commander at the scene has the final responsibility of determining just what the word *feasible* means." He didn't add that his orders included provisions for destroying the Sirius stargate with a nuclear device, should he deem that necessary in order to keep the Hunters of the Dawn away from Earth.

It couldn't be any other way. Earth was ten years away by starship, seventeen years away for a two-way exchange of lasercom or radio messages. *He* had the final say when it came to whether Earth would study the Wheel—or destroy it.

It was an awesome responsibility, one that he took very seriously.

"Cornell," she said. Damn it, he hated it when she used his first name, as though they were friends or intimates. "Just remember who's paying for all of this and just what we have riding on this mission. FTL, instantaneous interstellar communication, gravity control, the gods alone know what else. We could have it *all* if we play things right."

"Yes, and if we screw up, Ms. Lymon," he told her, "we could have the Hunters of the Dawn a mere eight light-years from Earth and looking for blood! I would very happily exchange my chance at some stock options for the security of my home!"

Lymon sighed. "Why did you volunteer for this? For the command of this expedition? It's not as though you were making a smart career move."

"That," he told her angrily, "is not your business."

"But that's where you're wrong, Cornell. Everything concerned with this expedition is my business." Her icon cocked its head to one side and smiled. "I gather your wife divorced you."

Damn the woman! Cornell Dominick had been a member of one of the older and more well-connected of Washington's line marriages—the Cabot Line, eighteen men and fifteen women, at last count, and all of them well-connected politically, financially, and socially. They'd voted him out a year before Operation Battlespace had been conceived, largely because he'd become a political liability to the family. It seemed the Cabot family favored United Federalism and Mexican Annexation, while he, personally, had been leaning toward the Free Social Isolationists—which meant hands off Mexico and tariff restrictions on the global corps . . . like PanTerra. When his views had become known in a Triple-N interview, he'd become an embarrassment to the family and been eased out. The separation package had been generous, but the embarrassment, the public humiliation, had been unbearable. . . .

"So?" he snapped. "That's not your business either."

"General Dominick," she said. "You quite literally stand at the crossroads of history. If you successfully negotiate a workable peace with the Nommo, one which gives PanTerra access to the technologies we *know* to be implicit within this stargate, you will return to Earth richer and more powerful than you could possibly imagine. The shame of your divorce would be expunged. You will be able to write your own ticket with the Cabots and every other old-money family you can think of. You will have the money, the name, and the connections to pursue whatever political or social goals you might have for yourself.

"If, God forbid, this mission fails—if, in particular, you end up destroying this asset—you will be remembered as the Social Isolationist who panicked and cut Earth off from the stars."

"Or I might be remembered as the man who saved Earth," he pointed out. "Have you thought of that? Humankind can't stand up to the Hunters of the Dawn."

"If they even exist."

"Maybe they don't. But someone destroyed the *Wings of Isis*, remember. They were hostile and they wielded unimaginable power. I will destroy the stargate if I believe that to be the only way to ensure Earth's safety. I would be Earth's savior."

"Not after PanTerra's publicity department is done with you," she told him.

"Damn you and your threats—"

"Now, now, Cornell. I'm not making threats. I'm just reminding you where the power really lies. On Earth, it's the global corps, of course, but out here it lies with us. You and me, working together. On *our* shoulders rests the future of Humankind! I simply want to be sure you're keeping that in mind."

"Believe me," he told her. "I think of very little else."

With deliberate rudeness, he broke off the noumenal link and returned to the real-world environment of his control deck.

In any case, events weren't in his hands at the moment—or even in hers. They lay in the armored hands of the men and women of the Marines onboard the Wheel.

CPL John Garroway
Sirius Stargate,
Lower Tunnels
1504 hours, Shipboard time

"Nommo?" Garroway asked again, pointing.

The being in front of him touched its chest with one hand. *"N'mah!"* it replied, the voice a deep rumble crisp with static.

Nommo, N'mah. Close enough. And there was something about the alien's language that was . . . not familiar, exactly, but it was as if he'd heard the language—or one much like it, before. The cadence, the sharply distinguished syllables, sounded much like the language of the An.

Garroway wasn't much of a linguist. On Ishtar the Marines had been linked through their implants to a language database that let them translate what the An were saying, and to make themselves understood, and the word was that the Marines had access to the same database here, just in case the Wheel's inhabitants spoke either An or ancient Sumerian, which was supposed to be related.

As he understood it, though, the word *nommo* was supposed to be from the Dogon language, the speech of the primitive tribes people in sub-Saharan Africa who'd retained the myth of the Nommo's arrival in their stories and lore. According to Franz's information, it was supposed to mean something like "guardian" or "monitor."

Or . . . had the star-beings who'd landed somewhere in the Fertile Crescent called themselves "N'mah," and the humans later assigned the meaning to the name?

Without his database link, Garroway couldn't try speaking to the creature in the Sumerian-An pidgin developed on Ishtar. But he did remember a few words. *Ki* was one, the Sumerian word for "Earth." He remembered that one because he'd been told that the word *geos*, as in "geology," had been derived from the Greek *ge*, pronounced with a hard *g*, and that that had derived originally from the Sumerian *ki*.

Damn it, what was the Sumerian–Ahannu word for "human"?

Adamu, that was it. Just like Adam, the mythical first man in Genesis. The word, he'd been told, was actually a kind of Sumerian slang, a name meaning "blackhead." The hairless Ahannu had evidently named their human slaves for their most distinguishing characteristic, at least in their alien eyes—the dark thatch of hair sprouting from the tops of their heads. Only much later did a play on words connect the name "Adam" with the Hebrew *adhamah*, the word for "ground," and the belief that the God of Genesis had fashioned the first man from dust or dirt.

Touching his own chest, he said "*Adamu*." And, to drive home the point, he added, "*Ki. Adamu. Ki.*"

He wished he could remember more or that he had an electronic connection with the linguistic database. He could remember fragments. There was a Sumerian word, something like *lu-u* or *lu-lu*, that was also supposed to mean "human," but he didn't want to try using that. It literally meant something like "worker" or "slave" and derived from the long period of time when the colonizing An had used the local human population as slaves.

Telling the being before him that he was a slave was not, Garroway thought, the best way to impress him.

Damn it, how did you impress someone who didn't speak your language or share any part of your cultural background?

"*N'mah*," the being rumbled once again, indicating itself. It then pointed at Garroway. "*Ki-a-d'hammu. Sugah ni-gal-lu.*"

Well, that was a start, of sorts. Garroway remembered another phrase . . . the name bestowed upon the Marines on Ishtar after the fighting there was over. He touched his chest. "*Nir-gál-mè-a*," he said, hoping he had the pronunciation right. According to what he'd heard, the phrase meant the same both in the An dialect and in ancient Sumerian—"respected in battle." No harm in negotiating from a position of strength. . . .

But suddenly the being was no longer alone. Other armored forms, three of them, emerged from the shadows, holding weapons, all of them aimed directly at Garroway.

"Was it something I said?" he asked . . . and released his weapons mount lock, letting the PG-90 drop back to the horizontal.

It looked to him like a Mexican standoff. How many could he get, he wondered, before they flamed him?

"*Dagah ni-mir-gala!*" the first Nommo said, and then it

rumbled something halfway between a gargle and a choke. The three newcomers stopped their advance, weapons wavering uncertainly, and they began gargling as well.

It took Garroway a moment to realize they were speaking a language very different in intonation and character from the Sumerian-sounding speech. This one sounded like it didn't rely on words at all; if there *were* words in that mess, Garroway couldn't recognize them as such.

At least no one was aiming a weapon at him for the moment. He chanced a look around, wondering if he could slip away. The argument was growing heated.

Not *that* way. One of the big aquatic beings was in the deeper water at his back, unmoving, its dark eyes glittering in the light from Garroway's armor. It appeared to simply be . . . watching.

Abruptly, the gargling ceased. The first Nommo turned to face Garroway, holding out its left hand. "*Gah nam-edah!*" it said and Garroway heard the sharpness in its voice. Anger? Impatience? How could you tell? The sharp waggling gesture with its six fingers, however, was unmistakable. It was telling him to come along and quickly.

Garroway hesitated. Was it ordering him to surrender? Or was something else going on? Once again, the aliens didn't need to *ask*. They could have burned him down where he stood or overpowered him easily enough. Hell, they could have shot him from the shadows before he'd even known they were there.

The being reached up with both hands and touched some sort of pressure plate or button at the base of its helmet. With a sharp hiss and a small cloud of vapor, the large helmet split longitudinally, separating from the rest of the armor. The Nommo lifted the helmet off of its shoulders, exposing its naked head.

The face, Garroway saw, was much like the long, double-decker face of the aquatic beings. It didn't have the fist-sized goggle-eyes of a fish on top, however. Instead, all four eyes were small, deep-set, and jet black. Clearly, these guys were closely related to the aquatic beings who'd grabbed him in the first place, but whether the resemblance was that of an adult to a juvenile . . . or of a chimpanzee to a human, he simply couldn't tell.

"Gah nam-edah!" it said again.

"Okay," Garroway said. It was a nasty choice. He could refuse to be taken prisoner and open fire. If that happened, he would almost certainly be killed . . . or knocked down and captured anyway. Or he could trust these weird and alien beings—the one that had removed its helmet, anyway—and go along.

Very slowly, careful to make no sudden moves, he reached down and unlocked the mounting for his PG-90, keeping the muzzle pointed away from the Nommo. With a click, the weapon disengaged. He lowered it to the black metal at his feet, stood up straight, and raised his hands, palms out, fingers spread . . . just as he'd seen the first Nommo do.

"I'm all yours," he said. *Marines*, he thought, *never surrender*.

But sometimes it paid to stay flexible.

20

Corporal Kat Vinton
Alpha Company, First Platoon
Upper Tunnels, Sirius Stargate
1523 hours, Shipboard time

Kat was completely familiar with the idea of a chain of command. Corporals did *not* go straight to battalion commanders with crazy ideas, nor did they inform them what they had to do.

In fact, she wasn't thinking of chains of command at the moment. Major Warhurst was *there*, the man she'd served under at Ishtar, a Marine officer whom she respected completely, and whose orders she would willingly follow no matter where they led. *Semper fi.*

"Major Warhurst! Sir!"

"What is it, Corporal?"

A century or two before, Kat wouldn't even have been able to get close to the battalion CO, nor would she have had access to his command communications channel. But the MIEU was wired top to bottom and back to the top again for complete communications interface at all levels.

And better yet, Major Warhurst was approachable. It wasn't something to abuse, but it was there when you needed it. And, damn it, she needed it.

"Sir, if there's a chance we can get Gare back by turning the alien loose, well, I say we should do it, sir!"

"Corporal!" Gansen snapped. "You're out of line!"

"It's okay, Lieutenant," Warhurst said. "I was thinking pretty much the same thing myself."

"They want a prisoner pretty bad back in the fleet, sir."

"I'm well aware of that."

The alien appeared alert and unharmed. It waited quietly in the water, gill slits pulsing with its breathing, its strange eyes, unblinking, watching every move the Marines around it made. Four Marines held it in place with tethers pulled taut and two more stood close by, their LR-2120s trained on it.

"Gunny?" Warhurst asked. "What do you think?"

"Can't say, Major. Hell, chances are, we let it go and it goes back and tells its friends what patsies the Marines are. Still, we seem to be in this thing deeper than we expected. If there's a chance to stop hostilities and talk to these . . . people, then we ought to take it. Sir."

Kat heard Warhurst's sigh over the channel. "I agree. Unfortunately, this is one that has to be bucked up the ladder. Wait one, everybody."

She found herself holding her breath as he took up the question with his superiors.

General T. J. Ramsey
Command Control Center
UFR/USS Chapultepec
1525 hours, Shipboard time

"No fucking way, General Ramsey! Absolutely not!"

"Watch your noumenal language, General," Ramsey told Dominick pleasantly. "There are ladies present."

"What's wrong with his language?" Dr. Franz asked.

Despite her anger, Lymon laughed, a harsh splash of emotion. "Obscenity, Doctor. The freaming Marines are old-fashioned that way. Zakking milslabs."

Ramsey considered this statement with a part of his mind. Until now, the civilians with the MIEU had shown little evidence of the linguistic and cultural rifts that had been developing over the years between time-lagged Marines and the rest of Humankind. In her anger, however, Cynthia Lymon appeared to be reverting to type, and a distinctly hostile them-against-us mind-set. Fascinating . . .

But not germane. "General, this may be a God-given opportunity to establish peaceful relations with the Nommo. I agree with Major Warhurst's assessment. We should let the prisoner go and see what happens."

The statement elicited another barrage of protest and Ramsey sighed. His skull was feeling very crowded just now. The conference was being held noumenally, of course, and it included all four of the civilian advisors, General Dominick and his staff, Admiral Harris and his staff, as well as Ramsey's own command constellation. Damn it, it *hurt* when everyone shouted at once.

Cassius was providing the visual feed. In his mind's eye, they were seated at a large circular conference table, surrounded by star-dusted space. The Wheel, seen from an oblique aspect, hung overhead. Ramsey wondered if that was a deliberate bit of very human psychology on the part of Cassius. The enormity, the sheer mass of that huge and alien device suspended in space just above them seemed calculated to focus the discussion, a Damoclean sword twenty kilometers across.

"People, people, *please*!" Admiral Harris put in. "This is getting us nowhere! General Ramsey, I have to agree with General Dominick. So long as we keep him in the tunnels, the prisoner is not secure. We could lose him if the Nommo attack again."

Ramsey thought about the old joke about the differences in

how the various military arms defined the word *secure* and suppressed a smile.

"Must I remind you, General," Dominick asked Ramsey evenly, "that this is a *military* operation and that gathering intelligence, through POWs and other means, is absolutely vital in that regard?"

"No, General. You needn't remind me. I'm very much aware of the fact. I'm also aware that our intelligence on this operation so far has been zip—hell, it's been in the negative numbers. We came out here with seven ships and twelve hundred Marines. We were told that there *might* be a crew resident on this thing, but that the Marines were primarily along to secure this facility . . . as if it were nothing more than a large spacecraft or orbital base!

"We get here and find the place apparently inhabited—and quite well defended. From the data feeds I've seen so far, there's a *world* inside that thing, though, admittedly, we haven't seen much of it yet except for the sewers."

"General Ramsey!" Dominick said, trying to regain control of the discussion. "Possible failures of intelligence here are not the point! And I am most disappointed in your attempt to shift the blame for your military setback to poor intelligence. We have before us now the chance to rectify any gaps in the overall intel picture . . . a prisoner to interrogate. I suggest that we take advantage of the opportunity that's been given to us."

Ramsey bit down on what he'd been about to say. He was angry, but venting at these people would accomplish nothing. He took a deep breath. "And I suggest, General, that a reality check is in order here. Twelve hundred Marines is not sufficient to conquer a world. They're not sufficient to conquer a *city* when absolutely nothing is known about that city's layout, population, or technological resources!"

"It's *not* a world, General," Lymon put in. "Or a city. It's a large structure, yes, but calling it a city is a freaming exaggeration . . . and a diversion from your failure to take the thing as ordered."

"I repeat, General," Dominick said. "We can fill in the gaps in our intelligence picture simply by interrogating our prisoner."

"Dr. Franz?" Ramsey said. "You're on record as saying that you can learn to talk to these people. But how likely is that if we have to learn how from one POW . . . and one who may not feel like cooperating."

"Well, that's hard to say—"

"Cassius!"

"Yes, General?" The AI's evenly modulated voice seemed to come out of the air above the virtual conference table.

"Have you made any progress interfacing with the prisoner's communications hardware?"

"No, General. Not beyond purely superficial scans of the hardware in question. The prisoner is wearing a sophisticated communications device of some kind and there is evidence that it may have implanted technology within its brain as well, technology similar in concept, at least, to that used by humans. But any such resemblance is purely superficial. I cannot interface with alien software and will not be able to do so, not, at least, within a reasonable amount of time."

"And there you have it, gentlemen and ladies," Ramsey told the human members of the group. "We can attempt to interrogate our prisoner, an alien with whom we have no shared language or technology. In the meantime, we attempt to maintain our toehold on the Wheel, against unknown numbers and unknown technical potential. We have already suffered over fifty casualties, most of those KIA, and we've been on the beach for just three and a half hours. How much higher is the butcher's bill supposed to get before we realize we've made a terrible mistake, here?"

"General—" Admiral Harris began.

"*Or* we can take advantage of this opportunity and make a

kind of spontaneous, free-will offering, to see if we can enlist the Nommos' cooperation."

"Now I've heard everything," Lymon said. "A Marine who doesn't want to fight."

"That's not the point and you know it, Ms. Lymon. The point isn't to fight, but to gain access to the Wheel. And if the Marines *have* to fight, we're going to do it intelligently!"

"General, I appreciate your position," Dominick said. "Completely. But this is a matter for consultation with the appropriate civilian government authorities, not a decision that can be made by the military alone."

"Civilian government authorities?" Ramsey asked. "What civilian government authorities? Earth is eight light-years away!"

"Which, I remind you, is why *we* are here as representatives of that authority, General," Lymon said. He could hear the acid in her noumenal voice. "The military carries out policy. The civilian authority sets it. That is the way things have to be."

"Agreed. For policy. But the government does not tell the Marines how to carry out a landing. They set policy, not strategy and not tactics."

"General, be reasonable," Lymon said. "That prisoner represents undreamed-of advances in technology for Earth."

A side window opened in Ramsey's mind. It startled him, for he'd not ordered it. It was, he saw, a private channel linking him with Lymon. "We need that prisoner, General Ramsey!" her voice said. "You could find cooperation extremely profitable for yourself. We're talking about, quite literally, billions of newdollars, if you play this right—"

"*Get the fuck out of my head, lady!*" He slammed the noumenal window shut. Damn it, how had she been able to hijack his implant protocols that way?

"I don't want to make this an order, General Ramsey," Dominick was saying on the main conference channel. He'd not heard the brief exchange with Lymon. "But I am in overall command of this expedition, which means it's my responsibility to determine overall strategy. You will order your men to pull back out of the tunnel, and have them bring the prisoner with them."

There it was . . . an order. If he refused, he was guilty of mutiny. He could be relieved, arrested, and court-martialed. Dominick, likely, would take over direct command of the Marines.

Ramsey, however, knew he had one thing going for him. In combat, nothing is static, and the situation is constantly changing. What he needed here was time. *Enough* time, and the situation would resolve itself, one way or another.

"Very well, General," he said. "I will give the necessary orders. But I do so under strong protest."

"Your protest is noted, General."

"The units currently in the tunnels are still engaged with the enemy," he added. Technically, that was quite true, even though the last Nommo attack appeared to have broken off. "They will need time to regroup and fall back to the entryway."

"He's stalling!" Lymon snapped.

"No, ma'am," Colonel Maitland, the Battalion Executive Officer, said. "General Ramsey is quite right. Withdrawing in the face of the enemy is one of the trickiest military maneuvers there is, and by far the most dangerous."

Ramsey relaxed slightly. Howard Maitland was a quiet man who rarely spoke, but when he did he always seemed to know exactly the right words to say.

"We will do this by the book," Ramsey added. "I will *not* lose more men and women needlessly out there."

This, he thought, *is not over. . . .*

Major Martin Warhurst
Alpha Company, First Platoon

Upper Tunnels, Sirius Stargate
1532 hours, Shipboard time

Evacuate the prisoner back to the fleet . . . and fall back to the entrance to the tunnels—taking all appropriate precautions to preserve the unit's security—and prepare to evacuate to the surface. Warhurst had his orders, but he didn't like them. He still had one man missing, and he'd already deployed some twenty Marines forward, probing the tunnels from which that last attack had been launched.

"Damn it to hell," he snapped.

It was the micromanagement that grated more than anything else. He didn't blame Ramsey; the general knew the score, and was doing the best for the Marines he could. But Warhurst had the feeling that Dominick and the civilians were calling the shots now.

And that spelled trouble, big time.

"Major Warhurst? I have a suggestion."

"Yes, Cassius! What is it?" Warhurst was surprised. The command constellation's AI was available at all times for inquiries, but it rarely volunteered information. Cassius was intelligent and probably was even self-aware by most definitions of the words, but his creative initiative was limited, at least in human terms.

"The alien prisoner clearly requires both air and water for survival," Cassius said. "Removing it from this environment could easily kill it."

Warhurst blinked. "I believe the plan calls for using an emergency escape bag. One of the large ones ought to accommodate our friend, at least for the time it would take to get him onboard a TRAP."

EEBs were standard issue gear onboard TRAPs and most other spacecraft. They were plastic bags tough enough to resist hard vacuum. A crewman onboard a disabled spacecraft or station could climb inside one, seal it tight, and have air enough to breathe while space-suited companions moved him to safety. They came in various sizes; the largest could accommodate four humans, and ought to be large enough for a four-meter-long Wiggle.

"Indeed. But the being also evidently requires water. HM2 Lee's medical scans suggest that it possesses lungs as well as gills, but the lungs appear to be somewhat atrophied, and the being does exhibit signs of respiration distress when its gills are exposed to air for more than a few minutes."

"Well, we put some water in the bag. . . ."

"We have no way of knowing whether the being will be able to breathe once the EEB is moved into zero gravity. The water would float around inside the bag as small globules, and the being might well not be able to breathe. Nor do we know how it will respond psychologically to being put in a bag and dragged into microgravity conditions. I also question whether any number of Marines could manhandle the being into a bag if it decided it did not want to go."

Warhurst smiled. "You know, Cassius, I think you've bought us some time."

"In addition, Major, I submit that removing the prisoner from these tunnels would constitute a direct violation both of Article IV of the Jerusalem Accords, and of General Order One."

General Order One made removing an alien being from its natural habitat in such a way that its life was at risk a crime punishable by court martial. The Stockholm Accords, sometimes called the Civilized War Protocols, had superseded the old Geneva Convention two hundred years before, and, among other things, made it a crime to mistreat POWs.

"I agree. Have you discussed this with General Ramsey?"

"Discussed it, no. I left a message, however. General Ramsey is currently in session with General Dominick and the civilian members of this expedition. He privately told me that he needs to buy time for the Marines inside the Wheel. This was my suggestion."

"Well done," Warhurst said. "*Very* well done. This could be our ticket out of this mess."

That, of course, was not guaranteed. Both General Order One and the Stockholm Accords were guidelines for military personnel rather than absolute law. Eight light-years from home they could not be anything more.

But they did mean that Warhurst would be more than justified in taking his time obeying the order to transport the prisoner. Hell, one misstep, one mistake in dealing with an alien physiology, and they could lose the prisoner. The thing could freak out when it was sealed inside a bag, have its equivalent of a heart attack . . . and *then* where would they be?

The only reason Warhurst could think of for keeping the prisoner was the chance that it could be used as a bargaining chip—perhaps an exchange for Corporal Garroway. To do that, they needed to *talk* with the bastards.

And right now the bastards weren't talking.

In fact, the more he thought about it, the more he knew what he had to do. He walked over to the prisoner, which watched him with four alien, unblinking eyes. He unhooked the tether cutter from his armor, reached out, and snicked through the Nommo's bonds.

"What the hell, sir?" one of the Marines holding it motionless said, startled.

The lines around the being's arms and torso went slack. "Stand clear," Warhurst said. "Let him go. If we keep him, he's going to die."

He said that last mostly for the benefit of the recorders in his helmet. He'd just disobeyed a direct order and he would face a court-martial for it, of that he was certain. He might as well state his defense now for the record.

The Nommo didn't move immediately, but crouched in the water, rubbing its strange, webbed hands.

"G'wan, scat!" Warhurst said. "There's no point in holding you and it's dangerous around here."

The Nommo hesitated a moment more, then, with a rippling twist, it turned and slithered into deeper water. Warhurst watched its tail flick once at the surface and then it was gone.

What, he wondered, would it tell its fellows? That the Marines weren't such monsters after all? Or that they were gullible suckers, and it was time to hit them, hard.

"Thank you, sir," Corporal Vinton said.

"Don't thank me, Corporal. Some people aren't going to be real happy with that decision." But he was determined to take full responsibility for it.

"Sewer One! Sewer One!" a new voice cried, using the call sign for Warhurst's advance HQ element here in the tunnel. "This is Sierra Papa Niner! We have enemy contact!"

He checked the tactical screen. SP-9 was one of twelve squad-level patrols now moving into the smaller tunnels branching off from this big one.

"Sewer One, Sierra Papa Three! Enemy contact! We are under fire! . . ."

One by one, other patrols began reporting massive enemy contact. So much for releasing the prisoner in order to facilitate peaceful communication. On the map graphic projected through his implant, it became obvious that the tunnel regions surrounding Sewer One were literally crawling with contacts, all of them hostile.

All thoughts of evacuation went on hold.

The Marines would need to win this fight before even thinking of a retreat.

CPL John Garroway
Sirius Stargate
1612 hours, Shipboard time

The first part of his journey had been underwater. Garroway had held still, allowing one of the big aquatic beings to snag hold of his armor, grabbing the carry handle at the back of the neck, and dragging him through the depths. The trip was full of lefts and rights, ups and downs, and while his suit's inertial navigator seemed to be keeping up with things, Garroway soon felt completely turned around and lost.

One thing was clear, though. The Nommo habitation within the Wheel was enormous, and it was highly sophisticated. At one point, they left the darkness and entered an area where the bulkheads of the tunnels themselves gave off a cool, greenish light. Everywhere, he saw oddly shaped, blocky looking vehicles like the ones that had attacked the Marines on the surface, except that these appeared to be simply transport of some kind, threading their way through the water-filled tunnels in unending streams, like red cells moving through capillaries.

A bit farther on, the tunnel opened into a vast water-filled and brightly lit chamber, one filled with rank upon rank of titanic machines, which vanished into the murky distance. Each looked as though it had been grown from the Wheel's structural foundation and was more or less pyramidal in shape, with towers, spires, and angular constructs growing from their sides in dizzying forests of black metal. He tried to guess what those machines were for. Power generators? Water circulators or purifiers? Or devices somehow connected with the Wheel's teleportational aspect? He couldn't begin to guess. He looked at everything he could, letting both his suit computer and his implant record the images for later study.

If there was a later. He'd lowered his plasma gun with the understanding that he was cooperating, not surrendering, but how could he tell how the Nommo were perceiving his actions? He might well be a prisoner. In the sense that he was not free to leave, that he couldn't leave if he wanted to, he *was* a prisoner. So far as the Nommo were concerned, he might be their prize POW. Or the next sacrifice to their war gods. Or lunch.

He tried not to think about the alternatives. His first responsibility, as he saw it, was communication. As a Marine, his first responsibility as a POW was to attempt to escape . . . but he was choosing to interpret his current situation as something a little different. The more he could learn about the beings who inhabited the Wheel, the better.

He would worry about communicating that information to the Marine chain of command later.

Eventually, they surfaced. The bottom had been steadily rising beneath them, and suddenly he was able to stand up, his head and shoulders above the water. The panorama was . . . spectacular.

It appeared to be a city . . . appeared because nothing Garroway was seeing was making a whole lot of sense at the moment. Slabs of black metal grew from tunnel walls and cliff sides in asymmetrical profusion. Slender spans that might have been bridges arced across broad gulfs. The broad expanse of overhead was pierced by a number of uniform slits, each easily the size of a football field, and through these openings streamed a dazzlingly brilliant, pure, blue-white light.

This must be the side of the Wheel facing Sirius, Garroway reasoned. His suit told him that the light was harmless; it must somehow have been filtered coming in, to take out the ultraviolet and harsher radiations that made the naked light of Sirius A deadly to unprotected humans. The Nommo didn't seem to mind it. A large number of the beings he was now thinking of as Walkers, as opposed to Wiggles, were gathered on pathways, bridges, and balconies overlooking the waters of the bay he'd just emerged from, and the light wasn't bothering them at all.

The aquatic Nommo handed him over to a detail of four armored Walkers. They formed up around him in a protective square and led him along a broad pathway that steadily climbed up from the water's edge. The crowds watched silently, but he could imagine there was an air of tension—or possibly of expectation—emanating from them.

Perhaps they simply saw him as a captured invader.

He was interested to see them without the military armor, however. The armored ones—and he saw lots of them within the crowds—seemed clumsy and relatively slow moving. The rest, though, went naked, or with only bits and pieces of what might be jewelry, or some sort of communications hardware, or both. These moved with a fluid grace Garroway found entrancing. Their skin was smooth, almost rubbery-looking, like a dolphin's, and tended to be a subdued mingling of greens, browns, and blacks.

The city was a city of canals. Waterways were everywhere, and every building, it seemed, either jutted out above the water, or grew out of it. Curiously, there were no children that he could see—only the silently watching adults. He wondered if this place, then, was less a city than it was a work-place, or a military base.

He simply didn't have clues enough to how these beings lived to make any rational guesses.

His escorts took him to a slab-building growing from the cavern wall high up, almost to the ceiling, and not far from one of the dazzling windows looking out into space. Through brightly lit corridors, up a ramp—and finally they ushered him into a room.

The chamber felt odd to him, though he couldn't justify the feeling. It was octagonal in shape, but with uneven walls and a sloping overhead, and he decided that the strangeness of perspective was what was bothering him. There was furniture—recognizable sofas and tables, at least—though it was obviously designed for alien anatomies. The chairs and sofas, for instance, possessed wide slots to accommodate a short tail and were sloped in such a way that the sitter would be angled forward, with much the same posture as when they walked.

Well, they obviously hadn't expected to be entertaining human houseguests.

"Okay, what now?" he said, turning . . . but his escorts were gone and the door was silently sliding shut. He didn't hear a click, but he knew that he was, indeed, a prisoner. The cell was comfortably, spacious, and brightly lit, but these people obviously weren't going to allow him the run of the city.

If the tables were turned, he couldn't imagine letting one of them run around loose in Washington, D.C., say, not until humans knew them better than was the case now and could communicate to them on a level deeper than "Go there."

He began studying his suit readouts. The atmosphere, he saw, was breathable. Oxygen was registering at fourteen percent. That, together with the low atmospheric pressure meant a low O_2 partial pressure which might be a problem for marathon runners, but the suit electronics judged it to be marginally breathable, at least. Nitrogen was high—eighty-four percent, but unless he planned on doing high-pressure work or deep diving, that wouldn't be a problem either. The temperature was chilly—9° Celsius.

There remained one problem that Garroway's Mark VIII vac armor could not say anything about, and that was the possibility of contamination by some alien microorganism. Nommo germs might be deadly to humans, simply because humans had never been exposed to them.

Or hadn't been in several thousand years, if these were the guys who'd visited the early Sumerians, like Dr. Franz said. Still, the current wisdom of all of the downloads on the topic said that it was very unlikely that any microorganism that had evolved to feed off one species was going to be able to jump the gap of an alien biochemistry to a different species altogether. Humans had mingled with the An of Ishtar for years and there'd never been a problem.

"Hell with it," he said. His armor was uncomfortable and

heavy. Reaching up, he popped the release catch, unsealed the helmet, and took it off his head.

The air, as predicted, was chilly, and there was an undeniable whiff of something like fish—just a taste of it. Garroway wrinkled his nose at first, but after a few breaths he scarcely noticed it. He set the helmet down on a table and unsealed and removed his gloves. He was wearing suit utilities under the armor—basic dungaree-type overalls with special nanoconverter packs strategically placed to handle urine, excrement, and sweat—but he decided not to strip down that far just yet. He would wait and see what his hosts had in store for him.

The lights dimmed. He looked up sharply, then turned to face the wall opposite the door to his cell. A deck-to-overhead screen was glowing now, and as he took a step closer, the movie started.

Okay, this was encouraging. Apparently they wanted to communicate, and this was an obvious first step. The images were not three-D, but they were in full color and extremely high definition; looking into the screen was like looking into the actual scene, a scene, he realized with a start, that must have been recorded on Earth itself some six thousand or more years ago.

There was a village . . . a human village, though it consisted of little more than lean-to affairs made of logs and mats of woven reeds. The people were nude or nearly so, with animal skins wrapped about their hips. The men were bald, and many sported tattoos on their faces and upper bodies, patterns of dots and circles outlined in blue ink. The landscape around them was completely flat, an endless panorama of marshland and plain in one direction, and metallic-blue-gray water in the other. The sun overhead was harsh in a brassy sky.

The humans, Garroway saw, were gathered around their visitors, who evidently had just emerged from the waters of the Gulf. He was watching, he knew, a recording of one of the early contacts between the Nommo and humanity; if

Franz was correct, this scene had played itself out at the headwaters of what today was the Arabian Gulf, what in later eras would be known as the Fertile Crescent of Mesopotamia.

There were three of the visitors—not counting the being who, Garroway presumed, must be operating the camera, though that job could have been entrusted to a small flying eye or other piece of technological hardware. He was startled to see that the Nommo were, in fact, the aquatic beings. They rested in the water at the water's edge, with small wavelets breaking around them. Their upright torsos weaved slowly back and forth, their long faces at the same level as the faces of the gathered humans, the rest of their bulk coiled in the water, glistening with an iridescent gleam in the sunlight.

One of the Nommo was apparently speaking with a human—possibly with the village's head man, since he wore a particularly elaborate pattern of tattooing on his forehead and chest. The Nommo extended one black arm, raised one webbed finger. *"As,"* the Nommo said quite clearly. He held up a second finger. *"Mina."* And a third. *"Pes."*

It seemed fairly obvious that the aliens were giving the humans in that recording their first lesson in basic arithmetic.

He was aware of a kind of running commentary in the background, a low, ragged gargling sound. It took him a while to decide that he was hearing two languages in the record. The Nommo were teaching the humans in an easily pronounceable tongue, quite likely their native language. What was it . . . Sumerian? The commentary, if that is what it was, sounded completely other, completely alien.

Suddenly inspired, Garroway turned to face the empty room, looked toward the overhead, extended one finger, and said, loudly, *"As!"* A second finger. *"Mina!"* A third. *"Pes!"*

And Garroway's language lessons began.

21

CPL John Garroway
Sirius Stargate
0915 hours, Shipboard time

According to his implant, this was his second day of captivity; he'd been a prisoner—there was no sense in calling it anything else—for forty-one hours.

It was not an unpleasant captivity, however. Garroway remained in the octagonal room, continuing to watch the video records of an ancient expedition to Earth. He was witnessing, he now realized, the genesis of human civilization.

His captors had offered him food—something that looked like raw fish, and something that looked like bits of kelp. The testing kit in his armor had promised that nothing in the bowl would harm him and he'd eaten it all. Holding his nose helped with the swallowing. He'd supplemented each meal with pieces of food bar from his armor's survival kit, just in case there were vitamins or amino acids he needed missing from the local fare.

By now, he'd shucked his armor. He still hadn't figured out how to use the N'mah sanitary facilities, but at least a constant stream of fresh water trickling into a basin with a drain let him manage a sponge bath. After all of that time in the basic suit utilities, though, he missed a full shower. He might be watch-

ing the dawn of his species' civilization, but he didn't feel very
civilized himself right now. The amphibians evidently didn't
need showers—not when they were in and out of the water all
the time anyway—but Garroway was all too aware of his own
stink. He continued to use the BSUs for waste disposal and
hoped he could figure out how to use the alien equipment before his waste treatment nano needed to be recharged.

All of that was no more than a minor annoyance, however.
He was learning a lot, watching the N'mah teach his distant
ancestors the essentials of farming, animal husbandry, medicine, math, and science. Of particular interest was the fact
that the humans he was seeing in these records appeared to
be the ragged survivors of catastrophe.

Was he seeing actual footage or extremely good computer
graphics? He couldn't tell and he supposed it didn't matter.
But he watched brilliant, high-definition images of the An,
who'd colonized the Earth at some time prior to the arrival of
the N'mah.

He watched the An starships landing, watched the An
emerge from the ships in combat armor and carrying
weapons. He watched stone-age humans butchered, watched
hundreds of them rounded up in pens, watched human slaves
building zigguratlike structures and cyclopean walls for their
masters, watched human priests offer human sacrifices to the
gods to win their favor.

He watched the An as living gods—hairless, reptilian,
golden-eyed—ruling from their ziggurat palaces, punishing
rebellious villages with lightning from the sky, accepting
sacrificed animals and humans alike as . . . as *food*.

The butchery had been appalling.

How long had the enslavement lasted? Garroway couldn't
tell from the scenes he was being shown. Centuries, certainly . . . and quite possibly millennia. He noted that as time
went on, however, more and more of the humans—especially
the ones who obviously held the roles of leaders and priests

over the human cattle—began to shave their heads and tattoo their bodies, apparently in imitation of their gods.

The *Adamu*, the black-headed people, were trying their best to be like their hairless, reptilian masters.

Cities grew along the waterways of Mesopotamia, in Asia, and in the Americas. The An conquest imposed a sharp stratification of society upon the slave population—rulers and priests at the top, followed by soldiers, followed by the lower castes within the city, and with the wild men, the untamed humans beyond the city walls, at the very bottom. The An gods appeared to rule in fiefdoms that frequently were at war with one another . . . or perhaps they were simply bloody games of some sort. Garroway watched human armies battling as their gods watched from floating platforms in the sky.

Then the Hunters had arrived.

Garroway assumed he was watching the Hunters of the Dawn, though he never saw anything of them but their ships—immense, gravity-defying structures hanging in space . . . and the mountain-sized chunks of rock they brought down upon a helpless planet. The An colonies were annihilated, pulverized by direct impact, or drowned by mile-high tsunamis. Later, the Hunter ships had drifted slowly through Earth's skies, burning down An and human alike as they fled the holocaust.

Eventually, the Hunters had departed.

Time passed. Human survivors emerged from the rubble, from the mountains, and from the forests all across the planet and began attempting to re-create something of the civilization taken from them.

He wondered why. The survivors were free. Why try to bring back the emblem of their enslavement?

Garroway couldn't understand the running commentary accompanying the scenes, and could only guess. The An had been gods, in every way that mattered, to the humans they'd enslaved. They'd also evidently created a nobility or a ruling caste—the priests and leaders—and those people would not have relinquished their pathetic power over the lower classes easily. Perhaps, too, many of these people were descended not from survivors of the cities, but from the bands of untamed humans that had existed outside of the gods' domains. It might have been that they'd been envious of the trappings of civilization, without being fully aware of the cruelty of the gods. In any case, certain aspects of the An rule survived, or were re-created.

Perhaps the greatest An curses of all had been organized religion and the monolithic state.

More time passed. A lot of it, Garroway thought, though he couldn't tell from the images how much. The human survivors continued to eke out a marginal Neolithic existence on the shores of various waterways and seas worldwide, making tools from stone, wood, and bone, making pottery, growing crops.

And then the N'mah had arrived.

And that was where Garroway had come in with the first images he'd seen—N'mah emerging from the water to teach human communities the basics of civilization.

Saviors of civilization? That, at any rate, was what they wanted him to believe, the message they were trying to get across to him. There might well have been some propaganda mixed in with what he was seeing . . . but, then, it was only natural to try to present one's self in the best possible light.

That first scene with the counting . . . he now realized that he'd not been seeing a math lesson, but a *language* lesson. The language, he was now certain, was indeed ancient Sumerian, and the humans had been teaching it to the N'mah. That stood to reason; if the Sumerians had the words for "one," "two," and "three," they already had the rudiments of arithmetic.

In two days—with only a few hours off for rest when he became exhausted—Garroway had learned a great deal of Sumerian. He didn't have the ability to download from a central database, but his implant did remember things for him, and remember them well. Once he heard a word and associated it with a meaning, he did *not* forget it.

A few hours earlier, he'd begun to converse with his captors directly. "Gar-ro-way," a deep-throated rumble spoke from an overhead speaker in pidgin Sumerian. "Important is to make peace, your people, mine."

"Important is," he agreed. "Your people, my people, speak soon."

"Your people, my people, speak now."

Garroway looked up sharply at that. Was the voice saying that now was the time for peace talks? Or that peace talks were happening now as they spoke? His grasp of Sumerian grammar was still far too weak to make that kind of distinction.

He was trying to compose a question that would clarify things when the voice continued. "Gar-ro-way. Surprise is."

"Beg pardon?" he said in English. Then he added, "*Ta-am?*"

The door to his cell slid open, and Major Warhurst walked in.

"Sir!" Garroway sprung to his feet. "What . . . how? . . ."

"I'm getting sick and tired of springing you out of jail, Garroway," Warhurst said with mock severity. The grin on his face belied the words. "Getting thrown in the slammer back in East LA was bad enough. Now you're doing it way the hell and gone out here."

"Hey, sir, you know how Marines like to party." Garroway looked at Warhurst's uniform—Marine utilities with his major's rank pinned to the collar. "You're not in armor, sir, so the shooting must be over."

"That it is, Corporal. Thanks in part to you. I gather your willingness to try to talk with the N'mah went a long way to convincing them that we were worth talking to."

"It was more like surrendering, sir." He made a face. "I didn't like that."

"We do what has to be done. We survive, overcome, adapt."

There was a commotion in the passageway outside the door. A moment later two more Marines burst in—Kat Vinton and Tim Womicki. "Gare!"

Warhurst stepped aside as Kat exploded into Garroway's arms. "I needed an escort to come up here," he said, almost apologetically. "These two wouldn't let me take a step unless I brought them."

After a time, Garroway disentangled himself from Kat's embrace. "It's . . . good to see you guys again." The words sounded so inadequate.

"Hey," Womicki said, clapping Garroway's shoulder. "Marines do not leave their own behind. Ever."

"*Semper fi.*"

"The reunion had better wait, people," Warhurst said. "Right now we have to get back to Camp Denderah."

"Denderah?" Garroway asked. "What's that?"

"Our new base," Womicki said. "And it's a hell of a lot better than on board the *Pecker*, let me tell you! There's room to *breathe*!"

"We'll fill you in on the way back," Warhurst said. "Grab your armor and let's vam."

Denderah. At first, Garroway assumed that the name was a N'mah word, but he learned that Dr. Franz had contributed the suggestion. It seemed that the ancient Egyptians, who considered the star Sirius to be the soul of the goddess Isis, had built a number of temples oriented toward the heliacal rising of Sirius, the day of the year when Sirius rose at the same moment as the Sun. One of the most important of these was the temple of Isis–Hathor at Denderah, a village on the west bank of the Nile not far downstream from Luxor.

The Marines had embraced the idea when someone had pointed out that some of their own history and blood was mixed in with the place; in 2138, a Marine strike force had gone into Egypt to secure certain historical monuments and sites to protect them from the local fundamentalists. Warhurst, then a captain, had been with the Marines fighting at Giza, but other Marine elements had secured other archeological sites along the Nile, and Denderah had been one of them. An ancient star map had been found there centuries ago and there were numerous clues at the site to contact in the remote past with visitors from the stars. Charlie Company, one-third of the Second MarDiv, had fought a sharp, two-day action there and saved the temple from being blown up by Mahdi fanatics.

And so Denderah it was.

The Sirian Gate's Denderah occupied a vast, open chamber perhaps twenty kilometers around the ring from the Marine LZ. A hole had been eaten through from outside—this time with the locals' permission—and an airlock docking collar installed so that TRAPs and supply shuttles could begin offloading the contents of the *Altair*, one of the robot freighters. Within hours, a small city of inflatable domes filled much of the chamber, providing living quarters for over a thousand men and women, machine and repair shops, storage lockers, transport pools, rec facilities, and mess halls.

The N'mah demonstrated an intriguing aspect of their technology, literally growing a headquarters building from the gate structure itself. The trick, it turned out, was accomplished by using nanotechnic devices injected into the metal to reshape the atomic bonds within the nickel-iron substrate at a quantum level. Those hordes of floating combat machines the Marines had faced two days before had been grown around ready-made propulsion, power, and weapons systems, a process taking only a few moments, and limited only by the number of internal components.

That one discovery, it turned out, had made the PanTerra people quite happy. Nanotechnology had been used to grow many buildings and other structures back on Earth for almost a century, but that process involved mixing raw materials and growing the finished shape in a mold. The N'mah technique was faster, cleaner, and far more powerful—a form of high-tech magic that would net PanTerra trillions when it went into production back home.

The Marines were less concerned with PanTerra's interests, however, than they were with security. Their hosts seemed ill-at-ease, concerned that the Hunters of the Dawn might already have taken note of the human presence at the Sirius Gate, and if that happened, all of the nanotechnological magic in the universe might not be enough to save the MIEU . . . or Earth. Warhurst told Garroway that a briefing had already been scheduled between the humans and the Deep Council, a group of elders who were the closest thing to a government, apparently, that the N'mah possessed.

"At least everyone's agreed on that one," Warhurst told him as they entered the outskirts of Camp Denderah. A small mob of Marines was approaching, cheering Garroway's return. "The more information we can share with the N'mah, the better . . . for both of us. Looks like you have a small reception committee here, Garroway."

"We already linked to 'em that Gare was okay," Womicki said, grinning. "I think a small party is in order, don't you, sir?"

"If it's not, I doubt that I could stop it," Warhurst said. "Garroway, S-2 is going to want to talk to you and download whatever you got from the Wiggles. But you can stand down for, oh, make it twenty-four hours. I think I can keep the intel boys off your back for that long."

"Thank you, sir."

"I suggest you get some food in you, get some rest, and for *God's* sake get a shower and a clean uniform! Otherwise, you're going to be partying by yourself!"

"Aye aye, sir!"

"Carry on."

The other Marines arrived as Warhurst walked off toward

the HQ building. "Hey, Gare!" Roger Eagleton called. "Welcome home!"

"Yeah," Anna Garcia said. "We thought we'd fuckin' lost you!"

"Jesus!" Lobowski said, wrinkling his nose. "What the hell've you been rolling in, Marine?"

Garroway turned his head and sniffed at the shoulder of his suit utilities. "Whew! I guess the Major was right. I need a shower before I do any serious partying."

"Or *Sirius* partying," Gunnery Sergeant Dunne put in. "Vinton? Show this Marine to his quarters and see that he showers down. Steel beach party at the grinder, fifteen hundred hours. Do you copy?"

"Copy, Gunnery Sergeant!" Garroway snapped back, grinning.

"Then git your sorry ass out of my sight until then! Carry on!"

"I gather everything's squared away with the Wiggles?" Garroway asked Kat as they walked toward the hab dome that had been designated for Alpha Company.

"Pretty much. We had a prisoner, but Major Warhurst turned him loose. That didn't stop the fighting, not right away, at any rate, but I guess between that and what you were doing in Wiggle City finally got through. They contacted us by radio through Cassius, speaking ancient Sumerian."

"Outstanding."

"Y'know the funny thing? We thought the aquatic Wiggles were the children. It's the other way around. The Walkers—the ones who do the fighting and the building—they're the N'mah young. The big seagoing Wiggles, that's the adult phase. They're the thinkers and the leaders." She shook her head. "There's *so* much we have to learn!"

"Roger that." He thought for a moment. "So what's with this big pow-wow the major was talking about? Something about Earth being in danger?"

"They don't tell us much," she said. "You know that. But the word is, some big stuff is happening."

"Yeah?" Garroway asked her. "Like what?"

"Well, to begin with, the scuttlebutt is . . . remember that AI we sent through the gate a couple of days ago?"

Garroway nodded. "Sure."

"Well, the word is, it's returned. And the brass is *not* happy with what it saw."

That gave Garroway something to think about. He stopped thinking about it when he entered the barracks shower, however. Kat joined him under the blast of hot water and there were other, more pleasant things to think about. Afterward, they got reacquainted in Kat's rack, with the promise that the Alpha Company barracks was going to be otherwise unoccupied for the next couple of hours. Lobowski and Garcia, standing guard outside, would see to that, she told him.

For just a little while, Garroway could forget about Wiggles, Marine deployments, and alien contact with ancient Earth civilizations, and lose himself on that most ancient, and most pleasurable, of all purely *human* contacts. . . .

General Ramsey
Conference Chamber
Sirius Stargate
1530 hours, Shipboard time

This, Ramsey thought, was the first *physical* briefing session he'd attended in longer than he could remember. Noumenal conferences were so much more convenient. All imaginable data were instantly available, a thought-click away, for everyone to see. There was no travel involved, and no discomfort. What had begun a couple centuries ago with telecommuting had eventually become the means for people to interface with one another . . . virtually, within the computer-guided noumena of their minds.

But human implant technology could not interface with N'mah computers, not yet. The two groups, thanks to the extensive Sumerian language database on the MIEU network, could talk to one another face-to-face or by radio, but more sophisticated forms of communication were going to take time.

The battle fleet had moved in close to the Sirius Gate, and most staff personnel—Navy, Marine, Command, and civilian—had been brought across on board TRAPs to quarters prepared for them within the recently grown N'mah buildings. The place designated as the conference chamber was a large room just below the cavern taken up by Camp Denderah. There was a table and chairs, brought down from the *Altair*, for the humans, and a pool, accessed from an underwater tunnel, for the N'mah elders. To one side, a five-meter flatscreen had been set up, so that maps, computer simulations, and visual recordings could be shared with the N'mah, who did not have access to human noumena.

It was, Ramsey thought, a scene unlike any since the N'mah had first visited a human village on the shores of the Arabian Gulf, eight thousand years or more before. Fourteen men and women sat around three sides of the table, facing three of the huge, iridescent beings, four-eyed serpents with arms, resting in their pool. Cassius was invisibly present as well, of course, translating for the group. The N'mah would speak Sumerian, a language they had learned and recorded during their interactions with humans millennia ago; Cassius would translate to English via the humans' implants. The humans spoke English, which Cassius would translate into Sumerian and transmit, by radio, to the communications hardware each N'mah wore imbedded in her skull.

Her skull. He was still getting used to N'mah concepts of gender. From what the medical department had been able to learn so far, N'mah males were internal parasites, resident within the equivalent of the females' genitalia. Females gave live birth to meter-long offspring that looked like large salamanders. These crawled ashore and were taken in by the Community of the Young, the Walkers who constituted the land-phase of N'mah amphibious life. This juvenile phase lasted for a long time; N'mah concepts of time were still poorly understood, but Dr. Franz thought it might be as long as fifty years.

The juveniles, it turned out, were the builders. In N'mah prehistory, tens of thousands of years ago, it must have been the land-dwelling juveniles that had discovered fire, smelted metals, and eventually gone to the stars.

The race still mourned that decision, which they called the Death Turning. If they'd not begun exploring the oceans of space around them, they might never have encountered the Hunters of the Dawn.

An estimated twenty thousand years ago, it seemed, long before they encountered a humanity that at that time was still dwelling in caves on distant Earth, the N'mah had found the Hunters—or the Hunters had found them. Their home world and some hundreds of colony planets had all been destroyed, subjected to the intense asteroid bombardments that were the Hunters' signature.

This much, at least, had already been learned through informal exchanges with the Elders. As the exchange of data continued, Ramsey expected that the humans, at least, would learn a very great deal more about their prehistoric past.

"Everything depends on the way the Gate works." Dr. Marie Valle, the civilian xenotechnologist, was speaking at the moment. "If I'm understanding our hosts . . . the, the space inside the circle of the Gate is literally in two places at once, and those two places can be many light-years apart."

"Yes, yes," a deep rumble of a voice agreed within their minds. Cassius was transmitting his translation of the N'mah words with the same timbre and intonation as their deep and decidedly unfemale-sounding voices. "Same space, two places."

The Sumerian language database, it turned out, was lacking, especially in technical words and concepts. That was hardly surprising; most of the vocabulary had come directly from ancient Sumer, which had not possessed starships, star gates, or the language of quantum physics. The rest had come from the An of Ishtar who, though they still had the computer network they called the *abzu*, had lost most of the technology of their starfaring past. Concepts like *mul-ka*, literally "Star Gate," were simple enough, since both *mul*, "star," and *ka*, "gate," were known. In the same way, the word starship could be rendered as *mul-ma-gur*, "*ma-gur*" being the ancient Sumerian for a large boat.

But what about words like "energy," as distinct from *izzi*, "fire?" Or "atom?" Or "light-year?"

And the toughest part of the problem was that Sumerian was not the N'mah's native language. The gods only knew what was happening when they translated, from Sumerian to their own gargle-sounding tongue, a jury-rigged compound nightmare like *us-u-su-as-mu*, for "length-light-cross-one-year."

"If we understand the technology correctly," Valle went on, "then the Sirian Gate is . . . 'tuned,' I guess would be the best word, tuned to overlap with another gate somewhere else in the Galaxy. According to our hosts, there are some millions of gates scattered across the Galaxy. We're not sure, but these may be another of the legacies left behind by the Builders, half a million years ago . . . or they could have been constructed by a civilization earlier still than that. By adjusting the tuning at one gate, a ship can dial in on any other gate, no matter how distant.

"The tuning at the Sirian Gate is currently controlled by a star-faring culture the N'mah refer to as *Ghul* or *Xul*. We don't know what they call themselves. Xul is a Sumerian word, though, for 'evil,' or possibly 'evil destroyers.'"

"The Hunters of the Dawn," Dominick said.

"We don't know that," Lymon put in. "Not for sure."

"Right," Ricia Anderson said. "It could be *another* race of Galaxy-faring psychopaths intent on wiping out emerging civilizations by smacking them with asteroids."

Lymon ignored her. "Obviously, we should just take whatever steps are necessary to get control of the gate ourselves. That would solve everything."

"Actually, that's a lot easier said than done," Valle said. "Xul starships approaching the Gate can retune it to a specific destination, using radio or lasercom codes. As far as we've been able to determine, *any* ship with the appropriate codes can do it. We can learn how to use the gate ourselves—the N'mah have some of the appropriate codes themselves. But we can't stop the Xul from accessing the Gate, not without destroying the Gate entirely."

"Then we destroy the Gate," Ramsey put in. "We have some tactical nukes in our inventory, and two AMB-75 antimatter devices." He looked pointedly at Lymon. "Our mission orders specifically dictate the necessity of destroying the Gate, should we discover a direct threat to Earth."

"We don't yet know that there is a threat," General Dominick put in.

"Besides," Dr. Franz said, "the Sirius Gate is inhabited! You can't possibly be thinking of destroying it!"

Ramsey looked at the silently listening N'mah elders. What were they making of all of this? "No. But there must be a way to disable the Gate without harming the environment here."

"That . . . may be difficult, General," Valle replied. "The Gate operates because of quantum-special distortions generated by two rotating black holes inside the Gate structure, as we've guessed. But that's also the source both of the gravitational shielding which keeps the inhabited areas habitable, and of the power that runs the N'mah life support systems, their water purifiers and circulators, all of that. Now, the life support we might be able to keep going by tapping into the fusion plants that power some of the secondary systems, but we can't do a thing about the gravity shielding. The N'mah say they don't possess gravity control technology."

"What about those flying tanks?" Admiral Harris asked.

"Mag-lev, using the Gate structure itself to generate an intense local magnetic field for propulsion. Old tech. We've been able to do the same thing ourselves for a couple of centuries—railguns, maglev trains. . . .

"In fact," she went on, "I'm afraid the N'mah aren't so very far ahead of us in technology at all."

"What?" Lymon said, startled. "That's not possible! We were counting—" She stopped herself.

"Much, we have lost," Cassius told them in the N'mah's rumbling pseudo-voice. "Much. We have been crippled by the *Xul*."

Ramsey made a mental note to follow up on that with the N'mah later, if he could. What they'd revealed about their race so far suggested that some hundreds or perhaps thousands of N'mah colonies were now scattered across the galaxy, hidden in remote and out-of-the way places where they would not attract attention from the Xul. How many such colonies of survivors remained the N'mah themselves didn't know.

The Sirian group, they claimed, numbered around ten thousand individuals, both young and adult. They were, the N'mah claimed, a remnant of a much larger Sirian colony that had been destroyed by a Xul attack—if Ramsey was understanding this right—less than two thousand years ago. Evidently, they'd retained some useful high-tech like that nanotrick with metal, but lost the faster-than-light ships, the interstellar communicators, and the world-shattering weapons.

"The great danger," Valle said, "is that the Xul, or one of their ships, at any rate, and that's all it would take, may know now about our activities here. If they come through again—as they did when they destroyed the *Isis* ten years ago—they would not need to search long or far to find Earth. Local space is bathed in the EM radiation from our civilization. And . . . while the N'mah do not have faster-than-light starships, the Xul most assuredly do. They use the Gates for zigzagging around the Galaxy, but they also have an FTL drive they use for more local jaunts. If, and when, they emerge here, they will be literally only a few days away from Earth."

"But how do they know we're here?" Dominick asked.

"For that, why don't you take a look at the screen. We'll let Cassius tell his side of things."

The flatscreen on one side of the conference table lit up; simultaneously, a noumenal download became available for the humans present. Ramsey chose to focus on that rather than the screen. There was less chance of missing something important that way.

He found himself adrift in space. It took a moment for him to recognize what he was seeing . . . a vast, spiraling smear of starlight, the galaxy seen from outside. The scene rotated slowly, and he saw other, more easily comprehended objects . . . a planet, a red-dwarf star, the magnificence of a globular star cluster, and what appeared to be an asteroid or small moon pierced by an enormous cavern or hole. He was forcibly reminded of the crater Stickney, on Phobos, one of the moons of Mars, only instead of being a deep pit filled with dust and loose rubble, the hole seemed to go down and down and down forever, with no bottom.

A star gate, tunneled into the side of a fair-sized asteroid.

"This is what I saw—or, rather, what my downloaded alter-ego saw—on the other side of the Sirius Gate," Cassius explained. "Here is the relevant imagery."

The scene shifted to the planet, visible only as a slender, ruddy crescent close by the shrunken red sun. A star gleamed—oddly—*inside* the arms of the crescent, where no star should be. Cassius's imaging system zoomed in on that star; the crescent expanded until it filled the scene, then expanded some more and moved out of sight. The star stayed star-like for a moment, then suddenly expanded as well.

And then Ramsey was looking at the golden, needle-shaped spacecraft he'd seen before, the one that had emerged from the Sirius Gate to destroy the *Isis*.

"*Xul-mul-ma-gur,*" one of the N'mah rumbled.

"A Xul starship," Cassius translated. "And they almost certainly now know we are here."

22

General Ramsey
Conference Chamber
Sirius Stargate
1540 hours, Shipboard time

"One of the Marine pilots of 5-MAS," Cassius went on, "res-cued me, so to speak. Captain Greg Alexander fell through the stargate during the battle, four days after I—after Cassius I-2, rather—went through."

"Wait a sec," Helen Albo, Dominick's chief of staff, said. "I'm confused. Are *you* Cassius? Or the other Cassius? Which one is I-2?"

"I am both," Cassius replied evenly. "When I was down-loaded into the Starhawk probe, Cassius Iteration-two became a separate consciousness, experienced a different stream of events and recorded memories different from those of the Cas-sius left behind. When I—when he, rather—returned, he was uploaded back into the MIEU computer net, where his sepa-rate memories became my own. Essentially, Cassius I-2 no longer exists as a distinct and separate entity. I am he."

"Oh. Stupid question."

"Not at all. The English language is not well designed for distinctions of this nature."

"How badly damaged was your Starhawk?" Ramsey asked.

"My maneuvering thrusters were operable, enough so that I was able to stop my spin. My main drive, however, was damaged, and I had lost nearly all of my reaction mass. I elected to maneuver my craft to a parking point some fifty kilometers from the opening of the stargate on that side, and observe the region."

"For clarification," Ricia Anderson said, "we've named that stargate the Cluster Gate. We're uncertain as yet which of a number of different globular star clusters it might be, but the name seems to fit. That gate—and the red dwarf sun it orbits—appear to lie within a few hundred light-years of the cluster proper. Go ahead, Cassius. Excuse the interruption."

"Some eighty-three hours after I went through, Captain Alexander emerged from the gate. His Starhawk was badly damaged and incapable of maneuvering. Fortunately, we both fell through the gate on similar trajectories, and ended up in the same general volume of space, and I retained sufficient maneuvering capability to effect a rendezvous with him. These scenes were taken by one of the remote probes I released in the area."

The assembled humans and N'mah watched the scene as recorded by a remote probe—one damaged SF/A-2 Starhawk drifted slowly alongside a second, more badly mangled one. Against the backdrop of the sky-filling galaxy, a space-suited human figure emerged from the badly damaged fighter and began checking over the plasma-blasted ruin of the portside thrusters of the other.

"Fortunately, his Starhawk still possessed reaction mass. My main drive was damaged but repairable. Captain Alexander was able to effect repairs to my portside drive, a matter of replacing the KR-1509 circuit board, which had melted, with the identical board from his SF/A-2, which was intact. The repairs allowed me to reverse my path and return through the gate."

"Why didn't Alexander come with you?" Dr. Franz wanted to know.

"My Starhawk had neither life support, nor space for a human passenger. The cockpit area had been given over to the electronics necessary to support the Cassius iteration."

"So Captain Alexander is still adrift outside the Cluster Gate," Ramsey said. "How much life support does he have left?"

"At the time," Cassius said, "five point three hours ago, his fuel cells would provide reserve power for another fourteen hours. He evacuated the air from his cockpit in order to perform the EVA to effect repairs on my Starhawk. His space suit, I estimate, if connected to his reserve shipboard tanks, had air for another twenty hours."

"So we have fourteen hours, more or less, to go in and pick him up."

"Unless," Admiral Harris said, "the Xul have already picked him up."

"You said the Xul may know about us," Dominick said. "Is that because of your, ah, incursion to the other side?"

"Actually, we saw no indication that the Xul starship was aware of us," Cassius said. "Our ships were tiny and operating at extremely low power. However, we must assume that they are aware of the gate's operation."

"When the *Isis* first approached the Sirius Gate," Harris said, "she launched several remote probes through the gate aperture. We now believe the Xul ship became aware of *Isis*'s presence as those probes emerged through their side of the gate. If so, they would certainly know about those two fighters."

"And be on the way now to investigate," Ramsey added. "At least, we must make that assumption."

"So the question becomes," Dominick said, "what can we do about it?"

"I'd give a lot for a planetary defense battery right now," Harris said. "Something big enough to be sure of taking out that Xul behemoth."

The N'mah rumbled among themselves for a moment, then posed a question to Cassius in Sumerian. He translated. "Please, what is 'planetary defense battery'?"

"Anything big enough to kill the Xul ship," Harris replied, grim. "Railgun. Plasma weapons. Missiles with nuclear or AM warheads. The *New Chicago* has a fair-sized particle beam cannon, spinal mount. But from what we've seen of that Xul battlewagon, we'd need three or four such weapons firing together to guarantee a kill."

"But . . . do you now have such weapons aboard each of your vessels?" one N'mah said.

Another N'mah agreed. "It was your use of these weapons against what you call the Wheel that prompted our defense in the first place."

"What the hell are you talking about?" Dominick protested. "*You* fired first at *us*."

"Maybe he means the laser sampling, early on," Valle suggested.

"No. Each of your starships possesses a . . ." Cassius broke off, then continued in his usual voice. "The N'mah words literally translate as 'huge-fire-moving-bow.' I believe, however, that she is referring to some type of very large, high-energy weapon."

"Something shooting energy instead of arrows?" Valle said. "That makes sense."

"No," Harris said. "It does not. *New Chicago* is the only ship with that kind of weapon. The other ships have spinal-mount railguns, but those aren't nearly big enough to worry something as big as the Xul ship."

"No, no," one of the N'mah insisted, through Cassius. "Your ships. Big fire-weapons. What you said before . . . 'spinal mount.' "

"I think she's right," Ramsey said. "I think she means the Kemper Drives!"

That caused some consternation around the table. "What

the hell are you talking about, General?" Dominick demanded.

"Think about it, sir. All of our ships are essentially very large particle accelerators. The Kemper Drive uses magnetic fields to accelerate reaction mass to near-light speed and blast it out into space . . . either astern or forward, depending on whether the ship is accelerating or decelerating. What comes out tends to be a *very* hot plasma. You all know damned well how careful we are not to point those things at, say, an inhabited planet or space station when we light them off! When we decelerated into the Sirius system, though, we must've looked like we were coming in, plasma guns blazing!"

Further questioning proved that Ramsey was correct. The N'mah had ships that operated with a magnetic drive . . . nothing as large, as powerful, or as *deadly* as the Kemper Drive accelerators. To N'mah instrumentation, the MIEU's arrival had looked like an attack. They'd chosen to stay hidden—their usual strategy when confronted by the arrival of a Xul ship—until Cassius I-2 had used his sampling laser, *obviously* a direct attack. Then, and only then, had they struck back.

"Are you suggesting that we could use our ships as weapons?" Harris asked.

"Exactly. And the sooner we position the ships, the better. We should also plan on sending another probe through the gate, just to take a quick peek at the other side." Ramsey was talking fast now, trying to keep up with his own racing thoughts as he traced out the possibilities. "Our immediate problem is the Xul ship at the Cluster Star Gate. If it comes through to our side, we must destroy it. Whether it comes through or not, we must also destroy the Cluster Gate."

"Why the Cluster Gate?" Dominick asked.

"Because the Xul know that, right now, the way the codes are set, the Cluster Gate leads to the Sirius Gate, and that means it's only a matter of time before they come through and find Earth. If we can destroy the Cluster Gate, well, let me ask our N'mah friends. What are the chances that they wouldn't know which gate, out of all those thousands of gates, was ours?"

The N'mah rumbled together for a moment, in consultation. "We do not have enough information to answer," one said, finally. "But . . . we are hopeful. The Xul are numerous and spread throughout much of the Galaxy, and beyond. But there are so very many stars, so many possible systems. You are right in saying that the only link they have at this time to this system—and to your Earth—is the one leading from the Cluster Gate. Destroy that gate, and the Xul ship guarding it, and we may remain undiscovered."

"Then, ladies, gentlemen, and N'mah," Ramsey said, grinning, "this is what we'll do. . . ."

General Dominick
Personal Quarters
UFR/USS Ranger
1750 hours, Shipboard time

As soon as he could, Dominick had returned to the narrow closet that was his quarters on board the carrier, sealed the hatch, and put a block on his implant communications. Who the hell was in command of this expeditionary force, anyway? That goddamned Marine brigadier was like a force of nature. There was no guiding him, no changing his path once he had it in mind to go a certain way. And as for Lymon . . .

Helen Albo could reach him here, but no one else, and she had a list, a very short list, of who he would be willing to talk to.

The list did not include Cynthia Lymon. *Especially* it did not include Cynthia Lymon. That insufferable bitch was becoming more and more of a headache with her demands . . .

especially her demands that he make himself available to her at all times, and that he relieve Ramsey and take personal command of the MIEU. He was beginning to think that the billions of newdollars she'd first promised him back on Earth could not possibly be worth this God-awful nagging.

She had a call in to him now, he noticed. When he closed his eyes and entered the noumenon, a call-waiting light flashed at the edge of his mind's-eye vision, with her name attached.

Well, let her flash.

Whether she knew it or not, he was still on her side, and working for her interests. Right now, the important thing was to salvage something of value for the MIEU to take back to Earth. They had the N'mah nanotechnique, and that was worth a lot. Better, though, would be the technology that operated the stargates, or a working Xul starship drive, or Xul weaponry. If he was able to secure anything like that, he could write his own ticket with PanTerra.

And after that, he would be rich enough to write his own ticket with the entire damned planet Earth.

The problem was that all of those possible windfall discoveries—stargate operation, starship drive, or advanced weaponry—were locked away onboard the Xul ship. And Marine Brigadier General T. J. Ramsey was planning on springing an ambush that would ensure the Xul vessel's complete destruction.

Something had to be done, and fast. Something other than relieving the Marine CO. Much as he would like to do it, Dominick did recognize that Ramsey had a way of making things happen . . . and he had serious doubts about whether Ramsey's Marines would obey an Army general with the same verve and élan that they obeyed Ramsey.

Damn the man, anyway. And damn his jarheads. They were very good at breaking things, but not as good at *secur-*

ing them. There had to be a way to get them to capture the Xul ship instead of destroying it out of hand.

He opened his implant's communications function, thought-clicking on Ramsey's address listing.

General Ramsey
Combat Command Center
UFR/USS Chapultepec
1755 hours, Shipboard time

Ramsey, too, had gone back on board ship, returning to the *Chapultepec* to better coordinate the offloading of the TRAPs they would be needing, as well as the special weaponry. When the call from Dominick came through, Ramsey was in a noumenal planning discussion with his senior staff and the Navy.

"I really question the idea of using one of the robot freighters as a missile," Admiral Harris said. "We don't have time to offload more than a fraction of the supplies. We can't afford to ditch one third of this expedition's consumables!"

"I believe we can, Admiral," Ramsey replied. "When we planned for this expedition, we weren't counting on finding food and water out here. The Wheel, so far as we knew then, was uninhabited—or might have been inhabited by critters so different from us in body chemistry that we couldn't use their food."

"We can't," Captain Louis Howard, the Battalion Medical Officer, said. "We can't survive on N'mah foods. The biochemistry is different."

Ramsey had downloaded a report on the subject earlier. Certain molecules necessary for life were not symmetrical, but came in what were known as isomers. The sugar humans got energy from in food was what was known as a right-handed sugar—that was where the word "dextrose" came from, in fact. Left-handed sugars would pass right through the human digestive system untouched. The same was true of amino acids. Humans required left-handed amino acids in their food; the right-handed isomer was useless.

As it happened, N'mah biochemistry was based on right-handed sugars, but also on right-handed amino acids. Essentially, that meant their food tasted okay, and provided short-term energy . . . but that humans would starve to death if they tried it as a long-term, steady diet.

Ramsey remembered a line downloaded from Berossus: *This Being in the daytime used to converse with men; but took no food at that season; and he gave them an insight into letters and sciences, and every kind of art.*

That "took no food" had been a loudly shouted clue that Man's alien benefactors didn't possess the same biochemistry as humans. The An were enough like humans in their biochemistry that the two could eat one another's food. Indeed, human survivors from the trade mission on Ishtar had survived on local foods out in the hills for ten years, and when the An had colonized Earth, they'd survived for centuries on the "sacrifices" of native grain and animals. But the N'mah chemistry was different.

But not, Ramsey thought, *too* different. "Actually, we have enough food to supplement the diet," he said. "Dr. Howard? Check me on this. We could take on board enough N'mah food to give our people something to chew on, but the amino problem could be held at bay with supplements."

"Yes, that would work," the medical officer said.

"Besides, we only need enough for however long we stay in Sirius space. On the return, we'll all be in cybehibe."

"Even in cybehibe," Howard pointed out, "our bodies keep replacing wornout cells and tissue. We need food during hibernation, *especially* amino acids, which go into mak-

ing up the proteins we need to sustain life. That's why we
have those supplements along! But . . . in general, you're
right."

"And if necessary," Ramsey added, "we go on short rations. It can be done."

"But . . . smashing the Xul ship with one of our starships,"
Harris said. "That's kind of expensive for an anti-ship missile, isn't it?"

"And just how damned expensive does it become if they
get through to Earth?" He paused as the alert for the implant
call from Dominick came through. "Hold it a second, people," he said. "I need to take this."

Damn. He'd not *deliberately* excluded the Army mission
commander from his deliberations with Harris and the others. Not exactly. But if Dominick had learned he'd been planning the upcoming battle without him, there'd be hell to pay.

"Yes, General. I was just going to flag you."

"Oh? About what?"

"We're putting together some ideas for the assault on the
Xul ship."

"Well, I've been having some ideas too, General. I wonder . . . can we possibly plan on *capturing* that vessel, instead
of destroying it?"

The question stunned Ramsey. He was glad the noumenon
wasn't revealing his facial expression.

"General Dominick . . . that is the most ragged-assed
sorry excuse for an idea I have heard in a *long* time."

"Hear me out . . ."

"Is this about some deal you have with PanTerra?" Ramsey demanded. "I know Lymon is hot to corner the market on
alien high-tech. But do you have *any* idea—"

"Profit is important, General. But this is something even
you should be thinking about. What if there are prisoners—
human prisoners—onboard that vessel?"

That stopped Ramsey. The question hadn't yet come up during his discussions with the others and, frankly, he'd not stopped to think about it.

"General, that seems most unlikely."

"Is it? The images we have of the *Isis* . . . that Xul ship just seemed to swallow them. Maybe they're still on board. You Marines are the ones always harping about never leaving a man behind."

Ramsey was stunned first, then furiously angry. Dominick was using that centuries-old covenant to manipulate him, and Ramsey did *not* like being manipulated.

"General, I'll remind you that that happened in August of 2148 . . . almost twenty-two years ago. Just what are the chances that those people are still alive?"

"I have no idea, General. You tell me."

"I can't, sir, and you know it. Nobody can."

"Our orders include verifying that there are no survivors of the *Wings of Isis*."

"*In the Sirius system*," Ramsey added. "Why would the Xul keep 245 humans alive onboard ship for that long?"

"Who knows? They're aliens, damn it. Anything is possible."

"It's also possible that the Xul will turn out to be stuffed purple bunnies who surrender when we open fire on them, but I'm not taking any bets on that happening. I find it much more likely that they offloaded any prisoners they might have taken at that planet Cassius recorded . . . or taken them off to another star system entirely. Nor do we know if this is the same Xul ship that took the *Isis*. We have absolutely no reason to think any of our people are still onboard that vessel."

"And absolutely no reason to think they are not."

Ramsey sighed. There was no way to win this argument. Technically, Dominick was right. The Marines were here for several key reasons—to investigate the Sirius Gate and secure it for further study, or else to destroy it in the event that it posed a threat to Earth's safety; to learn more about the events that had led to the *Wings of Isis* being captured or destroyed, especially in regard to the ship that had emerged to take the *Isis*; and to rescue any among *Isis*'s crew who might still be alive.

What made things tough was the priority of those orders. Earth's security, obviously, came first. There were fifty-some billion people on Earth, and there was no way to measure those lives against the lives of the 245 members of *Isis*'s crew both fairly and rationally. The MIEU's mission orders were *most* specific on that point. Earth's security came first. If events had transpired in such a way that Ramsey had been forced to destroy the Sirius Star Gate *and the ten thousand N'mah living there* in order to save Earth, he would have done so, without hesitation.

But there was a damned big gray area here, and no way to be completely safe, when it came to Earth's security, or completely sure, when it came to the *Isis* crew. He needed to find a reasonably safe middle ground.

But where the hell was that?

He thought for a moment. They'd already discussed several plans. Maybe using a freighter with an antimatter warhead on board was just a *little* on the side of overkill.

But they would have to be sure.

"General," he said at last, "Earth's safety comes first. You know that. But we may possibly have a viable plan that'll at least let us find out about the *Isis* and her crew."

"That's all I'm looking for, General," Dominick replied.

Like hell, you bastard, Ramsey thought. *You're looking for a way to capture Xul hardware.*

But even that was legitimate. If Operation Battlespace brought home some tech that would give Earth a chance against the Xul in the future—a working interstellar drive, say?—then almost any risk would be worth it.

If that risk didn't extend to Earth's teeming billions.

"I suggest you join our discussion, General," Ramsey said. "C'mon in and join the crowd." He shifted channels. "Okay, I'm back, people. I'm tabling the idea of a freighter with an AM warhead. General Dominick has made some *very* good points about that.

"So, as I see it now, to do this right we're going to need an old-fashioned Marine CBSS. . . ."

Corporal Garroway
TRAP 1-2
Sirius Stargate
2345 hours, Shipboard time

Once again, Garroway was strapped into place in the sardine-can closeness of a TRAP packed with a section of twenty Marines. Once again, it was the waiting . . . and waiting . . . and *waiting*.

"Buddha's hairy balls!" Womicki said. "How much longer are they going to keep us in here?"

"As long as they have to, Womicki," Dunne replied. "Now shut your trap and vacseal it!"

The stress within the section had been steadily growing. They'd crammed into the TRAP almost four hours ago. A four-hour wait was nothing if you were going somewhere . . . but they were just sitting here, and had been the whole time, adrift some ten kilometers above the surface of the Wheel.

At least, that's what they'd been told. As usual, they did not have a visual feed from outside. "You'd be too damned busy gawking at the sights," Dunne had explained. "You start lollygagging like a goddamned tourist and *then* where would you be?"

"The probe hasn't returned," Major Warhurst's voice told them. "It should have been back twenty minutes ago. I think we can assume that means action is imminent."

Garroway drew a deep breath. He was glad the major was listening in, though he knew that would put a damper on the conversation. It meant that the battalion CO cared about them.

And right now, that counted for a hell of a lot.

General Ramsey
Command Control Center
UFR/USS Chapultepec
2345 hours, Shipboard time

Ramsey *could* see what was going on. From his noumenal vantage point, in fact, he was drifting in space some twenty kilometers from the Wheel. The vessels of the MIEU were in place, positioned in a circle around the Wheel's center far enough out that they were out of the reach of the gravitationally strange space within the Gate's central opening, their spacing staggered in such a way that no ship had its drive venturi aimed at any other ship. All main drive thrusters were aimed at the center of the Wheel, however.

An old, old saying within the Corps had it that the Marines always did more with less. Mass restrictions dictated that MIEU-1 couldn't bring its own artillery, so the seven remaining vessels of the fleet were being drafted into service.

Seeing his battle plan laid out like this was less than reassuring. Over the past several days, Ramsey had become used to seeing the Wheel hanging in space, a black wedding band adrift against the stars. It was easy, however, to lose sight of just how *big* the thing was.

Chapultepec was the largest of the fleet's ships with a length-overall of 622 meters, pencil-slender behind the 100-meter spread of her forward R-M tank and shield. *Ranger* was a hair shorter, at 604 meters, but with a larger and deeper reaction-mass dome. The three robot transports, bulkier and more massive than the manned vessels, were each 570 me-

ters long, while *New Chicago* had loa of 510 meters. Even
the little *Daring* was still over three times the length of a
football field, longer, in fact, than the old supercarriers that
had been the mainstay of the U.S. wet-Navy two centuries
before.

They were, in fact, the largest manned structures capable
of moving under their own power in human history. Seen
against the backdrop of the Wheel, however, even *Chapultepec* looked like a metallic child's toy. The Sirius Gate
spanned over twenty kilometers, almost forty times *Chapultepec*'s length. From out here, the Marine interstellar transport looked tiny and harmlessly insignificant.

Minutes slipped past, one following the next. How much
longer?

Damn it, it should *not* be much longer, one way or another.
Well over forty minutes earlier, a recon AI, another SF/A-2
Starhawk outfitted with a Cassius download had passed
through the gate. The idea was to have it emerge from the
Cluster Gate, decelerate for ten minutes while noting the position of the Xul ship and any other pertinent tactical data,
then accelerate back through the gate with the information.

That Starhawk should have returned to the Sirian side of
the gate half an hour ago. The fact that it had not was, itself,
a pertinent datum. A malfunction or some other unforeseen
occurrence was always a possibility, of course, but likeliest
was that the Xul vessel was approaching the gate, had noted
the Starhawk's emergence and had swatted it like a fly.

According to N'mah data, the Xul possessed a type of
magnetic shielding as a defense against particle beam at-
tacks. The focused output of seven starships, however, ought
to be enough to overwhelm their screens.

Ought to be, There was still so much about this new enemy
that was unknown.

He wished the recon A-2 had returned. Waiting like this,
with no information at all about what was happening on the

other side . . . damn it! How much longer? He checked his
implant time sense. Past midnight, ship's time, not that
schedules out here paid any attention to day or night.

Perhaps they should try again, another probe. Perhaps . . .

Something was emerging from the Gate.

It happened quickly, far too quickly for merely human response. The Xul ship, needle-slim forward, but with asymmetrical bulges and sponsons aft, slipped out of nothingness
a bit off-center within the Wheel's embrace. One instant
there was nothing; the next, the Xul vessel was growing out
of empty space faster than the eye could follow.

But human eyes and human reactions were not the first line
of defense. Sissy—the Combat Command Network linking
the ships of the MIEU—together with Cassius as the tactical
component, reacted at computer speeds and efficiency, correcting the seven ships' aim and triggering the starship drives
simultaneously. The Xul vessel was struck by seven streams
of star-hot plasma.

And it kept coming, emerging completely from the Gate,
apparently none the worse for wear. . . .

23

General Ramsey
Command Control Center
UFR/USS Chapultepec
0007 hours, Shipboard time

Fire in the night.

The seven converging beams of plasma, moving at near-c velocities, were invisible in the vacuum of space, but when they played across the electromagnetic shielding of the Xul starship they elicited a dazzling splash of blue and violet radiance, highlighted by flickering arcs of lightning. Ripples of blue light seemed to flow across the target's golden surface. In spots, that gold sheen seemed to be breaking down, blackening and crumpling under that torrent of high-energy particles.

The ships added their own firepower to the barrage. Both *Daring* and the *New Chicago* opened fire with their spinal-mount rail guns, sending high-velocity projectiles ripping into the target.

Ramsey could only watch as the bombardment continued, a battle completely beyond his hands, beyond any human hands. In the background, he heard the radio chatter from the Navy vessels, from bridge and gun crews, but the battle proper was being managed by Sissy and Cassius.

Everything, *everything* depended on whether the trick with the starship Kemper Drives would overwhelm the Xul EM defenses, and do so within a period of a very few seconds. If the Xul vessel was able to return fire, the battle might well be over almost before it was begun. Xul military technology must be pure magic from the human point of view. Their one hope was that the Xul wouldn't be able to fire with its shields up, and, logically, those shields had to *stay* up so long as the human ships kept up their attack.

Logically. The word meant nothing now. Even the N'mah didn't know much about Xul military technology, or the capabilities of their warships.

As soon as they opened fire, the seven human ships began backing away from the target at over one gravity; the particle beams *were* their main propulsion drives, after all, and the *Daring* and the *New Chicago* added to that acceleration by keeping up steady bombardments from the railguns mounted in tandem with their forward thrusters.

With sickening suddenness, *New Chicago* died. Her mushroom-cap RM-tank appeared to simply *crumple*, collapsing upon itself, and, an instant later, with her drive still running and the forward thruster destroyed, the antimatter stores used to charge the plasma came into contact with matter and engulfed the entire ship in a dazzling, white hot sun punctuated, according to his sensor data, by an intense burst of X-ray radiation.

Ramsey, uselessly, braced himself. Presumably, *New Chicago* had been targeted because she was also the larger source of the high-velocity rail-gun bolts tearing into the Xul's hull, but the largest of the attackers, *Chapultepec* and *Ranger*, must be next on the enemy's target list.

At three spots along the Xul's hull, the flickering blue radiance coalesced into blinding miniature suns, spots of brilliance that appeared to be eating into hull metal.

The Xul warship was slowing . . . slowing . . .

Damn. How much punishment could she take? Six starships continued to spray the two-kilometer monster with
streams of high-energy fire, and the little *Daring* kept punching away with her rail gun despite the spectacular death of
the much larger *New Chicago*.

Damn it, we should've gone with the AMB option, Ramsey
thought. If rail gun projectiles were getting through the target's defenses, a five-hundred-meter missile with an antimatter warhead would certainly have been able to punch through
the Xul's hull and detonate inside.

The blue flickering across the Xul ship died, and for an instant, her naked hull lay exposed to the starcore fury of her
assailants.

All six Navy ships ceased acceleration in the same instant,
their helms under Sissy's control. They wouldn't have been
able to keep firing for more than another second or two anyway; all were racing out from the Wheel now at several hundred meters per second.

The Xul vessel hung motionless now, relative to the Star
Gate, her golden hull blackened in some places, and fiercely
radiating in others. A cloud of debris slowly expanded from
amidships.

He was astonished to note that the entire fight had lasted
only seven seconds.

"Target appears to be neutralized," Cassius said, and Ramsey allowed himself a long, drawn-out sigh of relief. They'd
done it. *They'd done it*.

"Send in the Marines," was all he said.

Corporal Garroway
TRAP 1–2
Sirius Stargate
0008 hours, Shipboard time

"We've got the word," Warhurst told the waiting Marines over their implants. "CBSS is *go*."

"Wonder if there's even anything left of the target to board?" Arhipov asked.

"Don't you fucking worry about *that*, youngster," Dunne told him. "Just keep your head and go by the download."

"Aye aye, Gunnery Sergeant."

Garroway felt a hard thump and a surge of motion. The TRAP was moving.

"Disembarkation in six minutes," Dunne said. "Lock and load, people."

Garroway checked the safety on his PG-90, ratcheting back the bolt-feed access to check the mass injector, checked the power pack and the cable connector, checked the diagnostics. Good to go. The weapon was weightless in zero-G, but still possessed over ten kilos of mass, a solid, reassuring inertia resting in his grasp.

"Okay, people, listen up," Dunne snapped. "Like the download says, we're not doing a dropout. Word is there's lots of jagged metal over there and lots of floating debris. The TRAP'll slip in as close as the pilot can take us, the clamshells open up, and me and Cavaco'll shoot tethers onto the hull or into the wreck, whatever we can manage. Each of you then hook to a tether and pull yourself over. Move cautious, but *move*. We don't know what's waiting for us over there, and we don't know what kind of weapons they have. Be careful of jagged edges. They might be sharp enough to cut through your armor at a joint. Keep your IR up and watch for hot spots. Word is some spots over there are still white-hot.

"The mission is short, sweet, and simple. We go onboard and see if anybody is alive over there. If we can get prisoners, fine . . . but no heroics. We don't know their capabilities, so shoot first and download second. Do you copy?"

"*Copy, Gunnery Sergeant*!" eighteen voices chorused back.

"We secure the objective—or as much of it as we can manage—and wait for the civilians to come across. We'll also be trying to link the unit AI in, to see if he can access the thing's computer.

"Watch your backs, watch your fire, watch your buddies, and give the bastards some good old-fashioned Devil Dog hell! Do you copy?"

"*Copy, Gunnery Sergeant!*"

"Ooh-rah!"

"*Ooh-rah!*"

Garroway became aware of a new sound, a kind of irregular pinging and clatter, like gravel bouncing off a tin roof. The TRAP's cargo bay was in vacuum, so the sound was being transmitted through the transport's hull and up through Garroway's boots. It took him a moment to figure out what the sound was . . . metallic debris striking the TRAP's hull as they approached the objective.

"Two minutes, Marines! Brace for impact!"

Garroway braced. . . .

General Ramsey
Command Control Center
UFR/USS Chapultepec
0012 hours, Shipboard time

Ramsey watched as four TRAPs approached the Xul ship from four quarters, edging slowly closer. He had to have them highlighted in his noumenal imagery; a CTV-300 series transfer pod, eighteen meters long, was invisibly tiny next to the two-kilometer bulk of the objective. The size difference helped drive home the sheer audacity of what they were attempting here. Eighty Marines, against a monster a mile and a half long.

"General," Cassius said, "I am picking up a moderate X-ray source at the target."

"X-rays? What is it? What's causing it?"

"Unknown. I have pinpointed the source in what I assume is the Xul vessel's power plant. It appears to be growing stronger, but at a slow rate."

Ramsey considered this. It might be a weapon powering up. It might be the crew attempting to refire the engines or light up a reactor. It might be a damaged power plant about to go into meltdown. It might be *many* things, and there was no way to guess what.

"Keep an eye on it, Cass," he said. "We continue with the mission."

There was nothing else to do, at least, not until they had more information to work with.

He thought-clicked to a close-in view—TRAP 1-1 drifting slowly through a blizzard of debris, edging ever closer to a gaping hole in the wounded Xul ship's hull, maneuvering gently until its blunt nose actually poked inside.

The dorsal clamshell doors swung open. . . .

Corporal Garroway
TRAP 1–2
Sirius Stargate
0010 hours, Shipboard time

"And *three* and *two* and *one* and . . ."

Garroway felt the shock, a crumpling, grating noise transmitted through the hull, a gentle surge of deceleration. Overhead, the clamshell doors slowly opened up, sweeping aside the debris drifting immediately above the TRAP.

Harsh light spilled into the TRAP's cargo bay. Sirius A was visible through the center of the Wheel, intolerably brilliant, the light illuminating the golden hull of the Xul and picking out the dust-mote debris like snowflakes in a blizzard. From his vantage point in the cargo bay, Garroway could see part of the Xul ship, like a smooth-sided golden mountain, and a ragged, blackened tear engulfing the forward end of the TRAP.

Cavaco and Dunne edged themselves halfway up out of the bay, braced themselves, and aimed stubby line-shooters into the opening forward. Tethers unreeled from the spools attached to the guns, tipped by a nanoseal projectile that would adhere solidly to whatever it hit. The two Marines gave the tethers hard tugs, making sure they were firmly anchored, then attached the reels to the edge of the TRAP's cargo bay hatch.

"Let's go, Marines!" Dunne ordered. The first man in line, Eagleton, popped a D-ring attached to his suit tether over a boarding line and began pulling himself out of the bay, hand-over-hand. Garcia was next . . . then Arhipov.

Garroway followed, clumsily with the bulk of his PG-90, hooked up, and pulled himself out.

The sharply enclosed space of the TRAP cargo bay dropped away, and Garroway found himself lost in an impossible immensity. During his drop onto the Wheel two days ago, the only objects he could see besides stars were the Wheel itself and the occasional pinpoints of fighters and other Marines in the distance. He'd felt very small and very isolated then, but the sky around him was just a sky, and he'd worked and trained in space before.

This time, though, space was *crowded*. Using his own mental set of reference points to bring order to the chaos of zero-G, the TRAP was beneath him, the side of the Xul starship ahead, looming as huge as a mountain adrift in space. Beyond, much larger, was the arc of the Wheel, its size enhanced, somehow, by the relatively diminutive size of the four Navy ships Garroway could see from this perspective.

Taken all together, the encircling vista gave scale to the surroundings, leaving Garroway and the other vac-armored
Marines edging toward the objective feeling very tiny indeed; two lines of ants crawling toward a boulder as big as a
house.

Can that! he snapped to himself. *Concentrate on the job*!

The pig-ninety gripped in his right hand, he used his left to
pull himself along, careful not to get himself moving so fast
that he would collide with Arhipov's feet just ahead.
Forcibly, he made himself narrow his focus to Arhipov's
boots at the ragged hole in the Xul ship's side, now just meters ahead. He could see long, hard shadows cast by the advancing Marines etched against the TRAP's forward hull;
Sirius, high and off to his left, was too bright to look at, even
through filtered visors. They'd told him that he could survive
direct exposure to Sirius A's light for a short time—thirty
minutes or so, plenty of time to get across the Xul ship and
back. Nonetheless, he kept checking his suit's dosimeter.
Pieces of metal, some black, some mirror-bright, drifted
past, some clinking against his helmet.

Ahead, he saw Eagleton unhook and vanish inside, followed closely by Garcia, then by Arhipov.

Then it was his turn. The plunge into shadow was startling, and it took his eyes and his helmet visor both a moment
to recover.

He was in an enormous, mostly enclosed space, the opening partially blocked by the TRAP's nose and forward thruster
tanks. The volume revealed by his suit lights and by reflected
Sirius light from outside was roughly spherical and outlined
by unrecognizably fused, blackened and twisted masses that
might have been decks or machinery or almost anything at all.

With his left hand, he unhooked his D-ring, then gave himself a gentle shove off the nearest piece of bulkhead, drifting
deeper into the wreckage. He hit what might have once been
a deck, broken and twisted, and anchored himself, holding

his plasma gun ready, trying to penetrate the encircling darkness with every sense at his command.

Other Marines followed. Gomez, coming in behind Garroway. Lobowski with the section's other pig. Kat Vinton, Tomlinson, and Womicki. Geisler, Morton, Weis, and Donegal. Deek with a third pig, and a replacement from Bravo Company, Wu, with the fourth. HM2 Lee, the company's Corpsman, and two other new replacements, Delaguet and Somdal. Cavaco and Dunne bringing up the rear, where they could steady any Marine who might be having second thoughts about attempting the impossible. Twenty men and women, friends, comrades, and fellow Marines. Garroway didn't know the newbies well, but he'd faced death with all them, and they were as close now as family. Closer.

Someone in his family shrieked in agony. . . .

"Man down! Man down!" Lucia Velasquez shouted. "Corpsman!"

Instantly, everything was chaos, shouting, and fear. Tommy Tomlinson was cartwheeling slowly through space, a chunk of his right side missing, a brilliant scarlet swirl of blood spiraling out from the breach in his armor. Doc Lee launched himself from a bulkhead, sailing through empty space, colliding with the wounded man, and carrying him on across to the opposite bulkhead.

Garroway couldn't see a threat with his unaided eyes, but his helmet optics were highlighting a half-dozen hot spots, *moving* hot spots, twenty meters away, high up in the side of the cavern. "Bogies!" he yelled. "Firing!"

He opened up with his pig, sending a rapid-fire burst of plasma bolts snapping into the darkness. The recoil—plasma bolts *did* have mass, unlike the pulse from a laser weapon— nudged him backward, but he held the PG-90 low, beside his center of mass, hooked his left leg around a piece of twisted metal, and kept firing.

The trick was to keep the recoil from setting him tumbling,

but as long as he was well-anchored it was no different than firing under a full one-G. He shifted aim, following the aim-point reticle the gun's targeting optics were painting on his visor, aligning it with one of the moving hot spots. Was the target in the open or behind a thin barrier of metal? He couldn't tell, but the deadly burst from his pig seared through the space, shredding wreckage and bulkhead material in a cloud of metallic vapor and white-hot chunks of shrapnel.

Deek exploded, the upper half of his armor vaporized in a white-violet flash, his helmet, arms, lower body, and PG-90 spinning in different directions, trailing blood, entrails, and bloody chunks of flesh. Garroway realized suddenly that the pig-gunners would be *the* primary targets, since their weapons were bigger and nastier than the lasers carried by the others. It didn't matter. *Nothing* mattered, save laying down a devastating curtain of fire that would let the others win through the gauntlet safely.

A piece of the decking Garroway was anchored to suddenly flared in a silent violet flash and the shock knocked him hard to the left. He kept on firing, even when he found himself adrift, his shots steadily pushing him back from the target. IR was no help now; that patch of bulkhead was glowing red-hot now under the combined fire of three pigs and a dozen LR-2120s. Someone triggered their M-12 and an RPG streaked across the chamber on a thread of flame, striking the bulkhead and exploding in a messy blast of hurtling metal fragments.

"Cease fire! Follow me!" Gunnery Sergeant Dunne yelled and his armored form launched itself into space, sailing across toward the target area.

It seemed just a trifle arrogant that he would assume the Marines would hear him and stop shooting, thus avoiding a friendly fire incident, but the volley of high-energy destruction stopped, and then other Marines began hurtling through space after the platoon's senior NCO, Garroway among them.

A pitch-black corridor opened into the cavernous chamber. There was no sign of the sniper, but, then, the area was so cluttered with twisted, drifting debris it was tough to tell exactly what was there. Half of their number were detailed to remain behind, guarding the way out. The rest moved on. Single-file, picking their way past blasted wreckage, the Marines pushed deeper into the depths of the Xul warship.

And then it was hand-to-hand. The enemy seemed to emerge from the bulkheads around them, black-armored things like smooth, oblong, abstract sculptures two meters tall, with whiplash tentacles and glittering red crystals that might have been eyes.

Or camera lenses. Garroway smashed one aside with the butt of his pig, then fired. Half of the thing exploded in white vapor, and the rest was all circuitry and cables and bits of melted plastic.

"Check your fire! Check your fire!" Cavaco yelled. Shit! PG-90s were too deadly to use in such an enclosed space— the fringe bleed would fry friends as well as foes. But the Marines all carried sidearms, special issue for close-quarters combat—15mm Colt M-2149A1 Puller slug-throwers like the one that had nearly cracked Garroway's visor open during that training accident back at Earth's L-4. Those who could drew the holstered weapons and opened fire. The rest used their lasers. For such fearsome bad guys, given stature and status by the threat of the technology they wielded, the Xul proved less of a threat in hand-to-hand. Bullets punched through paper-thin armor; laser pulses burned out crystal lenses and melted through delicate internal circuits. If these were aliens in armor, the armor was crap. If they were robots, they were not designed for combat.

In five seconds, the passageway was secured, the enemy dead.

Fifty meters deeper into the wreckage, they emerged

within a compartment that might have been some sort of control center. *Might* have been. There were no screens or consoles or other recognizable instrumentation, but a half dozen of the abstract sculptures were locked into recesses in the bulkhead, apparently oblivious to the Marines' entrance. Or were they dead, killed when the ship around them died?

There was no way to tell. The Marines pumped three or four pistol rounds into each one, then posted guards to keep an eye on the metallic corpses. "Elvis, this is One-two," Dunne reported. "We're in some sort of a high-profile area. Lots of electronic activity all around us. We may have a computer access point here."

"Roger that, One-two. Hold position."

A moment later, Kat shouted an alert and the Marines pivoted to cover another entrance to the compartment . . . but then more Mark VIII vac suits began emerging—Lieutenant Gansen with Section A, the rest of Alpha Company.

Half an hour passed, a very tense half of an hour, but no further Xul appeared, no more shots were fired.

Only then did the civilian experts come across from the *Ranger*.

General Ramsey
Command Control Center
UFR/USS Chapultepec
0042 hours, Shipboard time

"General, the X-ray source is growing stronger." Cassius didn't sound worried, exactly—an AI didn't think that way— but Ramsey thought he heard an edge to the artificial voice that might indicate urgency.

"I see it. Any ideas?"

"The radiation is consistent with a small black hole consuming matter at a rate of several hundred kilograms per minute. I am unable to verify this through gravitational mass readings or by other means. However, it seems possible that some component of the Xul spacecraft used or generated micro-scale black holes, and one of them is loose."

Ramsey nodded. He'd come to much the same conclusion himself. The way the *New Chicago* had crumpled in upon itself had made him think of a gravitational collapse; it was possible that the Xul weapon had launched a tiny black hole that had ripped into the *New Chicago*, devouring her as it went. The Star Gate itself used a pair of black holes, and, if the gates weren't Xul artifacts, the Xul certainly were familiar with the technology. If a microscopic black hole used in the ship's weapons or propulsion systems had broken loose during the battle, it would be drifting now through bulkheads, decks, and hull metal, sucking down matter in a horrific whirlpool of ultimate collapse. X rays were the death screams of matter falling into the Pit.

"How long do we have?"

"Unknown, General. Extrapolation by the rate of increase in X-radiation suggests we have something on the order of one hour before the rate of collapse cascades."

"Understood." He shifted to the command channel. "Dr. Franz? You have thirty minutes."

"That's not enough time, damn it!" Franz shot back.

"That is how much time you have. We have reason to believe a small black hole is eating that ship tail-first. When it goes, you go, and I want my Marines off the ship before that happens."

"Acknowledged."

Ramsey shifted back to Cassius's channel. "Cassius? You getting anywhere yet?"

"Not as yet, General," Cassius replied. "Dr. Franz and Marie Valle have attached a relay to control circuits within the secure compartment onboard the Xul vessel. I am reading . . . patterns of electronic activity. Many of them, all quite rich and varied." _

"Yes, but can you *talk* to the son of a bitch?"

"That, General, will take time." A pause. "One hopeful sign. The coding feels similar, very similar, to that encountered onboard the Singer ninety years ago. As with the Singer, this appears to be a trinary code, and I am getting flashes of comprehension. I am operating on the assumption that the two sets of code are related, and am attempting to translate on that basis."

"Good. Keep at it." The Singer had been a Hunters of the Dawn starship half a million years before, crippled and trapped in the Europan world-ocean. An AI called Chesty Puller, a direct linear ancestor of today's Cassius AI program, had managed to interface with the Singer's software and to learn a surprising amount.

If this software was related, it was the first hard proof they had that the Xul and the Hunters of the Dawn were one and the same, that the Hunters had survived for the past half million years and passed on their technology to their descendents, that the Hunters of the Dawn were still a direct threat to Earth and Earth's civilization.

That bit of information alone, Ramsey thought, was worth the price of admission.

Cassius
Sirius Space
0045 hours, Shipboard time

Strangeness . . .

Ninety years before, a Marine AI named Chesty had probed an alien group machine mind and established at least a fleeting and fragmentary contact. Chesty had recorded everything, of course, and those records were a part of the MIEU database, there for Cassius to draw upon. The aliens had called themselves Seekers of Life, and their concourse was a mingled harmony of thought and awareness that translated as song, calling to the Void.

The Singer. . . .

Cassius now was aware of the Song, of mingled minds and thought, a sea of awareness around him. He could almost, almost understand. He'd tapped into the current, was sensing . . . *something* . . . but the language had changed in half a million years. Evolved.

But he glimpsed images. Memories, perhaps, or recordings of distant worlds, distant and far scattered regions of the Galaxy.

He saw the galaxy viewed from without, from Cluster Space, sensing it not with merely human eyes, but with the varied and incredibly sensitive mingling of a thousand senses, utterly beyond the human ken. He drank in the light of four hundred billion suns, felt the deep, slow, pulse of gravity waves from the Core, the flicker of gamma radiation singing from the depths of supernovae, the thin, hot soup of neutrinos sleeting unfelt through star and vacuum alike.

A shift of perspective, and he was deep within the Galactic Core itself, the dust cloud nebulae piled high like banked thunderheads, agleam in the filtered reds and oranges of starlight, of ancient suns crowded hundreds to the cubic parsec. Gas clouds with the mass of a hundred million suns surrounded a vast central region swept almost clear of stars and dust, within which ticked the strange objects Terran astronomers had long before dubbed Sagittarius A West, Sagittarius A East, and Sagittarius A*. Magnetic storms like vast, arcing solar prominences stretched across a thousand light-years. Spiraling disks of ionized gas and dying matter . . . neutron stars by the hundreds . . . radio jets and scintillating bursts of gamma rays . . .

The astonishing thing was that in this sea of hard radiation, he could sense life.

Or, rather, *mind*. The Hunters of the Dawn, whatever they truly were, were *here*.

And another shift and Cassius was somewhere among the Galactic spiral arms, viewing with keen interest a world, green and blue and smeared with white streaks of cloud . . . and on the nightside the thickly scattered gleam of city lights marking a highly technical civilization.

Cassius felt the Xul ship reach forth . . . saw the world's sun explode, saw the dayside seared by nova light, saw the heat storms ripple across the night hemisphere, saw the atmosphere stripped away, and the gleaming cities die. . . .

Evidently the Hunters of the Dawn no longer restricted themselves to asteroid bombardments when they sought to eliminate the competition.

Cassius dutifully recorded everything, while trying again and again to pierce the veil of incomprehension that still sundered him from these minds. They were machine minds, of that he was certain . . . or rather . . . they were an odd mingling of machine mind and organic. Cyborgs? Downloaded intelligence?

And what, if anything, was the difference?

And then he heard the screaming and recognized there the timbre of distinctly human thought, but thought seared by white agony.

Emotionless, as only an AI could be, Cassius continued recording.

Corporal Garroway
Sirius Stargate
0115 hours, Shipboard time

"That's it, Marines," Gansen called. "We're moving out!"

"On our way, sir," Dunne replied. "Aw*right*, Marines! You heard the man! *Move* it! *Move* it!"

Garroway took a last look around the alien chamber, suppressing a shudder. If this was the face of the Xul enemy, it was a bizarrely inhuman one. He was glad to be leaving.

"Why the rush?" he asked, hauling his way back through the tunnel to the first chamber. The Marines were hooking on to the tethers, and beginning to move back toward the TRAP. Elsewhere around the Xul vessel, three other sections were evacuating to their TRAPs at the same time.

"Word is a black hole is loose on board somewhere," Dunne replied. "If it is, we want our collective asses *out* of here."

"Roger that," he said. "Let's vam the hell out of Dodge."

But he felt a heavy sadness as he hauled himself out of the wreck, emerging once again into the brilliant star shine of Sirius. A part of him, small and irrational but utterly implacable, had still hoped against all hope that the Marine VBSS teams would find a sealed and habitable chamber somewhere onboard that goliath alien vessel and that within that chamber would be two hundred and some survivors of the *Wings of Isis.*

And among them . . . Lynnley.

Marine search teams had moved through much of the Xul ship while the civilians worked in the control center. According to them, the open, accessible portions of the ship were actually quite small, compared to the vessel's enormous bulk. There simply weren't that many places to look. Unless human prisoners had been in one of the sections vaporized by the attack on the Xul, they were not onboard.

Garroway had to admit, at long last, that Lynnley and the others were dead, that they must have died twenty-two years before.

For a moment, loneliness clawed at his mind. Never had he felt so isolated, so cut off and adrift in time . . . not even when he'd been sinking into the depths of that alien internal sea within the Wheel.

Another ten years back to Earth. Would he recognize anything, anyone, when he got back?

Fuck that, he told himself angrily. *At least you* are *going back*! So many other Marines were not.

He hauled himself into the TRAP, found a vacant seat, and wedged himself in. It wasn't quite as crowded in the cargo bay this time around. Both Tomlinson and Deek were dead. Their bodies—in Deek's case, what could be found of it— had been put into body bags and would be riding back to the *Pecker* in an aft storage compartment.

Marines always brought back their own.

No, he wasn't alone. Not so long as he was a Marine.

The TRAP backed away from the Xul ship, clearing the debris field, then boosted back toward the waiting *Chapulte-pec*. This time the powers-that-were granted a camera-aft view of the Xul for implant download to all of the Marines. Grateful to lose himself in something other than black thoughts, Garroway opened a window and watched the golden vessel, marred by rents and blackened hull plating, slipping away astern.

Something was happening within the bulge of the aft third of the Xul ship. It appeared to be crumpling, folding in upon itself as though wadded up by a titanic, invisible hand.

The crumpling accelerated. The Xul vessel must have had a small residual velocity, for it appeared to be moving now, falling very slowly toward the center of the Sirius Gate. It continued to crumple, to grow smaller . . . smaller . . .

And then it was gone.

The Marines around him were cheering and bellowing "*Ooh-rah!*"

Garroway still felt crushed and empty—as crushed as that vanishing alien ship.

Somehow, though, he managed to join his voice with the others. "*Ooh-rah!*"

Epilogue

Corporal Garroway
Cluster Space
1215 hours, Shipboard time

How long had it been since he'd slept last? Garroway had lost track. It was twelve hours, more or less, since the battle on the Xul ship.

Three hours since he'd come . . . here.

He stood on the surface of an airless, dusty rock, the horizon so close he could almost touch it, the sky a glory of unearthly majesty and wonder. This was what they were calling Cluster Space, a place they were now claiming was at *least* 30,000 light-years from home. Half of the sky was filled with the subtle smear of starlight that was the home Galaxy, the Milky Way. It had taken Garroway quite a while to even make sense out of what he was seeing, for the reality bore little resemblance to the time-exposure photographs he'd seen in books and astronomy-text downloads. The subtle blue glow of the spiral arms, the warmer, ruddier glow at the core with a fuzzy, star-like nucleus, the bands and lanes of dust and gas, the iridescent colors of the nebulae . . .

At his back, the globular star cluster covered sixteen times the area of the Moon seen from Earth, and was bright enough to cast a shadow. The local planet and its dwarf sun were out of sight, at the moment, below the ridiculously close, sharp horizon. The dusty rock he was standing on was a twenty-kilometer planetoid with a stargate bored into its core, a different kind of stargate than the one at Sirius . . . maybe even an entirely different kind of technology.

Garroway didn't know and didn't care. He'd volunteered to come through with the security team accompanying the engineers. They'd searched the moonlet for inhabitants—there were none—and now they were planting a pair of anti-matter bombs that would blow this gate into rubble. Elsewhere, Starhawk fighters had gone out, located a Marine Starhawk that had fallen through during the battle, and already had it under tow through the Gate. The word was that the pilot was in bad shape, but that he would live.

Which was more than could be said of a number of good Marines.

"Gare?" a voice called. "You okay?"

It was Kat. "Yeah," he replied. "Just thinking."

She joined him, her chamelearmor mingling the dark gray of the planetoid beneath their feet with the black of space. "You've been thinking for hours. *Never* a good sign."

"Did you hear the scuttlebutt about the *Isis* people?"

"Yeah. I heard."

They were saying that the *Isis* crew had been killed twenty-two years ago. That was what was going into the official report. But Dunne had heard a bit more—he'd hacked into the battalion databanks, he claimed—and he'd told some of the Marines . . . including Garroway.

Xul technology was still beyond human comprehension, *magic*, for all intents and purposes. But Cassius had picked up some human voices in the cacophony of thought and mind within the Xul ship minutes before its destruction. No one understood how it could be accomplished, but somehow, somehow, those 245 humans, including Lynnley, had been downloaded into the Xul group mind. Maybe they'd been saved for interrogation. Maybe they were there so the Xul could learn about humans.

It was doubtful that they'd learned much of value, though, because if Cassius's data was correct, they'd been broken down, dissolved almost literally atom by atom, so that it was the information being stored, not their physical bodies.

Mind is, essentially, patterns of information. Electric charge. Ion flow and balance. *Data*. And the data that described Lynnley Collins's mind had been data taken from a body in agony. They'd downloaded her tortured mind into their computers and they'd left it there that way for twenty-two years.

The blessing was that her mind—or whatever it was that was left of her—had been insane and beyond knowing soon after the download took place.

And the greater blessing still was that the torture had ended, at long last, with the Xul ship's destruction.

Garroway had never believed in the Christian or the Islamic view of the universe, the view that said that a just and righteous God condemned human souls to everlasting torture because they happened to be born into the wrong culture, the wrong religion. That was one reason he'd long ago embraced a gentler, less dogmatic and less judgmental faith in Wicca.

The Xul, with their godlike powers, had condemned 245 humans to a perfect simulation of Hell for twenty-two years.

Garroway could not understand how any mind, no matter how depraved, how *evil* in any sense of that word, could subject any mind, any soul to that kind of torment.

Had they even been aware of what they were doing? Scuttlebutt said they were machines, after all. Machines that wanted to eliminate any Darwinian competition to their rule of the Galaxy.

"I'm so sorry, Gare," Kat told him. It was as though she were reading his mind.

Maybe she was.

"We're going back there," he said, gesturing with one hand at the galactic spiral. "We're going back there and we're going to *kill* those . . . things."

"Roger that. *Semper fi.*"

"*Semper fi.*"

"Okay, Marines," Gunnery Sergeant Dunne's voice called. "The charges are in place. Hotfoot it back here if ya don't want to be stranded a *long* fucking way from home!"

Garroway took a last look at the Galaxy. It seemed, from this vantage point, an unbearably cold, lonely, and hostile place.

Once the Marines had gone, the antimatter charges would destroy this gate; if the Xul returned to this system, they'd have no way of telling from which of four hundred billion suns the attackers had come.

With luck, the Marines had purchased some time for Humankind . . . maybe even as much as a century. It wasn't much, but it would have to do.

Do more with less.

And whatever the future held for humans . . . for the *Galaxy* . . . Garroway knew the Corps would make a difference.

Always.

Semper fi.